April 19

[handwritten entry, illegible]

April 20

[handwritten entry, illegible]

April 21

[handwritten entry, illegible]

THE CATBIRD SEAT

Rebecca Hollingsworth

THE CATBIRD SEAT

A NOVEL

REBECCA HOLLINGSWORTH

GREENLEAF
BOOK GROUP PRESS

Published by Greenleaf Book Group Press
Austin, Texas
www.gbgpress.com

Distributed by Greenleaf Book Group

For ordering information or special discounts for bulk purchases, please contact Greenleaf Book Group at PO Box 91869, Austin, TX 78709, 512.891.6100.

Design and composition by Greenleaf Book Group
Cover design by Greenleaf Book Group and Kim Lance
Cover Images: ©iStockphoto.com/gurkoao,
©iStockphoto.com/Color_Brush, ©iStockphoto.com/arxichtu4ki,
©iStockphoto.com/RedDaxLuma

Publisher's Cataloging-in-Publication data is available.

Print ISBN: 978-1-62634-915-5

eBook ISBN: 978-1-62634-916-2

Part of the Tree Neutral® program, which offsets the number of trees consumed in the production and printing of this book by taking proactive steps, such as planting trees in direct proportion to the number of trees used: www.treeneutral.com

TreeNeutral

Printed in the United States of America on acid-free paper

22 23 24 25 26 27   10 9 8 7 6 5 4 3 2 1

First Edition

For
Sheila Low-Beer

"Power does not corrupt.
Fear corrupts . . . perhaps the fear
of a loss of power."

—John Steinbeck

AUTHOR'S NOTE

In 1976, as my mother walked from the mailbox, she started reading a letter from my sister who was attending school in New York City. When she got to the part where Jill mentioned dating a Black musician, Mother dropped to the ground. My brother, who happened to be visiting, rushed her to the hospital; apparently she'd had some sort of anxiety spell.

When Mother got back home, the first thing she did was to take down from the living room wall a large oil portrait of Jill, which she carried to the backyard and hacked to pieces with a hatchet.

I was born in 1945 and grew up in Pinellas Park, Florida—every bit as backward as Bessemer, Alabama, or Greenwood, Mississippi, in regard to acceptance of the races into one harmonious society. As a child, one of the first curiosities I encountered was the two drinking fountains in the A&P grocery store, one marked *White* and the other, *Colored*. When I asked about it, Mother waved it off, as it was just one of life's commonalities—not worth an explanation. Thus began my indoctrination in an existence where little regarding race was challenged, questioned, or debated by the people I knew. People did not talk about how things should be but just said "that's how it is."

White people were aware of "Coloreds" (the accepted term for African Americans at the time), but they were no more familiar to us than the dark-skinned Africans featured in *National Geographic*. White society had been very effective, during years of effort, in creating total unfamiliarity between the races. Colored people lived on the other side of the tracks, leading their own lives of which most of us White people had not a clue. There were the privileged few White families who had Colored help, but they were not "like members of the family," as Whites in that position liked to say.

Whites and Blacks were on separate, and unequal, paths. There is no question that my sister's boyfriend, who had the audacity to cross some color line into my family's White sanctuary, was why Mother went berserk with the hatchet. Reading my sister's letter, in that instant she must have realized her life was about to change if the relationship persisted (which it did, to marriage), and she would be forced to face interacting with a living, breathing human being who happened to be Colored—something she had never remotely considered.

Earlier, in 1954, the US Supreme Court had ruled in *Brown vs. Board of Education* to put an end to school segregation. But it was not until in my senior year in high school, in 1963, that the first dark-skinned student enrolled—a first in my school and a first in the county. To tone down the expected adverse reaction, the school administration quickly let it be known this student was "Hawaiian." His father had once been stationed in Hawaii while in the US Air Force. From this weak connection, the deception was created.

The White students accepted this story because the young man was not lazy, sneaky, over-sexed, or possessing a tendency to draw a knife when provoked—all traits many of us had been raised to believe were endemic to Blacks. My mother would say of them that "they like to cut," as if this was in their DNA. These and other negative characteristics belonged to all who made up the Colored race—or so we had been taught from an early age by our parents and from all the derogatory signs all around us.

Only when the school yearbook came out, showing our "Hawaiian" was from Washington, DC, did it occur to the White crowd that he was actually Colored. As a first experience for many of the White students to get to know someone who was Black, it was a positive one (even though it was a trick). But this was not enough to reverse a childhood of ingrained myths regarding Black people; it was easy to think of him as just an exception out of a whole society of "inferior" beings.

When I left the South to pursue my career in advertising in New York City in 1968, I took the South with me. The new environment did little to change my beliefs. The North did not open my eyes to a more diverse existence. There were the same dual societies—Black housing somewhere away, mostly Whites in the workplace, little social mixing, all very much the same as I was used to at home. Without embarrassment or reprisal, I was more than happy to carry on my Southerness in Yankeetown, just as *ya'll* stayed prominently in my vocabulary.

When I returned home to visit, I'd buy a handful of Dixie postcards from Woolworths to send back to friends in New York—cards depicting Black folks picking cotton, or cartoon cards with shoeless, big-lipped Blacks being chased by alligators—all for a little giggle. This was done without the burden of conscience because, like most White Southerners, I had bought into the common myth, to the caricature spread around about Blacks. It is easy to be disrespectful about people with whom you are totally unfamiliar.

After my stint in the North, I went South again, living for thirty-five years in Atlanta and then Charleston, South Carolina, where I have been living for twenty-odd years. It wasn't until the year 2000 that I was jarred into taking my head out of the sand to notice the current state of affairs regarding race. For far too long, I had allowed myself to think of racial disparity as someone else's problem. But now I started to face the fact that there was a big chunk of our population being ignored—something I had long accepted in my life. Up to that point, I was content in my ignorance. But of all things, it was the flack over the Confederate flag flying above the South Carolina State House that caught my attention.

In Charleston, you can't escape the Civil War. Every year there was the Confederate Ball, with the men in re-enactment gray dress uniforms and the women in hoop skirts—with young Black people serving the canapés. Tours of the many old plantations did brisk business in showing off the romantic-sounding way of life in the antebellum South. Slave cabins had been preserved, but little was made of that part of the history. Charlestonians, in jest, for many years referred to the Civil War as "The Late Unpleasantness."

But something clicked in 2000. Black people in Columbia, the state capital, had hit a tipping point in their exasperation over having to see the Confederate flag flying every day since 1961 from the State House dome along with the American and state flags.

The NAACP got involved, and under their leadership the question as to whether the flag should stay or be taken down evolved into a demonstration, with media coverage that spread nationwide. The issue of the Confederate flag picked up momentum, raising questions well beyond the appropriateness of it flying from the State House. The immediate reactions from both sides were largely sentimental—one side claimed the flag represented Southern pride, while opponents came back with the accusation that Southern pride was a smokescreen for die-hard racial prejudice. One placard seemed to me to isolate the opposing views—*Your Pride Is My Prejudice*.

As the demonstration intensified, it became evident that the Confederate flag was the tip of the iceberg—what was really at issue was the South's culpability in Black oppression. As I saw it, the South was on trial.

I listened to a lot of voices, read about how others defined the South. But it felt hollow and it became clear I was going about it all wrong. There is the sentimental, nostalgic Southern story laden with a catalogue of gentility—good manners, respect for the old folks, sweet tea, and the like. That part of the story has been skillfully told by Eudora Welty, William Faulkner, and others who could beautifully weave a tale of relationships among quirky eccentrics. However, the same place where people dished out unparalleled compassion was also where people acted out with some of the most egregious cruelty ever experienced in the country. It was this contradiction I needed to explore, hoping to gain some understanding. On top of it all, what part did I and my family play by just standing by?

As the demonstration over the Confederate flag heated up, so did the rhetoric. There was a lot to take in coming from both sides regarding whether the flag was to go or stay. It was clear that most participants were getting hung up on sentiment, and I knew that in order to understand racism, the discussion was going to have to go way beyond feelings and there would be no escaping the issue of slavery—and also the unfulfilled promise that "all men are created equal."

Once I got into the history, things started to jell for me. I started to get some answers as to how the past influenced the present. Complete understanding would involve deciphering all the complexities, untangling all the contradictions of racism. After many years, I think I can say I've made some progress—enough to know I may have gained some insight, which I hope to share in this book.

Let me note that this book contains two parallel stories. Chapters about the Confederate flag controversy in 2000—so immersed in the issue of slavery—alternate with chapters that tell the story of events in the relationship between a slave and master in 1857. Since I sincerely believe all history is human history, I felt an honest portrayal of the dynamics between these two characters would bring a new, fresh look at a complex relationship, not often presented in this way.

1

DESPITE THE EARLY MORNING HOUR and the humidity lying heavy in the air, a handful of people on the street below hustled along at a steady pace going to any one of the surrounding buildings. Meanwhile on the fifth floor of the parking garage, a no-account compact car eased into a slot against the outer wall, but no one got out. Gil Culkin sat motionless behind the wheel in a profound state of concentration, staring ahead—focusing on nothing. In her work she was accustomed to deep thought and analysis of data before putting meaning to a particular issue of study. However, this was different. This was personal, uncomfortable territory where she had to find answers from within herself.

At thirty-six, she was settled into that comfortable place where it was no longer necessary to contemplate who she was as a human being—that place where she had convinced herself she was a decent person.

Now Gil was submerged in her head and totally unaware of her upper body being taken over with sweat, inevitable in June in Columbia, South Carolina, if you chose to dally in the elements without the benefit of air-conditioning. Her car was out of coolant.

Columbia was a city that carried the slogan "Famously Hot." The Chamber of Commerce had been trying for years to change this to something more inviting, but nevertheless, "Famously Hot" stuck. From the beginning of June until the end of October, Columbia was hot no matter how anyone tried to sugarcoat it.

In the early morning, after the slight downtick of the temperature overnight, the humidity converted to a slick film over grass, or running beads of moisture on glass, or a slurry of dampness on concrete that mixed with grit and made the unholiest sound when walked on. Even after the morning burn-off, this humidity was not gone but felt in other ways. The hot vapor formed beads above upper lips and accumulated on scalps until it ran in rivulets through the hair down behind collars or sought lower ground in the valley of cleavage.

Columbia had no relief at all from heat and humidity for a good five months of the year. There was no cool breeze coming off any large body of water, no crisp air sweeping down from some majestic mountain. Columbia was inland and flat. If you could not tolerate still and muggy, then you had better stop at the North Carolina border and not venture any farther south.

For Gil, what set her back had started earlier that morning at the gym. Racial prejudice was the kind of thing she vaguely knew to exist, something she had seen in others. So when it emerged within her own space that morning, it caught her off guard.

She was in the middle of her standing Tuesday morning workout when her trainer, Max, glanced around to see if anybody was in earshot. Their conversation usually centered on new restaurants in town, or his kids—light stuff—but when his voice lowered, it was clear the idle chat was about to deepen. Max had worked with Gil for three years and knew her to be a straight shooter—she would be truthful about what she thought.

Max said he had recently been interviewing applicants for an open trainer position. The candidates were impressive. All had degrees in some form of sports training. However—somehow Gil almost saw it coming—the most qualified, fit, and personable candidate was Black. Max asked if she thought any of the clients would have a problem working with a Black trainer. Without stopping to consider, Gil told him that yes, she thought there would be a problem.

Max had already asked the question of one client's daughter, to check how she imagined her well-heeled parents would take it. Every month, they laid out a big chunk of change for three weekly sessions for themselves and their adult son and daughter. The small gym would struggle financially if they walked out the door. In the daughter's opinion, her parents would balk at the prospect of a Black trainer.

Along with Gil's spontaneous remark, Max had what he needed to justify telling the young man the gym was looking for someone to handle the growing need for balance training for their senior women clients, and that position could best be filled by a female trainer.

Immediately Gil regretted her response—something hung on in her mind like a betrayal, but of what was not clear. She thought for a second to tell Max maybe she spoke too quickly, but by then he was again focused on her exercise routine, so she tried to shrug it off. Besides, with the world still rotating on its axis, she asked herself why she was getting so worked up.

By nature and training Gil was not usually spontaneous. The things that came out of her mouth were usually thoroughly scrutinized. It was uncharacteristic for her to react off the cuff—to rely on a gut response and not her intellect. So everything about her answer didn't sit right to the extent that the rest of the session with Max was a blur.

She questioned what had just happened that had upset her equilibrium. One thing was clear. She had not thought it out, had not considered implications. Not the least of these was that her answer probably—no, definitely—cost the young man a job. This fact horrified her when put plainly.

As soon as she answered Max's question, Gil started to feel uneasy. Here it was the year 2000—the beginning of a new millennium—and there still remained a cultural divide between the races when there should already have been big changes in old habits and standards. Instead, when presented with the question of including a Black man in her White environment, she had responded negatively, and this was a jolt to what she thought she knew of herself.

Max had asked whether in her opinion a Black trainer would in some way jeopardize the gym. Put that way—Gil was a natural problem solver—her thoughts went directly to the good of the gym and not to the best solution with all parties considered.

A Black trainer would change the dynamics of the small gym, where open conversation was freewheeling. Clients worked out in close proximity and joined the talk if a topic interested them. Conversation regarding issues relating to race was not taboo. With a large Black population in Columbia, there was bound to be frequent news of matters concerning race—which could become fodder for conversation at the gym. Oftentimes comments were not favorable to the Black viewpoint. The White clientele might take offense at having to censor their conversation.

Not that issues of race were a preoccupation of the gym's White clientele. They were all familiar with Black housekeepers or an occasional hired bartender for a party, but none of them had a clue what were the concerns or struggles that existed among Blacks, in the Black community. Whenever the subject of race came up, their comments were without serious thought—more idle chat, a filler for dead air.

The week before, someone had commented on a bill introduced at the State House requiring a clean drug test for anyone applying for state welfare benefits. The clutch talking about it thought the drug test made a lot of sense. Their consensus was that objection to the bill was just another case where Blacks saw discrimination under every bush, and that the Black community should accept that there were a lot of deadbeats who needed to be cut out of the system.

Right after Gil answered his question, Max moved on to some story about one of his kids. His decision about the Black applicant was sealed and he was easily able to clear his mind of it and move on. However, Gil could think of nothing other than her negative reaction to the idea of a Black trainer.

That she was an expert on the history of the most oppressive institution of humankind—slavery—made it all the more astonishing to Gil that she would find fault with incorporating a Black staff member into the gym. She held the position of Chief of Research in Southern Studies at the Caroliniana Library within the University of South Carolina library system. She could speak with great authority about the two hundred thousand slaves who entered her state through the port of Charleston (Charles Town until 1783) to be sold as chattel to the highest bidder.

Gil had a PhD in Southern studies and had written her doctoral thesis on Charles Pinckney, the leading voice for the proslavery position at the 1787 Constitutional Convention. So, her response rejecting a Black trainer was a shock to her and a reminder that no one escapes the highly charged issue of race—it was a stinging reminder that racial issues still existed and were not just a phenomenon of the past. She was surprised to see that no matter how fine-tuned her own intellect was on race, early influences and experiences remained and contributed to personal bias that had the strong potential to defy natural instinct toward logic and decency.

Gil's mind went to the American Founding Fathers' desire to define the principles of a nation independent from Britain. They aimed to create something new and unique, a contrast to their motherland. There would be religious tolerance, representative government, and, above all, individual rights and freedoms. In their Declaration of Independence it was stated that "all men are created equal." However, anyone could see the contradiction between that and how the "Negro" had always been treated in America, especially in the South. Just then there was a demonstration going on in Columbia over the Confederate flag, which Gil began to see as hundreds of years of history landing on the steps of the State House. It was a train of thought she would have to further explore.

When Max first asked her about the Black trainer, not only did she think about censoring conversation, but something else crossed her mind—something more visceral. It was the unfamiliarity of Black hands. She would never elaborate this point with Max because she had never before thought of how much skin color held a charge, and it sounded petty. But Gil could not excuse as slight the importance of the most basic form of communication—touch—largely denied between the races through years of orchestrated separation. Just a generation back, in her mother's time, it was considered a great offense—illegal even—for Black people to lean over a public drinking fountain to sip cool water.

Gil got to thinking that throughout history, looking different held great power. Black people carried around with them, just in their skin color, a reminder of centuries of slavery. Still sitting in her car, trying to get a grip on the episode at the gym, Gil started to think about her experience visiting her ninety-two-year-old grandmother in an assisted living facility.

Growing up in a small town just outside of Greenville, South Carolina, her paternal grandmother had very little direct contact with Black folks. Plenty of Black people were in and around Greenville, but in her time they were only background in the landscape of her life. In the four years since her grandmother moved into the facility, Gil found it interesting and sometimes amusing to watch the evolution in her grandmother's relationship with the staff—predominantly Black women. In the beginning the old grandmother was quick to criticize—to her, the women were rough, slow, and inattentive. Above all, according to her, she had nothing in common with them. There was nothing they could talk about. But over time Gil saw a remarkable transition. Before too long, the grandmother knew about the attendants' families. And the Black attendants knew all about Gil, her job, and accomplishments.

———

ON THAT TUESDAY MORNING, for the first time Gil began questioning her personal take on race and realizing that although she had studied slavery in an academic setting, hands-on was different. She was very familiar with the history of race in South Carolina, but now it was clear: Her studies had not helped her much in real life.

Getting out of the Ford Escort, Gil tucked her shoulder-length hair around the back of her ears. Though her hair color was naturally the deep red of aged mahogany, people still referred to her as a redhead.

Gil could easily be described as natural in appearance. She wore a little lipstick but no other makeup, mainly to avoid the fuss that went along with the application. Except for a touch of moisturizer put on in the morning, she did nothing to her nearly flawless skin—not china-doll but naturally healthy looking. With the thickness of her brows and lashes and her large hazel eyes, what she was born with was enough to call her attractive.

For clothes she preferred comfort over fashion. She leaned toward anything she could move around freely in, so her wardrobe consisted mostly of full skirts falling just below her knees. Again, with her God-given height of five foot, seven inches and trim body type, wardrobe could not improve on what was already there. Her only adornment was a simple sterling chain around her neck with an old British farthing her father had once found with a metal detector and had made up for her into a pendant.

She had the sure-footedness of an athlete—there was no sign of tentativeness or being off-balance, only confidence when she moved. She walked with conviction, like a woman who knew where she was going.

Standing beside the car, Gil fumbled with the heavy and awkward assortment of material for the hike to her office. Years ago she had expected that once she got her doctorate, all the lugging would stop. But when she became a professional in the field of Southern History and Culture, it only got worse. She had her routine down pat—the leather satchel went over the right shoulder, leaving her arms free to cradle a big brown accordion folder in one arm and an oversize File-a-Flex that doubled as a notebook and purse in the other. Both folder and File-a-Flex bulged beyond their capacity to properly fasten as designed. She took a quick glance at her watch and saw that the time she had just spent in the car lost in thought had after all not done much damage to her schedule. However, she still faced passing the demonstration at the State House. Until today it had seemed just an inconvenience to have to maneuver around the protestors, but now the implications on race were starting to come into focus and the demonstration took on more meaning.

Having grown up after the Civil Rights Movement of the '50s and '60s—that was her mother's era—Gil hadn't quite known what to think when unrest started brewing amongst Black people in Columbia regarding, of all things, the Confederate flag. But today, when she began to consider, she started to understand why they wanted to see the flag gone. The Confederate flag—along with the South Carolina state flag and the Stars and Stripes—had been there over the State House all along since 1961, when it had been raised to commemorate the centennial of the beginning of the Civil War. The morning ritual to fly all three flags continued for the next thirty-eight years.

When the issue flared up in late 1999, most White people were so accustomed to the Confederate flag being there that they did not even notice it. Gil herself—even with her background in Southern Studies—had not paid any attention to the flag of the Confederacy or placed any significance on it flying above the State House, although she passed it at least twice a day on her way to and from the Caroliniana. If she had thought about it, Gil would have imagined that long ago the Confederate flag had ceased to be emotionally charged. It seemed to be of interest only to hobbyist Civil War re-enactors and Old Miss football fans.

Gil did not realize that the flag had not gone unnoticed by Black folks. There had been several instances between 1970 and 1980 when Black lawmakers had called for the removal of the Confederate flag, but up against an overwhelming bloc of White state legislators, they were ignored. In 1994, Black ministers and the national chairman of the NAACP threatened to boycott the state if the flag did not come down, but their efforts fizzled out. That same year the Black mayor of Columbia appealed to the legislature for removal of the flag, but his request was met by the addition of two more Confederate flags on the State House grounds.

In 1997, White South Carolina governor David Beasley, under pressure from Black leaders, pledged to have the flag removed from atop the State House. But both the House and Senate rejected Beasley's plan. The next year, in the race for governor, both Beasley and his challenger promised voters they would not revive the flag issue. Influenced by organizations such as the Sons of Confederate Veterans, they did not challenge White voters who showed they were quite content with the Confederate flag flying over the State House.

Black people simply did not have the political clout to have the flag removed until, in 1999, something clicked and they were no longer willing to tolerate the status quo. The time had come. The flag became to the general public something other than a mere cliché of the Old South. It represented something deeper that called into question what it meant to be a Southerner.

As she walked toward the garage stairwell, Gil, who had spent her whole life in the South and knew more than most of its history, started to examine her own place as a Southerner. With all of her vast knowledge of what made South Carolina the South Carolina it was, her experience earlier that morning at the gym made her realize that she could no longer be a dispassionate observer of history but that she herself was a participant in history. After she told Max she thought there would be a problem if a Black trainer came on board, for the first time she felt directly involved and responsible for something important and out of her ordinary experience.

At the same time, Gil realized that along with the question of the Confederate flag there was another issue riling Black folks regarding equality and respect. Decades before, during the Reagan administration, a long-fought movement to honor Martin Luther King with a paid federal holiday was signed into law, but not every state chose to implement it. From 1983 until 2000 South Carolina employees could choose between celebrating King Day or any one of three traditional Confederate holidays. Anger festered over the state's holdout against observing Martin Luther King Day. In the spring of 2000 the governor of South Carolina finally signed a bill to make King Day an official state holiday. South Carolina was the last state in the Union to do so.

In the United States, issues of race had been swept under the rug for years. Black people were finally willing to attempt to force issues and try to get them out in the open. Now the Confederate flag, flying over the State House in Columbia, South Carolina, had become the vehicle to shine a light on race.

With the NAACP leadership prominent in the King Day campaign and the Confederate flag issue, things soon began to jell into the makings of a movement. From the beginning of the demonstration, Gil had noticed the NAACP at the State House daily setting up folding tables and chairs as a sort of command post to hand out leaflets and talk to the press. How long it would last was anyone's guess.

The protest not only remained in the public eye, but it had really caught on. The immediate issue of the Confederate flag boiled down to one thing—whether or not it should be taken down from the public building where it had been flying along with the American and state flags since 1961.

As a historian, Gil knew that behind the immediate issue were hundreds of years of slavery and racism and decades of struggle in the evolution of civil rights in the United States. There had been some advancement in awareness regarding civil rights, but suddenly the Confederate flag in Columbia hit a big nerve. From the first moment when the local chapter of the NAACP made its official statement about permanently taking it down, deep feelings—visceral feelings that perhaps had remained dormant for years—were stirred up. Not since the dramatic displays of hatred by Whites against Black children trying to attend all-White schools in the '50s and '60s had such passion been shown so openly by both sides.

———

THE TROUBLE STARTED when Black lawmakers first spotted the cover of the newly printed legislative manual with images of the Confederate flag prominently featured in the background. The time had come for a showdown regarding the flag, and it would grow to something deeper in meaning and would draw in both Black and White folks—what was needed all along.

The NAACP kept forcing the issue concerning the flag and soon found a willing partner to help promote the story—the national press, who were eager to challenge the South on race. A referendum on the flag quickly went nationwide with a broad audience eager to enjoy a good seat at the show of how the state that fired the first shots in the Civil War would deal with the race issue at the end of the twentieth century and in the year 2000, a hundred and thirty-five years after the War ended. Spectators from outside the South were very much engaged in the spectacle that, at times, bordered on comical in the beginning, before it got serious. To many White people beyond the South, race was a Southern problem.

Gil turned from her car and headed for the stairwell and the four flights to ground level. The garage elevator was out for the third week and so it irked her all the more that her prime reserved parking spot below—along with a handful of others—was "temporarily" commandeered to accommodate certain key participants in the demonstration. The Caroliniana leased a few parking spaces for staff and doled them out according to rank and seniority. With so many years under her belt, Gil qualified for a space on the ground floor. The disruption in the parking was originally supposed to last for only a couple of days, but the demonstration was still going strong after nearly a month.

With all the baggage of a pack mule, she emerged from the stairwell almost out of breath—only to have to see the Crown Victoria sitting pretty where her Ford Escort would ordinarily reside. The Vic was a buttery cream color and especially shiny and neat. The only thing foreign to the classic car was a maroon bumper sticker that read *JESUS IS LORD* in an ornate script like that on an ancient manuscript page.

The week before, Gil had cleared the stairs just as a tall Black man was unfolding himself out of the Vic. She had tried not to let him catch her looking at him for fear he would see her aggravation over the parking space, but while he fumbled with placards in the trunk, she got a good look. He was the Reverend Joe Pearl Joy, a late-night local televangelist—a favorite with insomniacs who found his soothing baritone voice just the ticket to fall into a deep sleep. The Reverend, a minor celebrity around Columbia, did not interest Gil beyond the annoyance that he had been given her plum parking spot, adding time and inconvenience onto her morning routine. Not only was she not the least curious about him; in his TV persona she thought him too showy for her taste.

The day she recognized him, Gil put on speed so that their walks toward the State House would not coincide. She intended to avoid any encounter. Now today Gil had to step it up, so she walked quickly out of the parking garage onto Main Street, heading to the Caroliniana. As she did every day, she would have to pass through the State House grounds before entering university property at the Horseshoe, the iconic loop connecting all the original university structures, of which the Caroliniana Library was one. She loved the majestic sight of the State House bathed by the sun in a golden light so that it glowed.

For the last few weeks, the demonstration had turned the city upside down, with traffic and a constant pounding of press coverage, both local and national—all over the Confederate flag that had been hoisted up the flagpole on the dome of the State House every day for the last thirty-eight years.

To Gil, the demonstrators on the steps of the State House created the visual impact of Black people in conflict with the Old South—the demonstrators silhouetted against the classical structure. The State House itself was a symbol of past Southern glory in the heyday of cotton. To Gil it was pure irony that Black people were trying to make their point in a place that had been built to glorify the South and the planter class.

———

UP TO THE LATE SEVENTEEN HUNDREDS, the South Carolina state capital was Charleston, but as settlement spread more and more inland, representatives to state government began to object to the extensive travel to the coastal capital and insisted on a more central location—at which time Columbia was considered. It was not an easy sell with delegates preferring the advantages of Charleston. Nevertheless, Columbia became the state capital in 1786, chosen for its central location in the state and easier access for the majority of the legislators.

James Hoban, a Philadelphia architect doing work in Charleston at the time, was asked to design the new capitol building in its new location in Columbia. He designed a handsome two-story wooden structure in a classical style. The main floor was for assembly and the ground level was used for delegate lodging, with crude beds and straw mattresses—usually two men to a bed. When the assembly was not in session and the delegates were away, goats were stabled down there.

The Hoban building in Columbia served the needs of the state adequately until a new wave of successful planters and merchants thought it was time for a grander State House. They had begun to use Columbia as a showplace for the riches brought about through cotton. With prices holding steady from demand coming from England, there was a new feeling of euphoria regarding their bright future. Nothing could possibly stop the momentum, was their sentiment. Neighborhoods of fine mansions were established—all with cotton money. With money came power, and the planters muscled their influence on the general assembly to focus on one thing—a new capitol building to represent the confidence and stability they felt.

In December 1851, a new building began in the fashionable Greek Revival style, designed to impress, with wide granite staircases ascending to two porticoes supported by stately Corinthian columns carved from native stone. The building would be the grandest and largest structure in the Upcountry.

The citizens of Columbia sensed from the perimeter footings that something remarkable was in the works. Crowds showed up daily to watch as up to five hundred workmen plied their trades. The free show took its place beside the other popular pastimes of the day—attending public hangings and watching spontaneous building fires.

Never before had granite been used in building construction in Columbia. Special tracks were laid to transport native granite from quarries at nearby Granby on the Congaree River. Immigrant stonecutters, masons, and carvers from Ireland were brought in for the finishes so vital in Greek-inspired architecture. The original small Irish community increased dramatically with the influx of the artisan craftsmen. Negro laborers were taken on for a small stipend. White locals saw this as taking jobs that could have been filled by White laborers, and they made their objections known.

The sheer weight of the granite made it necessary to develop ways to transport and manipulate the stone once it arrived by rail at the building site. Men, mules, and block and tackle were strained to the maximum. Tools were in the hands of people who had never before worked at that scale. The monolithic columns of native blue granite were among the largest in the world. Each and every column was carved from a single piece of stone forty-three feet long, weighing thirty-seven tons. Raising the massive columns into place was a major feat.

On February 17, 1865, at the end of the War, Sherman's Union Army shelled Columbia with light caliber cannons. Five shots hit the unfinished State House. The damage, not extensive, was never repaired but subsequently marked, years later, with brass stars to show the points of impact. A bronze statue of George Washington, already in place, took a beating. It sustained dents and abrasions from bricks and rocks. The bottom portion of Washington's cane was broken off and never repaired but remained shortened ever after.

Union soldiers dug trenches inside the partially completed building, filling them with explosives, intending to demolish what stood, but Sherman called off the plan, saying it was a waste of gunpowder and considering he was leaving it so poor, Columbia would never be able to recover.

Construction on the State House was not finally completed until after the turn of the century, but from 1869 it was in use. Two flags were flown from the beginning, the national Stars and Stripes and below it the South Carolina state flag. These remained and were joined by a third, the Confederate flag, in 1961.

———

AS SHE APPROACHED THE STATE HOUSE that Tuesday morning, Gil noticed the demonstration had grown from just the day before. According to the media, which had really stepped up coverage, people were starting to come from all over the country to add their voices according to their particular convictions regarding the display of the Confederate flag. Anyone could see that the flag issue was not going to blow over. It had fast become something that put a national spotlight on Columbia and Southerners.

Gil shifted her gaze from the demonstrators and up the wide granite steps, up to the portico, up the massive columns to the dome and the Confederate flag, unfurled in all its audacity.

She thought again how the cotton planters would roll over in their graves if they could see their State House, built to celebrate their achievements, as a backdrop for the demonstrators demanding equality and respect. The tables had turned, and now the Confederate flag and what it stood for were on the defensive. The flag issue stirred up something inside both White people and Black people that had been, up until then, largely unspoken, but festering nevertheless.

Gil continued walking briskly across the grounds of the State House toward the Caroliniana. She was carrying her smallpox report, due that morning, and while she had thoroughly enjoyed working on it, she was looking forward to her next assignment, whatever it might be. She was always happy to explore new areas of study—it was the main reason she loved her job so much. She seemed to never fall into a rut, working in Archives. Each new project was another chance to connect more dots in the puzzle to understand the influences from the past of South Carolina—clues to explaining present conditions.

Arriving at the Caroliniana, with some effort she opened one of the original heavy iron doors to the old building. It was these doors that came between Sherman's men and the Caroliniana's contents, the invaluable collection of books and artifacts recording the history of South Carolina that were already housed there when the Union troops arrived in Columbia.

From the entrance hall Gil took a left into Research and Archives, the place she had called home since the first day of her working life. This huge room was divided, with each of the staff having a personal space marked out by furniture chosen by each individual.

Within her own area, Gil followed her passion—to drop into the past life of the state. Actually doing the research was satisfying, but Gil had decided a long time ago that the real kick was to see how the past traveled through time and influenced later days. Gil got great pleasure when she noticed—as most people did not—past circumstances taking up residence in the now.

The enormous room was conducive to her work. It had remained almost unchanged in design for one hundred and fifty years. Throughout the Caroliniana, plaster walls were spared any violation by nail or hook. Picture moulding surrounded the perimeter of the forty-by-fifty-foot room. From this picture moulding were strung thin wires to framed images with themes of South Carolina history. On the wall with the longest uninterrupted open space hung an outsized engraving entitled *General Marion Inviting a British Officer to Share His Meal*. The print showed Francis Marion, a South Carolina Revolutionary soldier, motioning a captive British Redcoat toward a meager meal of a few sweet potatoes cooked over a campfire. It was said that the British officer, after being freed in a prisoner exchange, resigned the campaign and returned to England, explaining that there was no way such an army of American patriots, willing to live in such simplicity, could ever be defeated.

———

NO ONE MORE EPITOMIZED how a bunch of ragtag scrappers from the backwoods of the Carolina colony could prevail against the British Empire than Marion. While in the local militia—mandatory for all able young men to fend off Indians hostile to settlers in the region—he encountered Cherokees, who were very successful in their tactic of striking with no advance warning and then retreating to the woods and swamps where none of the militia thought it safe to pursue. This was the guerrilla warfare Marion adopted in fighting the British in the South. The method was most effective against an army that preferred to march across open terrain. Marion's men shot from the protection of the tree line and then disappeared into the wetlands. Stories of Marion and his band disappearing seemingly into thin air earned him the nickname Swamp Fox.

The British efforts to tame and dominate the Southern colonies failed precisely due to the fundamental differences in their battle technique. The British always made a spectacle out of battle: They announced time and place, played drum and fife, wore brightly colored uniforms and marched to attack in regimental parade formation. Marion's band was stealthy and camouflaged, and they attacked without warning—all tactics instrumental in running the British out of the South.

———

MOST OF THE REMAINING FURNISHINGS in Archives appeared as though they came from an old courthouse, and very likely they did. No chairs were of the ergonomic type found at Staples but were from some issue back before anyone could remember—the barrel-backed barrister style often used by juries in courthouses all over the South. There were worktables ideal for rolling out plats and maps. Other furniture, including book trolleys, were made of quarter-sawn oak from the days of the Arts and Crafts movement, a movement that was an "up yours" to mass production where machines replaced skilled craftsmen.

This old-fashioned style suited everyone just fine in Research and Archives, where their days were spent digging back into history while shutting out the hectic contemporary world. The individuals under this roof had gravitated to this place by different paths but with the same purpose. Everyone had a passion to clarify the circumstances, conditions, and forces that had come together to create the uniqueness of South Carolina.

Walking in, Gil greeted her colleagues as usual.

—Hey, fiends!

She headed toward her own domain, anxious to release the heavy canvas and leather tote that was especially hefty from the weight of the final draft of the monthlong smallpox project she had taken home the night before for a final look before today's deadline. Somebody shouted out that since she was later than usual, they all thought she was dead. She assured them she was alive, well, and ready to kick their butts just on general principle.

———

IN ACADEMIA, PEOPLE OFTEN took themselves too seriously, but not at Archives. They secretly named their little area "The Shit Hole." But not to show too much hilarity and offend the Friends of the Library—the benefactors—should they get wind of it, the name was shortened to "The Hole."

Thanks to a staff cutback two years earlier, Gil's office setup was larger than the others' after she swallowed the adjoining empty space. Too, working there all of her professional life—over a decade—had given her plenty of time to snag a couple of choice vintage oak cabinets from McKissick Museum at the head of the Horseshoe when they were having a major cleanout. The prize was a big piece, circa 1910, with a base of map drawers and a cabinet on top with glass-paneled doors. Her personal collection of reference books—including McGrady's four-volume *History of South Carolina*, Washington's *Southern Tour of 1791,* and a first edition of David Ramsay's two-volume history of the state—were locked up in the top portion of the cabinet. Her own great-grandfather's S-curve rolltop desk filled most of the remaining space. The built-in cubbyholes fit all the fiddly stuff that Gil needed—folded state maps, pocket dictionary, a jeweler's ocular to see very fine print or details of vintage photos. Her university-issue desktop monitor sat on a book trolley that she could roll into working position when it was necessary to use it. There was a lot of stuff, but all in its place to suit her sensibility to organize.

Tools of the trade—reference books, rolled maps, accordion folders from completed projects—were tucked neatly into every available nook of Gil's space. Personal items—an antique wooden, jointed boy ready to do a jig once a crank was employed, pearlized medicine bottles dug up during childhood excursions with her father, and a glass dome over a motley-looking stuffed indigo bunting—softened the hard look of academia. This was Gil's own workspace and it wrapped her in comfort and serenity.

Gil had her professional world exactly as she wanted it—no more, no less. She had the seniority and credentials to be the head of the whole Caroliniana. She was offered the position several times but passed on the opportunity in favor of her passion for historic research over administrative duties. Gil was not interested in writing the grants, schmoozing the donors, or playing footsie with the higher-ups at the university. That job went to Chip Limehouse, ten years her junior, who was more than happy to play the game in his ambition not only to head up the Caroliniana, but one day to be head of the whole library system of USC.

Minutes after Gil arrived, Chip came through the door, exchanging pleasantries along the way, heading toward Gil with a big smile. He always smiled when he knew she would be passing off a project.

––––––

CHIP HAD CHARLESTON GENTILITY bred in from a long line of "South of Broaders" or the "Lucky Sperm Club." All the boys of his class began learning good graces at a young age at Miss Child's School of Manners and Social Skills where every week, early Saturday, they would practice the two-step with other boys as their partners until they tried out the real thing at the October Carolina Ball when they were sixteen.

Chip wore the uniform of the South Carolina gentleman—cotton button-down shirt in pale blue, yellow, or stark white; khaki pants;

tasseled loafers, often without socks. A navy blazer was always on the ready just in case there was some "do" after work. He spoke with a distinct Lowcountry accent, which had a tinge of old English. Some said the old English came from the isolation during colonial times, when the mother tongue was baked in.

Every young man of South Carolina privilege had a large, extended family of cousins, aunts, and uncles who were socially intermingled since most stayed in the region and didn't go "wandering off" out of state. He could, from memory, recite the highlights of the family tree back to the first Limehouse, who sailed into Charleston Harbor in the early seventeen hundreds. Chip knew the name of the family silver and China patterns. He heard all about them and their legacy dished out at the Thanksgiving table from the time he could first hold a fork properly. He would no doubt inherit the lot and pass it along to his Limehouse offspring.

———

NOW CHIP APPROACHED GIL in exaggerated slow motion, and, referring to the report she had been hard at work on for the past month, sang out in a falsetto.

—It's tiiiime!

He was anxious over this one because of its importance and short deadline for a report with so much complexity. It could well have been a doctoral thesis for someone other than Gil.

The university was hosting a conference on public health. The key-note speech was to be on the history of smallpox in South Carolina. Gil had found that inoculation, a controversial practice abandoned earlier in England because it was widely thought to be against God's will, completely stopped an epidemic in Charleston in 1738, and that word of the Charleston success initiated the revival of the procedure in London.

Soon after Chip ran off with the smallpox report to deliver it to the conference chairman, he was back at Gil's desk with a box made of acid-free cardboard used for preserving delicate, aged documents.

—Take two deep breaths!

They both exaggerated a couple of puffs.

—Okay. Enough slacking off. Let's get back to work.

He flipped the hinged lid and lifted out a folder, also of acid-free card stock.

—Suit up!

At Chip's command, they both put on cotton gloves to handle the perishable material in the folder, to protect it from oil on the human hand that can eat at fragile documents.

From the folder Chip retrieved two small clutch notebooks, alike in style and size. One had originally been dark blue, the other maroon. From age and use the overall color of each was so deep they were almost black. Their size was much like a modern-day checkbook. The thin leather covers had a tab to slip into a slit, making for a flimsy closure arrangement.

Gil recognized the type immediately since many of these had come across her desk over the years. They were personal journals for record-keeping, to note down information of commerce or as a diary to hold personal thoughts. Either way, at the end of the day someone would take a moment to record the number of pounds of cotton picked or a visit from a young gentleman caller. This small-format journal was popular with soldiers during the Civil War, and the surviving examples held critical eyewitness observations in real-time situations. Archives had eight such diaries of Confederate soldiers, which were summoned out of Special Collections with some regularity to assist authors writing about the Civil War.

Chip told Gil that these notebooks had been found wedged between some rafters of a house that was getting ready to be torn down. They were brought to him by a walk-in. That is, somebody had simply walked in the door and handed them over with no interest in follow-up, merely saying that if the university wanted them, they could have them. The donor was so disinterested, he didn't even wait around for the form that most people requested for tax purposes. So there the two diaries sat with nothing known of them.

Chip explained that he had taken a quick look and had seen one was used for an accounting of property, while the other was a daily diary for the year 1857. Gil's assignment was to look at the daily diary, written in pencil and hard to read. Gil picked up the maroon folder and opened it to the first page. It read, *William R. Medlin, Clio, South Carolina.*

2

Sky clear for the first turn
April 16, 1857

MEDLIN SURVEYED THE YARD between the house and barn and began to contemplate the months that lay ahead, when he had to plant, nurture, and bring to market a successful yield of cotton. This was not another day of waiting. This was the first day of the new season and he knew very well what lay ahead even before the process began. Without really thinking it out, he knew from experience that it would take everything he had in him to see it to the end. In the pit of his stomach he could feel the anxiety that always came with the first day—brought on by knowing it was only a matter of time before forces of nature would offer up some challenge to test his will. Posted at the gin was a sign: *Cotton—where uncertainty is certain*. Everyone passing through the gin knew exactly what it meant.

A layer of mist hung a couple of feet above the ground, obliterating from sight all except a diffused view of the dark earth beneath. As the fog settled on the damp earth, already heavy with dew, it made a muddy surface ready to collect impressions of everything traveling across it. By noon the hot sun would render the yard a record of the morning's activity—crusty evidence of man, dog, and mule.

On the roof, still holding heat from the day before, the morning fog converted to condensation that traveled in rivulets to the edge of the roof and ran down in a steady flow to the ground. Medlin stood just in from the overhang to avoid the stream of chilly water.

William R. Medlin—called Medlin since his early schooldays to tell him from another William in his class—was not obviously distinctive in appearance or spirit. He was not a man who stood out with skills to persuade, nor was he known to hold opinions strongly defended against men of town—councilmen, lawyers and dodgers. His debates were not outwardly expressed but kept within himself.

Medlin was a small cotton farmer, which by category of occupation was one of a solitary existence. The farmer stood alone in trying to cope with the very thing that threw influence over everything he did—the unpredictability of nature. With farming, to predict the certainty of rain or foretell impending drought was the folly of a fool. With the ways of nature, there was only uncertainty that left the men of the soil robbed of confidence and security, longing for stability. Most farmers' eyes gave away constant weariness and fear. And so it was with Medlin.

He was average in most ways that a man would be described—average height and build. He showed the usual signs of ruddy wear as found in all who tilled the soil under the burning sun. At the corners of his eyes and between his brows were deep creases from the constant squint to protect against the blinding sun. This made him look older than his forty-three years.

His trousers, when first bought, were stiff but after much wear had the feel of shammy. Shirts were all similar in color, beige or gray—unsurprising for a person who put little thought to clothing. Of his hat, he was definite. He wore it from sunup to the evening meal when he took it off and hung it on a hook just inside the kitchen door. To most who knew him, he would look odd without it—a slouch that he wore slightly cocked to the right and forward, down to his brow. There was no hatband but instead, where the wide brim met the crown, there was a band of darker felt stained from years of sweat. From the brow up, his skin was pale where his hat gave protection against the burn of the sun.

That first morning of the new season, he stood for a while looking out at the yard and then stepped into a slimy combination of grass and mud, which immediately engulfed his boot to well above the sole. Each step made a sucking sound as the mud reluctantly gave up its hold. By the time he reached the barn, the mud had collected into large clods of clay. A couple of stomps relieved him of most of the burden.

He made his way to the back wall of the nearly dark barn where the tack hung over wooden pegs just as he had left it at the end of last season. The leather bridles were stiff, in the same shape they had been when hung months ago like dead cats left forgotten. During the long period of dormancy the harness and leads had grown a dusty layer of mold. A ready jar of wax and tung oil applied with a sack rag made quick work of the mold. After a few swipes, the leather once again felt limp and pliable.

Baugh and Wylie, a pair of seven-year-old draft mules, threw their heads back in defiance as they first took sight of Medlin coming their way in the pasture. They knew their idle days were over for the season. Fattened on field corn and grass, their bloated bellies made it difficult to bolt, so they stayed in place stomping gashes into the ground as he approached. He considerately held the two snaffle bits in his clenched hand to warm the cold metal, all to minimize the shock of the animals' reacquaintance with the gear. Still, they flinched wildly at the bridle coming over their heads. Medlin rigged the pair into a team while they gradually accepted their loss of freedom and readied for utility. All adjustments made, the mules felt the familiar command of the reins and through instinct and experience started for the field.

At the near southeastern corner of the field, Medlin stopped where he had left the plowshare the previous day after sanding and oiling it to knock back the rust that had set in over the winter. He had put the rasp to the blade to refine the cutting edge, ready for the first break of the soil. Now Medlin attached the plowshare and assumed his position, and the three were assembled into one unit. He slid the reins through his fingers until they met the notches he had made in the leather years earlier to mark the exact position for optimal tension in the leads.

Knowing all was ready, Medlin gave a slight tug on the reins reinforced with a short, shrill whistle. All lunged forward into a dance of man, beast, and metal—a dance performed by similar combinations for thousands of years in fields well beyond Marlboro County and in lands far beyond Medlin's imagination, the dance familiar to all who had ever tilled the soil.

Medlin had bought the pair of sorrel mules from a man in Bennettsville who bred mules for the money that he put under his mattress in case his own cotton crop for the year was a failure. A mule resulted from the union of a male donkey—a jack—and a female horse—a mare. Having a few of each, he handled the local demand for young hardy draft mules. His mares were from sturdy draft horse stock, necessary to bear desirable heavyweight offspring, and for that his mules were the most sought after in Marlboro County.

———

MULES USED FOR FARMING were far superior to the horse. The hooves of the mule were harder, and its skin was sturdier to hold up against sun and rain. Moreover, mules required less food than horses, and mules were patient and lived longer than horses. Charles Darwin, the father of the theory of evolution, was befuddled by the mule: "The mule always appears to me a most surprising animal. That a hybrid should possess more reason, memory, obstinacy, social affection, powers of muscular endurance, and length of life, than either of its parents, seems to indicate that art here has outdone nature."

The number of mules bred in America rose from fifty-eight individuals several years after the Revolutionary War to well over one million by 1850. This was largely credited to George Washington, who had heard of the value of the mule to agriculture in Spain. The Spanish government prohibited the exportation of their particularly fine strain of male donkeys. Nevertheless, Washington convinced King Charles III of Spain to send him a Spanish jack, which he named Royal Gift. A year later Marquis de Lafayette sent Washington a black Maltese jack as a present. For the last fifteen years of his life, Washington enthusiastically bred the animals to his own mares, producing a line of large, strong mules that he named the American Mammoth Jackstock. The fifty-eight he produced at Mount Vernon were the forerunners of the mules that formed the backbone of American agriculture. Mules became indispensable on farms in the agrarian South. A pair of mules could plow sixteen acres a day. They were invaluable at harvest time, after which they turned around and delivered the crop to market.

––––––

ON THAT FIRST MORNING OF THE NEW SEASON, Medlin's blade turned over the loamy soil. Early farmers of the sandy, dry mix common to the Upstate of South Carolina found that it proved perfect to grow a healthy crop of green seed, short-staple cotton—provided that all other influences were in total cooperation.

Halfway along the first row, Medlin looked away and took in the thirty-plus acres laid out by his father's father many decades before. He tried to superimpose the image of a lush crop of plants laden with big bolls ready for the first pick, but his mind was unable to make the leap, leaving him with the grim reality of the actual condition of the field. Left alone for months, it was—as always at the start of the season—overrun with vines, thistle, and spent stalks.

Medlin set to thinking what it was going to take to tame and reclaim the field and then to grow a healthy crop. He started an imaginary list of all the obstacles he would encounter and how he could beat down each one. The list was random and unwieldy, so he grouped all considerations under three main headings: insects, weeds, and weather.

Insects, about to suck the life out of the plants or the roots even before they had a chance to mature, would have to be battled at every stage of the process. To make matters worse, he knew that some pests were already deep within the very ground under his feet, lying in protective cocoons ready to emerge when the plants were at their most succulent and vulnerable.

––––––

A FEW YEARS BEFORE, planters had been eager to share tried, successful remedies. A new spirit spread through the region, a collective enthusiasm to refine the application of scientific principles to agriculture. Just two years earlier, in 1855, the Agricultural Society of South Carolina had been established. Their charter read, *Let us once get a cozy seat by the*

*fireside of the humblest farmer of the country, and we will endeavor to make him feel
that we are one of his own circle and indispensable to his success and happiness.*

The Society developed new, hardy seed stock and experimented with
exotic cotton plants from abroad. However, the issue of predator insects
remained. The Society studied new strains of cotton that it hoped would
be resistant to damaging infestations, but in the end it could produce
nothing that would materially eradicate the insect problem.

The initial rush of optimism brought on by the Society quickly played
out. Since there was nothing new to report, enthusiasm waned and the
Society's influence fizzled. For a short time, the farmer felt his lowly yeoman
status had been elevated. But he soon slipped back into the hard reality,
knowing that he was destined to continue to toil, once again, in isolation.

———

MEDLIN SET ABOUT THINKING of how nature could be so artful
in creating a situation where one destructive insect would be done in
and conquered to the benefit of another. Flies and moths could be successfully driven out with bonfires of dry stalks and brush, only to have
the method attract other species, in particular beneficial wasps from
neighboring farms, which would swoop in and feed easily on stunned
caterpillars. Or how could nature produce a creature that would first
use the cotton leaf as protection for its cocoon only to later consume
its host shelter to stay alive?

What force of nature had devised the armyworm that played such
devilment on the farmer? Eating little in their first stages, the small
worms could easily go undetected, but at maturity they became vora-
cious and could defoliate a crop overnight. However, the armyworm did
not go unchallenged. When certain species of flies descended onto a
field full of armyworms, they laid their eggs directly on the worms. The
hatched flies were parasitic, sucking the life out of the caterpillars. But
again the farmer lost. The flies laid their eggs on the armyworms only
after the worms finished feeding on the cotton leaves.

Suddenly Baugh and Wylie balked at a stubborn root mass, jolting
Medlin back to matters at hand. He was thankful to take his mind off
the threat of insects, a subject too exhaustive to conclude. A slight raise

in the plow handles drove the sharp blade under the tangled mass, cutting it free.

It was imperative they keep an even pace at breaking the still moist soil to ensure the ease with which the blade kept moving. It was on Medlin to keep a sharp eye out for obstacles in their path that had potential to slow progress.

This day was passing like all first days of the season, turning over the remnants of last year's crop and the new, hardy tangle of weeds that had been allowed to grow at their own will over the dormant months. It was now just a matter of sheer endurance until the September pick. That's if he was not wiped out by all manner of threats beforehand. There was always some threat.

The team made its way through two more rows with the work quickening now that all three were back to their familiar cadence after months of a slothful existence. Medlin set his mind on the second item on his list of things that could be ruinous if neglected—weeds. On account of several early "frog strangling" downpours, the weeds now flourished into a riot of spread and tangle. They had completely taken over the field and had to be turned over by the plow, pulled out by the roots and burned to reclaim the soil.

All through his upbringing, Medlin had been taught that God had created everything for a purpose. He could understand this for such phenomena as female birds blending with twigs and the like to protect their nests, or a hawk's crooked beak fashioned to tear prey, but for the life of him he could not imagine what was the good of a weed. The field was overrun with tall dog fennel, bull nettle, and moth mullein, all equipped with barbed thorns and/or onerous roots. To what positive end had God purposed these demonous plants?

The morning glory vines, plentiful before him, were a specimen not so easily judged. On one hand, in Bennettsville Medlin had seen rather attractive morning glory trained on trellises and fences for ornament. But here in the field it was the first culprit to bind the plow to a stop for untangling. Further, it was in the vine's fiendish nature for new seed to hibernate under the soil until tilling awakened its explosive growth cycle.

Normally, Medlin would not ruminate over such things, but during long solitary hours in the field it was almost inevitable that he would fret over the complexities of God's Grand Design.

Medlin looked down at the cuffs of his trousers, covered with cockleburs and beggar's lice. It was a sad conclusion to the subject of weeds. The sight of these clinging seed pods and prickly thorns only drove home the realization that for the rest of his life he would be a dirt farmer. No society or any other force would make his life into anything other than what it was—backbreaking work that would not ever be different than what it was at that moment.

Knowing there would be no end to it, Medlin laid off the subject of weeds and settled on the third and final category. If the weeds and insects had not the advantage of conditions just right for overwhelming the young plants with their various appetites, there was one more foe, and against this foe there could be no combat. One more foe that gave little warning and left the farmer powerless against its effects—weather.

Weather was all about balance, a delicate balance that could easily be tipped in the wrong direction, that could, sure as anything, wipe out all efforts thus far. No one but God Almighty had control in this matter. A successful cotton crop was totally dependent on a chance that the required amount of rain would fall on the right side of the scale. These were odds that even the most skilled gambler would pass.

If the rain came freely, the water easily penetrated the sandy soil, nurturing the roots that in turn rewarded the plant with all the soil had to give. But, when the scale tipped cruelly, clouds came and passed over, sharing nothing, and then the sun came and stayed, leaving the plants to burn and die of thirst. The soil crusted and cracked until it resembled a gator's back. After that any rain was shrugged off by the parched soil and redirected away from the plant roots so that it could not do any good. Without water the leaves turned brittle on the stalk. The plants lost all strength to live and nothing the farmer could do could save them.

When the clouds came and brought rain early, the plants flourished at first, giving the farmer hope—but maybe only for a little while. Too much rain and the roots began to drown and rot, leaving the young immature plants drooping to the ground. There was nothing the farmer could do to save that crop. The only thing left to him was to turn the doomed plants under and start again if there happened to be enough time left in the season. And there rarely was. Only time to wait for next year.

One thing was inescapable, and Medlin was reminded of it at the start of every season—the soil was getting played out, not able to fully support the plants with the nutriments they required. Every year he could see the yield go down.

Medlin contemplated the uncertainty of growing cotton. This he could do with little difficulty with last year's disaster still on his mind. Half the crop had succumbed to flooding. Too much rain for the soil to handle. Rain like we have never seen before, said the men with time on their hands huddling at the gin and sharing their collective misery.

An unsuccessful season had to be followed with the demoralizing job of raising enough money to fund startup for the next season. There was a time when factors had money to loan with payment in cotton when it came in, but when the yields became so uncertain, that source dried up.

Lending institutions like the bank were the only places to go for money. The total Medlin owed was troublesomely high. He had the slight comfort that everybody was in the same predicament of debt. Owing money to stay afloat had become the norm in the cotton culture.

The shift to debt came around 1850 in the guise of a windfall. England's appetite for raw cotton from the American South was insatiable, so small production farmers and big spread planters alike got on the cotton tread-mill. Planters increased their land holdings and slave stock. Small farmers hired more labor if they could or just worked much harder if they couldn't. Everybody tried to keep up with demand. Blinded by the prospect of immediate returns rolling in, they thought they could outrun the debt.

Meanwhile, the newly prosperous Southerners became prideful. With their wealth came confidence and even arrogance. There was a general feeling of accomplishment and a notion that they were beholden to no one.

Too busy to notice the precarious position they were putting themselves in, they assumed that the risks they were taking would not go against them, that the many possible adversities would not materialize—but of course they did. An overly rainy season, drought, out-of-control insect infestations—gradually yeoman farmers and planters alike got more and more in debt.

In its brief period of influence the Agricultural Society warned against having nothing to fall back on if and when an entire cotton crop failed. They suggested the idea of adding cattle or pigs, or breaking up the cotton fields and growing some wheat or corn—but growers could think only of cotton, which was demanded in ever-increasing quantities by the textile mills.

Cotton men went to the bank for relief year after year. The banks were making loans with Northern money. While the South stayed an agrarian society, the North gravitated to profitable, dependable industrial production. The North was flush with money and Southerners became dependent on the loans backed by the North.

By the mid-1850s, the soil in South Carolina was not fit to produce as it once had. More and more cotton was being grown farther South, in Mississippi and Alabama, where the soil was still rich—not yet done to death. But South Carolina farmers and planters continued to throw good money after bad as they tried to hang on, as they got further into debt.

Eventually Northern financiers owned a sizable portion of Southern debt. At the same time a powerful abolition movement had taken hold in some parts of the North. In their fight to rid the country of slavery the abolitionists spread their influence through lectures and far-reaching publications like *The Liberator*.

Large cotton production was almost totally dependent on slave labor, so it was plain to see that the South wanted no part in giving up their slaves. With the North having a big financial position in Southern loans along with the Northern abolition initiative that threatened to spread to the South, a fierce mutual resentment set in. Southerners resented what they saw as Northern meddling. Although not as dependent on slave labor as the big planters, small production farmers, too, were aware of the Northern influence. Powerless, they were swept into the threat that life as they knew it was under scrutiny and had the potential to undergo devastating change.

———

MEDLIN THOUGHT OF THESE THINGS as he deftly steered the team. Another row completed, the threesome—Medlin, Baugh, and

Wylie—were well settled into a familiar rhythm that suited all. The heads of the mules were swaying left and right in unison. From his vantage point, Medlin had long observed that when the front half of a mule went in one direction, the rump went in another. The motion and countermotion, along with the rhythmic slapping of the leads against the animals' flanks, put Medlin into a dreamlike trance.

Mindlessly watching the blade cut through the soil, Medlin suddenly caught sight of an oddity that drew him back into the present moment. A scarlet bead shone against a slab of fresh-cut soil. He startled Baugh and Wylie with a quick, unexpected tug on the reins just in time before the find would be folded back into the soil and perpetual hibernation. He leaned down and with his index finger loosened and freed the camphor berry–sized bead from the wall of earth. This was no less than the curiosity he had experienced a handful of times. With spit-moistened fingers he massaged the beauty to a jewel-like state. Held to the sun, it glistened like a ruby. From the Cheraw Indians, would be a good guess. The tribe had been charmed by ambitious settlers with trinkets like this Venetian glass bead, only to be unceremoniously driven off their land into obscurity. He put the bead into his pocket. Later he and Clara Anne would play out the ritual of placing this new find into a tin to join the others—all taken from this same soil.

Several more passes with little to distract. Then the upcoming trip to Bennettsville and all that the Bennettsville visits represented started to creep into Medlin's mind.

He briefly released his hands from the plow, letting Baugh and Wylie take it alone while he put another roll in his sleeves, hoping it would change the direction of his thinking. But even the flush of a small covey of quail hardly rocked the rhythmic gait of the mules and failed to distract him from the dreaded subject.

His thoughts about Bennettsville always opened onto a seemingly peaceful scene that could fool anyone into thinking of harmony and tranquility. Over the many years of torturous visits to his in-laws, the routine stayed the same. The Bristows sat in wicker rockers on one end of their big side porch while Medlin—in a rocker but not rocking—sat on the other far end, away from the elderly couple. Caleb and Daniel roughhoused in the side yard. Their father thought the play was a bit rougher than it should be when Daniel was a toddler of four and his big brother was nine. Lydia always sat in a neutral position between, on a bench swing suspended from the ceiling by a chain, as though the two factions were separated by an imaginary boundary with Lydia undecided. Clara Anne, as long as she was a little girl, huddled alongside of her mother. All sat in strained silence waiting for someone to address a subject of some commonality. But rather than speaking up, they preferred the awkward silence as they sipped cane-sweetened lemonade.

———

THE BRISTOW HOME WAS ON MAIN, the avenue where most of the upper crust of Bennettsville resided and where Lydia had been born and raised. Everything about Lydia's banker father seemed bland and meaningless to Medlin, a small cotton farmer who worked with his hands. His daily life was more about survival than gentility. Medlin viewed his father-in-law banker's work with a fair amount of skepticism. Moving numbers from one column to another seemed not about money but just empty signs representing the real thing.

It was not at all as Medlin knew the ways of money—cash for cotton. If you beat out strangling rain, drought, insects, and weeds, your reward was something you could feel and stick in your pocket after making a fair sell. The notion of what was honest, genuine work was at the very core of the relationship between the two men and would forever mark their approach to each other. The banker lorded his station as he saw it, whereas the farmer avoided any reference to his own low rung on the ladder as society deemed it.

During those visits to the Bristow in-laws, Lydia could see in Medlin's eyes what the working man would not defend, but she would pile on instead of backing off. Her father always picked at the differences to open wider the wound and welcomed his daughter to join in, which she gladly did. Lydia had learned the sniping in Bennettsville and taken it back to the farm, where after a time, experiencing little resistance, she felt justified—even entitled—in her mean-spirited behavior.

———

WITHOUT ANY WARNING, Baugh and Wylie broke from their rhythmic cadence, snapping Medlin back to consciousness. The animals reared back as much as the gear would allow. Their jaws opened wide and allowed their tongues to shoot from mouths despite the bit. He had never seen their eyeballs so exposed with the lids rolled back in total terror. Baugh's front hooves wildly pawed the air, then slammed into the soil with unusual power. Wylie was cow kicking, as Medlin fought to take control of the reins.

Over the commotion, he had heard the distinct sound of a rattle—like dried seeds in a shaken gourd—but all three knew otherwise. A female rattlesnake had crawled out from loose brush. Even before he regained control, it was over. The mules had stomped the life out of the four-foot-long female and the fist-sized knot of her young, who were no larger than earthworms.

He tried to calm the mules while checking for punctures on their lower shins. He could see none, but he would check for swelling throughout the day.

How had he missed the musky smell of the nest that would have warned him? Thoughts of Bennettsville had occupied his attention so fully that he was unaware of immediate danger. Medlin was frightened to think that he had put the trusted animals in such a vulnerable state. He would have to put all thinking aside and concentrate on breaking the soil.

Except for a couple of erratic head-jerks, the mules were gradually regaining their composure. Medlin checked all buckles and cinches to see if any had been wrenched loose. He spoke calming words of assurance that all was right again.

He resumed his position at the plow. While he fidgeted with the reins, something caught his eye. A red-tailed hawk was swerving this way and that to shake an attack by a pair of mockingbirds. The hawk soared high and dived low with no success against the constant harassment of the much smaller birds. The trio flew almost out of sight and then the mockingbirds peeled off to go back where they came from, seemingly satisfied they had won the battle. He had witnessed this many times but never figured out why the much larger bird, equipped with a dangerous hooked beak, did not turn and make quick work of the harassing mockingbirds.

A subtle flick of the wrist sent a signal to Baugh and Wylie to move forward. In a short time, though he kept fighting the urge, Medlin's thoughts returned to Bennettsville and, this time, back to the beginning.

———

LYDIA BRISTOW AND WILLIAM MEDLIN were from two alien orbits whose paths were unlikely ever to align, cross, or intersect. They were of different status and natural disposition. But their paths tangled and knotted. That they were ill suited should not have been a surprise, but they were young and they did not look deeply into their future together.

The only true commonality of the two was that the ancestors of both families were part of the Great Migration in the sixteen hundreds from the British Isles—England, Ireland, Scotland, and Wales. Not all followed the same path to America. Most came through ports in Pennsylvania and Delaware from Belfast, where transport agents put together numerous ships to cross the ocean in the safety of others. Not as many crossed the Atlantic in single ships with destinations in Virginia, South Carolina, and Georgia. But all immigrants from the British Isles came for a new start—for the most part, they were people of the soil or those who had a desire to seek out opportunities in commerce. The main difference between the two families, Medlins and Bristows, was that one continued to follow traditions relating to the land and hard toil while the other soon chose to leave the farm and go into business.

———

THE EARLY BRISTOWS SETTLED in the Carolina colony in a village called Carlisle, but later Bristows moved twenty miles away to Bennettsville, the flourishing town that was already the center of business in the region, where the Cotton Exchange in season attracted wagons piled high. These wagons often formed a line three blocks long for the weigh-in.

The business atmosphere of Bennettsville was compatible with the Bristow interests. The family preferred to support the farming industry rather than farm themselves. Lydia's Grandfather Bristow grew to prominence and wealth in the lending business—mostly catering to the financial needs of the burgeoning cotton industry. Lydia's father, Hugh Coit Bristow, followed his father into the family banking trade.

Through diligence and family connections, young Bristow advanced from lowly scribe to Vice President, Chief Loan Officer. He married Miss Mary Anne Quick, chosen from a class compatible with his own. She was a good marriage candidate, a young woman trained to run a home and handle social responsibilities for the young man on the way up.

It was on prestigious Main Street that young Bristow built a fine home to demonstrate his prominence at the Bennettsville Bank. The grand house on Main Street in Bennettsville was a world apart from the farm in Clio where Medlin grew up. His wife's life before they married was very different from his.

———

LYDIA ANNE BRISTOW WAS BORN into a home of privilege. She was the focus of her doting parents. There were no siblings, due to complications during a difficult birth, forcing Mrs. Bristow to bear the scrutiny of others toward a mother of a single child.

The Bristows hovered over their lone child. The fledgling Lydia grew under close supervision—too close to allow her to venture out to explore beyond the watchful eyes of her parents.

Not only did the parents protect Lydia from all negatives the world had to dish out, but they also showered her with praise of her beauty and deportment—neither of which she had. She was, in fact, plain and awkward, no beauty.

Moreover, since her parents were quite a bit older than those of her peers, their guidance of her wardrobe was not toward the current style. Mr. and Mrs. Bristow were not as aware of the latest fashion as they had once been.

Being an only child, Lydia had nothing and nobody to consider but herself, and the parents supported her self-centeredness. Around the house her mood was closely monitored. She discovered this could be used to her advantage. She was cunning in knowing that any swing in her mood would prompt some action by the parents. To appear happy suggested she was in want of nothing, so she showed herself to be in a constant state of discontent—a manipulation she carried on with much success.

The Bristows shielded their daughter from any hint of her shortcomings, but deep inside they were very much aware that Lydia was below average in presentation. With dread, they knew that one day their daughter's limitations would matter. With Lydia approaching marrying age, the day was soon coming when she would be judged by others in cruel ways.

All phases of her maturity followed the timeworn customs of her class. As a critical time in Lydia's development approached, the parents were ready to assist, knowing it would take the combined effort of all to get through it successfully. As a girl of Southern gentility, Lydia was expected to develop fitness and desirability to match with a young man from the same social level—with matrimony as the goal. She would be competing with all the other girls her age to be chosen as a wife within a narrow field of boys from the good families.

From the age of sixteen, girls were thrown into a vortex of domestic and academic training and preparation to hone their matchability to young men who initially would take only passing notice of what was happening until the pressures of custom and ritual would ensnare them.

A steady round of social activities commenced so that the young people could scrutinize one another. Lydia did not take to the cultural ritual enthusiastically. She determined that the entire process was made to serve the interests of the young men. Their wants. Their needs. The notion that the young ladies had in some way to prove their worthiness seemed pathetic to Lydia. To put in effort to be considered desirable went counter to her upbringing, where she had had to prove nothing, yet still was the center of attention. If this were not enough to repel Lydia, she sensed that the customary ritual was really a competition among the young ladies—to be chosen by some suitable young man was what it was all about.

Mrs. Bristow deeply loved her daughter, but her love was not full of pride. Pride necessarily would be driven by something special about her daughter, but Lydia demonstrated nothing to be proud of. Not deterred, the mother threw herself headlong into her job to mold, train, and tutor

Lydia, despite knowing it would be especially challenging given what she had to work with.

With Lydia loath to enter the competition to win over a future husband, Mrs. Bristow had first to put the girl in the right frame of mind. The mother started with a concept she only half believed herself. She suggested to her daughter that beauty was the work of pure luck, but to look and act dignified was a far higher quality over natural beauty. Lydia took to heart her mother's hint that her gifts were far superior to a pretty face. Armed with this notion, Lydia looked down on pretty girls from her lofty perch. She viewed their giggles and flirtations as mindless twaddle such as was found in more common circles.

The clutch of Bennettsville's popular girls considered Lydia haughty and managed to exclude her whenever tradition did not mandate her presence. She saw the snub as a demonstration of pure jealousy and paid it no mind. She made a point not to let it bother her but chose to go about her life independent of the comfort of close friends.

Because those most responsible for molding Lydia's thoughts and views were her parents, by her mid-teens she had become a reflection of a generation before her own. She was a fuddy-duddy with backward ideas—not one of the young girls entering that phase in their development when they thought anyone out of step with their perceived brilliance suffered from some lameness of mind.

With little that could be done regarding the daughter's God-given personal visage, Mrs. Bristow went to work to prepare the girl in other ways. Lydia was introduced to advanced skills in aspects of homemaking. In the floral arts, she was able to assemble more-than-adequate arrangements of seasonal flowers. She was taught needle arts—crewel, needlepoint—with mediocre results, due to unimaginative color choices and poor drafting skills.

Mrs. Bristow thought it important that Lydia learn to run a household, so on occasion she let the girl instruct Jewel, the slave housemaid, as to her duties for the day. Soon it became clear that Lydia was too harsh in her instruction. Usually it ended with Jewel in a sulk lasting for a few days. Mrs. Bristow made a mental note to teach Lydia the more effective points in handling the slaves.

———

THE SOCIAL SEASON STARTED, with dances arranged where partners were not by choice but randomly assigned to assure that every girl had an introduction to every boy. Lydia enjoyed everything at first. She loved dancing, especially the reels. She felt free to give in to the music and she enjoyed feeling her skirt swinging wildly, counter to her body motion so that it slapped against her stockinged legs. She could let herself go in ways that were not encouraged at home, where it wasn't considered lady-like to make the wild movements that were perfectly acceptable on the dance floor. She had so much fun at the first two dances, she forgot what was to come and what it was all about—a competition for her future.

The boys had not caught on to the seriousness of it all when the round of dances began, not realizing that they had entered the path to marriage and responsibility. Until they saw it for what it was, they jokingly called the selection process "cutting one from the herd."

By the fourth event of the season, successes were measured by the filling of dance cards. Initially Lydia—based on dancing alone—held her own. However, as the season progressed, when the boys became more serious about honing their choices, her desirability fell off to the prettier girls—to the ones who had picked up on the power of the giggle, the girlishness, the tease.

The Bristows grilled her after each dance, trying to get a fix on her acceptability into society. They could see by her dance card that it was not good. They had been encouraged early on, but by midseason the sulking took over. Lydia started saying it was stupid and she wanted to quit going to the dances. But quitting was not an option. Her parents made it clear to Lydia that she had to buck up and try harder.

Before panic set in, there seemed to be a turn for the better. Jesse White, of the lumber Whites, appeared to take an interest in Lydia. The attention of the handsome young man surprised everyone, including the Bristows. But they started to think that by the grace of God perhaps their fears were unfounded.

Jesse asked Lydia for the prized last dance at the final two cotillion balls before Christmas. Jesse had taken his position as Lydia's most serious prospect. He was by her side at the parties, and for everybody who was keeping score, he was Lydia's steady beau.

Jesse seemed to the Bristows to have all the qualities that fit hand in glove with Lydia's proclivities. He appeared shy, while Lydia desired to lead. She felt comfortable with Jesse, and she seemed to maintain her accustomed position as the center of attention. With Jesse, she did not fear being subject to the direction and whim of the man. In her mind, she had chosen him and that suited her just fine. The New Year was approaching, which meant commitments to matrimony would be finalized between families with the official announcement to be made in the spring.

But while Jesse appeared shy, much was going on behind his vacant eyes. What appeared to be a character to please, to accommodate, was a young man with his own plan. Jesse found Lydia a perfect candidate with whom he could mark time—get through the season safely until he could find a way to introduce Miss Emily Gilbert, a young woman of modest background, who had been the object of his affection since they had met by chance at her father's produce stand the previous summer.

Lydia was tolerable for his purpose, but as the New Year approached she became demanding and tedious to Jesse. He was more and more anxious to extricate himself from the pathetic girl who flaunted her beau around Bennettsville. Jesse was miserable—he had not yet found the right moment to uncover his true love to his well-to-do parents.

Completely unaware of Jesse's true plan, Lydia continued to preen and cavort with the increasingly quiet Jesse by her side. The peers of her class were stumped at her success. She seemed to have so few positive qualities with which to reel in a catch like Jesse, but they were too aware of the competition winding down to give it much thought—it was down to the wire and all the girls were concerned about their own fate.

Never mind that Jesse had not openly discussed an engagement. His attentiveness clearly demonstrated his intentions to wishful thinkers like the Bristows. Lydia pegged Jesse as a realist, not a romantic. He would be the type to first formalize things through a visit with her father to lay out his intentions and then ask permission for her hand.

Any day now, Jesse would be received into the house and ushered into the library where Mr. Bristow would be waiting. No other prospect ever entered Lydia's mind.

She did not hint of an actual engagement to the other girls, choosing instead to look forward to enjoying the full effect when the official announcement would be made. But she simply had to share her certain prospect with her mother so they could begin to lay the groundwork for what would be a wedding like none other in Marlboro County. Mrs. Bristow waited for the right occasion to share the confidence with Mr. Bristow. He tried not to let his expression betray his surprise that Lydia could please the White boy.

At the first opportunity, Mrs. Bristow went to the buffet in the dining room, where she could not resist running her hand over the bone china tea service, which had been sitting in wait for just this very occasion. She detected a slight film of dust on the surface. It would take a careful wash with mild soap and a damp cloth to return it to the inherent translucency of hard paste porcelain.

She took note to tell Jewel to take more care in her dusting. Mrs. Bristow decided she would be firm but not too harsh since the girl was just a Negro and therefore hadn't the capacity to feel the reverence fitting for such finery. However, Jewel was going to have to step up to the pressures of advanced entertaining that were sure to come after the announcement of the blessed engagement.

Mrs. Bristow's head was swimming with a great variety of things that would need her attention. She took out the small pad of paper and pencil that she always kept in her apron. The mounting number of items could very well surpass her memory. First on the list: *Talk to Jewel and Henry about more effort.*

To slow her racing mind, Mrs. Bristow took a step back to admire the tea service on the buffet and experience the same rush of pride she first felt when her parents presented it to her on the eve of her own marriage. She knew the history by heart—the tea set was Worcester porcelain from the region of England most known for the grandest of porcelains. The delicateness of the clay body, from mines in Cornwall, had a slight greenish cast to look as nearly as possible like China trade hard paste. It took years of experimentation in England to come to rival the porcelains of ancient China.

George III and Queen Charlotte visited the Worcester factory in 1788 and were so impressed by the quality of the wares that they granted to the manufacturer the coveted title of Royal Porcelain Works, thereby establishing it as the choice of nobility seeking the best in the land. The brass medallion with the royal crest, affixed to the front facade of the factory, signaled that only the exceptional could be found within.

Mrs. Bristow's parents, on their grand tour through Europe, came upon the Worcester tea set in a shop in London. They dismissed the patterns of wide appeal—mostly hand-painted florals. Porcelains of Chinese influence, very popular at the time, also left them unimpressed. But when they first sighted "Feather," they knew that it was their image of forward thinking. Feather was delicately adorned with exquisitely hand-painted single feathers of game birds—grouse, pheasant, and gamecock. Each feather was painted with such accuracy that it was possible to identify the exact species of bird from which it came.

Although she had so much to do, Mrs. Bristow allowed herself to linger awhile gazing at the elegant tea set. After all, she had looked forward to passing it on to her daughter for so many years and now the occasion was near. Presently she turned her attention back to the pad still on the ready. She wrote, *Tea with Mrs. White*. A tea with just the two mothers would be the perfect time to blend ideas regarding the wedding and to forge a bond.

She put the notepad to service again as she wrote, *New uniforms for Jewel and Henry*. The appearance of the slaves and their performance in the presence of the Whites were of concern. There was no room for their antics around the Whites.

———

BOTH JEWEL AND HENRY had been in service with the family since well before Lydia was born. The slaves grew up on the cotton plantation—owned by the Quicks—where Mrs. Bristow spent her childhood. Upon her marriage to Mr. Bristow, the two had been a wedding gift from her parents. Jewel's own mother had been nursemaid to baby girl Quick and over time became the housemaid. Jewel performed the same functions in the Bristow home, nursing Lydia, then doing exclusively housekeeping duties. Henry, like Jewel in bondage to the Quicks and then a wedding gift to the Bristows, had been in charge of livery on the Quick plantation. But with the transfer to the town-dwelling newlyweds, his duties changed to include errands and pick-up and delivery of everything from groceries to handwritten notes. On those rare occasions when visitors came, he would be called on to usher in guests from the front door.

The universe of the two slaves was limited to the Quick and Bristow households where, over time, they learned the vulnerabilities of their masters and used them to their advantage. They had secret hiding places and plenty of effective comebacks as to why tasks had not been fully satisfied. In such a limited environment, putting one over on the Missus, who doled out the work, became an amusing game. Henry and Jewel played the game so well that the Bristows rarely detected what was going on right under their noses.

––––

HOWEVER, THE UPCOMING ENGAGEMENT put Mrs. Bristow on high alert and she felt this was the time to tune up the staff. She couldn't bear the thought of the house girl assisting at the tea in her raggedy service dress. Through time the crisp white had turned to a dingy yellow, but no one had seemed to take note of it until this point. Mrs. Bristow thought how horrifying it was that she should let slide the unraveling of the girl's hem and had only now noticed that Jewel's dress was worn so thin, her undergarment was visible, clear as day.

Too, Henry's livery jacket was taking on a telltale shine due to too many years put to a hot iron. It did not take a close look to notice the frayed collar from the constant rub of his nappy whiskers. How could she have not noticed the scruffy condition of her slaves? Mrs. White could take one look at them and think that the running of the Bristow home was far from adequate and, worse, would reflect on Lydia's poor training in running a household.

She turned the matter of her own neglect onto the slaves and concluded it was her good nature that had opened the door for the pair to become slovenly and way too familiar. When was the last time she had been addressed with proper respect as Ma'am? She began to feel aggrieved.

—Oh yes, this is going to change, and quick!

Getting her back up and devising a plan of action could have left her in a state of nervous agitation, but surprisingly she felt energized. She was starting to experience a major shift away from the feelings of stagnation that had left her emotionally paralyzed for a long time. Then lately she had been in a constant state of crippling fear that her only daughter would be husbandless and childless. She had dreaded the inevitable whispers of pity by neighbors, friends, and family.

Meanwhile, all through the fall and winter social season, Jesse White's parents hounded him about who he had taken a shine to. He once mentioned Lydia's name briefly without elaborating, but although she was startled, that was all Mrs. White needed to hear to believe that things had become serious with Miss Lydia Anne Bristow. It was always like pulling teeth to get anything out of the boy, so for him to come up with a name was as good as a commitment. Without an announcement to the rest of the family, Mrs. White took it upon herself to have a sit-down with Lydia's mother to compare notes about their young ones.

Mrs. Bristow was not surprised when a hand-delivered note from Mrs. White arrived at her door. The mothers would meet on neutral ground—the customary August Moon Teahouse—to save their homes for the official engagement and then wedding announcement. In talking together, both mothers were delighted to find, as they had suspected, there was mutual intention between the children to advance toward matrimony. On parting, the women shared a hearty embrace, with both feeling there would be years ahead with mutual experiences together, not the least being grandchildren.

The day came when the Bristows extended an invitation to the Whites to get together for tea to formalize the engagement—it seemed to the mothers a natural progression through the months of social events coming down to the pairing of the next generation of the good families of Bennettsville.

On the other hand, Jesse was dreading the day. Ever since the idea of engagement to Lydia occurred to his mother, his nights had been fitful. He would fight back images of the upcoming engagement, then fall asleep only to dream the same dream night after night. He was always in a skiff being swept toward a perilous waterfall. Generally he would awake and feel relieved it was merely a dream, only to realize a moment later that the reality was worse than the nightmare. He became sullen and standoffish. He woke up the day of the engagement feeling sick with dread.

———

MRS. BRISTOW LOOKED at the carefully set table on the veranda. At the sight of the elegant tea set on the ready, looking so special as only the finest of porcelains could look, her spirits lifted. Jewel came onto the porch to lay out the slivers of fresh lemon on a silver dish. The slave girl wore her new service dress. Knowing that Henry would open the door for the Whites looking crisp as he should in his new set of clothes just topped off the satisfaction that Mrs. Bristow had dreamed of since her child was a toddler. She said it out loud.

—Oh happy day!

Mr. Bristow and Lydia arrived on the porch at the exact moment the front door knocker sounded, as though this were a stage play. Henry ushered Mr. and Mrs. White out onto the porch. They looked in stark contrast to the occasion—their eyes to the ground and glum. They said that Jesse should be along any minute, adding that the boy had never been late for anything so important and asking for his actions to be excused. This was certainly not how he had been raised. Tea was poured with everyone in cordial conversation waiting for the young man to arrive. Jewel had been given strict instructions to serve flutes of champagne for a toast as soon as Jesse was there.

After half an hour, everyone tried not to show panic. When the door knocker finally sounded, Mrs. White's quiet exclamation could barely be heard.

—Thank God!

Henry came carrying a silver tray bearing a telegram addressed to Mr. White. Without looking at it first, he read out loud. *Father, I never meant to hurt anyone. I have gone to Charleston with the young lady I intend to marry.*

Lydia slumped over in the wicker rocker and tried to catch her breath. Both mothers rushed to steady the girl, who looked about to faint.

―――――

MEDLIN'S PARENTS BOTH DIED YOUNG when Medlin was in his very early twenties. He lived on alone, taking care of the farm, after his brother Tom went off to Charleston to find work in the trading business—less stable even than farming but always with the outside chance of making a fortune. After a couple of years, although he didn't much mind the solitude and was quite happy going out by himself hunting and fishing, Medlin began to think that perhaps he had better find a wife. So he started walking to Bennettsville to attend Lyceum, where young people gathered on Saturday nights for a poetry reading or lecture followed by refreshments and dancing.

However, he did not really enjoy being there. After a little while he would escape to an outside porch to avoid the awkwardness of mixing with people he didn't know at all well. One evening, he was totally unprepared for the young woman who came out from the hall and engaged him in conversation. Lydia was her name and she, too, was uncomfortable with the frivolous atmosphere and the idle chitchat taking place within. Immediately Medlin thought he saw in the young woman the melancholy or aloofness—he couldn't tell which—that he recognized in himself.

From that first Saturday evening on, though they met only at the Lyceum, the two developed a bond. Each felt safe in the company of the other, and that allowed them both to handle their anxiety to mingle with other young people. Lydia loved to dance and once she had young Medlin by her side, there was not a reel she didn't drag him into. Before long, Medlin was her crutch to fit in and he went along with it.

Pretty soon, they married, not because of passion but more that it was the thing to do, and Lydia was very anxious to get a husband after the fiasco of Jesse. However, once Lydia had the security of being a married woman, she started to throw away her husband emotionally and openly looked down on him. Medlin withdrew more and more into himself. Although they produced three children, they both realized too late that it wasn't enough just to hold each other up in the face of social pressures—there had to be more for a happy marriage, but there wasn't.

Medlin got to prefer his solitude to being in Lydia's company, so even with all the problems he worried over when he was alone, he was content to be out in the field working by himself on that first day of the season.

———

APPROACHING THE END OF ANOTHER ROW and still thinking about Bennettsville, he suddenly felt faint. The last thing he could remember as he got ready to put Baugh and Wylie into the turn was a sharp pain in his gut. Then everything started swimming before his eyes. The next thing he knew he was lying in the fresh-cut furrow, and he heard the mules blowing out snorts of air from their nostrils and the jingle of the tack hardware as they threw their heads back and forth. Baugh and Wiley stomped their big hooves into the ground—they were impatient.

Medlin opened his eyes to the odd perspective on the plow from the dirt up and beyond, to the underbellies of the mules. With his right arm still tangled in the leads, he was able to force himself into a sitting position. As he tried to assess his situation, he deduced he had had a spell of sorts and had gone down. After a couple of paces—once they felt they were under no control—the mules had stopped, but before coming to a good full stop they had dragged Medlin a few yards. He spit out dirt and blood from a cut to his lip, where he had hit the spade on his way down. He applied some pressure with his thumb to his gut below his navel and suddenly sucked in air from the pain.

He managed to get on his feet, using the plow for leverage. Baugh and Wiley both strained to look around to see about the delay. He considered whether to continue, but he could barely stand in a hunch—the only position his bowel would permit. He could tell he had fouled his britches. The flies had already taken their attention away from the mules and were buzzing around him.

Disheartened, he turned the mules toward the barn and hoped Lydia would be busy at something away from the house so that she would not make sport of his condition.

THE DAY AFTER CHIP GAVE GIL THE TWO DIARIES, she drove to work anxious to get started. She parked the car and then made directly for the stairwell and the four flights to ground level. Again, she did not even consider the elevator—it had been out of service for weeks. Heading down the stairs, she could hear the grit mixed with condensation under her flats. On the ground floor, there sat the Vic in her parking spot, but she wasn't going to stew over it, so she walked quickly out of the dim parking garage and into the morning light.

There it was, right ahead, the capitol—the State House—bathed in a golden sunlight, as it always was on a clear morning in June. No one else on the street would give it the slightest notice, but Gil thought the sight was magnificent. Atop the rotunda flew the three flags. For the first time she noticed that in color and design the flags complemented one another as though they had always been intended to be presented as a set. Through a quirk of history, both the Stars and Stripes and the Confederate flag were some combination of identical shades of red, white, and blue. The dark blue and white of the South Carolina state flag fit right in.

With her knowledge of South Carolina's past, Gil could not help but think that if a narrative would be put to this group of flags, the result would be a history of the state. To her they were a fitting exclamation point above the State House.

ONE OF THE THIRTEEN STRIPES on the American flag representing the first colonies belonged to South Carolina. The stripe had been hard to come by. Gil thought about how on the road to American independence many individuals representing the state experienced loss and hardship and even death. Of the four South Carolina signers of the Declaration of Independence, one fell ill on his way back to South Carolina from Philadelphia, where the delegates had spent months hashing out details of the Declaration. Exhausted and hoping to regain his health, in Charleston he boarded a ship going to the West Indies. The ship was lost at sea. The other three were captured and imprisoned for a year when Charleston was overtaken and occupied by the British in 1780 during the Revolution. The extensive holdings of all three were seized, their confiscated slaves representing a large portion of their wealth.

That South Carolina would commit to the cause of independence from Britain was surprising given a sustained attachment to the motherland and a nostalgia for everything British. England was referred to as "home." Charleston, a thriving coastal port, was where most newcomers concentrated, setting up housekeeping with the trappings of their homeland. Every day ships were at the port offloading books, textiles, porcelains, and every manner of remembrances of the lifestyle in England.

WHEN CHARLES PINCKNEY FROM CHARLESTON arrived in Philadelphia in 1787 for the Constitutional Convention, years after the Declaration of Independence, he was only twenty-nine. The older seasoned and veteran delegates did not expect much from him. They were wrong. He spoke often—over one hundred times—and by the end had added immensely to the final draft. The separation of church and state and trial by jury were just two concepts that he contributed. In all, thirty-two provisions within the Constitution could be credited to Charles Pinckney.

All Southern delegates were on guard against any action to limit slavery. Pinckney led the negotiation to prevent Congress from making any attempt to limit the slave trade for a minimum of twenty years. He threatened that South Carolina would withdraw all participation if there were any change in policy regarding slavery and pointed out that the other slave states would surely follow. The word *slavery* did not appear at all in the Constitution.

The colony of South Carolina, while rich and powerful, was largely unknown to the Founding Fathers in Philadelphia. Later, in 1791, Washington passed through on his Southern tour, but during the 1780s there was virtually no travel to the region from the North. South Carolina was the most prosperous of the thirteen, with a port to rival all others in colonial America, but because of the difficulty of the long sail to get to it, South Carolina remained apart and distant from the Northern hotbeds of activity regarding independence.

The colony was also somewhat isolated from adjoining colonies. The colony of Georgia was right next to South Carolina, but there was such a wide difference in basic culture that there was little exchange between them. The southernmost colony was established as a haven for lowly debtors sent to the New World to work off their financial obligations, and for ne'er-do-wells who were a drain on society back in Britain. Leaders of the Georgia experiment felt that for many the abuse of drink had been the culprit, so they forbade the use of hard spirits. But in South Carolina, especially in Charleston, a good Madeira or Scotch whiskey was thoroughly enjoyed.

———

GIL HAD ALWAYS THOUGHT that the practical isolation of the colony of South Carolina had a hand in the strong streak of independence and the characteristic of stubborn self-reliance that would show themselves through the state's history. Without the advantages of closeness to the Northern colonies and little in common with Georgia, South Carolina went about developing on its own. The port of Charleston thrived. The colony encouraged the worship of all religions. Prosperity was within the reach of those willing to work. South Carolina did well for itself and with success came pride and a little arrogance from the conviction that the success was achieved without help from outside.

For decades, the colony grew without incident under British rule, but by 1765 the British began to look to the colonies to start paying their own way. Parliament passed the Stamp Act requiring all newspapers, commercial bills, and legal documents to bear a stamp purchased from British agents. Resistance was so strong that the tax was withdrawn. However, in 1767 the British levied a tax on tea and other commodities with the Townshend Revenue Act. Boston and Charleston each staged a "tea party" on their docks and tossed tea into their harbors in protest.

All thirteen colonies did not combine forces in a revolution against the British at the same time. But when South Carolinians concluded they objected to being exploited and denied Parliamentary representation, they joined the other colonies in the risky project to take up arms against the greatest power of that time, the British Empire.

As Gil continued down Main toward the State House and the Caroliniana, she considered the middle flag—the South Carolina state flag. It was simple in design, a white palmetto tree and a white crescent on a dark indigo-blue field. There was a lot of history in this flag, too. For starters, the palmetto tree.

———

ON JUNE 28, 1776, after chasing George Washington around Boston and New York, the British set their sights on the South for what they thought would be a quick encounter. They desperately needed a victory under their belts. With nine men-of-war—a fifty-gun flagship and eight other well-armed vessels—they sailed into position just outside Charleston Harbor, bearing the collective firepower of three hundred cannon. A sandy strip of land at the mouth of the harbor was where the South Carolina forces had their barely fortified line of defense.

Colonel William Moultrie was in command of the fort, which was not much more than piled up sand on a nothing spit of land called Sullivan's Island. When the British made their appearance, Sullivan's was mainly a quarantine station for African slaves before they were taken across the harbor to be auctioned in Charleston.

Colonel Moultrie had gained much of his military experience over sandy terrain, chasing runaway slaves—whom he either killed or recaptured. When not running down slaves, Moultrie was mainly charged with chasing off local native Indians and confiscating their land for White settlers to turn into farmland. Going against a heavily armed fleet of British warships was another thing altogether. Up until he faced this powerful enemy, his foes had been the defenseless. To make matters worse, Moultrie's troops were wholly unprepared for the engagement.

Caught unexpectedly with little to protect the fort, Moultrie ordered his men to cut and stack trunks of the palmetto trees that were plentiful close by the fortification. The spongy logs were very effective in deflecting the cannon balls that came in by the hundreds. In the end, the little fort held. The British, bombarded from the shore, never made it past Sullivan's Island. The fleet, soundly beaten, retreated in defeat. The action was a major victory for the American upstarts early in the Revolutionary War. The story of the spongy native palmetto was not forgotten but honored with placement on the state flag of South Carolina.

The field of the South Carolina flag was indigo blue, widely thought to honor a teenage girl who miraculously and almost single-handedly saved the stagnant South Carolina economy.

———

COLONEL GEORGE LUCAS SAILED into the harbor of Charleston in 1738 with his wife and two young daughters. His two sons were in England getting their education. Lucas had been serving in the British Army stationed in Antigua, in the British West Indies, but when tensions between Spain and England in the Caribbean Islands flared up, he took his family to a safer environment in Charleston. He purchased three working plantations and the fifty-five slaves included in the transaction.

One year after arriving in Charleston, Colonel Lucas accepted an appointment as lieutenant governor back in Antigua and returned to the British West Indies, leaving his sixteen-year-old daughter, Eliza, to take charge of his three plantations. His wife could be of no help since she was gravely ill and bedridden. The other daughter was just a child, leaving the mature-for-her-age Eliza to take full responsibility for running the estate. On top of everything, before he left he confided to Eliza that the plantations could not survive economically solely on the existing rice operation and that it was up to her to develop a new cash crop in order to keep the estate going and pay down the substantial debt incurred upon purchase of the properties.

With England in the midst of a textile boom, it made sense to investigate the much-needed production of cloth dyes. To the British, deep blue from the indigo plant was a particular favorite coloring for uniforms, work clothes, and fine garments. The climate and soil were ideal in the West Indies to grow indigo, where the production of the blue dye had mushroomed into a thriving business. Knowing the West Indies climate to be similar in the Lowcountry, her father sent Eliza a small packet of indigo seeds for experimentation.

Eliza and a trusted slave named Quash diligently went to work to grow a test crop of the indigo plant. Although the first attempt produced healthy plants, an early frost set in, killing the whole lot. The father sent more seeds from Antigua, along with an expert in growing indigo there. This seasoned veteran observed the ambition of the girl and saw her potential to become a dangerous competitor for his business back home, so he tried to sabotage her operation with erroneous guidance that would guarantee disaster. Quash, working side by side with Eliza, caught on to the ruse and the man was run off on the next ship heading south.

Eliza and Quash worked for three years until they were able to produce, with confidence, indigo dye. Their production of dye started with plants, which were harvested and boiled into a slurry of dense dye and then dried into cakes. Eliza was generous and shared seeds and expertise with neighboring planters. In just a few years, ships left the port of Charleston with holds full of cakes of indigo, bound for an insatiable market at textile finishing houses in England. The volume of dye grew dramatically from 5,000 pounds in 1746 to 130,000 pounds two years later. Before the Revolutionary War, indigo dye made up one-third of the total exports of the Southern colony and drastically improved the economic status of the planters by supplementing the wealth they gained from growing rice.

———

GIL LOVED THE THOUGHT that the color of indigo would be chosen for the background of the South Carolina flag—a nod to the untiring, precocious efforts of a girl who made such an enormous contribution to her adopted state.

The last of the three flags—the Confederate flag—waving over the State House in the soft breeze under the American and South Carolina flags looked to Gil rather attractive with its prominent white stars on blue bands crossed on the red field—the same three colors as on the Stars and Stripes. But then she caught herself and thought that the flag was attractive only if you didn't consider all the baggage that came along with it. That third flag was the reason why day after day there were crowds of people gathered at the State House.

Yet despite what the Confederate flag represented, to Gil's eye the three flags together did make an attractive-looking group in the early, crisp light of the sun.

———

THE CONFEDERATE FLAG was not originally the official flag of the Confederacy. The first flag intended to represent the states that seceded from the Union was called the "Stars and Bars." It had three broad horizontal stripes, alternating red and white. The canton—top hoist corner—was blue with thirteen stars in a circle, each representing a state of the Confederacy. However, this first Confederate flag had an unacceptable flaw in battle—commanders could not immediately differentiate the Confederate flag from the American flag of the Union, and so they were unable to follow the progress of their men in the field.

Needing to make a quick interim change, the Confederacy adopted Robert E. Lee's Northern Virginia battle flag. With its Southern Cross so prominent on a field of red, it was easily distinguishable in battle. Still trying to come up with a unique official flag, the Confederate Congress selected a design with Lee's battle flag as the canton against a pure white background, which some thought fitting because "as a people we are fighting to maintain the Heaven-ordained supremacy of the white man over the inferior or colored race."

But just as the first flag did not work on the field of battle, so it was with the second—there was too good a chance, with the majority of the flag in white, that it would be mistaken for the traditional white flag of truce. The design was then altered by adding a broad vertical stripe of red to stand out on the white field. This flag was officially adopted a month before the end of the War in 1865—but by then there were far more pressing issues than settling on the national flag of the Confederacy. From the end of the War onward, the interim flag—Lee's Northern Virginia battle flag—was used as the symbol of the Confederacy.

———

GIL WALKED ACROSS GERVAIS STREET and onto the State House grounds, where for nearly four weeks various factions had been setting up daily. The debate over the Confederate flag and about the South seemed to have the power to draw people in, both Black and White. As the demonstration had become more organized, the controversy had gained momentum and rolled along, adding layers of complexity—legacy pride, oppression, systemic racism, entitlement, alienation. White Southerners felt they were unfairly perceived by outsiders as a tribe of "ignorant crackers"—a reputation they couldn't shake. No matter how much effort was spent to replace the old image with views of a progressive "New South," it was all being challenged, right out in the open now. The South needed to prove William Faulkner wrong when he said, "The past is never dead. It's not even past."

At the least, the flag shook people out of a state of apathy and complacency dating from the days of Martin Luther King. Not since the height of the Civil Rights Movement, decades earlier, had there been serious contemplation of society's commitment to racial equality. With the issue of the Confederate flag, people began waking up again—thinking about the significance of this symbol of the Confederacy displayed on a government building.

The flag meant different things to different people. To some it represented the legacy of a justified rebellion when the South was in fear of

losing a way of life, while for others it represented both White supremacy and the bitter oppression of slavery. Now Gil noticed demonstrators
carrying placards with two opposing messages—one: *Your Heritage Is My
Slavery*; the other: *Pride Not Prejudice*.

Gil came to the conclusion that everybody was getting hung up on
the Civil War as though that was the basis of the whole reason for racial
discord. Many people, both scholars and the average citizen, were trying
to make sense of the issues on race, and their thinking began and stayed
on the War itself, but Gil knew it was more than that and had much
deeper roots.

In Gil's mind, too much emphasis was being placed on two questions
that seemed to emerge in the context of the Civil War—was the War
about states' rights or slavery? And was Lincoln really dedicated to abol-
ishing slavery or was he more set on saving the Union? Who to blame for
the War seemed to be a question monopolizing discussions. For Gil it was
more meaningful to look at what had led up to the conflict. To concentrate
on the Civil War alone was to focus on the result of what had come before.
To understand fully, one had to follow the treatment of the Negro back to
the sixteen hundreds. To start with the Civil War would be to ignore the
vital fact that the War was a result of what had led up to it.

Gil was certain there was a thread of continuity running from White
Europeans' superior attitude toward the Negro starting long before the
first colony in America, strung all the way through to Columbia in
2000 when Black people were being faced with seeing the Confederate
flag on the State House, a reminder of their history steeped in racism,
where they were branded as inferior. Although Gil tried to look at the
issue of the flag with the cold eye of an academic, she wasn't altogether successful. While she contemplated the big picture of racism in
America—its origin and progression—it surprised her to see that from
a personal perspective, she wasn't much different from many others in
that she was not firm on how she thought about race.

She hadn't given race much thought until after her conversation with
Max at the gym when she said there would be a problem hiring a Black
trainer. It horrified her to think she herself was a contributor to racial inequality. It had come time when Gil and most all other Southerners—many for

the first time—had to face racism, and it couldn't be done without individual soul-searching and drawing on family background.

Despite Gil's certainty that the Civil War—or "The War Between the States," "The War of Northern Aggression," or just "The War"—was not merely the fulcrum of racism in America, it remained the main focus of the demonstration. Most especially, the press could not resist making the Civil War the centerpiece of its reporting—it offered endless opportunities to glom onto a colorful sideshow of Southern crazies acting the fool. There were interviews with rednecks unaware or not caring about their display of ignorance. "Political correctness" came into play when Confederate flag boxer shorts, worn by an off-duty cop and posted on his Facebook page, got him fired. Meanwhile Stuckey's, a large chain of tourist traps found mostly along Southern highways, quickly replenished their supply of Dixie trinkets. These—Confederate flags, as well as tee shirts and ball caps with the messages "Live and Die in Dixie," "Forget? Hell No!" or "Born White and by the Grace of God, Southern"—all flew off the shelves.

———

IN 1953, MAURICE BESSINGER opened a barbecue joint called Piggie Park. It was wildly successful. Eventually he had a chain of eight, where a large side of White supremacy was served up along with the food. Stacked up at the entrance to every restaurant there were tracts claiming among other things that Africans "appreciated" enslavement because of the "better life" they found in America.

A Baptist, Bessinger was also head of the National Association for the Preservation of White People. He refused to serve Black people until he was sued. *Newman v. Piggie Park Enterprises Inc.* went all the way to the United States Supreme Court. Bessinger's defense was that his religious beliefs compelled him to oppose any integration of the races whatsoever. The Court did not agree.

The loss in court did not dampen Bessinger's promotion of White supremacy. He stuck to his notion that God gave slaves to White people—that slavery was God's will and therefore it could not be evil or unjust. He urged the president of the University of South Carolina to cancel a Stevie Wonder concert, insisting that "jungle music is for jungle people."

During the demonstration against the Confederate flag in 2000, Bessinger defiantly raised the largest Confederate flags he could find over each of his restaurants. The press covered the die-hard White supremacist as an example of a perfect Southern racist.

Bessinger's commercially produced mustard sauce that he called Carolina Gold sold well against a crowd of competitors with labels like Swamp, Q Shack, and Booger Holler—all names suggesting old-time recipes from the piney woods of Dixie. But under pressure from customers over his racist antics, large grocery chains suddenly pulled Carolina Gold from the shelves. Walmart, Winn Dixie, Kroger, Publix, and others distanced themselves from anything Bessinger. The fall happened fast. Before he grasped what was going on, the financial losses were devastating.

The barbecue man freely spoke his mind about White supremacy for decades with no thought of how it would feel if people spoke their minds by punishing him through his business. He had not seen the changes coming. The Old South as he thought he knew it no longer existed. His assumption of a united Dixie was outdated.

———

IN THEIR EFFORTS to get the Confederate flag taken down from the top of the State House, the NAACP had decided on a strategy where the state would feel the sting if it didn't comply—they went for financial consequences. They settled on the threat of a boycott against the state of South Carolina. At the beginning it appeared that this would have little real impact in that it would keep only Black tourists away from the state, but when the net grew a lot wider, with cancellations of conventions and conferences, the tone and the economic consequences turned more serious. Sure enough, the opposition—those in favor of keeping the Confederate flag flying over the State House—first hearing of the boycott thought it would mean just a negligible loss of a few Black sympathizers. They failed to see the potential for big losses.

The NCAA (National Collegiate Athletic Association) Final Four Tournament was considering Greenville for 2002 but abruptly pulled out of negotiations after the demonstration started to heat up. The Bureau of Tourism and Trade in Charleston felt they were close to inking a deal with the National AMA (American Medical Association) convention, but suddenly all communication stopped. Big trouble due to the boycott set in for the state. The stakes were proving higher than any-one expected. Still, supporters of the flag just dug in their heels—deeper. Members of the legislature who were not sure how they felt decided to wait it out to see which way the constituents would go. The governor, too, waited to see how the country would weigh in—it could get ugly if the whole country was wrangled into the flag flak, and at all costs the governor didn't want ugly.

———

AS GIL WALKED BY THE STATE HOUSE, she couldn't help seeing that the NAACP organizers of the demonstration had stepped up in num-bers. The national coverage had grown and so had the demonstration. From her viewpoint it appeared they looked more organized. Early on it seemed there was a lot of standing around as people did when it was not clear what was what and who was supposed to be doing what. Now there were no idle clutches of demonstrators, but hustle in the pace and an air of immediacy and purpose. The only group not busy with some task was made up of a few people on the landing of the State House seeking the attention of the tall man Gil knew to be the owner of the Vic—the man who was using her parking space, the onetime-wrestler-turned-late-night-television-preacher who seemed to be showing up lately on the national news as the talking head representing the position of the NAACP.

———

A WOMAN ON THE SIDEWALK crossing the State House grounds caught Joe Pearl's eye. He had a good line of sight from the landing midway up the State House steps. It registered that this was the same woman who passed by every morning at just about this time or a little earlier and again later in the afternoon. And he recalled seeing her in the parking garage.

This morning Gil drew his attention same as anyone would take notice of a cardinal over a mockingbird. Her red hair made her an anomaly among the others scurrying on the path. It wasn't so red that she ever had to hear anybody call her carrot top, but any description of her appearance would have to start with her natural hair color. Gil herself saw it as being a bit of a burden. It added a layer of unwanted complication to her life, as it forced her to consider the color of clothes. She could never just throw on any pastel—pastels washed her out. And red, out of the question. So her go-to was any one in a collection of full skirts of densely colored patterns.

Before Joe was pulled into action by several people who wanted to bend his ear about this and that, he took another glance and noticed how free the woman with the red hair seemed to be. Her gait was swift and her skirt looked as if it had a hard time keeping up as it billowed out behind in the slight breeze. He wished he could be like that—free.

———

JOE PEARL'S STORY WAS LEGEND around Columbia. In his younger days he had a lucrative career in professional wrestling. He was a favorite amongst both White and Black folks, mostly because of his persona as a legit fighter against an array of opponents who had reputations built on showmanship over skill. He went by the name The Mighty Joe, where others chose names to support their image as badasses in the ring: Dick the Bruiser, The Vicious Viking, and Igor the Terrible. But one night Joe was thrown from the ring, and despite all the training to tuck and roll, when he hit the concrete he crushed his number four and five vertebrae like—as the doctor described it—a shattered teacup. His wrestling days were over.

During his lengthy stay in the hospital and rehab just to get walking again, there appeared before him a blinding white light with the message that he was to become a "shepherd of men."

Joe was always very well-dressed. He had his suits made to measure by a tailor whom everybody called "The Jew," whose shop was in the seediest part of town. There was no sign out front, but customers looking for quality could find him. The man moved about the shop always with a tape measure around his neck and three or four straight pins sticking out of his closed lips like someone with a toothpick. The Jew handled the expensive cloth with respect and reverence, but the best that could be said of the shop was that it was a dump. Out the back door in the alley was parked his S-Class Mercedes.

It was not hard to tell that under Joe's beautiful custom-tailored suit was a body that was well maintained. Joe thought of the gym like his second home. His real home was a decent townhouse in a better-than-decent neighborhood, but it was in fact only a place to sleep and reflect on the upcoming sermon for his TV show—as anyone could see by the blank walls and sparse furnishings.

On the counter separating the kitchen from the living room lay a decorative paper bag with limp blue-and-white streamers on the handle and a hangtag saying *Welcome to Thornwood*. The bag contained coupons to the closest dry cleaner, a free scented candle from a nearby housewares shop, and an eyeglass cleaning shammy with the name of the neighborhood oculist imprinted on it. The bag had remained untouched since he put it there two years earlier when he first moved in.

In the second bedroom were a desk, a chair on casters, and a plastic carpet protector under the chair. Against the wall opposite the window were a three-drawer filing cabinet and a low bookshelf unit holding Christian reference books, including a particularly thick volume entitled *The Bible Tells Us So*. This was the room where Joe wrote his scripts for his late-night television show, *Pearls of Joy*.

He was of the freakish height of six foot, ten inches. With both height and brawn, Joe looked like a cross between Tarzan and the Hulk. Other men at the gym would fake breaks in their routine to catch a glimpse of his magnificent body in action. The only special consideration in his workout was for his lower back, held together with titanium pins. He did pull-ups instead of crunches, which got the job done on the abdominals. On occasion when the back gave him fits, he carried, for support, a tall walking stick fashioned more like a crooked shepherd's staff than a cane.

Joe held on to some of the show business of a professional wrestler. His shoulder-length straight hair, combed back with a healthy application of Baxter's Pomade, looked like a helmet of patent leather. He carried it off well where on others it could look clownish. But of all the physical characteristics that made Joe really stand out was a subtle oddity that people stopped to wonder at—his hazel eyes.

When he was talking one-to-one, his conversation style was thoughtful and controlled, whereas on his television show he was greatly animated—walking with deliberation from one side of the raised stage to the other, all along sharing his message with exaggerated enunciation to emphasize key points. He had learned in the ring how to hold the attention of an audience.

He wore a small gold cross stud in his left earlobe and on his right hand a large Super Bowl–sized ring, custom-made to his own exact specifications. Upon close inspection, the size fifteen platinum ring had an embedded black pearl surrounded by an engraved wreath of thorns.

It would be a safe bet that the Reverend Joseph Pearl Joy was a descendant of slaves. According to his mother, on neither side of the family was there ever any speculation that their people might have come from somewhere other than within one hundred miles of Columbia. Of the Joys, on the father's side there were aunts, uncles, and cousins in Newberry, just fifty miles up the highway. More likely than not these Joys worked on cotton plantations for generations. Of Joe's father, not much was known since he had not stuck around long. In fact he was gone before Joe was born.

Joe's mother was vague about exactly where her own people were from. She knew that a good number of relatives had left the area during what was known as the Great Migration, when one-third of the Black population in the South went North to escape Jim Crow and find better-paying jobs in industrialized America. Many of those in her family who had headed North ended up in Chicago.

The origin of the name Joy was a matter of some spiritual pride to Joe. After the Civil War, emancipated slaves had to choose a last name by which to register as free men. The name was strictly of their choosing. Some assumed the name of their former master. Others took the name of a past president such as Washington or Jefferson, and some chose based on their state of mind when newly freed. Joe liked to speculate that his ancestor felt joy at being emancipated from slavery. *Pearl*, on the other hand, was purely the invention of a young

Joe who thought *Pearl* would look good on a fight-promotion poster and sound good coming from the microphone as he was being introduced into the ring.

Joe was raised by a mother who had little to offer a prospective employer, but she was street smart and had ways to get around a mostly blank resume. She had two children to feed, their fathers long gone. Irma got a job stocking shelves at a county-run food bank, where she took advantage of overripe fruit and vegetables, as well as on-the-brink milk given out free to employees. Food stamps took care of the rest.

Irma's wages fell just below the line of sustainability, so she qualified for subsidized housing. The family of three piled in with her sister and her sister's two kids for the yearlong delay while paperwork passed through the system. Finally they were accepted into Green Hill. Their two-story, two-bedroom brick unit, along with the other 184 same such units, were designed by government engineers. They were built with no consideration toward style or comfort but only to minimize square footage and to maximize the number of beings that could be accommodated. When Green Hill went up in the 1970s, there was no regulation requiring air-conditioning, but after a government study—one seemed to roll around every decade or so—indicated cool air was a basic necessity, window units were installed. They droned on in a constant loud hum throughout the complex during the hot months. From clotheslines strung behind the units hung mismatched sheets and pillowcases. The original plan made no allowance for clothes dryers, considered a frill by the government people.

The exterior grounds were spare, with an occasional bush that might be a rare survivor from the original landscaping in place during the ribbon-cutting ceremony decades before. On the other hand, water oaks, planted as saplings as part of the grand plan, grew some forty feet tall, blanketing the ground in shade, making it impossible for grass to grow anywhere. The only thing left underneath was bare earth, which the old-timers swept with a broom to keep their own little areas tidy. Nothing else but clotheslines interrupted the otherwise nude landscape.

Government subsidized housing came with rules. How stringently they were enforced depended on the whim of those in power at the

Housing Authority. The HA maintained a right to monitor tenant compliance and they had full power to act swiftly in case of violations. There were random checks for what the regulations referred to as *changes in household*, meant to determine whether any unauthorized man had taken up residence. It seemed that weekly there was a small pile of someone's sole possessions in life out at the curb after the tenant ignored two notices of eviction just hoping that Housing would give them a break—which they never did.

Equally monitored was undeclared income that could upset the hardship qualification and prove a tenant ineligible for low-income housing. Someone running a tiny beauty shop out of the unit or selling a little fresh produce, eggs, milk, or snacks as a convenience for other tenants would learn the hard way that anything of the sort was forbidden. Noncompliance not only resulted in losing the privilege to remain at Green Hill but would also go very badly toward anyone applying for assisted public housing elsewhere or at a later date.

With such high risks of losing housing, there was an overall suspicion among Green Hill tenants of anybody and everybody coming into the project, especially White people, who most represented snooping personnel from the Housing Authority or Child Protective Services. Suspicion extended to busybody neighbors who were seen as possible informants to the agencies in exchange for special favors. Therefore very few friendships were struck in Green Hill. Worst of all, once a family signed on at Green Hill or any other project like it, they would be capping off a life filled with bad luck, bad decisions, or both as they slid down the dark rabbit hole, with recovery near impossible. There was no reversal of fortunes in Green Hill that anyone living there could remember, no one they could see as an example that it wasn't futile to hope and dream for anything better.

However, as a teenager Joe got lucky. One Saturday morning Felicia Muirhead, age forty-eight, picked her way across a broken concrete sidewalk to find an apartment number. From the second she entered the Green Hill complex her every move was monitored through numerous parted blinds. She was on a mission from Olin Mills, her employer. Olin had recently launched a child-mentoring program, which they called

Hands Out To Our Neighbors, an initiative to counter critics who said Olin ignored the low-income community that existed practically in the shadow of the mill. The mission statement, pinned to the company bulletin board: *To transform Green Hill into a community of multigenerational and socially stable individuals and families.*

Every department got a memo from the head office saying they were expecting one hundred percent participation from every division, a tactic Olin used each year when the United Way drive rolled around, knowing no one would want to be an opt-out spoiler. Everyone in Logistics, Felicia's department, had kids of their own except for her, and all said they figured with their own broods to put up with, they were already doing their part for the youth of the world—thank you very much. That left only Felicia to comply with the directive, which was ironic considering she had not one altruistic or nurturing bone in her body. Her one priority was herself. But she was loyal to Olin, who she thought couldn't function without her, so she signed up.

When filling out the forms for Hands Out, she was immediately tripped up by the question of whether she wanted to mentor a boy or a girl. She was stumped, since she didn't have a clue about what to do with either. Felicia had no affinity for the girliness of shopping for clothes with a young girl and thought the boyish activity of playing sports was a waste of good time. She ticked off the box marked *girl* not because she had knowledge of how to provide guidance to a girl, but because the only edge was that at one time she had been one.

When the mother, Irma, got the call from HR at Olin Mills about the possibility of her daughter being a "neighbor partner"—that was the term the company was using over "kids at risk"—she jumped on it. Anything that would get the girl out of her hair, even if it was for just a Saturday morning, was more than fine with her. The sixteen-year-old had become more and more of a pain in the ass. Her smart back talk was one thing, but when Child Protective Services started nosing around after someone anonymously called in to report a situation going on where the girl was running wild in the neighborhood late at night, Irma attempted to rein in her daughter's antics, knowing that such a report could lead to trouble with Housing.

The CPS report noted sightings of the girl hanging around the convenience store across from Green Hill and it went on that she was disappearing into the back alley with males to engage in—they didn't know what all. The mother saw a segment of *Dr. Phil* about young girls with missing male role models who often looked for love in all the wrong places. But it didn't really matter where her daughter's problem came from—it was what it was. Irma thought maybe this new mentoring plan could somehow knock some sense into her daughter, so she gave her consent to be on a list of "partner" parents.

Felicia found the unit and knocked on the door. With the sun shining against the screen, she couldn't quite make out the figure who consumed the entire space in the frame of the door. She asked to see the girl who Olin had assigned her, only to find that the word had not gotten back to the program organizers at her office that the girl was pregnant and had been shipped out to her grandmother's.

When Felicia first entered the grounds of Green Hill, she had determined she would get herself into the apartment no matter what. If the mother, the signee, was at work, maybe the young girl would be resistant and put her off; so first, she told herself, *Get in.* When this large figure at the door told her the girl had moved, as was Felicia's way she automatically continued with her original plan to get inside.

As Joe Joy first peered out the screen door at the White lady dressed in a pale blue sweater set with her hand extended for a handshake, there was no indication that anything good would come of the stranger. An unannounced White person at the door rarely went to the positive. But before he could head her off, there she was already perched on the couch in the unexpected beginning of a relationship that would defy all conventional and cultural differences between the two and create a bond that would last for decades.

Felicia never could have conceived of the situation she now found herself in—a teenage Black boy, a near giant at a good two hundred and fifty pounds, and her diminutive self at one hundred ten pounds, five feet three in modest heels. Plus, he was closer than she was comfortable with. The boy was sitting on an ottoman right in front of her. Truth be told, young people scared her. Right from the get-go she wondered how she had ever signed up for this mess. Her aim now was to get out of that apartment as quick as possible, but her polite Southern upbringing prevented her from just bolting. The only thing she could come up with was to ask him a question.

—What's your passion?

Passion—the word to Joe was mixed up with sex, so he froze for a moment until she saw his confusion and rephrased it.

—What interests you?

Felicia counted on a show of disinterest to give her the excuse to get the hell out of there, but instead Joe sort of laughed and said he had never been asked such a thing. To her surprise, she was drawn in and went further, probing for ambitions and inclinations. With more articulation than she expected from him, he said he liked to talk to people, that talking came naturally and that if you approach people honestly, the rejection most people expect back doesn't come.

Oftentimes in school, students were called upon to sell tickets to raise money for the school band or for the wrestling team to travel out of town for meets. He, Joe, always was at the top of the posted performance charts for number of sales. He said that in spite of this, he was usually misjudged and pestered to do things based on his size alone, like trying out for front lineman on the football team, but was rarely considered for anything requiring the softer skills. He wanted to run for class president, but everybody went for the popular, pretty White boy.

Felicia saw that she, too, had misjudged and found it quite smart of him, at such a young age, to have discovered something it took her much longer to realize—if you put people at ease right off, they will let you in with far less resistance. And he showed he was a realist when he didn't accept losing to the White boy as an excuse to give up on life.

Felicia was in the apartment for an hour and already a plan was taking shape in her head—baby steps at first, but a plan nevertheless. With summer break coming up, she said, there was no time like the present to get a job in an area that interested him and might lead to something later. She stressed positioning where one job would lead to another until inertia would propel him into meaningful, fulfilling employment. It was the first time Joe became aware that maybe his life could be managed and not have life manage him. Within two weeks, dressed in a size 3X white shirt and tie and carrying a resume typed up nicely, Joe interviewed for a summer job at a Verizon store for a decent salary with a bonus program for performance in sales of phones and service plans.

Even after he landed the Verizon job, Felicia and Joe got together once a week, meeting now at her house where the White lady's presence would not be constantly watched as at Green Hill. And they did not meet only to discuss a career path—Felicia taught him the fine points of dating such as pulling out the girl's chair when called for, napkin in the lap, and good table manners. For this they role-played at white tablecloth restaurants. Joe knew some of it was old school, but he didn't just blindly go along with it. He grasped the overall lesson—he picked up on the chance that it might set him apart, that he could avoid being stereotyped as a young man from the projects.

Joe's mother was always suspicious of the White lady's motives in taking an interest in her son, since she had never been extended any sign of the same in her lifetime. Despite the cold shoulder, Felicia and Joe continued their weekly sessions. Felicia never lost heart, even through the setback to her efforts for Joe to buy his first car. She gave Joe money to match his contribution from his summer job only to find Irma, to bail out her boyfriend from jail, had emptied the tin box where Joe kept it stored away in his sock drawer. Felicia told Joe that life was full of disappointments and the best thing to do was start over by opening a savings account—which they used until the needed $1,850 was achieved and the car was his.

Felicia was not about molding Joe into something of her own personal design, so when at twenty-two he was approached to go on the wrestling circuit with the World Wrestling Federation for crazy money, she hired a lawyer who went through the contract to be sure it was on the up-and-up. If Joe performed anywhere near Columbia, Felicia would be ringside, enjoying every minute, sitting in the VIP seat that Joe had waiting for her. She was onto the fake blood and the spitting out of fake teeth, but if ever Joe were wronged, there was no one louder in protest.

They both benefitted from the relationship. Helping Joe gave Felicia's life purpose beyond any satisfaction she got from her job at Olin Mills. It gave each of them the opportunity to experience life beyond the confines of their own environments. But mostly, they shared in the humanness of each other.

4

Tom & me board the
Eastern for Charl & Savannah
May 5, 1857

MEDLIN SAT IN THE ROCKER in the front room reading the latest circular from the South Carolina Agricultural Association. He was most comfortable out of the way near the fireplace. It was after supper and he was tired, but it was still broad daylight—too early to go to bed. He was not paying much attention to Lydia, once again, telling Clara Anne about the tea service and how it was to be the girl's once she got married. Medlin had heard the story dozens of times, so it was easy to tune it out.

Clara Anne sat next to her mother on the settee. Her young mind was not willing to take it all in again. Instead, her attention fixed on the fair-haired boy at school whom she had not much noticed until February 14. On Valentine's Day a card showed up unexpectedly on her desk, signed with only a hand-drawn heart under the printed message, *Be Mine*. By March, he started tugging at her braid from his desk directly behind hers. From that, intuition told her he was the source of the anonymous valentine.

Clara Anne was daydreaming about the boy when she came to and heard her mother was in full stride about the time when her own grandparents, on the European grand tour, happened to stroll into a porcelain shop with the Royal Seal displayed out front showing the Crown approved of the quality within. Lydia looked at her daughter for a sign that the girl was appreciative of her future bounty, so Clara Anne took a lingering gaze at the tea set resting for all to see on the mantel.

She wondered if this was going to be the long version or the short. The short story would only be of her great-grandparents' delighted discovery of the tea set and that one day this elegant symbol of refinement would be hers. The extended one would be all about the discovery, as well as the tea culture with all the rituals that went with it.

The tea set was so important to Lydia. It represented the finer things of life. She hounded Medlin to make the trip to Bennettsville as often as they could so the girl could, as they say, "soak up some culture."

Clara Anne snapped back into the moment when she heard her mother quiz her.

—Does the hostess ever fold her napkin?

With that, she knew this would be the long version, so she braced for the tedium of being tutored about the tea ritual. Right off, tea was always served at four. Lydia made it clear that anyone who varied the timeworn tradition must surely have grown up in a barn. Clara Anne let out a sigh, which she hoped no one could hear. Her mother began to yammer on about etiquette in the case of an honored guest. Clara Anne didn't think she could bear it, so she began to focus again on the boy.

Lydia had been taught manners in Bennettsville, where there was often an honored guest. She did not worry about the very unlikely possibility that her daughter Clara Anne would serve tea as a young married woman in Clio, where no one saw the need to serve tea. In Lydia's plan, Clara Anne would not marry someone from Clio. She would not choose from the slim pickings in that hick town. She would marry a farmer—over her mother's dead body.

Lydia repeated that no one should ever get up to leave a tea before the honored guest and that it would be up to the hostess to signal the end was at hand when she picked up her napkin and placed it loosely to the left of her cake plate.

Medlin could take it no longer and muttered under his breath something about letting the girl be, when Lydia launched into a point she had made many times—the point that the tea service indicated a connection to high breeding, which would become important when Clara Anne would have to demonstrate some appeal to attract a boy of means. Of course, she would be presented in Bennettsville—certainly not in Clio. The elaborate tea service would put distance between her and the humble cotton farm existence.

Lydia's bitterness regarding their low status always landed the final punch to Medlin with a cruel taunt.

—You might not give a whit about the future of the boys, but with God as my witness, I will move heaven and earth to be sure that Clara Anne escapes Clio into the hands of a good family!

Just as Lydia finished her tirade, Daniel ran in to announce to his father that the pair of bald eagles were back again for the third year in a row. Daniel had put his eyes to the sky for weeks waiting for the eagles to return to the nest. Medlin, still shaken by Lydia's ability to hurt, tried to show joy at Daniel's news. He told the boy he had the talents of the Cherokee to carry within him the ways of God's natural world.

Medlin rose out of the chair and boy and father started to roughhouse. Both were enjoying the merriment of male play. Daniel pulled away toward the fireplace and Medlin lunged to take hold. In his lunge for Daniel, Medlin's shoulder lifted up the heavy mantel from its pegs—the mantel he had cut and planed from a downed maple years earlier.

The lighter teacups and saucers hit the floor first, and showing the delicacy of the fine paste porcelain, they shattered into a hundred small shards. The teapot first landed on Daniel's back. As it bounced toward the floor, its lid came free and shot the full length of the room, landing at Lydia's feet in pieces. Lydia's face was frozen in horror. Clara Anne let out a scream. Medlin grabbed for the creamer with his left hand, but only snagged the handle, which snapped off as the main part crashed to the floor. Simultaneously with his right hand, he bobbled the large sugar bowl up into the air with just enough time to pull it into his chest with such force that one of its handles snapped off. The last to break was the lid of the sugar bowl, which dislodged from its host and was the exclamation mark as it bounced alone, first safely onto his boot but then hitting the floor and shattering.

No one could move as the calamity worked its way through their minds and settled into horrifying reality. There was one common thought—there would be a change.

A week after it happened, breaking the tea service was still on Medlin's mind—he was sure it would plague him until the day he died. To add to his foul state of mind, Lydia's cutting jibe about his not giving a whit about the boys' futures still hung heavy on his mind. He had not shared his thoughts on the matter with Lydia, but college money for the boys was a constant worry along with the ever-present list of other worries. Contemplating his financial position every year when he squared the expenses against what he cleared after he tallied the total sales for his cotton, his intention was always to put away some portion for the boys' education. However, for the past two years he had barely broken even after he accounted for the next year's household expenses and the seed money necessary to start all over again. And then there was the rolling debt that seemed to increase over time.

As Medlin continued to stew over the broken tea set and money matters, his younger brother Tom came through Clio after brokering the hardship sale of a farm in McColl, fifteen miles away. He arrived with an idea he wanted to pass on to Medlin.

Tom was high as a kite over a forthcoming slave auction in Savannah. In just a few days, the largest number of slaves ever were to go on the block at one time—463. Tom was planning to go to Savannah for the slave auction. He simply could not miss something that was bound to be talked about for years to come. Now he wanted to convince Medlin to get in on it by going along and buying a few slaves that he could then turn over for a quick buck a few days later at another sale in Mobile, where the big money was.

When Tom got to Clio the brothers had a long talk—away from Lydia and the kids—with Medlin getting a lot off his chest about money and the lack of it, most especially about the impending need for college money for Caleb. Tom could hardly believe it. Now was the perfect time for him to spring his idea about making quick money through the upcoming auction in Savannah. He laid out the idea to Medlin, mentioning all the positives, making it sound like a sure thing—it would take a week at the most for Medlin to have the money needed for Caleb's tuition at college. Medlin made it clear that the idea would have to be put to Lydia for approval.

Lydia had disliked Tom from the first time she met him when he showed up at her wedding drunk as a coot. So when she was presented with the auction idea, her eyes went to a disapproving squint. She was skeptical of anything Tom was a part of. Even before the idea could be fully told, Lydia chimed in contemptuously.

—Hmpf! My husband doesn't have it in him to do any such a thing!

This and her often repeated accusation that he did not care about the boys' future—which she had last made right before the tea set fell from the mantel—cut deep and rolled over and over in Medlin's head.

Out of sheer defiance, Medlin answered Lydia's insult.

—Well, I think it's a fine idea to make some money for Caleb to go to that school in Columbia.

Both Lydia and Tom were astonished to hear Medlin go on to say that after all, the boy was near seventeen and it was none too early to get squared up to make that happen. All that evening and the next morning until the brothers left Clio, Medlin put on a show of enthusiasm for turning a few slaves into quick cash. Yet in the pit of his stomach he knew the idea was beyond his natural inclinations. He sensed it would be a fiasco, but it was too late to back out.

———

WITH EVERY ROTATION OF THE IRON WHEELS, mile after mile, Medlin's dread grew. As soon as the brothers boarded the train in Bennettsville, bound for Charleston and on to Savannah, the shooting pains in his gut sharply increased. Tom, on the other hand, was in a jubilant mood, as was clear from his constant chatter starting the moment they settled in their seats.

—Big brother, why so gloomy? This'll be a hell of a lot of fun. And you're all down in the mouth. Just think, you'll have your pick of more nigger slaves than we'll ever see in one place in our whole life. You know, it'll be at the only place they could find big enough, the Big Oval racetrack.

—I don't see it as anything other than a chance to send Caleb to school.

—Just gettin' away from that wife of yours for a few days should make you feel good. Anyway, this auction is on account that Northern fool Butler is broke. God, there's nothin' I love to see more than a Yankee down on their luck. I hope he's there. I wanna get a look at that son-of-a-bitch.

Medlin, sick of hearing it, interrupted.

—Tom, I swear to God, if you don't shut up I'm going to smash you right in the face!

The force of his own voice surprised him, and he quickly shifted his weight away, made a pillow of his slouch hat, and pretended he was going to sleep. Tom fell silent.

———

PIERCE BUTLER HOPED TO SLIP QUIETLY back into his comfortable life in Philadelphia once he shed his failing Southern holdings and settled with pressing creditors.

Major Butler, the father, in declining health, had passed along his vast fortune in plantations—and what had been reported to be the largest number of slaves within one estate—to his two sons, Pierce and John. The value of all the property was divided evenly between the two sons, with Pierce named manager of the working plantations.

Out from under the watchful eye of the Old Major, the plantations soon were on a failing course. Pierce Butler was a Philadelphia lawyer who had neither the knowledge nor the inclination to put in the effort necessary to make a success of the large holdings, spread through Georgia and South Carolina. There were hired overseers, but unless rigorously supervised and held to account, they tended to engage in an assortment of nefarious activities, not the least of which was outright embezzlement. Pierce himself rarely traveled south, preferring to tend to his affairs in Philadelphia. In a short time, his neglect left the Southern properties in ruins.

Butler had to sell soon, before creditors could find ways to seek satisfaction through his personal wealth in the North. He had already commissioned real estate brokers to handle the sale of the several thousand acres of land and structures. He was willing to greatly reduce land prices to facilitate a quick sale, but he planned to make up the loss through a separate sale of the Butler estate's prized slave stock. He had been advised to present them through an auction, where the maximum value could be realized.

The 463 slaves would include men, women, children, and infants. Some were highly skilled at smithing, carpentry, and saddlery. Few or none of these would be unsalable, and in fact they were expected to bring top dollar. The rest were mostly prized field hands with valuable knowledge of the ways of rice and cotton production. A benefit to buyers was that the majority of the slaves had been born and lived all their lives on the Butler plantations, where they were accustomed to a relatively harmonious atmosphere, and showed little desire to escape to the uncertain, perilous life of a runaway.

Fugitive slaves were a nuisance and an added expense to chase after and discipline. The Old Major understood that a contented slave was more manageable and productive than one openly chafing under slavery, so he worked to provide what he saw as comfortable conditions. He built a small church on each plantation, issued plenty of salt pork weekly, and gave a new set of clothes every Christmas. He could think of nothing else that his slaves could possibly want.

The breakup of such a large estate was unusual and would bring out both interested buyers and the curious. But Pierce Butler had another feature that added even more interest to the auction—his wife, Fanny Kemble, a British stage actress, popular in both Europe and Up East America. True to her profession, Fanny was very theatrical in her appearance and manner, both on and off the stage. She was also known for her writing—mostly published journals of her travels, of which there were an exhaustive eleven volumes. The books sold well to readers anxious to follow her glamorous life.

Fanny, seeking a break from her busy social schedule in Philadelphia, traveled to a Butler plantation in Georgia, thinking to enjoy a rest in an atmosphere of Southern gentility. However, what she found was anything but the pampered life. She encountered intolerable heat and frightening bugs of both ground and air. The constant presence of bugs drove her to distraction. Special netting was fashioned to cover her bed for some relief against the flying variety that seemed to have the hideous nature of striking only at night.

After a very few weeks in Georgia, Fanny prepared to return North, but then she began to look about her. Immediately the writer in her felt compelled to report to the world. One day she heard a racket in the yard. Upon investigation, she found the houseboy had been given a hard lashing for stealing an egg from the larder. After that experience, she postponed any thought of returning to Philadelphia and started keeping a thorough account in her diary of what she saw to be the frequent mistreatment of the slaves.

This soon became a popular book called *Journal of a Residence on a Georgian Plantation*. Abolitionists embraced the book as an eyewitness account of the horrors that beset Southern slaves. The published diary burned like a hot poker in the eye of all Southerners who saw the author as just another uppity Yankee sticking her nose where it did not belong. Fanny's book depicting plantation slavery haunted Pierce Butler for the rest of his life. The Butler auction's serious buyers and the idly curious grew to unprecedented numbers, all eager to revel in the Butler muddle.

———

NOTICES ADVERTISING THE AUCTION were widely distributed from Virginia to Louisiana. To handle the anticipated increased passenger load, train cars were diverted from less traveled routes and coupled to coaches on the main lines coming into Savannah. Whores from Charleston were shuttled in to supplement the supply of what would be in high demand.

Talk in saloons and public houses was of nothing but the auction. Speculators in the slave trade found congenial company in familiar auction rivals with their mutual interest in the Butler sale. Everyone spoke of hammer-down prices. All agreed that the quality of the stock and the large number of attendees made bargains unlikely.

The business affairs of Pierce Butler were woven throughout discussions everywhere. His diminished position was not spoken of in terms of

pity, only spite. He was a Philadelphia Yankee who had come by a fortune not from sweat but through inheritance. There was nothing more
irksome than a Northerner gaining such advantage by merely being
born to it. Yankee money had failed, and they were glad. Everyone was
anxious to get a good look at Butler. It was rumored that he would be in
attendance at the Oval, but only Old Major Butler would appear briefly
at the auction.

————

WHEN THE TRAIN GROUND TO A HALT in the Savannah station,
passengers went into chaotic motion to grab their bags and be quickly
off, but with everyone of the same notion, the aisles became clogged.
Both brothers Medlin and Tom had a struggle to lift their gear from the
overhead rack while other passengers were pushing to get by. The pain
in Medlin's lower gut had been coming and going in waves ever since
they left Bennettsville, and he began to panic as he tried to think where
he could relieve himself if it went that far. The thought of quick accommodations was on his mind. However, Tom was intent on getting to the
auction as soon as possible.

Medlin could not remember how many years ago it had started, but
the spells brought on a familiar dialog within himself. It wasn't in a human
voice—more a presence—but it was every bit a communication. There
would be a back-and-forth at the onset of an episode, measuring its sever-
ity and laying plans to deal with it. The pain had a name. In the secret
dialog he called it "the miseries." Now Tom broke into his thoughts with
talk of transportation. This pulled Medlin from the inner dialog to address
pressing logistical issues. They would need a way to get to the auction.

In a field across from the station a couple of enterprising cotton dirt
farmers were offering rigs to let by the day. Tom applied his skills and
beat one of them down on a rickety buckboard, which he got for half
the asking price. The buckboard and two horses were on the far side of
their usefulness but would do. Medlin took the reins to divert his mind
from the miseries.

The direction was clear—everyone was following the same dusty
road and kicking up plumes of dust that rose above the trees like smoke

from a brushfire. The travelers all around seemed to be having a great time of it. Medlin could not hear exactly what they were saying, but the tone mingled with laughter gave the whole scene the air of a Sunday outing. Tom was in the same mood, and shouted out jocular comments to passersby, sharing in the holiday spirit. Even before boarding the train in Bennettsville, Medlin had already concluded to himself that buying slaves was a bad idea, but by then it was of course far too late. Now driving the buckboard, he stayed quiet and sullen, hoping some force would transport him back to the farm and the security of the field. It was no surprise to Medlin that the predicament was playing out this way when he took into account the influences from childhood that forged the dynamics between the two brothers. He felt hopeless, insecure, trapped.

———

MEDLIN AND TOM WERE IN EQUAL MEASURE the product of both parents, but they grew up as two different and even contradictory individuals. Medlin had his father's even disposition, which the mother saw as a weakness that would do him no good service as he encountered the harshness of life. Medlin was tallish, but was not what would be known as a beanpole. He was fair-skinned with a mop of shaggy, light hair so much akin to his father's that all who knew the elder as a young man said the two were of the exact same mold.

Tom was more of the stature of the mother. The father described Tom as closer to the ground and squarish, making him harder to knock down—amusing to all who heard it because it so well described him, especially the knocking down part. He had darker skin and hair than Medlin, making plausible the talk of Cherokee blood coming down on the mother's side. She saw more of herself in Tom and so favored him. She counseled the boy to consider all things as they would benefit his aim and interest. Tom should realize there was good as well as bad in most things, and he should weigh all in judgment before making decisions.

Tom was smaller and younger than Medlin. But the little brother was wiser in ways to look inside others and find the weaknesses to gain advantage. Medlin had a catalog of childhood experiences where Tom had gotten the upper hand.

Tom's shenanigans found an easy mark in a mind so naive and witless to manipulation as Medlin's. Medlin had a mental chronicle of Tom's manipulations. He noticed that any small pleasure that came his way could quickly turn to gloom once the story started to play. As a young man he already began thinking that maybe he was not meant to live without the burden of low spirits.

———

As THEY TRAVELED THE THREE MILES to the track, other wagons joined the crowd, but some travelers were on foot. These pedestrians were covered in dust as the thick surrounding brush kept the footpath close to the road. There were young boys with fathers who thought it a good idea to flash before their sons the realities of life—the Butler auction was much like their first drink of whiskey, a rite of passage.

The road ended at a large field surrounding the racetrack. There was a great deal of confusion in the huge crowd. With the push from behind, there was no choice for Medlin but to go forward. The horses started to panic. Medlin gave them a sharp, strong pull back, hoping vainly that such a command would check their desire to bolt.

He was totally powerless when suddenly he felt a tug at his pantleg. He looked down.

—Half dollar and I'll take care of 'em!

Even before Medlin answered, a small person grabbed the harness and expertly pulled the rig into a makeshift corral of stakes and rope. Only then did Medlin fix his attention on the strange-looking creature that had pulled them to safety. The man looked to be more weasel than human, with a pointy snout, weak chin, and close-set eyes. He was not a boy as Medlin first thought, but a very small man, maybe mid-forties. His jockey cap made it clear that he was of the horse-racing trade, though past his prime—a track rat, always hanging around looking to make a little change as a breeze or a groom.

—Half dollar, sir?

The Weasel stuck out his small, calloused hand. By the time Medlin and Tom jumped down, the horses were hitched and the Weasel was making for the satchel in the back of the buck as part of his duty for the fee. Medlin quickly grabbed it away, knowing his cash bid money was just inside. Unfazed, the Weasel launched into excited chatter about the goings-on at the auction.

—We don't see this kinda thing much around here. You here to buy some niggers? They got over four hundred of 'em. Have you heard about Hutto? He's the biggest nigger in the whole world, and he's here. Maybe somebody'll buy 'im for a circus. I hope to get a look at 'im myself!

The racetrack was encircled with posts, each carrying a banner with the pattern and vivid colors of the silks of local jockeys. Above the gate was an arched sign, saying, in big letters rimmed in gold, *Savannah Downs* and under that: *The Sport of Kings.* Leaving the buck and horses in the care of the Weasel, the two brothers walked through the gate and worked their way to a vacant spot far to the right to escape the incoming flow and to plan their next maneuver. They decided to register first so that they would be free to inspect the stock.

Asbill & Smythe, out of Savannah, had been commissioned by the Butler estate to handle all aspects of the auction—hire the auctioneer, manage the readiness of the slaves, process securities of potential bidders, and issue bidding paddles. Since Medlin had cash, there was only the paddle to deal with.

The slaves were confined in wooden pens and sheds erected principally for racehorses. No mattresses for sleep or benches to sit were provided, so the bundles holding all their worldly possessions would have to do as the only thing the slaves had against the muddy ground. They had been brought to Savannah a week earlier. Every day, gangs were marched the three miles to the track until the complete stock was there and ready for inspection.

Tom and Medlin followed the flow of onlookers past stall after stall of poor wretches on display. Each slave had a placard hung from a cord around the neck with a number that corresponded to the catalog. From adults to infants—all had been assigned a unique number. Families stood shoulder to shoulder for inspection, with children pulled from safe hiding behind the skirts of their mothers, because they, too, were to be judged on fitness. Some were enduring rough treatment—their mouths were forced open to show teeth, and they were commanded to walk up and back to check for lameness. Backs were bared to show any signs of the lash. Questions were asked of the women as to prospects for childbearing. Attempting to disguise advanced age, handlers had rubbed coal dust over gray hair, but sweat from the hot sun betrayed the practice.

Grief was in the air. Some sobbed openly. Others huddled in small groups, trying to console one another, knowing that in hours they would likely be separated forever.

All along, shouts of the most vile nature rang out from the more brutish element of the crowd. They wanted to spur a reaction, but the slaves' grief was too deep for this abuse to be effective.

One crowded stall had a most curious spectacle in play. *No. 87*, a well-looking, fit slave, approached a buyer he judged might be of decent temperament and made great efforts to persuade the man to buy his whole family. Wisely, he did not appeal to the man's charity but to his desire for a good purchase. *No. 87* went to work telling of his family members' usefulness. He said his wife, *No. 88*, was an excellent laundress. She gave an awkward curtsey. He went on to say that though there was but one child, there would in all likelihood be more babies. Of *No. 89*, he said she was presently only a small child but soon she could be useful in the field. Tom found all this most amusing and laughed out loud, leading others to join in. Medlin sensed the man's desperation, a feeling he himself had experienced to some degree.

The crowd pushed forward. Ahead were more pens with more examinations of fitness going on: teeth assessed and bodies checked for lice. Slaves were pinched and there was open groping of the women and sometimes of female children. Tom fell to a system of grading the stock and began a string of comments about how to make the best judgment of value. Medlin could look no more.

He purposely slipped from Tom's side and caught the flow going in another direction—toward the auction tent. Near the entrance were two large corrals that were normally used by jockeys to mount up. One was reserved for the first lots of slaves to go on the block. For enticement, these were among the most valuable slaves, and would set a precedent for prices.

At the far side of this corral, almost out of sight, was an elderly White gentleman in the company of the Negroes. His dress showed him to be a man of wealth. Someone whispered that this was Major Butler. The gentleman took something from a canvas sack held on the ready at his side by a man in the livery of a body servant. The Old Major went from one slave to another, offering to each what Medlin could tell was a coin. By the size, he deduced it to be a silver dollar. There were no eager outstretched hands, but each offering was accepted with a curtsy or bend at the waist. Words were exchanged but no one could hear what was said or the nature of the exchange, though it could be observed to be one of mutual regard.

Outside the second pen, right next to the entrance to the auction tent, was a knot of people all straining to look inside the locked gate. Whereas the adjoining enclosure was crowded with slaves, this one looked empty. Medlin was pushed along until he was right beside the gate. There was a sign with big red letters: *HUTTO*.

In the back of the pen there stood unmistakably the object of the hullabaloo that the weaselly stablehand had talked about—a man so large he resembled a reared-up bear. To grasp Hutto's size, Medlin put him into comparison with a draft horse and decided the man's middle would reach the withers of a horse of seventeen hands. His head, body, and limbs were in proportion to his tallness so he looked like an ordinary man, though freakishly huge.

His clothes were not of standard issue but of homespun lamb's wool, dyed brown with hickory nuts, made custom to his proportion on the plantation. Any plantation laundress had such skills. Hutto's enormous shoes were of thick leather, cut crudely—a construction not of the cobbler but of the saddler and the blacksmith.

Hutto did not face the crowd but stood showing only his broad back. He looked to be alone, but Medlin could see that there were slender arms coming from behind, encircling one leg. They looked to be a little child's arms, but all sense of familiar proportion and scale was gone. A small face partly appeared, only clearing one eye, and quickly darted back out of sight behind Hutto's leg. In that fleeting instant, knobs of hair tied with strips of rag revealed it was a girl-child. Two ruffians leaning against the gate started shouting out vile, slangy names that seemed to have no effect until they hurled the worst slur they could think of.

—Congo nigger baby!

Hutto slowly made a quarter turn and glowered in the direction of the shouting.

His skin was blue-black—the color locals called Congo Black—stretched tightly across a forehead that looked like ebony wood sanded smooth. His eyes were deep-set and now had an expression of hatred, and the strong jaw rippled with muscles tightened by clenched teeth. As Hutto turned, another figure was exposed—a woman, obviously the child's mother. At Hutto's menacing look, all bawdy insults stopped, and the crowd moved on.

———

THE AUCTIONEER CHOSEN BY ASBILL & SMYTHE for the Butler auction was W. Poulnott & Associates out of Charleston. Wally Poulnott was not always an auctioneer and he had not always looked the way he did on the day of the Butler auction, though everyone who knew him or of him could picture him in no other way.

To describe him, first thing, would be to speak of his small size. He went right on looking like a boy even when he was not. Some people of his size took advantage of the characteristic—became jockeys or chimney sweeps—but Wally was suited for neither. Labor, either skilled or no, was out of the question, seeing how his strength was that of a weak boy.

Wally tried to compensate for his weakness and insignificance by adopting outlandish attire—a colorful velvet cap, striped tunic, and flouncy pantaloons. His only occupation as a youth was walking around town, dressed in this eccentric costume. Loitering around the courthouse, he became a familiar sight to the legal traffic. One day, a lawyer approached and made Wally a job offer. He was to deliver documents to clients, as the lawyer no longer saw benefit in releasing his staff to do such work for he suspected it opened them to lollygagging. The job suited Wally perfectly. He was paid by the delivery, so he did not dawdle. Alive to the advantage of standing out, he continued to wear his costume. He presented every delivery with a quick jig.

The young Poulnott became very familiar with the flow of business around Charleston. Sometimes, if delivering an unsealed document, he would dart into an alleyway and have a look at the contents.

It was clear that the commodities business, especially the slave trade, was very robust. A good many of Wally's deliveries were to the area around State and Chalmers, where by now there were thirty-five wholesalers. For many years the city's most well-attended slave auction had been regularly held on the steps of the Exchange Building right at the end of Broad Street, but now this blocked the increasing traffic. The slave auction needed to move. On nearby Chalmers Street, there already existed a yard and two-story "nigger jail." Slaves fresh from the wharfs were held there until they were marched in chains to the Exchange Building on Broad Street to be sold. The Exchange auction made the logical move to its new location at Ryan Slave Mart, without a break from the weekly Saturday schedule.

Wally greatly enjoyed the fast-paced atmosphere around State and Chalmers. He liked the people associated with the slave trade. They laughed easily, loved a good story, and always had time for gossip. The auction itself satisfied their appetites in a jolly setting much like the traveling carnival that came to town once a year. Never did the pitifulness of the plight of the slaves interfere with the high spirits of the traders. Wally was drawn to this atmosphere, and he could be found every Saturday enjoying the spectacle at Ryan's.

He became interested in the bidding process and started to play a little game with himself to guess final hammer-down prices. He got quite good at it, but in short order it became clear that the success of an auction depended chiefly on the crowd. Each required a strategy—how could it be manipulated to get the best prices? A good auctioneer would start by spotting who was in attendance. If played right, even gawkers could be of assistance to goad or shame a bidder to stay in on a run-up. A skilled auctioneer maximized prices and created an atmosphere that guaranteed future crowds. Wally thrived on the energy, the spectacle, but mostly he was intrigued by the artistry of the auctioneer in manipulating the crowd.

There were plenty of people working at Ryan's—handlers, promoters, clerks, and of course auctioneers. Then there were the people who kept the jail and cookhouse going at the back of the lot. Three cooks prepared the one meal a day for the slaves—usually fat-back with crowder peas, grits, or johnnycakes.

Almost everybody knew Wally, first from the delivery business, but after he started coming around to the auctions, he made a point of befriending everyone from auctioneers to cooks. Soon he became a fixture around the place, with privileges to move about in areas usually reserved for paid staff. People felt comfortable enough with him to share gossip of all kinds—tidbits involving customers (both buyers and sellers) and even petty grievances within the Ryan gates.

Ryan's appreciated Wally's manner and costume. They hired him to put on a little show before the auction to put the crowd into a jolly frame of mind. Before long he added a few comments shouted out to regular bidders. If he saw a way to stir up a little friendly rivalry, he by all means did it with provocative comments.

—Johnny, you're not gonna let Malcolm get the better of you this week, are ya?

Crowds increased and people came earlier to catch the Wally show. By auction time the tempo would be at a high buzz, with spirited bidding commencing right off with the first lot. Ryan's was making more money than ever before. They asked Wally what it would take to have him quit delivering for the lawyer and come on board permanently. He had already thought about it, so his answer came quick. He made it clear that he was not willing to be just a song-and-dance man—he wanted to continue his act to hype the crowd, but he also wanted to combine it, to make it part of the overall presentation of a full-fledged auctioneer. He threw in the fib that there was another promising offer from elsewhere that he was considering. Immediately a deal was struck, even though the Ryan people were suspicious of the allusion to another offer. They admired Wally for using it and saw it as a good sign that he could be cagey in dealmaking. Wally soon determined that if he could do only auctioneering, that would suit him just fine. There would always be work—the slave business was booming.

Two years after he first got to Ryan's he conducted an auction to move a premium gang of fresh-to-the-market slaves from a plantation in the Upstate. The Africans had been loaded into wagons bound for auction in Charleston. By the time they arrived at Ryan's, they had worked up fierce anger, showing it in the pens with scowls and every manner that came to them to appear unsalable. Among their number was a man, also to be sold, who gathered them around and spoke sternly of the unfortunate outcome of such behavior. Wally watched and heard him tell his fellow slaves that their display would only lower prices and attract only the roughest speculators, who would have no trouble "correcting" them in fiendish ways. His counsel was so persuasive that all attempted to show their worthiness on the auction platform. What looked to be a hard sell instead went satisfactorily and resulted in a good commission. Wally, impressed with the insightful young slave, purchased him for his own use. His name was Bingo.

The two worked well together, with Bingo handling the slaves. Wally had no taste for that part of the business. No one ever heard Wally refer to Negroes with any sentiment, only as prices. Their plight, well-being, or future beyond the hammer-down was of no interest to him. He bought Bingo to handle the slaves.

Though between Wally and Bingo there was for a long time never the threat of the lash, Bingo was clear as to the limitations of the relationship. They took no meals together. Nor did they share thoughts. Bingo lived in a shed in the yard and was never invited across the threshold of Wally's house.

Bingo had a taste for show, which perhaps rubbed off from Wally, or maybe he always had it but was unable to act on it until now. Like his master, he fashioned a fanciful costume, punctuated by a top hat. Wally was rarely to be seen without Bingo at his side.

After five years at Ryan's with Bingo there to handle the slaves, Wally felt free to establish his own strictly auctioneering business. Ryan's had branched out into all facets of the slave trade—handling bonds, transport, and bidding for absentee clients. Wally wanted to stay on the boards and do nothing but call auctions. He named his new firm W. Poulnott & Associates—though there were no associates other than Bingo, whom Wally would never consider as anything other than property. Wally's reputation for attracting attendees and wringing out the best prices made him the most sought-after auctioneer in the region. So it was no surprise to anyone when the auctioneering firm W. Poulnott & Associates was chosen for the Butler auction.

———

Tom caught up with Medlin just before the surging crowd pushed them into the auction tent. Momentum spit them out dead center in front of the platform—close enough to stick a hand out to touch the wooden planks where soon there would be a parade of lost souls.

Tom had been drinking, as was told by the sweet, musky scent of his breath, easily detected at close quarters. He had already run into acquaintances from Charleston. He told Medlin that the consensus regarding bargain prices was tipped toward slim, that the crowd gathered knew too much to let a lot pass below market price, and some had come a long way and were under pressure not to go home empty-handed. On hearing this, Medlin's shoulders relaxed and dropped a bit as he realized that just possibly he would be out of it. The day before, in Bennettsville, he had emptied the bank account, leaving nothing for next season's startup. Lydia was furious at the idea of taking any risk at all to try to make quick cash. If the venture was unsuccessful—or even if it was successful—she would no doubt take an opportunity to belittle her husband with a string of examples tossed out to mingle with other past disappointments. She would have no problem expressing herself, even in front of the children.

Now finding himself actually in the auction tent, Medlin heard the gavel come down hard on the podium with a loud rap that snapped him to attention. An impassive representative from Asbill announced basic auction terms and policy. His voice droned above the crowd, not yet totally quieted. He recited the rules of the procedure in a flat tone, as someone who had done it so many times that it was clear it was not meant to inform but rather was only mandatory. All sales were final. All buyers were responsible for transportation, which had to be completed by the end of the day of purchase. All would usually be offered first as families where a family was established—a policy set by management. The announcer did not say that this policy about families was not for humanitarian reasons but rather for assuring the sale of the aged or unserviceable along with younger and healthier family members.

There was still an effort to get the swell of people bottlenecked at the entrance into the tent. An animated Negro wearing a raggedy top hat was moving among stragglers and knots of men still in conversation blocking the entrance. Bingo twirled and high-stepped, singing a ditty as he hustled the crowd to move on in. Beside the sound of spitting tobacco, a few lingering hushed exchanges, and an occasional outburst of laugher, the crowd settled down. Suddenly Wally Poulnott burst onto the platform and immediately commenced a spasm of footwork in tandem with flailing his arms around wildly, more like in a fit than a rehearsed jig.

Medlin was close enough to pick up on some theatrical enhancements. Wally's boots had an exaggerated heel to gain the appearance of more height, but without much effect. His size was that of a boy that no high heel could compensate for. His attire was a combination of bright colors and in a style not seen on the street but suited more for the stage. The outlandish costume itself could be explained as a ploy to gain attention. The powder and rouge applied to his face gave him an overall deathlike appearance. Wally made a little speech about how everybody was not to hold back but have fun, and he summed it up with the command for which he was well known, his personal slogan.

—Now, talk to this ole boy!

Bingo joined Wally on the platform. Both shouted out in unison.

—Now, are you ready?

The crowd answered back with howls and chants.

Bingo brought up the first lot: an unmarried carpenter, announced to be highly skilled and fit. Wally advertised that he was equally proficient at both furniture-making and building. *Lot No. 1* was a prize and hammered down at $1,600. The first dozen lots were considered highly salable, as they had specific skills, put ahead to get the money flowing before things would slow when the bulk of the lots would be common field hands.

Most all the slaves climbed the steps dejectedly to a fate that they could not imagine, having never been beyond the confines of a Butler plantation. The most apprehensive and hesitant were prodded onto the platform by Bingo with the butt of a short whip known as a "black snake." After being sold, he ordered them to get back down the steps, where they stood, waiting to be claimed.

Medlin began to feel more relaxed, as it appeared prices were far too high for his modest purse. There was a cluster of men behind him with whom Tom joined in a conversation about correcting slaves who were bent on running off. Everything from whipping to branding was touted. One rough character broke in, saying that he had a great deal of experience with slaves who showed their mind. If they stepped to the end of his tolerance, he took out his pistol and shot them. He said it helped to do it once in a while as it showed the others what could come of such shenanigans. All who heard the story knew there was a big chance it was a total fabrication, made for effect, but it was received as though it was told by a wise man.

On the platform Wally drove hard, feeling the temperature of the crowd. He applied every trick he knew as a tonic to keep the energy up. He had been at this for a long time. One rule had come to him early in his auctioneering: Never let the people see the auction for the pitiful thing it was. Don't let the buying of these slaves get in the way of the amusement. It was Wally's mission to keep the crowd entertained, engaged, and enthusiastic.

Two field hands were sold back-to-back. One of them was blind in one eye but was still useful and went for $900. Next was a fit field hand who sold for $1,150. Right away Wally joked.

—Now, I always wondered what an eye was worth, and I just this minute found out—it's $250!

There had been a slight dip in the crowd's enthusiasm, but with that remark he had them back on track. Medlin, however, could not be swayed. No joke, no sleight of hand could divert him from the meaning of the display close enough to reach out and touch. Human beings were bought as if no different to cattle. He had never been to a slave auction before. He had seen many slaves, mostly at work in the fields. Even had rented some from a planter in Clio when he needed help for a big pick, but this auction had transformed them to something else—it had taken away any humanity. As they were paraded out, Medlin could tell by their eyes that they were not even the beings he had witnessed before in the pens. By the time the slaves were herded into the tent and onto the auction platform, the dullness had already set in. Most looked straight ahead, seemingly emotionless, fighting in the only way they could to not go mad. A few glanced in the direction of the highest bidder, hoping to see a glimmer of decency.

Lot No. 286 was the last to be sold on Thursday, with the rest to be auctioned the next day. Bingo lifted a light-skinned girl by her left arm onto the platform. Wally started right in.

—She may not be pretty, but her childbearing years are soon to come! Who's gonna bid me $200, huh? Come on now, y'all!

The auction program listed *No. 286* as *Youth, Dalia, possible house girl, blind in one eye*—as anyone could see by the leather patch strung tightly over the void socket. The leather was pliable and sunk in where an eye should have been, giving notice that there was no eyeball. The brute who boasted about shooting troublesome slaves whispered that he had heard how the girl had come to such a condition. Her mother ran away for a second time, and when she was tracked down with her four-year-old daughter in tow, the driver applied swift punishment by gouging out the little girl's eyeball. With a chuckle, the brute went further to tell how the bloody eyeball was thrown to the trail dogs as a reward for finding the two fugitives hiding behind a fallen tree. Then the driver shot the mother dead where she stood. The young girl was taken back to the plantation, where she became a companion to the master's youngest daughter. She was sold off to the Butlers at about age thirteen and put to work in the house before the Savannah sale.

Dalia was dressed no worse than the rest—her shift was clean and someone had taken pains to knot her hair with colorful strips of cloth. She was offered with no family, so it could be assumed that she was cared for as their collective own within the Butler slave quarters. With no one beside her, she swayed from side to side. Several ruffians began to clap to the rhythm of her body. Wally joined in with a little dance, calling again for an opening bid of $200. Although no one bid, he felt the curiosity of the crowd, so he kept it up until there was a distraction.

From behind Wally someone tossed a coin—a silver dollar—which landed on the platform and rolled on its side until it came to rest at his feet. And then came two more. Then one by one the silver dollars grew into a steady stream. Several coins rolled toward the front edge of the stage. At this, Wally dropped, first to his knees, then stretched out on his stomach to reach the coins, heedless of all the mud tracked in by the slaves. Wally lay scooping up bits of mud along with silver dollars, totally devoid of embarrassment. The coins could not be seen from a distance, so it appeared to most spectators that Wally was having some kind of seizure until the news spread that coins were being tossed from behind the platform. The crowd strained to see the source, and soon they realized that the slaves were throwing the coins.

A woman came onto the platform with her skirt hiked into a pouch holding more coins. She knelt and let them fall onto the floor. Bingo joined in the spectacle and started loading coins into his hat. The crowd went into a frenzy and started to chant.

—Dalia! Dalia! Dalia!

Wally struck down the gavel, hard, and shouted.

—This lucky little nigger girl has been bought by her own people and is now free! So get on out!

Dalia made her way to the back of the platform. She went down the steps, and disappeared into the crowd of slaves. A roar went up. People started filing out of the tent, knowing what they had just seen was almost unheard of. It would be talked about for a very long time and they could boast they were there when it happened.

————

THE WEASEL SHOWED TOM AND MEDLIN a nearby shed where they spent the night on the floor. Next morning, the second day of the auction, Medlin felt cheerful. Prices the day before made it clear his purse was too modest for any advantageous purchase, so they would soon be heading straight back to Clio and the normalcy that suited him. He had wanted to board the train home the evening before, but Tom insisted they see it through. The Weasel handled the rig again with much talk of the Dalia drama, and he couldn't resist going on about Hutto, of whom he had finally gotten a glimpse.

The Big Oval seemed different today—brighter—but it was just Medlin's mood. When Tom ran into old friends from Charleston, Medlin was surprised at how easily he joined into the jovial conversation. He got to thinking he needed to find more of this in Clio. In high spirits, the men passed a flask around. This appeared quite ordinary to them. At his turn, Medlin dropped back a swig and liked the ease of blending in.

The auction started. Wally's tone was unmistakable—things were going extremely well. He was making money. Those to be auctioned were quickly shuttled forward. There was a possibility it would end early. Hutto, the young Negro woman, and their child were still on display in the pen just outside the tent. Wally's plan was to hold Hutto until last to keep the crowd interested, and this was working. Very few people left the tent.

The brothers had found a place to stand just inside the tent so when the final gavel was struck they could beat the crowd to the wagon and head back to the train station. *Lots No. 457* and *458* were prodded onto the platform—a blacksmith and his wife, a housemaid. Wally had held several desirable lots for the end to maintain interest. As expected, the blacksmith and housemaid went for $1,800 and $1,300. Two more lots were quickly disposed of to a bidder from Alabama.

The time arrived for Hutto, but there was a delay—all designed by Wally to stoke anticipation. Then Hutto stooped to enter the tent but balked and did not go farther until his woman and child were close behind. All three slowly climbed the steps to the platform. When Hutto showed full size, the front row reared back from fear, to get a better look, or both. Even Wally, who looked like Tiny Tim next to the giant, felt his mouth drop open in astonishment. He quickly gathered himself, not wanting to miss the chance to whip up the crowd.

Fast as lightning, Wally somehow scrambled all the way up onto the tall podium. Now he was shoulder to shoulder with Hutto, who seemed even bigger in contrast. Wally was not opposed to making a mockery of his own stature if there was a point to it. Next, he hiked himself up onto Hutto's shoulders, waving to the audience, which was howling. Tom thought the scene hilarious and jumped up and down where he stood in pure joy. Hutto stood motionless and stunned.

When Wally felt he had taken the crowd as far as was in his power, he climbed off Hutto's back, down onto the top of the podium, and started the bidding.

—Now talk to this ole boy!

He could hardly be heard above the noise of the crowd. Bingo came forward on the platform, raising his hands to quiet everyone. To start,

Wally called out for $200, while Bingo pulled the woman and child aside. They were not going to be auctioned as a family.

—Do I hear $200 for the big nigger? Damn, he's the size of two niggers. You'll be getting two for the price of one!

But the crowd did not respond. Wally lowered it to $50 just to get some momentum going. A driver in the front row took the bid.

—Talk to this ole boy! Don't make me work this hard! Do I hear $100?

A paddle went up for $100.

—Do I hear $150?

After a slight pause someone in the back of the tent raised a paddle for $150.

—You got it. C'mon, people, this here's prime black gold! Who's gonna give $200 for the big nigger?

Tom, carried away by the energy around him, grabbed Medlin's paddle and shouted that Medlin wanted Hutto for $200.

As the tent full of people remained engrossed in the bidding, a most peculiar thing happened. Wally had climbed down off of Hutto, but he was still standing on top of the podium. In spite of his shackles, Hutto suddenly grabbed Wally with one hand by the throat and lifted him straight up like a doll. The crowd reacted with a collective gasp. People at the front scattered in panic and when some fell, others ran over them in a wild move toward the exit. Bingo himself, by instinct, jumped from the stage, but then jumped back up and started lashing at Hutto with his whip—with no effect. The driver standing just in front of the stage reached for his pistol, but he had clean forgotten that firearms had been confiscated at the door.

Wally frantically waved his arms and legs in the air. Hutto's big hand completely encircling his neck choked off any screams, but foam and spit came out of his mouth. His theater powder covered his blue-red face, but his eyes, bulging from their sockets, showed he was in much trouble. Leg shackles made it difficult for Hutto to hold up Wally and fend off Bingo. The more brutish traders leapt onto the platform to risk an assault on Hutto, who in their eyes had gone mad. They made a fruitless attempt to pry Hutto's fingers from Wally's neck. Desperately Bingo grabbed Hutto's girl and thrust her up before his face. Only when he saw the child did Hutto let go of the grip he had on Wally.

The little man dropped to the floor and wildly gasped for air until he recovered enough to scream.

—Put a bullet through that nigger! Get 'em outta here, all three of 'em!

Medlin yelled out over the crowd.

—He's not yours, I bought him!

Bingo himself picked up the gavel and slammed it down.

—All three sold for $200!

He jumped off the stage and made his way toward Medlin. Medlin gave Tom a shove toward the exit and told him to get the rig, while he fumbled for $200 from his pouch and slammed it into Bingo's out-stretched hand.

Hutto, bleeding from gashes to his face, gathered the woman and child, and they all three picked their way down the side steps of the stage toward Medlin, who took hold of the chains and elbowed his way through the throng of men who momentarily hung back, although they had not yet had enough. Hutto carried the child as he held his arm around the woman to protect her from the crush of people now rolling along toward the exit in a mass of elation and confusion. Hands reached out from everywhere to touch the big man. Medlin pushed through, with many calling out to him at once.

—Ya got yer hands full now!

—He's all yours, and the women to boot!

—What're ya gonna do with 'em?

Just outside the tent Tom had the wagon, with the Weasel holding the horses by their harness. The hitched pair pulled and snapped their heads around, almost taking the Weasel off his feet. Medlin got the three slaves into the back of the wagon. Then he jumped up in front with Tom. Hutto, the woman, and their child bounced around roughly in the wagon bed, with Medlin maneuvering the team through the crowd. People were running up to the wagon, reaching and grabbing to try and touch Hutto so they could boast about it later. Medlin had no choice but to force the team forward into the crowd. People had to make the decision to move aside or get run over.

The situation was alarming for the horses. They started to kick, their old legs stabbing the air, using energy they no longer had to spare. The two pulled wildly against each other.

Meanwhile, the crowd remained at a high pitch, shouts and claps all mixing into the sound of a mob out of control. The horses were in full panic with their eyeballs so exposed they looked as if they would fall out of the sockets at any moment. Both flailed about like wild mustangs feeling the saddle for the first time. The crowd completely encircled the rig, with no one considering that if the horses got free, some could be killed.

Suddenly there came an almost human scream from one of the horses and a crash so heavy the ground seemed to move—wood, metal, slapping of leather—and then stillness. Everyone pulled back into a big circle around the wagon and the air that had been so filled with noise went silent.

One horse struggled to stay up against the pull of the harness of the other lying motionless in the dirt, dead on its side. Its eyeballs looked as wild as they had before it collapsed. Its tongue fell fully extended from an open mouth. The horse died frozen in appearance as in the last moment of life.

Onlookers drifted away in stark silence with the image of the dead horse crowding out everything else. The Weasel freed the struggling horse from the binding tack. When it calmed down, he leaned over the dead horse, lifted the mane from out of its eyes and smoothed it, then ran his fingers thoughtfully across the velvety muzzle that had already started to lose warmth.

———

MANY YEARS LATER, on a Charleston spring evening, one of the better carriages—a splendid carriage with polished brass fittings and matching two-team—pulled up to the front of the theater. Such a carriage was a rare sight in Charleston after the War. Maneuvering around mountains of stone-and-brick rubble was a mere inconvenience compared to the more critical issue of just surviving. For years after the War many people, including children, still wandered the streets with nowhere to live. It was not safe to go out alone in the evening to take the air. Citizens started carrying small pocket pistols.

Evidence was everywhere that it would not be anytime soon, if ever, that life in Charleston would remotely resemble life before the devastating shelling by Union warships. The pattern of living of Mrs. Thomas Pinckney after she came back from Orangeburg to reclaim her grand home at 15 King Street was one glaring example of the reduced circumstances that most of the finer families found themselves in. At a brighter time, twenty-three slaves lived on the Pinckney property and served every need of the Mister and Missus. But now only one, Cecilia, remained. She stayed even though she had the chance to leave with the others. Maybe she stayed with the Missus out of loyalty, or maybe it was because she knew she would at least have a roof over her head—more than could be said of most freed slaves, who left their masters with their freedom and nothing else.

With no other income, the old Missus rented out rooms in the stately King Street home, known to have had the liveliest of social events in its own majestic ballroom. The Jew tailor Samms rented the entire carriage house. He ran his business on the ground floor, while living with his family in the loft above. Mrs. Pinckney and Cecilia lived behind the big house in the dependency—once used as a cookhouse and slave quarters. In the work kitchen the two elderly women made the terrapin soup that Cecilia delivered to customers in the neighborhood in a pail swaddled in cloth.

It was pitiful to those who had known her back in the heyday to see the Missus on Broad Street selling roses she made with her own hands from palm fronds, but in her, memories of her past grand life had long since dimmed and been replaced by the strong human instinct to survive.

Yet in the midst of widespread misfortune, a theater managed to spring from the ashes quicker than most establishments. Some families that were not tied to cotton came through the war years with their wealth intact, and they enjoyed the diversion of concerts and plays.

On that spring evening fifteen years after the War, when the elegant carriage came to a stop as the crowd rushed into the lobby with little time to spare, a fine-looking Negro man dressed in evening attire stepped down from the box, opened the carriage door, and offered his hand to a light-skinned Negro woman. She disembarked, lifting her gown slightly to expose scarlet-colored shoes worked with silver beading. The fabric of her scarlet dress was so abundant that it took special effort to clear the carriage door gracefully. Her luxuriant ensemble was of the likes rarely seen since the period of opulence before the troubles of wartime. One of her eyes was covered with a silk patch embroidered with the fine stitching of a flourished monogram: SD.

The elegant Negress passed through the lobby, attracting attention on the way to her own reserved box. By the number of tipped hats, it was plain she was well known to male patrons of the theater—but she was not acknowledged by wives, who looked away at the sight of the woman.

After the end of the War, with citizens trickling back into the city, the atmosphere was dreary. The popular Carolina Men's Social Club was in ruins. Once an oasis for all men of means, it was now a shell of a building, and it had been pegged for total removal. With only the company of their wives to pass the evenings, it was with great relief that men saw that an enterprising woman—who already ran a successful establishment for a more brutish clientele—would see the sound reasoning in elevating the status of the business to appeal to the club set.

Her new venture was called The Silver Dollar. Her original establishment, the less-polished emporium, she had named The Half Dollar. Both offered similar services, but it was the level of quality that distinguished one from the other. Gentlemen could enjoy a good cigar or cards in the company of their peers at The Silver Dollar, and there was always a bevy of attractive, well-dressed young ladies of the night who seemed overwhelmingly more amusing to these clients than their wives.

When speaking of their husbands' absence after dinner, the wives of The Silver Dollar clientele referred to "going out." That was what they heard their husbands say as they left home for a few hours in the evening.

At the theater the woman sat alone in the box with her escort standing at attention just behind her. His eyes were in constant motion, taking in patterns of movement throughout the theater. Down below and five rows back from center stage was a particularly boisterous group of men who caught the attention of the young sentinel. Wally Poulnott was at the center of the commotion. The group had been drinking, and took no mind of the aggravation of those seated nearby. Wally's hijinks and popularity had not wavered from his auction days, even considering he and his money had gone off to California as soon as the fighting started. He was now back in Charleston, retired and bored with no stage to mount. He no longer wore his outlandish costume, but he did settle on bright-colored cravats as his signature.

Bingo was no longer in the picture. All the years they worked the auctions Wally made it clear that Bingo was nothing more than a slave in a top hat. As the War grew closer, talk of freedom for slaves spread. Bingo thought more and more of freedom. Prodding and sometimes beating other Negroes to get them to move along at the auctions became more difficult now that he felt that they, too, could be secret dreamers.

After Hutto almost killed him at the famous Butler auction in Savannah, Wally started to carry in his belt a cat-o'-nine-tails. For good measure, he attached a lead ball to the end of each tail. Right before the War broke out he got violently angry and used this whip on Bingo, when, for the first time, Bingo refused to lay in hard on an old slave who was slow to mount the auction platform. Shortly thereafter, the firing on Fort Sumter prompted Wally to run off to California. Bingo broke into Wally's house and took the brutal whip that Wally had left behind. He waited for Wally to slink back into Charleston. He was patient. A few years after the War ended Wally did return. Bingo caught him trying to crawl into a window of the house, which had been left neglected and abandoned for five years, while Bingo continued living in the shed. Bingo got him good. He lashed at Wally's back until it ran blood and his shirt was in shreds. Bingo felt satisfied.

It would have been over except that Wally turned his head around with an insult he had sometimes used toward the slaves on the block.

—Bingo, you're nothin' but a dirty Congo nigger!

Bingo then took a hard swing at Wally's face. One lead ball took out a front tooth and cut a deep gash at the side of the mouth.

Charleston was lawless after the end of the War, so with rampant stealing going on, Wally's beating was of no consequence to authorities. The cut to his mouth healed badly, leaving a constant sneer or smile—depending on the interpretation of the viewer.

———

THE CONCERT PROGRAM THAT NIGHT was baroque pieces, chosen partly because of budgetary restrictions—the music required only two musicians, cello and harpsichord. Though it was by no means an orchestra such as Charleston once enjoyed, the duo still gave the impression the city was on the way back to some civility. At intermission, several gentlemen paid their respects to the woman in her private box. Always nearby stood the silent young man, whom she never acknowledged or introduced. It was clear that he was constantly aware of any activity near her.

The curtain came down at the end of the concert. There was a surge toward the lobby. The silent escort walked slightly ahead of the Negress, to part the crowd for her comfort and to make a path wide enough to accommodate her gown. As they cleared the stairs from the box level, their way coincided with Wally's party, still in boisterous animation. As the escort almost imperceptibly bumped into him, Wally let out a muffled cry and fell to the carpet. The elegant Negress rapidly stepped around him and continued toward the doors. Panic quickly swept through the lobby. In the confusion, most thought they were in imminent danger. Women were screaming. Several gentlemen left the side of their wives and along with the escort got Dalia immediately into her waiting carriage, and she was safely away.

Several men, one a doctor, knelt over Wally, who lay on his back, his contorted face to the ceiling. The doctor closely inspected his bulging eyes, particularly the pupils. Wally had spittle coming out of the side of his mouth. He tried to speak but couldn't. His body began to quake, and in his thrashing about a small patch of blood could be seen on the carpet. The doctor turned him on his side, and after some searching he saw the small slit where something narrow like the blade of a stiletto had entered the body. Within moments, Wally Poulnott lay still, dead.

5

GIL HAD SPENT THE PREVIOUS DAY starting her transcription of the diary Chip had given her on Tuesday. As she pulled into the parking garage she planned to continue transcribing but also to begin some research. After glaring briefly at the Vic in her prime parking spot, Gil took a left on Main, where her spirits brightened at the sight of the State House. The structure majestically monopolized the view. Most likely to the hurrying morning crowd the building was nothing more than an obstacle on their route to the office, but not to Gil.

The sun bathed the face of the State House in gold with deep shadows accenting the classical details so popular in the mid–eighteen hundreds. The grand impression was not an accident, but all as intended to strike pride in South Carolinians. For Gil, a sixth-generation native, it did just that. Seeing the State House and knowing its history added another layer to her everyday navigation through life.

History, mostly South Carolina history, had been Gil's passion since she was a young girl. It wasn't everybody who knew exactly what they wanted to do with their lives at the age of ten, but for Gil it was so. She knew it from the time she and her father, members of the Carolina Diggers club, first traveled down dusty back roads to small South Carolina towns to unearth old bottles and other small objects from the past.

Gil and her father had a system. Father did the digging, very gently so to not break any finds. Then he would baby out of the fresh soil each piece, which he would pass off to Gil, who would take a soft brush to it.

After a little experience she could easily distinguish an ink from a medicine bottle. What amazed her at that young age was that with a bit of work, she could uncover an artifact frozen in time that would be a clue to an existence left behind. After that, there was never a question as to her future pursuit of a life in history.

With one of the best schools of native history in the country, just fifty miles from her hometown of Greenville, there was also no question Gil would attend the University of South Carolina. The university's strength was Southern history, and it had an unparalleled collection of documents and artifacts. With a masters and doctorate program, there could be no better choice.

Growing up, Gil never really fit in, since her peers thought her too serious. She joined in on bike rides during the summer months, when the kids were gone from noon until suppertime, but when most would peel off to go to the park, Gil kept going by herself to explore old, abandoned shacks half covered in vines. Simple dwellings long gone to ruin, some had been home to Black sharecroppers who most likely abandoned them to follow work out of the fields and into the industrial North. Openings in the walls were stuffed with newspapers for insulation, showing the extreme hardship endured in days gone by. Most were just one room with a fireplace blackened from daily use for cooking and for heat. Some shacks were larger with two to three rooms, undoubtedly owned by poor White people. Among shards of plaster and broken furniture Gil once found a brochure with a printed cover of a robed man on a white horse with the headline *Ku Klux Klan—Today, Tomorrow and Forever.*

Through high school Gil remained neutral when the other girls would dwell on the subject of boys and their efforts to attract them. To the frustration of the girls, the boys liked Gil's company. They thought she was clever and interesting. And they were relaxed with her because there was not the tension they felt around the girls who had snagging a boyfriend on their mind.

When Gil got to the university in Columbia, she discovered there were others like herself—others who placed a lot of emphasis on their passion. She found that they, too, had felt like misfits in high school, and when they discovered each other, a group of about eight individuals clung together in both work and play, with a bond like they had never known before. True to their nature, they put study first, but they managed downtime, when they played as hard as anybody else. Not only Gil, but everyone discovered they had something to offer—their humor, wittiness, or silliness. Each of the eight young men and women made personal discoveries about themselves, and they felt free to express and explore them. Finding people like themselves made them feel they were okay for the first time. Gil began to date some. Although nothing of major consequence developed in her college years, she was relaxed enough that she felt open to something serious. If it didn't happen, then so be it.

The friends hung together through school at USC, but after that, most scattered across the country, pursuing advanced degrees or careers. Gil stayed with the doctorate program in Columbia, where like anyone in the history game she had a special relationship with time. She was fascinated with stepping into the mind and landscape of the past. Gil was forever intrigued by passing time, with its implications for the present. When she could see patterns within the transition to the present, that was where the big payoff was for her.

On her way to the university every morning, she drove across the rocky Congaree River with its mostly mud-laden water that flowed not with commanding force but meandered. Many thousands of years before, a glacier had stopped at this place and receded at the geological fall line, leaving a jagged, rocky confluence of rivers.

Most would drive over the bridge and pay the river no mind, but Gil had the gift to blink and see the Congaree maneuvering over granite boulders and gigging perch in side pools. She knew those rocks were the very reason Columbia had come to be where it was. Newcomers traveling by boat through the backcountry, looking for agreeable territory to settle down, came upon the unnavigable, rocky shoals of the Congaree. Rather than get off the river and portage around, it seemed reasonable enough to consider the spot their final destination, so many stayed and settled.

———

IT WAS UNLIKE HER TO DELAY her arrival at the Caroliniana and her busy day at work, but today Gil turned right after she crossed Gervais, to vary her routine and walk the complete circumference of the State House. She wanted to review the many monuments—some not more than a plaque in the grass, others large, scaled bigger than life size. The monuments had been scrutinized and some even vandalized of late.

In all, there were thirty-one, scattered throughout the grounds. Gil had meandered by most of the monuments before, not paying much attention, but with South Carolina under fire, everything took on more importance in her mind.

Now she found herself very intent on finding clues that might lead to answers to her growing questions about South Carolina's history of race. At a glance, some monuments might have seemed quite innocuous, but the demonstrators had already taken a close look and uncovered issues that added fuel to the fire already set and blazing over the Confederate flag.

In a prime spot at the southwest corner of the grounds stood a simple but impressive tribute to the South Carolinian Dr. James Marion Sims (1813–1883), donated by the Women's Auxiliary of the South Carolina Medical Association. A curved set of steps ascended to a granite block surmounted by a life-size bronze bust of the "Father of Gynecology." Dr. Sims's early research into women's gynecological issues and subsequent contribution in the form of his development of groundbreaking cures were very impressive. He invented numerous devices and instruments used in women's health. It was Sims who designed the speculum, which was thereafter the primary device used in women's pelvic examinations.

Sims also performed experimental surgeries seeking a cure for vesicovaginal fistula, a debilitating condition arising from complications of childbirth. He operated on enslaved women whom he bought for the purpose. Three slave women with fistulas were the subjects Dr. Sims chose for extensive experimentation. On one of those women he performed over thirty individual surgeries. None were given anesthesia, which at the time was not a fully accepted practice for surgery. Beyond the study of gynecological issues, Sims did a study of the cause of truism or lockjaw in children—for which he used a shoemaker's awl to manipulate the skulls of infants born to slave women—again, without anesthesia.

Gil was not surprised to see that the Sims monument, in its peaceful, shaded spot conducive to reflective thought, was emblazoned with red spray-painted swastikas—clearly a reference to unethical medical experiments preformed on concentration camp prisoners in Nazi Germany. Everything around the State House was being scrutinized because of the spotlight on the Confederate flag. Nothing was passed over in the search for evidence of violations against the human condition of slaves. And soon the focus on the Confederate flag grew to embrace all that was considered Southern.

Unlike Sims's bronze bust, Benjamin "Pitchfork" Tillman's monument was not in a peaceful nook. The eight-foot, full-body bronze sculpture, mounted on a five-foot-high marble pedestal, stood prominently beside a well-traveled walkway. The six-term senator was so well loved in the state that when the citizens were called upon in 1940 to contribute to the cost of the monument in a statewide campaign, money flowed in. The popular Tillman had only one eye, but this deficiency was made up for by his fiery personality, most especially demonstrated when he spoke on the subject of the Negro, which he called an "ignorant and debauched race" characterized by "barbarism, savagery, and cannibalism." He openly admitted to having burned out and killed many in his campaign to keep them from voting or making any other attempts to participate in mainstream society. With his jocular stories always designed to demean Black people, in life Tillman was the center of every crowd. He once said of Negroes, "They are not baboons, though some are so near akin to the monkey that scientists are yet looking for the missing link."

Even though Tillman died in 1918, his memory lingered on in the hearts of many White South Carolinians, until, in 1940, his monument was dedicated in front of a very large crowd of devotees. Before the demonstration over the Confederate flag, there was only one attempt to have it removed, when a Black congressman initiated a bill that went nowhere. But finally, with the demonstration going on, the tribute to Tillman, like the monument to Dr. Sims, was vandalized—spray-painted bright red, Coca-Cola red. Because of this vandalism, there were police keeping watch around the clock on all the threatened statuary. The Tillman monument went onto the long list of tributes to historical figures with racist views. They became the targets of a growing movement demanding that they be torn down.

Though the demonstration in Columbia originally focused solely on the Confederate flag flying atop the State House, there were so many other images construed as symbols of racism that objections to them grew throughout the South. In New Orleans, the City Council organized a task force to address monuments to Robert E. Lee, Jefferson Davis, and General P. G. T. Beauregard. To forestall controversy, the city government acted swiftly and had the monuments dismantled and hauled off in the dead of night.

Monuments dedicated to Confederate General Lee seemed to be all over Dixie, and almost everywhere these came under attack. Ironically, Lee himself had spoken out against memorials to the Lost Cause. Four years after the Civil War, he said, "I think it wiser not to keep open the sores of war but to follow the examples of those nations who endeavored to obliterate the marks of civil strife, to commit to oblivion the feelings engendered." Nevertheless, there were dozens of monuments honoring General Lee, not only throughout the South but all throughout the country.

———

IN 1864, A YEAR BEFORE THE END of the Civil War, Congress passed a law requiring each state to send statues of two of their notable citizens to be placed in the important National Statuary Hall, adjacent to the Capitol Rotunda. With the War still on, most states did not prioritize the project. Indeed, some did not get around to sending their statues to DC until decades later, well after the Confederate states had rejoined the Union. Virginia eventually sent a statue of George Washington. For their second statue, the Virginia General Assembly bypassed Jefferson and Madison and agreed on Robert E. Lee. Some representatives from states outside of the South were appalled, saying that Virginia had not decided upon a patriot but instead had sent a statue of one who had tried to destroy the nation. Many passionate objections to Lee's statue were made, but the objectors' hands were tied. The law left it up to the states which statues they sent to the National Statuary Hall. Georgia sent a statue of Alexander Stephens, vice president of the Confederacy.

Mississippi sent Jefferson Davis, president of the Confederacy. South Carolina chose Wade Hampton III, a highly decorated lieutenant general in the Confederate Army.

———

GIL BEGAN TO SEE THAT THE DISPLAY of White supremacist Civil War heroes had a long history before the Confederate flag controversy erupted. It took time for the South to rebuild after the War, but decades later, as money could be raised, monuments to symbols of the Confederacy sprang up all over the South. Tributes were erected throughout the twentieth century, indications that the South was long in the desire to continue to aggrandize the Civil War and not ready to throw in the towel in the Lost Cause.

As she continued looking at the monuments, it was obvious to Gil that there was no grand scheme or master plan for their placement. Most appeared to be put simply where there was a vacant space, but this was not the case in the positioning of the monument to one of the most loved and honored men of the state, Wade Hampton III. Man and horse, five times life size, struck a classic pose atop a massive marble block adorned with bronze plaques—each commemorating a Civil War battle in which he fought, including Gettysburg.

The Hampton monument originally had been placed elsewhere on the State House grounds, but in the 1970s, it was relocated to a more appropriate position in front of the six-story 1930s building named after the general. Gil passed beside the State House and continued on her route between the Wade Hampton and Calhoun buildings. She glanced over to the Hampton monument and thought that there would probably be calls for its removal before long. Hampton was one of the largest slaveholders in the Southeast before the War. He fought against the Union in some major battles and rose to the high rank of lieutenant general—all reasons why his monument would be in danger of teardown. Imposing in size and positioned prominently in a large open space—alone, without the clutter of anything else to fight for attention—the monument was awe-inspiring if the viewer were into the accomplishments of the man.

The Hampton sculpture stood in front of and introduced the Hampton building. To those who named the building in 1938, Hampton seemed perfectly natural to honor a man considered by those in power at the time a great hero in the history of South Carolina. No one passing by would pay the building any particular attention except for Gil, whose curiosity as to why it was on the prestigious National Registry had prompted her to look into its history.

Most buildings on the Registry were selected for superiority in architecture—something special that made them unique. But the Wade Hampton State Office Building was just a watered-down version of Classical Revival with a few Art Deco touches thrown in. It was a building of restraint, designed and built mainly for one purpose—to put people back to work during the Great Depression of the 1930s. The national Works Progress Administration (WPA) pumped grant money into projects that would get skilled craftsmen and artisans back into the job force. There were massive WPA projects throughout the country, like the one to install decorative tile throughout the New York City subway stations, done by accomplished but out-of-work tile setters.

That the Hampton State Office Building was built with WPA money had nothing to do with it being on the Registry. Gil read in the Registry documentation that the building was viewed as a symbol of the state's policy on segregation. The building originally housed state offices responsible for monitoring compliance with segregation laws. By the time the building was in full operation in 1938, the doctrine of "separate but equal" as set down in *Plessy v. Ferguson* had been the law of the land for over forty years. The building was a testament to how things were in the era of *Plessy*. On the basement level, as was laid out in the original blueprints, the three bathrooms were segregated—one for White women, one for White men, and one for "Colored."

When Gil once had an occasion to go to the basement of the Hampton building she noticed an up-to-date drinking fountain with a low, handicap-accessible version alongside. Since the old plaster walls had not been repainted, it was clear that there had once been two fountains, side by side. There was no question for Gil that years earlier there had been one drinking fountain for White people, and a separate one for Coloreds. Gil was horrified when she realized that such segregation had not happened in the distant past, when women wore long hoop skirts. This happened in her mother's time, when undoubtedly she would have witnessed the dual accommodations everywhere she went.

This morning, Gil walked alongside the monumental tribute to Hampton and admired the sculptor's skill in making the war hero larger than life—majestic, gallant, and strong—as he had once been portrayed in school books across South Carolina. Now Gil felt sure that this particular Hampton monument, along with other monuments to White supremacists, might soon be slated for removal. Wade Hampton had been a major slave owner, Confederate war hero, state governor, and US senator, but most passersby in 2000 had no idea who the man on the horse had been.

———

IN 1850, AN EMINENT HARVARD PROFESSOR of zoology and geology, Louis Agassiz, was in the South lecturing and collecting evidence to try to prove his theory of human origins or polygenism, which he called "God's Great Plan of Creation." For a lecture aid he commissioned an engraver to create a chart showing profiles of three "species" side by side—White man, African, and ape—and he pointed out what he deemed to be stark differences. The African's broad nose and lips, and the ape's cranial shelf above the eyes were to Agassiz evidence that he was correct in considering that they were two species distinct from the White man—unrelated to Homo sapiens. Further, he wanted to document these differences using a sensational technology—daguerrean photography—first developed in France, at the time almost unknown in America, that captured an image on glass with a clarity never before seen.

Agassiz's theory of polygenism was a popular topic on the lecture circuit. Southerners like planter Wade Hampton were most receptive to such thinking, as it reinforced the idea of inferiority that they used to justify slavery. Agassiz traveled to Charleston to address the Association for the Advancement of American Science, where he said that "the brain of the negro is that of the imperfect brain of a seven months infant in the womb of a white"—a statement his audience accepted as fact.

When Agassiz traveled on to Columbia to do field study on the "African species" he met Wade Hampton himself and Benjamin Taylor, both plantation owners who had large holdings of slaves and who were receptive to lending them out as props to support the popular theory of polygenism. Seven Congo slaves were chosen. They were pure African specimens, perfect for examination, perfect for memorializing on glass plates. Joseph Zealy, a Columbia daguerreotype photographer, was commissioned to make a record of the individual slaves. He posed them—both male and female—some stripped completely naked, others naked to the waist.

———

IN 1976—MORE THAN A CENTURY LATER—an employee of Harvard's Peabody Museum of Archeology and Ethnology, rummaging around in an obscure storage cabinet in the attic, came across the images, still in their leather cases marked *Zealy Studios*. The images had not been seen since Agassiz used them in the 1850s to try to justify his hypothesis on the creation of mankind.

After their discovery in 1976, the daguerreotypes were widely published and were said to be the best visual example of the harsh reality of slavery in the United States. The reason for which they were taken—to make a record to support Agassiz's "scientific" theory of polygenism—made them very compelling in contrast to the later "Sambo art" depicting a jovial Aunt Jemima or the kindly Uncle Remus. Because of the raw starkness and emotionless quality of Zealy's daguerreotypes, modern viewers like Gil found it hard to look at them, but at the same time they were unable to turn away.

———

LINGERING FOR A FEW MOMENTS beside the Hampton monument, Gil was reminded of the Agassiz connection and was sorry that others passing by were oblivious to the story, no doubt seeing the Hampton

monument as just another statue of a man on a horse. The connections, the twists and turns of a thread of continuity running through
time—these were what drew Gil so compellingly to the history game.

6

Negroes frightened of the train
May 7, 1857

THE SAVANNAH TRAIN DEPOT was experiencing beyond-normal activity with large groups of slaves and their handlers fresh from the Butler auction. The slaves were shuffling along, tethered together with lengths of chain that were joined to iron cuffs around their ankles. Some of the young males, in chains for the first time, balked at the arrangement, so they had the additional burden of shackles binding their wrists and were placed at the front of the procession for close observation. Handlers were on high alert after word spread that a slave of advanced age had somehow gotten loose from the bindings the evening before and, unable to cope with the fearsome surroundings, jumped purposely out in front of an oncoming train. It was thought that though the old man had been hammered down at a very modest price early in the auction, his death still meant money down the drain.

Women and young ones were given no special consideration. They, too, wore heavy leg irons, and had difficulty keeping up. Infants were cradled in their mothers' arms or strapped to their backs with swaths of cloth. Drivers made clear that if the infants in any way impeded progress, they would be abandoned. Even though it was an empty threat—after all, slave babies would one day be valuable property—the threat was enough to have mothers hold on tighter and muffle cries as best they could.

It was likely that none had ever experienced such rough treatment on the Butler plantations. The irons cut into the unaccustomed flesh, leaving wounds that bled so much that there was a red trail of blood marking the slaves' path. Audible protest would bring nothing but the lash. Adding to the unceasing commotion throughout the crowded station was the rhythm of the chain flailing at the floor as each gang worked at the same measure of movement to achieve the least resistance on the shackles. One stumble could be disastrous and pull others down.

The rhythmic beat of the chain slapping the floor was not unlike a rhythm from former days. After long hours in the field, everyone would join in around a fire and dance to the beat of a pigskin drum—ancestral rhythms carried in the soul with origins in Africa. But those old rhythms were not now on their minds in the Savannah depot. Their will to just survive had, for the time, replaced any hopes for joy or reminiscences of a happier time.

With so many ready to board the next train, crowds were shoved into any unoccupied space on the crowded station platform. The station itself was not much more than a huge shed with a plank floor and rough-hewn walls of wood of local species. The gable roof was held up by a series of posts and beams so as to make the wide reach across platforms and track possible. The roof was high to accommodate the plumes of smoke and steam billowing from locomotives.

The train people, knowing of the auction at the racetrack, had worked the schedule to put online two more passenger cars on Thursday and Friday to accommodate the large crowd expected, and four more boxcars to handle the great load of auctioned slaves heading north. It was imperative to get the slaves quickly to Charleston, where another auction was planned for the next day. Potential buyers, unwilling to make the trip to Savannah, would be anxious to inspect the fresh stock and get in with dealers, who were counting on a quick flip to recoup capital.

However, Tom had convinced Medlin that the big returns would be coming out of the Mobile auction houses. Medlin and the slaves would therefore get a train the next day to Mobile. They would part company, with Tom in Charleston—the hub for the Southeast. Tom knew that in Mobile, cotton prices had overtaken and surpassed those in South Carolina. Over the past two years, he had seen the cotton yield out of Carolina dwindling in volume and quality. It was obvious to anybody in the cotton business that the soil was petering out and losing out to the Gulf states, Alabama and Mississippi—states new to cotton, with rich soil not yet dogged to death. At the Butler auction Tom had seen new faces, people who were no doubt up from the Gulf trying to stock up in the push for slaves. Textile mills were calling for more and yet more cotton.

The Negroes would travel in boxcars—with hogs, cattle, and horses also on their way to auction. Regular passengers, accustomed to traveling the night train to arrive in Charleston to conduct business, were used to seeing a few enslaved people, but certainly not in these numbers. They were alarmed by the sight of so many in one place. Under normal circumstances, they looked forward to a quiet, sleepy ride to the city and to arriving refreshed and ready for a busy day of commerce. That evening they held kerchiefs over their noses and looked down at the platform so as not to catch sight of the tawdriness all around them in the station.

All muscle and power, the American Standard 414-0 locomotive had spent the better part of the afternoon in the yard, busily jockeying into position for the final coupling, and was now ready and waiting, just outside the station, for the conductor's signal to advance.

Medlin and Tom were positioned at the edge of the platform with Hutto, Celia, and Jama when the engine lurched forward and sounded its deafening whistle. All three tensed and felt almost on the verge of panic. Jama, held firmly by her hand by her mother, grabbed with her other hand the closest thing—Medlin's leg—and clung on tightly. All orifices of the locomotive spewed a combination of smoke, steam, and heat that rose quickly to the ceiling and rolled off it to fill the station and engulf everyone and everything in a blanket of grayness.

The three slaves, having nothing in their past to compare with such power, all shrank away from the tracks. They imagined this as the hell they had been told of, as described in the Bible.

Attached right behind the slow-moving locomotive came the tender. It was painted in gold letters spelling out *The Southern*. The style of lettering was known to trainmen as Bastard Railroad Gothic, and was used universally to identify all train lines at the time. As it passed, Medlin thought the painted tender looked too joyful—it would be suitable for a circus wagon rather than such a powerful train.

When the conductor motioned for all to board, the experienced slave handlers deftly removed the leg shackles and then rushed their gangs toward the livestock cars. The slaves scrambled to board as best they could. Medlin approached and saw that in the first boxcar, horses, tethered to an interior rail, were in high panic at the commotion. With their heads restrained by leather straps, their only defense was to kick at the slaves pouring into the already cramped space. The next car was no better. Medlin could hear hogs squealing in horror over the commotion.

He reversed himself through the surge of slaves being pushed to board the cars by the handlers. Pulling Hutto by his wrist shackles, Medlin worked his way back against the current of humanity. Celia held tightly to Hutto's pants waistband with one hand, and with the other she held on to Jama, now riding on her mother's back. Tom shouted above the noise that they were going the wrong direction, to which Medlin shouted something about finding another way for accommodations.

With Medlin in the lead, they entered the rear platform of the third passenger car. People were rushing into the first two cars and filling them to capacity. Before they spilled into the third, Medlin went in the direction of the porter, hoping to strike a deal for the three to be stowed in a small compartment he had noticed just inside the car and next to the rear platform. The door of this compartment was slightly open, enough to see it was meant for train business. It held various boxes, lanterns, and what looked to be a pull-down seat as refuge for the car porter. The trainman looked highly agitated when he saw Hutto, Celia, and Jama in his car and rushed down the aisle with his hands up in a pushback position. Tom stepped between the porter and Medlin and made a proposition. There was resistance until the porter accepted a half dollar. The three were directed into the cramped space and the door was shut. The arrangement was completed just before passengers entered the car looking for a comfortable seat.

Medlin and Tom settled onto bench seats just across from the closed compartment. Medlin felt uncomfortable over the tight quarters of his charges, but when Tom made the point that it was better than the box-car, he let it go. Tom instructed his older brother that in dealing with slaves it was best to think of them as animals and not be burdened with such things as their comfort.

Maybe the ride would be a chance for Medlin to sleep or, better, to turn his mind to the advancing ordeal that was starting to appear to have no end. If he could lay out to himself what was ahead, there was a pos-sibility that the plan could take the edge off his mounting fear. It was in his nature to try to anticipate the upcoming, the unexpected—a charac-teristic hewn from cotton farming.

Medlin was quiet, but with Charleston ahead, Tom could not help himself from spewing out tall tales of his past spent in roaming the bus-tling port city. He knew his brother would not be in the least interested, perhaps downright annoyed, but he carried on with a seamless string of stories that in other company would amuse and be met with other like tales—all embellished beyond any reality.

The train lunged forward as though it had been hit from behind by another engine, but it was the nature of such machines that they had no capacity for subtle stirring. As soon as they cleared the station Medlin turned toward the window, hoping the passing terrain would lull him into a dream state, but by now it was getting dark outside and the only thing he could see was his own face reflected back at him from the glass window. His hat, cocked forward, blocked the light from a hanging gas lamp, leaving half his face in shadow, featureless just north of his mouth. As he stared at his own image he reached out to touch the glass—almost to reassure himself that it was not someone else looking at him, judging. He stared for a good while at the ghostlike image that gave him a strange feeling that this face belonged to another man—a more sinister, uncaring man. A man with a character that would better serve him during this ordeal.

If he could just block out of his mind all other considerations except the practical utility of getting his three slaves to the auction in Mobile, he could go home with the money needed to start Caleb at college. For years he had been closely watching Tom for signs as to how to acquire a single-minded nature, as Tom possessed this practical feature. Medlin had always envied Tom's matter-of-fact attitude about life, all the while knowing it was never to be part of his own anxious approach to existence.

Clues to their personalities could be found in the early traits showing in the two boys before they became full-grown men. Medlin did not have to scrape very deep to examine the differences between himself and his brother. The contrasts were stark: Medlin was a plodder, a grinder, seeking the reward of a clear, predictable path—he meticulously took the time necessary to weigh all aspects of a problem so that he could easily make adjustments to counter adversity, should it arise. Tom, on the other hand, was spontaneous. He knew that any path was sure to be littered with unforeseen challenges requiring a quick response to avert otherwise inevitable disaster. Lying, blaming others, even resorting to violence were diversionary tactics in a life of spontaneity. Tom indulged in them all. And what was most shocking to Medlin was that Tom was so skilled at going through life with not a whit of self-consciousness or conscience regarding responsibility for his actions. A natural conclusion was that Medlin became a farmer and Tom a ruthless, scrappy commodities trader.

Now, on the train to Charleston, Medlin's only escape was sleep lulled by the cadence of the iron wheels hitting the junction between each twenty-foot length of rail in a brutish lullaby. But his sleep proved to be fitful and far from an opportunity to put his troubles to rest. Instead, there were foreboding dreams—dreams of being chased by an unknown assailant in a plot that was somehow exacerbated by his unpreparedness. Most of the time, the best he could do was half sleep, teetering between consciousness and extremely drowsy. Whenever there was a noticeable change in the cadence of the wheels along the track, he came fully to.

Every fifty miles, the locomotive depleted its wood supply. Every fifty miles, the firebox had to be stoked with 128 cubic feet of wood. So it was that every calculated stop spawned a small town. At each refueling station one or two passengers boarded the train for business or pleasure awaiting them in Charleston while train firemen quickly loaded wood. Having a cord—four by four by eight feet—available for each scheduled train was no easy feat. Pine was plentiful, but pine had too much resin that would quickly turn to a disaster in the hot box. Oak was the wood to have—lots of it.

Each stop had a modest station house. Had there not been a sign naming it, there would be no way of distinguishing one from another, as all stations were alike. After the sprawling Savannah station, these rural depots were scaled down to accommodate only the ticket window, a small waiting area and a platform with an overhang as protection from sun and rain. The sameness in the spartan design suggested that the rail company took comfort in all stations being alike. It seemed that before the refueling stations were built, in the interests of economy a single master plan was distributed so that all the stations would be built alike.

The only difference between one station and another was the setting. Most were adjacent to a little town consisting of a single thoroughfare with several mercantile shops and a bank. In contrast, a few stations stood in isolation, away from the settlements they serviced, leaving a mystery as to the town's existence. As the train approached each station stop, there was the screech of metal grinding on metal, brakes on wheels. The complete stop was always punctuated by a lunge forward for the passengers.

Medlin, on the outskirts of sleep, took notice of the new passengers coming on board the train. Without knowing the first thing about them, he felt a pang of envy at the casual way each newcomer approached the routine of travel. It showed that they were regulars, with nothing more to think about than meeting the train on time. Unlike him, none was responsible for three beings stuffed in a cramped compartment not much larger than a rabbit pen—the pen just a few feet away from the path of the new passengers as they casually sought a seat. None were—as Medlin was—about to make their way over unknown ground, far from home, to conduct business with people who were sure to sniff out his inexperience and weakness for fairness.

Medlin had been obsessed with the time of day since the minute they left Bennettsville. He felt some comfort in monitoring the time as the only thing familiar in what was becoming a desperate momentum forward. He had to resist taking out his pocket watch at every urge to look at the time, aware that to look at his watch with such frequency was getting to be a compulsion and the way of a madman. His father had given him this fine old watch—an English Liverpool, with an eighteen-carat-gold hunter case—just days before finally succumbing to lung disease.

Medlin was usually a bit self-conscious about taking the timepiece out of his pocket, because in his mind it was ostentatious in its heft and large size. Despite his desire to keep it concealed, his vest watch pocket could not totally contain it, as it crested into plain sight.

After a few hours Medlin opened his eyes and was surprised he had gotten some sleep after all, as he noticed the golden light of morning cutting across a brick building on what must have been the outskirts of Charleston. The train was starting to slow down, and passengers were already beginning to fill the aisles and fumble with their baggage. They moved quietly, out of consideration for the few who were still getting used to waking up, but there was an undercurrent of anticipation at disembarking and the rush that was sure to come with it. Once the train stopped fully, the passenger car emptied rapidly.

Tom was just coming to, stretching with a long audible yawn. The brothers devised a plan to time getting the slaves off from the rear platform the minute the train came to a complete stop. It was Tom's idea to hustle them on foot the three city blocks to the "nigger jail" adjacent to Ryan's Slave Mart, where they would be held until the next morning before again boarding a train, this time for Mobile. He and Medlin would spend the night at his rooming house in town.

The aim was to get to the jail before the large gangs held in the stock cars would also be requiring accommodations that Tom knew to be limited. Not all would need board, as some would immediately be up for the special auction at Ryan's when the first hammer would go down at ten o'clock that same morning.

Medlin opened the door of the compartment, where the three were already on their feet. Hutto was crouching under the low ceiling, and once he crossed into the passenger car, he struggled to stand up straight. Tom assessed the situation on the crowded platform and directed Medlin and the slaves to exit on the track side. The three men jumped to the ground. Celia and Jama were lifted down by Hutto. Following Tom, the group hurriedly left the train yard and traversed a series of alleys and side streets until they came out on Queen Street, just a block from Ryan's and the jail.

When it appeared that the plan to get to the jail was almost realized, Medlin was struck with an unbearable cramp in his gut, so severe he had to lean against a brick wall for support. Soon he slid into a heap on the pavement. Tom rushed to his side and knelt down close.

—What's the matter?

Medlin could not answer right then. He was in such pain he was barely aware of anything other than feeling as if he was being stabbed with a knife. After a few moments, he managed to sit up with his legs outstretched and his back propped against the wall. He came around enough to comprehend that the jail was almost in sight.

—Tom, you take these three and go on over to the jail, then come back here for me. I've got to just sit here for a spell. But I'll be okay. Go on, now, hurry up.

Medlin sat alone as fragments of his predicament began to spiral in a rush of quick passing images—getting on the train tomorrow at dawn bound for Mobile, negotiating a sale at the Mobile auction, going home, and facing Lydia if the price did not stand up to the effort. And there was the agonizing question whether his freshly planted fields would grow over in weeds before he could get back home.

7

G IL WAS HAPPY TO HAVE THE CHANCE to get out of town for ten days. The demonstration about the Confederate flag flying over the State House was still going strong and had now escalated into wild dimensions. Early on, the issue spread countrywide and was on front pages in all large market newspapers, as well as the lead story on news broadcasts.

Reporters and columnists put their slant on what the flag represented—some thoughtful, others bizarre. The issue went beyond just the subject of the flag. It widened to scrutiny of the whole South and all Southerners, in generalities that lumped the states below the Mason-Dixon Line and their inhabitants into one pot of collard greens.

The Ku Klux Klan enjoyed seeing the light of day. With their numbers dwindling, in recent years they had joined with neo-Nazi and other White supremacist organizations. When the Confederate flag controversy began, the KKK was one of the first organizations to surface and soak up as much attention as possible—which the media was happy to give.

With the South at large under attack, the media glommed on to anything Southern. A nationally popular television cook from Georgia who had built an empire dishing out Southern home recipes had it all come tumbling down suddenly. Asked if she had ever used the word "nigger," she answered truthfully that yes, she had once used the word in talking to her husband in her own home twenty-seven years earlier when she was a young bank teller. She described to her husband how that afternoon, a robber who was Black had held a gun to her head. Food Network, where she had pulled in big numbers of loyal viewers, dropped her from the roster within a week after the story broke. Her cookware line, sponsorships, and appearances were immediately cancelled—a sorry fate for a woman who started out to make a living preparing bag lunches that her two sons sold door to door.

Some national publications had no problem tying the incident of Southern cuisine to racism. A staff writer for *The Christian Science Monitor* suggested that the Georgia cook "may now be responsible for raising deeper questions about whether the marketing of Southern culture and cuisine comes with a side of bigotry." A *Time* magazine article said the woman made "a pile of money" promoting Southern culture, so "in return, she has an obligation to that culture . . . not to embody its worst, most shameful history and attitudes. Instead . . . she single-handedly affirmed people's worst suspicions of people who talk and eat like her."

Everyone living in Columbia was fed up with the traffic and a constant pounding in the news, so when Gil's Chandler cousin Heather suggested a trip to England to run down the ancestors on her mother's side, she gladly jumped at it. The trip would be mindless, brain-cleansing travel through beautiful countryside. It was just what Gil needed.

After blowing a few days in London, they traveled to Burnley—the town where the Chandler name was first recorded in the Domesday Book in 1086. At the Lancashire Records Room, Gil and Heather were able to locate the original family farm, where they found a mound of rubble. Both dug up a few pottery shards, hoping these were part of something some of the greats—times thirteen—had used to eat some tucker centuries before.

The trip almost at an end, Gil and Heather were packed for the shuttle flight out of Manchester to London, with five hours to kill. Someone suggested a garden tour in nearby Styal, where they found a Historic England protected site—a beautiful, wooded property with meandering gravel paths, stone walls, and a river running through. And there was an old textile mill, also open to tour.

Quarry Bank Mill looked from a distance just like so many the two cousins had grown up around—old mills were as familiar to them as a

Walmart. At home a few mills were still in use as mills, some were abandoned shells, others had been turned into fashionable condominiums, but all were part of the landscape in the Carolinas. Out of curiosity about the familiar-looking mill in England, they decided to skip seeing the grounds to tour the mill.

They were interested to see such similarity to Southern mills—red brick architecture with no frill or flourish but designed instead strictly to maximize space for the long stretch of spinning machines.

Once they were inside, it was obvious right off that there was no way to circumvent the scripted tour and meander at will—which was what Gil had hoped to do, since she had already toured so many historic buildings.

At the first station was a woman in period costume, sitting at a spinning wheel. She started by saying that well before the sixteen hundreds, the region was known for producing and processing wool. She continued that every home had a spinning wheel like the one she was working, where the women of the house spun wool into yarn for extra income. This continued with little change for many generations until flax and then cotton were introduced as substitutes for the coarse wool, which was more difficult to spin. With the conducive properties of cotton and a growing interest in cotton cloth, there began a big push to increase production.

Gil and Heather proceeded to the next display. The guide said that one spindle at a time on the wheel was no longer acceptable in the mid-seventeen hundreds, and that the race was on to find ways to have multiple spindles working at one time. Inventors fashioned a series of more efficient and faster machines. In a short time, output doubled, quadrupled, and well beyond. The machine on display, humming along under the hands of the demonstrator, spun sixteen spindles at once, powered by a foot treadle. There were several successive vintage models of looms for weaving to make the point that with the increase in cotton thread production, looms had to be designed to keep up.

Historians, trained to think without sentiment in a linear fashion, looked for the connections and implications of a series of events. So it broadsided Gil when the guide ended this part of the tour by pointing out that through the exploding growth in cotton thread and cloth production, the frenzy to keep up with demand for raw cotton put pressure on the Southern American planter to grow as much cotton as possible—which meant more slaves. Being so caught up with the English story, Gil had failed to think about America and the South as they were in the later seventeen hundreds yoked in a partnership with England that would have lasting repercussions, not only the Civil War but also events right down to the present, 2000. Gil had never before seen the vital connection of the English textile industry to slavery and the South. Before she could process this connection, it was time to move along on the tour.

Long before entering the final display, they could feel and hear it. The thick wooden floorboards vibrated under their feet and the sound was of something powerful, almost scary. Once they entered the main spinning room, likely eighty feet long, they were taken aback at the sight of a fully operational machine, spinning hundreds of spindles at one time, powered by the Bollin River, which they could see from the window. The vast machine depended on a belt attached to a water-wheel situated several floors below. It set off a series of motions of swing arms, gears, and twisting apparatus, all directing raw twisted cotton, snaking from drums stationed at intervals on the floor, through twists and turns until the cotton became a thin thread winding onto swiftly rotating spindles. An elderly man, likely a retired machinist, was in constant motion—tweaking, oiling, adjusting, and tightening—to keep the giant machine fed and moving.

Without even thinking, Gil instinctively knew she might be standing at the site that was the genesis of the powerful forces that, when once put in motion at home, would be so strong that they would eventually divide the United States. She already had the spark of an idea that there must be a connection between American slavery and the Industrial Revolution. She knew the Industrial Revolution had to do with hand-production methods advancing to machine production, but knowing that it was kicked off in the textile industry was something that had never occurred to her, that at the core of it would be cotton from the American South. By the time she got on the plane to London that afternoon, her head was spinning over thinking of the implications on slavery.

Gil was looking forward to research whether Quarry Bank was as important as she thought to the history of her home state. Could the cotton mills in England have turned the quiet countryside of upland South Carolina upside down under the "thrall of cotton"? It looked like the needs of the mill across the Atlantic were linked to the enormous increase in slaves in South Carolina between 1790 and the Civil War.

When Gil got back to Columbia from England, she put in as much time as she could spare to see if her instincts were right about Quarry Bank Mill and its influence on South Carolina. Gil started with cotton, which was the thing that Quarry Bank demanded in such enormous quantities. After reading that climate and soil conditions were ideal to grow cotton over immense regions of the entire world, Gil wondered why it was that the American South came to supply three-fourths of the British cotton market by 1860. She found the answer to be that America had the land, labor, and political stability so essential for growing cotton.

She learned that leaning on the South for cotton was not immediate. Until the 1780s, the need for cotton in the Lancashire Valley was adequately satisfied by planters in the Caribbean, Brazil, and India. North America as a source for cotton was not a consideration during the Revolutionary War, which did not officially end until 1783. Colonial cotton was grown at that time only for domestic use in modest quantities.

But all that was about to change. The two largest suppliers of raw cotton through the mid-1780s were India and Saint-Domingue. With political unrest in India and mass rebellion in Saint-Domingue, English textile merchants started to look elsewhere to find reliable cotton suppliers. As soon as the Revolutionary War was over, there began an interest in America as a major source of cotton.

The first recorded shipment of American cotton to arrive on the dock in Liverpool was in 1786. As an experiment in their search to find new vendors of raw cotton, British textile merchants Peel, Yates & Company ordered a small amount that arrived in a hold full of rice, tobacco, and timber. Customs agents, having never before seen cotton from North America, found it suspicious and impounded it, believing that cotton "cannot be imported from thence, it not being the Produce of the American States." No one could forecast that those first bags of raw cotton from the American South would, in a few years, grow to 36.5 million pounds, annually.

Gil found that the first reference to cotton in America was made by Spanish explorers, who wrote in the early fifteen hundreds of seeing native Indians growing cotton in Florida. A century later, in what was known as the first British colony, Jamestown, it was recorded that cotton was grown by "twenty and odd" Congolese, brought there in 1619.

Cotton was not grown for export until the end of the eighteenth century. Before the Revolution, as the population grew along the east coast, enterprising efforts produced much desired goods for the British market. Indigo, rice, and tobacco—but not cotton—were the most successful commodities to find eager buyers an ocean away. From the textile trade in England came wool and linen cloth to be made into clothing. But with the Revolutionary War, there was a complete shutdown of all trade between Britain and her rebellious colonies, leaving the goods of the fledgling colonies without a market and the fledgling colonies without a foreign source of needed goods.

Throughout the eight-year revolutionary conflict, the colonists had to provide for themselves, independent of their former motherland. Cut off from their source of wool and linen cloth, and using seeds from the Bahamas, American planters started to cultivate cotton in modest amounts for domestic use for clothing. It was too early to predict how cotton would change America, or how important it would become.

The war with Britain left America deeply in debt and the economy in shambles. To finance the war, the Continental Congress borrowed heavily from France, Spain, and the Netherlands. There was an enormous sum to be satisfied.

With nothing to transport, ships sat idle in what had once been bustling ports along the East Coast. Fields that had grown indigo, rice, and tobacco were neglected, or abandoned altogether, when the British market collapsed. America was in great and immediate need of something to get the economy going.

No one was more aware of the dire situation than George Washington and James Madison. Both were slave-owning tobacco farmers in Virginia and had personally been affected by the severe economic downturn. Both men were immersed in the rhythms of the international economy in their efforts to find a place in it for their new country. Each became aware of rising cotton prices and the demand for cotton emanating from the textile centers in Manchester, England. Each predicted that America would become the world's major cotton-growing country—that cotton would lead the country into prosperity. Negro slaves already working on tobacco plantations were portable and could easily be shipped south to convert their skills and labor to cotton production. Both Washington and Madison were convinced the country was destined for tremendous success through cotton. There were both ideal soil and the established plantation system with its slave labor that had been built for a tobacco business that was on the decline.

The first sign that cotton was taking hold was along the coast of Georgia and South Carolina, planted with premium-grade long-staple seeds from the Bahamas. This variety had a long fiber strand or staple, which spun into smooth, durable thread, making it into a luxuriant, soft cloth for fine clothing. It was called Sea Island cotton, named after the coastal islands where it was exclusively grown—where the soil and weather were ideal for cultivation. Long-staple cotton was a favorite of the Manchester market.

Southern coastal planters bought up all the land they could that was suitable to plant the long-staple until there was no more land available. While Sea Island cotton thrived in the soil and weather conditions of the coastal regions, it was unsuccessful farther inland in more loamy soil, where the short-staple variety flourished. In the early eighteen hundreds, the drive to acquire land to farm short-staple cotton expanded rapidly inland in Georgia and South Carolina, and beyond, in the biggest land grab in American history. Millions of acres had already been set aside for Creeks, Chickasaws, Choctaws, and Cherokees, but these people were very soon burned out and run off by planters eager to capitalize on the cotton push. With the encroachment of settlers into inland territory, plus the government's assistance in removing native people, open land suitable for cotton production seemed endless, especially after the Louisiana Purchase in 1803, which doubled the territory of the United States. The Louisiana Purchase was financed by Thomas Bering, British banker and one of the world's most successful cotton merchants.

Slaves, accustomed to tobacco production in Virginia, were eagerly bought up and shipped deeper south until the numbers in the southernmost states had doubled. Planters went into debt to buy as much acreage as they could. Pressure was on them to produce. As one contemporary historian described the atmosphere at the time, "All men in the South are slaves to cotton."

Short-staple cotton grew very well in the Upland, but there was one major problem. The tight boll of short-staple "blow" was made of 250,000 individual fibers, which clung stubbornly to the thirty-three seeds. Cleaning the raw cotton of the seeds and stem trash was done by slaves and took one-third to half of the labor required from planting the seed to getting the finished product to market. Planters were desperate to eliminate the bottleneck created by deseeding.

———

IN 1792, YOUNG ELI WHITNEY was on board a ship bound for Savannah, Georgia, where he expected to take up a tutoring position. He had just graduated from Yale with a degree in law, at his father's insistence. However, law was not particularly a passion. What the young man really liked to do was to tinker in his father's workshop. But to work with his hands was not considered a fitting occupation for a young man of Whitney's social class. As a tutor in Savannah he would be in the employ of a respectable family of high social status, and thus could postpone going into law.

Once he got to Savannah, Whitney found the tutoring position had dissolved, so he contacted the widow of Revolutionary hero Nathaniel Greene, Catherine Littlefield Greene, whom he had met on the sail down from Massachusetts, to accept her previous offer of a job as a companion to her young son on her plantation, Mulberry Grove. Whitney grew close to the family, and was present when they discussed what to plant in the upcoming season. Putting in cotton for the cash crop was considered, but then rejected, because cotton was too labor-intensive as to the extraction of the seeds to be profitable.

This conversation inspired Whitney. He went to work and put together a device made up of a hand-cranked roller with grabbing hooks that pulled cotton though a sieve made of wires tightly spaced to leave behind the seeds. He said he got the idea watching a cat trying to pull a chicken from a wire cage. The cat got only a pile of feathers. Right away, Whitney's invention was a huge success locally and beyond. Soon he made improvements to larger models powered by mule or water. It was a simple machine, but to all who saw it, it was exactly what was needed.

After Whitney's device was received with wild enthusiasm by the neighboring planters around Mulberry Grove, the young inventor thought he could make a great deal of money. He immediately submitted schematic drawings to the recently established National Patent Office.

He decided on a plan not to sell the gin outright, but to install the device throughout the South and charge user fees to be paid in cotton. This proved to be a mistake. What he did not count on was that planters resented what they thought were exorbitant fees. They pirated his design and built their own versions. Whitney fought the infringements against his patent on the gin with little success in a weak federal patent system that was full of loopholes. Laws changed in favor of the inventor a few years before his fourteen-year patent ran out, but it was too late. Bitter from his unsuccessful battle to protect his patent, Whitney would later say that he had also invented a gin for long-staple cotton, but that it would be a cold day in hell before he would share another time-saving device with those who had wrangled him out of a fortune.

In the end it was not the cotton gin that made Whitney rich, but his time-saving method of mass production. He invented an efficient way to manufacture muskets using interchangeable parts. It was his idea to first produce a stockpile of like parts and then complete a mass assembly, as opposed to making each musket one at a time. This was a totally new concept in those days. It was a first in mass production, a system much later generally credited to Henry Ford with his Model T. But the concept was Eli Whitney's.

———

LIKE EVERY SCHOOLCHILD, Gil had learned that Whitney invented the gin, but she had not realized the enormous effect it had on the South and the world economy. Nothing showed the impact of the gin like the increase in cotton exports. The modest amount of cotton exported from the American South three years before the invention of the gin would grow to 167.5 million pounds by 1820. The gin could process fifty pounds of cotton a day—the amount one slave could produce in a week before its invention.

But contrary to any idea that the demand for slaves would diminish, just the opposite happened. The number of slaves in cotton production went from 750,000 in 1790 to 1.8 million in 1820. Planters bought even more slaves, as well as more land, to capitalize on the gin now that slaves were freed from cleaning the cotton by hand. On the eve of the Civil War, the number of slaves in America would number over four million, most of these laboring in the cotton fields.

Under enormous pressure to produce, every planter had in the back of his mind that it could all tumble down with a drought, or with too much rain, or an early frost, or a late frost—any of which could happen when it was too late to begin again for the season. Or pests could descend onto the field and wipe out a season's planting. At every phase of the one hundred and sixty frost-free days needed for the cotton to grow to maturity, the planter would anxiously walk the fields looking for leaf spots, cocoons, yellowing—every manner of pestilence that would call for restless sleep. One tobacco planter said he had no disposition to gamble or play the lottery, so he did not raise cotton.

The Southern Cotton Association saw great risk in the one-crop system, and tried repeatedly to convince planters to diversify. One acting president stated, "Yet I tell you, the strongest financial institution for every farmer is a well filled corncrib and smokehouse." But no one listened—everyone was mesmerized by cotton and failed to prepare for disaster. As one cotton man put it, "We appear to have but one rule—that is, to make as much cotton as we can, and wear out as much land as we can."

If a plantation crop made it through unscathed, there would be cause for celebration—usually an outdoor feast when everyone on the plantation, including slaves, would take part. However, one experienced farmer said, "We feel rich after the crop is sold until we meet the people we owe."

Gil was convinced that standing in the spinning room at Quarry Bank Mill on that day at the end of her trip to England was like being at the epicenter of forces that would eventually lead to the devastating Civil War and cause many to brand as evil her state of birth and heart. For Gil, understanding the story of the growth of cotton in the South—her South—was to understand a lot about how it was inevitable that two opposing parties would face off now, in the year 2000, on the grounds of the State House in Columbia, South Carolina, over the Confederate flag. But it would take her some more time and thinking to understand just how the past had led to the present. By now she knew that the present was tied, intimately, to the history of cotton. And cotton was demanded in enormous quantities by Quarry Bank Mill.

Gil looked closely at Quarry Bank and its owner, Samuel Greg (1758–1834), whose vision to lock man and machine into a compatible unit of production, to pair technological advances with innovations in the use of labor, was the foundation of the Industrial Revolution.

———

IN 1784, GREG BUILT QUARRY BANK MILL alongside the Bollin River. On the labor side, he attracted domestic spinners by offering steady wages. He built the first mill village, a concept that eventually made its way to America, where remnants of mill housing could be seen right next to cotton mills all over the South. Greg's mill village offered comfortable housing close to the mill, with amenities far better than any on the farm. A community center, individual plots of land for family gardens, and scheduled visits by a doctor were all very enticing.

By 1800, the one-spindle-at-a-time on the cottage spinning wheel had grown to several thousand spindles working in unison at Quarry Bank. In addition to spinning thread, the mill began to produce cloth. It was a challenge to have enough labor. Adult workers filled the mill cottages to capacity, and so Greg was swift to accept the local vicar's suggestion to use parish orphans as labor. Ninety children (sixty girls, thirty boys), age nine to fifteen, went to work in the mill.

From the start, child labor proved very satisfactory to Greg for many reasons—children were nimble, able to dart under the rapidly spinning machines to repair a break in the yarn. Children were easy to keep in line and they were cheap. Their wages were tuppence a week, per head. The children worked twelve-hour shifts. When Greg ran out of local orphans, children from workhouses in Liverpool—dumped there for various tawdry reasons—were acquired until the number of children working in the mill matched adult labor. Child labor in the spinning room at Quarry Bank kept the vast factory humming along.

By all accounts, the Gregs viewed the orphan labor as a benefit to both themselves and the children, who, the Gregs vaguely envisioned, would be taught a trade instead of facing a dreary, knockabout exis- tence. The "Apprentice House" was constructed in close proximity to the mill to house the children in dormitory-style community housing. But, however agreeable the Gregs saw the arrangement, in actuality it was anything but a positive experience for children, who thought they had left the worst behind in the orphanage or workhouse. Employment at Quarry Bank evolved over time to be equally or even more punishing.

Samuel Greg and his wife Hannah were philanthropic, with a bent toward humanitarian issues. Mrs. Greg was active in African slavery abolition causes. Yet she put a blind eye toward the slave holdings of her husband on the West Indian sugar plantation he inherited. Despite the fact that the Gregs participated heavily in a system of exploitation of slaves on his plantation in Barbados, as well as of English children, the whole family was honored in their community for what was seen as their humanitarianism. The Gregs were known as benevolent employers, with over three hundred souls in their charge at Quarry Bank Mill.

By 1816, Quarry Bank was producing over 345,000 pounds of cloth annually. A decade later they were producing twice as much. All along, their raw-cotton agents in the American South were pressed hard from Manchester to send more. The mill had to be fed.

Gil was anxious to follow up on a remark made by the guide at Quarry

Bank that once the capacity of the spinning machines was maximized, pressure ratcheted up for even more cotton from the American South, which meant that many more slaves were needed by cotton planters.

Gil learned that the vast African slave trade, so vital to America's economy, benefited from a quirk of meteorology and geography. Ships left their home ports in Europe and sailed to the coast of Africa near the Equator, where they caught the easterly winds, known as the trade winds. With these winds at their backs, they cut three weeks from an otherwise two-month-long sail west. Thus, the trade route to and from the New World was triangular—Europe to Africa with finished goods, Africa to the Americas with slaves, and from the Americas back to Europe with holds full of sugar, rum, rice, tobacco, timber, indigo, and cotton. The high demand for slaves for the Caribbean and North American plantations was conveniently met. After the first part of their journey was completed in Africa, ships filled their holds with bought and kidnapped African slaves for the middle leg of the round trip, which became known as the Middle Passage.

———

GIL WONDERED HOW SLAVERY could have become so entrenched in the South, considering the stated ideals of the Founding Fathers. The belief that all men were created equal could hardly be reconciled with the idea of slaves as property. Gil realized that it was only by making the African into "the other," or even a different species—not a man—that slavery was rationalized and codified.

Those who stood to gain financially from the commercial success of the colonies made their case for slavery from numerous directions. Proponents used rationalization to try to convince society and themselves that slavery was justifiable. English philosophers and scientists put their mind to defining the slave. The concept of who was a slave was tested in references to history, to culture.

The Africans' dark skin went against them because of European cultural prejudices. In Europe black or darkness had long been associated with evil. There were many references in the Bible to godliness as white and evil as black. In the Bible, light was associated with God and truth, whereas darkness represented sin and the Devil. The bubonic plague that killed many millions of Europeans in the mid-fourteenth century was called the Black Death.

Further contributing to the Europeans' impression that the African was alien was that to the seventeenth-century Christian Englishman, the "heathenous" African had strange spiritual beliefs steeped in superstition and mystery, beliefs considered the antithesis of Christianity. Pro-slavery Englishmen viewed or judged the African as primitive and incapable of intellect or socialization. One Englishman wrote of the Africans as "wild, barbarous people who bore more than a passing similarity to animals."

Some tried to rationalize slavery by saying that the captured Africans were the spoils of a just war against aliens, against those unlike their own, and thus these captives were subject to slavery—a belief held over from the Middle Ages, with its wars against religious infidels, a concept with which the Europeans were quite familiar.

Some even put a positive spin on slave labor from the perspective of the slave. A prominent essayist, William Gilmore Simms, wrote, "Providence has placed him in our hands, for his good, and has paid us from his labor for our guardianship." It was a popular notion among White people that the slave should be thankful for being saved from the harsh conditions in Africa.

Such arguments were easily refuted, but by the mid-seventeen hundreds, the plantation system, with its complete dependence on slavery, was securely in place and thriving with inexorable momentum. The economic importance of slave labor in the American South and beyond was very evident. It was considered indispensable. Slavery had become very entrenched into every aspect of society, and paved the way for successful plantation owners to breathe the rarefied air of moneyed, powerful society. Slaves formed the basis and the engine of the young country's growing economy.

———

GIL WELL UNDERSTOOD THAT SLAVERY was the foundation of the US economy. Slavery was established in the sixteen hundreds, and completely entrenched in the agricultural states of the South by the late seventeen hundreds. The African was seen as the other—as not human. Still, Gil wondered how it was that in the face of anti-slavery sentiment the Founders had failed to deal with the issue of slavery in the Constitution. She asked herself why, if the theories of John Locke about individual human rights were foremost in the minds of the Founders, they had not stated either that all men, including Negroes, were created equal and had rights, or that they were not men—not humans—and therefore did not have rights. She learned that the Framers of the Constitution had struggled, but ultimately kicked the can down the road.

When she looked into it, Gil saw that there was nothing more revealing about what was on the minds of Americans regarding slavery than the Constitutional Convention in 1787, where a thorough record of the testimony of delegates in attendance showed to what extent slavery put its mark on something as important as the Constitution, which was intended to outline the true principles of the American people. Most Americans had great reverence for this document, which some thought was divinely inspired. But, on close inspection, Gil saw the Constitution to be the product of deep compromise. Over the issue of slavery there were threats by Southern states to desert the Convention, and there was an understanding by some in attendance that the union was formed at the expense of human rights.

After much debate over a measure that South Carolina's Charles Pinckney opposed as vesting Congress with the power of "meddling with the importance of Negroes," the entire Convention accepted that the purpose of the Convention was to create a political union—not a moral union—among the states. In the end, the draft text did not specifically state that the Constitution sanctioned or forbade slavery. Instead, the issue of slavery was carefully avoided.

The Constitution never mentioned the words *slaves* or *slavery*. Yet, the issue was all over the document, if only by implication. With all the debate, threats, and tension concerning slavery at the Convention, the Framers chose to leave out the words *Negro*, *African*, and *slave*, and instead use terms like *all other Persons*. In 1787, the delegates desperately needed a Constitution for guidance, then and into the future. Not mentioning slavery directly was a compromise with the Southern states.

Many signers of the Constitution said in private that they thought the institution of slavery was immoral, but they were unwilling to publicly stick their necks out to fight in favor of freedom for the Negro. Perhaps those who were anti-slavery assumed that slavery would not stand the test of time and would eventually be abolished. In any case, by the end of the Convention, all involved with the founding of the new nation knew that resolving the issue of slavery was not going to happen on their watch. For the time being, they were leaving it to future generations to deal with the problem.

Gil tried to imagine what it would have been like to be in the position of the early men of liberty, faced with the first dilemma that had the potential to bring all their efforts down before the nation was on firm footing—whether to risk it all on the issue of slavery, or turn a blind eye. They did turn a blind eye. Considering slaves as property became the accepted practice in America by the mid-seventeenth century—and slaves weighed heavily in the accounting of personal worth. James Madison always planned to free his hundred slaves when he retired, but then, as he started considering financial stability for his wife, he changed his mind. Soon after Madison's death, in 1836, his widow, Dolly, began selling off her slaves to generate cash as she needed it.

8

7:00 Clear sky
Board Wm Javey for Mobil
May 9, 1857

EVEN BEFORE THE SUN CLEARED THE HORIZON Tom took
his brother and the slaves to the Charleston train station. Medlin
felt somewhat recovered after the bout of the miseries the day
before. He handed Tom most of the cash remaining after the auction,
for safekeeping. Tom in turn handed Medlin a bundle of oilcloth that
held a revolver in a belted, worn holster.

—A gun is not to scare but to kill, so when you take aim keep that in
mind.

This was the first time Tom ever mentioned anything implying danger, much less the remotest chance he might need to kill somebody.

Medlin was familiar with rifles for hunting deer or for killing a rabid
dog or raccoon, but a revolver was a whole different thing. Before he
could ask a question, Tom had tipped the brim of his hat and was gone.
Medlin for a brief moment felt alone and overwhelmed, but the dread
was quickly replaced with the necessity to get secured on the train in a
hurry. He was now alone, a familiar place out of where he could work.

Medlin looked at the revolver. It appeared larger and heavier than
he thought such a gun would be. It was a Colt .44 caliber Navy model,
which Tom had acquired in a trade one time when he was looking for

an impressive firearm whose mere appearance would be likely to ward off possible trouble. It weighed over four pounds and had a particularly long barrel, for which Tom had adapted a holster by cutting a hole in the leather so that the muzzle protruded. Medlin now tried to belt it at his hip, but he was too slim. The belt, holster and heavy gun started sliding down toward his feet. There was no time to fiddle, so he just slung the whole thing over his head and pulled his left arm through, resting the belt on his right shoulder while the gun fell a little below his left armpit, making it necessary to reach across his chest to draw. He felt self-conscious wearing the revolver in such a roguish way, but there was no time to make any adjustment.

He secured space for Hutto, Celia, and Jama in a boxcar. This was conveniently the next car immediately coupled to the rear of his passenger car. They would have to rush. The train was scheduled to pull out in minutes.

Hutto, Celia, and Jama had already encountered a steam engine in the Savannah station, but this second experience was hardly less frightening. They could feel the platform quake under their feet from the power of the engine. The billowing steam produced a hot, gray cloud that nearly blocked out the view of the close-by engine, making the whole experience alarming. Such power was unimaginable. The only thing they had ever witnessed to manipulate iron was the plantation blacksmith, whose forge turned out horseshoes and farm tools—nothing bigger—so the manufacture of such a thing as a steam engine was beyond their comprehension.

The life of a slave was such that they might never experience what lay beyond the plantation. Slaves were taught to look only inward. It was purposely presented to them that the only freedom would come after their death, in heaven, and then only if they had been obedient in life. Traveling clergy were commissioned to bring this home in houses of worship established on the plantation grounds.

On the train platform was a muddle of slaves being herded by their handlers into the boxcars. In the turmoil was a mix of shouting and sounds of the lash. Medlin hurried his slaves into the first boxcar and to a tight, vacant spot just opposite the sliding door. He quickly secured Hutto's wrist shackles to a rail designed to tether livestock. This put his arms in an awkward, elevated position as he sat down on the straw floor, but there was no time to adjust for comfort. Both Celia and Jama clung to the big man and closed their eyes against the harsh scene. Medlin forced his way out of the boxcar through slaves and handlers who were now in near panic to secure any space left. He boarded the passenger car with only a couple of minutes to spare before there was a sudden lunge forward—the train was underway.

He tried to settle himself and his gear for the tedious ride to Mobile. The seats were covered in a coarse, prickly fabric chosen for durability rather than comfort and stuffed with horsehair that had long ago given up its cushioning quality. There were indentations showing where many a passenger had passed long hours of travel. The seat Medlin chose, at the back of the car and nearest the boxcar where Hutto, Celia, and Jama were secured, was fashioned like a bench to accommodate two passengers, facing forward. With no dividing armrest, he spread out across the whole width, hoping the car would not be full to capacity so that the conductor would force him to share the seat. The rows ahead were in sets of two ample bench seats, one side facing forward, the other facing backward, making seating for four. Four fellow travelers could sit in a congenial arrangement. A pullout panel made a surface for card playing or whatever they fancied to lighten the trip.

As Medlin first settled, four rough-looking men entered the car. They adjusted into the seats facing one another, a few rows ahead of him on the opposite side of the aisle. Once seated the two facing toward Medlin gave him a prolonged look. He had noticed them in the boxcar handling a gang with the same consideration as for sacks of grain. And they had taken notice of him. With their well-developed animal instincts they sensed that even though he was in their familiar environment, he was not of it. The large Colt worn rakishly under his left arm was a puzzlement that made Medlin a curiosity and worthy of a watchful eye.

The train pulled from the station, going slow at first while the slack between the cars worked its way out with thrusts and bangs until it settled into a steady pace with the clickety-clack of iron wheels on iron rails. Others in the passenger car fell into a doze, but Medlin sank deep into what might be called a "death sleep."

Some time later, he woke to the animated voices of the four men, now playing cards. He straightened himself up in his seat, and taking out his pocket watch saw that he had slept for three hours. As the day wore on and the four all took long pulls from a shared flask, they became boisterous. Medlin, monitoring their temperament, figured them to be at the edge of control. He noticed right off that despite their card playing, all glanced around to take the measure of the passengers around them. Medlin was the object of most of their attention, but he chalked this up to the Colt.

Late in the afternoon, one of the men, whose straggly beard poorly masked a face scarred by old red pockmarks or burns—too old to tell the difference—rose from his seat.

—I've got me a hanker'n for some dark-meat poontang.

He headed down the aisle until he was almost alongside Medlin. Not talking to anybody in particular, he made a general announcement.

—That nigger girl child'll do me just fine.

Another stride and he was reaching for the door leading to the landing between the cars. Medlin took a quick look toward the three remaining men and leapt toward the bearded man before he could fully open the door. He was astonished how quickly the other three men overpowered him. Before he could get into a defensive posture, Medlin was thrown to the floor, his face slammed headlong into the wooden planks with such force that his front tooth cut through his upper lip. One heavy boot was on his neck. Both his hands were forced behind his back, and with the third man sitting on his legs, he was completely immobilized.

The straggly bearded man—they called him Ronnie—passed on through the door to the open platform between cars. Helpless and with his face pressed against the floor, Medlin heard the sound of the rushing wind combined with the train going over the tracks, deafening until the door slammed shut.

Out on the exposed platform, Ronnie felt the metal plate under his feet shifting wildly as the train responded to the unevenness of the iron track. Along with being quite drunk, he was not used to standing on such an unstable surface, but he made his way to where he could stick his head out into the wind and looked around at the boxcar door. All along, his beard blew into his face with stinging whips against his cheeks. After a short assessment, he reached out and grabbed the iron ladder on the outside of the boxcar. He pulled himself across it to reach the sliding door. Still holding on to the ladder, he rested his left boot on the end of the roller door's channel guide and pulled up on the lever to disengage the door latch.

The train was at full throttle. Loblolly pines flashed by at a dizzying rate as the car rocked back and forth wildly. Ronnie took a quick look down to the tracks and the gravel berm, and then to the brush line, which started just where the track bed ended. For the first time he considered what a tenuous position he was in. On top of everything, his calves were quaking from fatigue.

With the latch in an open position, he slowly forced the rollers into motion to open the door. He slipped inside and hesitated. The only noise was from the outside—the loud train engine, the wind, and the clacking of the wheels. In the boxcar there was complete silence, and darkness except for the fluttering light coming through the open door. It took a moment for his eyes to adjust to the darkness while he ran his hand down the full length of his face to the beard, where he let his fingers gather it up and slide to the bottom like he was wringing water from it.

Ronnie could barely make anything out. He was just starting to register the bent knees and the two gigantic shoes, heels together and angled out creating a V where the end of a plank of coarse lumber rested, when all of a sudden, the lumber shot from its cocked position, hitting Ronnie with great force in his midsection and hurling his body backward and out the door. The force of the blow propelled him all the way to the tree line, where his body hit the trunk of a stout pine. When his head collided with the tree it sounded like an exploding melon. The speeding train hit an especially uneven place in the track where the boxcar rocked with such force the door slammed shut but did not latch, so after that it rolled open and shut, open and shut.

Meanwhile, the train conductor passed through on his rounds. He maneuvered around the men entangled on the floor in the aisle, not reacting, having learned long ago he had best stay strictly to train business.

Medlin made several last attempts to get free, but he could only manage enough strength to squirm. After a while he let his body go limp. Seeing that the fight had now gone out of him, the three men undid their hold, leaving his gun alone. They returned to their seats and got back into their card game. Medlin slowly managed to raise himself and collapsed into his seat. He tried to assess the degree of damage to his lip—he discovered a flap of skin where the tooth had broken through.

The orange sun sank low. Intermittent streams of golden light danced on the walls of the passenger car. It was well over an hour since Ronnie had left them. The three remaining ruffians began to discuss his where-abouts. The biggest and roughest of them got up, headed toward the door, and entered the radically shifting space between cars. There were only boxcars trailing behind their passenger car. The big scruffy man came to the conclusion that Ronnie had entered the first boxcar by using the ladder to get across to the door. Like Ronnie, he swung his body out to the exterior of the boxcar by grabbing ahold of the ladder. He saw that the door was open. He, too, balanced on the door channel.

With his boots resting precariously on the channel and his fingers grip-ping tightly to the doorway, he cautiously peered into the car and called out Ronnie's name. In contrast to the wheels clacking against the rails, it was silent inside the dark car. The scruffy man cautiously planted one foot on the floor just when the car responded to a jog in the track. The door recoiled violently toward the closed position, banging him into the latch hardware, then slid back open again. He barely saved himself from fall-ing and was calling out in pain when a shaft of lumber slammed into his right kneecap. His legs came out from under him, and his body dropped straight down onto the gravel berm below. The train rushed on.

———

IN THE PASSENGER CAR Medlin and the two remaining ruffians traveled on not knowing the fate of the others. It eventually became clear to the two that their companions would not be returning. With no expla-nation and no one they could blame, they came to the conclusion that whatever had happened to them, Medlin must be at the root. They kept shooting Medlin dark looks. One whispered in the other's ear that he was a dead man once they got to Mobile. Although he had not overheard the threat, Medlin felt increasingly uneasy and thought he had better get off the train when he could.

Shortly after midnight, Medlin felt the train slowing to a stop to replenish the wood and water supply for the steam engine. The two ruffians were asleep. He quietly rose, grabbed his gear, and stood on the step between cars waiting for the train to come to a complete stop. He noticed that the sign on the station said *Maryville*. There would just be enough time to roust Hutto, Celia, and Jama and take them off the boxcar, which was just what he did.

————

WHEN THEY LEFT THE TRAIN in the middle of the night, it was dark as ink except for a lantern in the station house, where the railroad night man sat fiddling with some papers. There was only one thing on Medlin's mind at that moment—to get away from the train and the ruffians. Although the remaining two had no clue as to the fate of their missing companions, they had made it very clear that they were convinced that Medlin was somehow a part of their mysterious absence.

Leaving the station platform, Medlin steered his charges onto the wagon road. It seemed like there was a chance the road would parallel the train to the next settlement. In the pitch dark, until his eyes could adjust to the very little light offered by the three-quarter moon, he had to feel the way more than anything. As they walked, Hutto, Celia, and Jama stayed a few paces back but managed to maintain the pace. Throughout the remainder of the night, Hutto, despite the wrist shackles, held on to Jama's arms as she rode on his back with her head resting on his shoulder, asleep. Celia was unbound and walked alongside, struggling to keep up with his long gait. Occasionally, she and Hutto talked in low tones, too low for Medlin to tell what they were saying.

In the monotony of the foot travel Medlin had time to think. It didn't take long for the reality of their predicament to wash over him. Two days earlier, his mind would have gone in the direction of blame for the whole thing, and that would have been toward Tom, but now he had the full weight on his shoulders—there was no point in blaming.

Before the morning sun began to show on the horizon, Medlin had a bout of the miseries, which sent him rushing into the woods to relieve himself. The miseries usually came on with little warning. The shooting pains in his gut ended with a shaking in his hands and sweating all over. In half an hour, all symptoms could be gone, but the threat he might have another bout stayed in his mind.

There was no alternative but to just walk the two-rut wagon road until Medlin could conjure up something of a plan. As the sun glowed golden in the early morning, the terrain showed itself to be different than seen from the train at sundown the night before. The flatness had given way to higher ground, and ahead there were mountains that shone a pale blue green in the morning light—the color giving just a hint of size and distance. Medlin assumed that the track bed followed the low line—the path of least resistance—through the mountain range ahead. He could hear and feel a growling in his stomach. He had not eaten since the day before. As to Hutto, Celia, and Jama, Medlin did not know if they had eaten anything at all in the boxcar.

Medlin started to build a list in his head of what they needed once they came into the next town and found a store selling groceries and dry goods. As the list grew, he considered several scenarios, with changes in thinking as to how many days they might be on foot until he would feel safe boarding the train to Mobile again. He began to wonder if the story of the two lost men would actually travel to susceptible ears, or if such a tale would roll off sensible people, who would consider the source and dismiss it. So much was unknown—they might have to spend two days or more on foot. There could be no one answer as to what they would need to sustain them, so Medlin figured he would face it and decide when he stood before the store clerk.

As they walked, both men began to take notice of differences in terrain, vegetation, smells, and even birds from what was familiar. Medlin had some experience of higher elevations, but Hutto knew only of flat South Carolina and Georgia coastal land with its sandy soil. The smell here was different. There were lots of moist, decaying leaves turning to mulch mingled with the sweet scent of wildflowers—a lush smell that was new for both Medlin and Hutto.

The previous day, Medlin had noticed a sign at one of the water-and-wood stops, announcing that they had passed into Alabama. He could observe at the time very few changes in the terrain, but now they were walking, he could see that the land was very different.

Medlin and Hutto, always aware of conditions for planting, noticed the ground right around them seemed too rocky to be suitable for cultivating. What they didn't know was that to the south, where they were heading, sediment runoff over millions of years had formed a vast coastal plain of rich soil. That soil, along with a long hot season, made perfect conditions for growing cotton.

Medlin had not paid attention to the blisters on both his heels, but now he began to feel the pain. He sat on a fallen tree trunk and pulled off his boots. He was surprised to discover that these boots he wore every day on the farm had not coped well with the steady pounding on the trek from Maryville. They had rubbed enough to create big slabs of skin, broken blisters still attached at the top, translucent and pale. After reaching to the ground and fiddling through the top layer of vegetation, he lifted a handful of moist leaves clumped together. He placed a thick layer between his raw wounds and the socks, put on his boots, and stomped the ground several times to test the effect. It was not ideal, but he would keep going. No choice.

Hutto, Celia, and Jama had stopped abruptly when Medlin had begun to inspect his wounds. They huddled together, with Jama holding fast to Hutto's leg. She was in a tight position, wedged between her parents. Medlin, for the first time, looked to the disposition of their feet, curious as to how they held up on the long walk. The three wore shoes, of sorts. Because of the size, Hutto's shoes were no doubt made on the Butler plantation by someone charged with the keeping of saddles and tack, someone like the farrier, good with a heavy needle to repair leather but with only barely adequate skills to provide for Hutto the crudest protection from the harsh ground. The shoes of Jama and Celia were store-bought, likely of the yearly issue.

———

SHOES WERE OFTEN PURCHASED from a catalog that offered all supplies necessary to provide for slaves. The Missus ordered a new set of clothes once a year for each charge. Shoes were included, since a pair would rarely hold together past a season in the field. Most often the issue would be distributed at Christmastime, during a celebration when the Master and Missus would make an appearance and say a couple of words as to their hope of a fine crop in the new year. Often a bolt of cloth, usually a plaid, was on the list for the women to hand stitch into headscarves, aprons—and dolls if they had children. And in the same catalog there were items for correction—whips with names for each style, such as cat-o'-nine-tails or black snake. Shackles of all sorts along with an array of implements used to punish or discourage the runaway were offered in the catalog. Items were accompanied by engraved illustrations so the buyers could see what was available.

———

HUTTO'S SHOES, TOO LARGE to be offered in any catalog, were made of three slabs of thick leather sewn onto a sole—one on each side and meeting at the top of the foot with hide laces to hold them in place. The third patch of leather covered the heel and was stitched to the side pieces. Hutto's toes jutted from a gap at the front. Celia's shoes were more like sandals in that they exposed her heel—with straps rather than wide slabs of leather. But what kept the three from having any blisters or rub wounds was the condition of their skin. Their feet were indeed less like tender skin and more like dried leather from long days in the field.

Jama had on crude shoes, almost worn out. Likely, they were passed on from feet that had outgrown them. She was quite young, but she would have already experienced working in the field, where she needed protection against the ground covered in the clutter of thorns and plant stalks. Her first task would have been salvaging any loose cotton blow dropped during the pick.

———

THE FOUR TRAVELERS KEPT WALKING until the sun was directly above. Medlin's watch verified it was near noonday. When they came across streams, they slurped water from their cupped hands, but as yet there was no food. Ever since at least noon the day before, none of them had eaten anything.

Soon a few wagons hauling produce overtook them, heading in the same direction. People nodded to them, but nobody seemed to take any particular interest in the unusual sight.

As they went on, Medlin got to thinking how odd it was that he had never addressed his charges—never said one word to them in the three days since they became his property, except to give some brief command. The family had spoken to each other only in low tones. To get a measure of his talk, Medlin asked Hutto if the child needed to rest for a spell. Hutto answered in a deeper voice than expected that, no, if necessary he would carry the child so as to please the Master.

—Don't call me Master.

—Then what would you go by?

—Call me Sir.

—Yes, Sir.

Medlin did not think of himself as a master and felt very uncomfortable with being called such. He was just a poor dirt farmer in need of cash for his boy to go to school. He preferred no label or identification, as he felt it would put him square into a role that he never intended. He probably should keep his distance. He now remembered Tom's warning that he would be better off with a complete separation. From now on he would try to think of them only as property.

The road showed signs of increased use until finally they entered a town called Newnan, according to the name of the bank—The Bank of Newnan. Smaller lettering under the name said, *No Customer Too Small.* People were bustling about their business.

The sight of Negroes was rare in Newnan. There were plenty in boxcars passing through bound for the auction houses in Mobile, but seeing them on foot, out in their town, was rare. Hutto, with his enormous size, was especially a curiosity. Citizens busy with their chores stopped to stare, and then surreptitiously continued their surveillance until the White man entered the general store fronting the town square. Some dallied around outside the screen door of the store.

Hutto, Celia, and Jama followed Medlin inside and toward the counter, but stopped several paces behind him. There was a customer chatting with the clerk, but when the woman saw panic in the clerk's eyes, she turned around to see what was distracting him. Breaking off the conversation, she headed for the door at a fast clip.

Medlin stepped up to the counter and took a measured look at the shelves, to get his thoughts together. Then he rattled off the dry goods he wanted—two water bladders, a canteen, a short-handled camp shovel, two blankets, a duffle, a rucksack, a waxed cotton tarp, two leather straps cut to four foot each, two tin cups, a fourteen-inch skillet, a watertight tin kit of flint and matches, two tin forks, a big spoon and a three-quart cook pot. The clerk had a hard time keeping up, but managed to note it all on a piece of brown butcher paper.

Then Medlin started off with the food needed. This was harder to settle on, because he had no idea how long they would be on foot, but he was hungry and was influenced by the huge pit in his stomach. The clerk tore off another piece of butcher paper and began to write quickly as Medlin said what he wanted: two pounds of dried field peas, two tins of biscuits, two pounds of cornmeal, a pound of coffee, sugar, potted lard, four knobs of beef jerky, four tins of potted meat, a two-pound slab of lean salt pork, cut in four pieces. The clerk looked up and out from under his eyeshade to see if that was it. Medlin gave him a nod. The clerk went into action, pulling things off shelves, weighing peas and cornmeal before they were tipped from the scale into bags.

Hutto, Celia, and Jama stood motionless all the while, but their eyes were surveying the surroundings, taking in cans with labels of bright colors, jars of visible wonders, bolts of cloth with patterns of flowers and designs for no purpose other than to please. That a person could choose from what was offered was all new.

Jama was looking intently at a nearby glass case, where there were bins of individual round balls of different colors—colors like she had never seen. And in the same colors were long, shiny sticks, standing upright and sprouting from a jar. Other pieces were individually wrapped in paper twisted at both ends. Medlin noticed her attention and told the clerk to add to his order—five cents worth of hard candy sticks.

The clerk took a total for it all, and while Medlin fished in his money pouch to draw out cash to pay, all the items were laid out on the counter. The dry goods were stuffed into the duffle, with the shovel,

pot, and skillet strapped to the outside by the leather cords. Foodstuffs
went into the rucksack. As they left the store, a gaggle of townsfolk
parted for them to pass.

The train station was at the end of the block. Medlin thought it
was a risk to travel by rail right then—the story may have spread that
two men were missing and that a White man with three Negroes,
one extremely large, may be at fault. But, to continue on foot by the
road, they had to pass the station, where the southbound train had
just pulled in. As they approached, slaves were being hustled out of
two boxcars. A couple of handlers were roaming through the crowd
carrying a large pail of water and a dipper. The slaves drank in a most
desperate way, since the men passed quickly. Some of the slaves moved
a short distance to the edge of the berm of the track bed, pissing on
bushes below. Others were squatting to do their hard business. Women
and children separated themselves from the men and squatted while
hiking their skirts up. Suddenly the train whistle blew, and all were
herded back into the boxcars at a panicky pace. Medlin could hear
the slap of leather on skin and rough shouted curses. He turned and
started heading out of town. Hutto, Celia, and Jama, transfixed by
what they saw before them, did not react immediately. However, very
soon they followed him.

Medlin filled the water bladders and canteen at the public well with a
spigot of fresh water flowing into a trough used mainly for horses. They
each hurriedly drank some water. Medlin opened a tin of biscuits and
took out one for each. Then they picked up their walk. After an hour,
the road veered off away from the railroad track. Still hungry, Medlin
decided to stop for a spell and eat something. He sat down on a log and
motioned the others to settle down nearby. After reaching into the rucksack he drew out the tin of biscuits and one hank of beef jerky. Taking
out his penknife, he laid the jerky on a patch of smooth wood where the
bark had sloughed off and sawed it into four pieces. They all sat in silence
while they each ate a biscuit with jerky and drank from the bladders.
Medlin gave Hutto a second biscuit.

Medlin was uncomfortable in the quiet, but he wondered to himself
what there was to talk about. That he had taken charge of them and now

was utterly without a plan? He would have to come up with something, but for now all he could think of was to follow the train. Sweat beads formed on his upper lip, and he knew what was coming. He ran into the woods, and finding cover behind a stand of brush he squatted to relieve himself. He had to lean against a tree to wait for his legs to feel less like jelly, and for the shooting pains in his gut to subside.

After a short period while Medlin settled himself, they set out on the road once more. For the first time in his life, Hutto encountered rock—something totally unknown. He picked up a shard and inspected it as he continued walking. It was hard and cool in his hand.

With a mountain in sight ahead, Medlin hoped the road they were on was not far from the path of the train. Sure enough, in a while the tracks appeared down below, heading into a very narrow cut ordered by engineers as a path for the train to get through the mountain. Medlin now wanted to stay with the train, so he contemplated the steep slope from the road to the tracks. He figured it could be done if they concentrated on digging in their heels to keep upright. Jama, riding on her father's back, hung tight around his neck. Loose shale under their feet made it impossible to avoid sliding, but they all made it down without a tumble.

When they got to the train bed, for a while they followed alongside the tracks until the way became so narrow, with sheer rock on either side, that they could stretch out their arms and touch the wall and tracks at the same time. It had crossed the mind of everyone that if a train should appear, there would be no room to escape. They hurried through the narrow pass, almost holding their breath until they were safe.

Finally, the walls of the cut were not as severely high—they were coming out to the other side of the mountain. They met one last obstacle. They had to cross a wooden trestle bridge over a furiously rushing river. The bridge, strictly designed for trains, was a labyrinth of crisscross wooden supports for managing the load. The four had to carefully watch their step and not get distracted by the wide gaps, through which they could see the racing water below. Once they made it safely to the other side, Medlin decided, with the sun low on the horizon, they should set up camp by the river. With some trial and error, they found an animal trail leading down to the water and a suitable place to make camp.

Medlin dug a shallow hole, protected it with a ring of small rocks and placed dried twigs into a pyramid, then lit a fire. He took out from the rucksack lard, pork and cornmeal. There was not enough time to cook the field peas. Celia, without instruction, reached for the pot. After boiling some water and adding cornmeal, she soon had mush ready. Medlin heated the skillet and went to work frying up pork in a glob of lard. Mixing the results into the pot and skillet, he handed a fork to Hutto to share with Celia and Jama, took one for himself, and they all satisfied their hunger.

Medlin made coffee after the meal, and with the blankets, everyone sat around the fire. In his diary for May 10, Medlin noted *Good day of travel.* He rummaged through the rucksack and brought out a stick of bright red hard candy. He broke off about a knuckle length and held it up until Jama was nudged by Celia to see it. Instantly, she recognized it as from the shop. He handed it to her. Until he made a gesture with his hand to his mouth, she wasn't quite sure what to do with it. She put it into her mouth and mixed it with saliva that turned into cherry-flavored syrup. The adults watched as the pleasure of the discovery of the candy came over her. She ran the syrup all through her mouth and smiled at the same time. Both Hutto and Celia started to laugh but checked themselves as they waited to see the reaction from Medlin. Then they all three laughed, openly. It occurred to Medlin that the candy was perhaps an unknown pleasure to both Hutto and Celia, so he broke off two more pieces, which he handed to them. Their reaction to the candy was as wondrous as that of the young girl, and Medlin watched with much amusement and satisfaction.

9

G IL HAD HER MAIL DELIVERED at the university. It made sense since she spent more of her waking hours at the Caroliniana than at her two-bedroom, one-bath house on Singleton Terrace.

She settled down at her desk to do the sort—bills, junk, and legit correspondence—when she came upon a bulging number-ten envelope with the address in her mother's distinctive handwriting. As she held it between her hands, she noticed the stamp with an illustration of a bird, a bright red cardinal from the US Postal Service series on state birds. Her mother loved birds.

A pang of alarm came over Gil at first seeing the letter, because she had just talked to her mother, as always, on Friday, before the weekend. She routinely placed a call to her mother on Fridays at precisely five p.m., ever since the incident a few years earlier, when Gil was already in her thirties and her mother had the "premonition."

At seven on a Sunday morning, Mrs. Culkin was so anxious that she could wait no longer. She called her daughter's home to quell the unexplainable fear that something was terribly wrong and that Gil was, as she described it to herself, "in trouble." When there was no answer, her panic went into high gear. She had the names and numbers of several of Gil's friends—friends Gil had known since childhood—and she spread the word through them that Gil was somehow in danger. The friends, convinced of the accuracy of mother's intuition, called everybody they knew acquainted with Gil who could join in the hunt. One friend who had a key threw on some clothes and raced over to Gil's house, only to find two hungry cats and a well-made bed.

Of the many who had been alerted, only one, a boyfriend of one of the friends, showed any sense in the matter, when he asked if she was missing or just not at home. Gil was not at home but sleeping soundly at the townhouse of a new man in her life—in the early stage of exploration and trial. She hadn't shared his existence with anyone, because at that time in the relationship it could go either way—no reason to talk about it if it might fizzle out. His phone rang, and they both were startled out of a deep sleep. When he rolled over and said the call was for her, she was gobsmacked—nobody knew where she was. Seems among her friends, somebody knew somebody, who knew somebody, who had noticed Gil's car parked in the neighborhood, and somebody knew who lived there and had his number.

When she called her mother back and stammered out some tale about staying out late with girlfriends and after some drinking deciding to crash on a couch, she felt foolish that in her thirties she caved to such scrutiny by her mother, who lived seventy miles away across the state but could still run her down.

So after that, every Friday afternoon at five Gil would call her mother so they could talk about what she had on tap for that weekend and what was on her mother's mind. This worked well to forestall any anxiety—cut down on any more chance for premonitions. But that the mother held sway over her remained as a burr under Gil's saddle. For a long time, it irked her that she knew that the mother knew of the power she had over her.

Her friends spoke about trials with their own mothers, and she found that all of her friends had stories to tell. She herself couldn't go as far as one friend, who described her own mother as the one who "created the wounds, so she knows where to throw the salt"—too harsh for Gil, but there was some familiarity in it. Nevertheless, Gil drove to see her mother about once a month for the weekend, just to make sure things were all right at her mother's home.

Gil's relationship with her mother had its ups and downs—the downs had never gotten to the point of estranged silence between them, but Gil was always just a little guarded. The dips usually involved the mother's need to control her only child. Gil started to set the limits to the mother's butting into her life at about the time her mother went overboard to run her down simply because she wasn't home. Somebody at that point had told Gil that she let her mother into her life beyond what was healthy. From then on, Gil looked for balance as to what she shared—what would sustain a loving, caring relationship but still retain some independence.

Gil's mother felt the change immediately. She was not used to her daughter holding back, so she pushed hard to take the reins as before, but she soon saw that Gil was recoiling, so she gave in to the new order. After a while the new dynamic between them grew comfortable—Gil did not have to throw up barriers anymore, and the mother actually liked that she did not have to work so hard to keep tabs.

The previous year, during one of Gil's visits, the relationship started to change again. Or rather it developed further. Why her mother all of a sudden opened up with her was unclear, but out of nowhere stories of her past started flowing. Evidently there were things she wanted to get off her chest. The mother told Gil about how oppressive it was to grow up in the country, ten miles outside of Florence. Her parents—Gil's grandparents—had a general store in town where they sold everything from chicken feed to canned goods. Nana tended the store and Pop Pop almost single-handedly worked the forty-acre tobacco farm. Gil remembered visiting them regularly up until she went to college. She had fond memories of the place—catfishing with her grandfather Pop Pop and learning to make buttermilk biscuits with Nana. After a weekend or sometimes a whole week during spring break, Gil would leave the farm rested and renewed after enjoying the simple life in the country.

However, her mother's memories were of boredom, stifling oppression. When she was in her late teens, she would ride her bike two miles down the country road to visit the closest kid her age, a boy who was every bit as bored as she was. Eventually she got to the part of the story where she said that they had sex and she got pregnant. Gil was startled, because this was the first she had ever heard of it, plus she never envisioned her mother in any kind of human drama. Gil had never thought of her mother other than as it related to herself—Gil had never thought about her mother as a young girl, teenager, or young woman.

The story continued with all four of the parents getting together to discuss what was to be done. It was decided that the teenage Mary Ellen Chandler would disappear just before her senior year with the excuse that she had been called to take care of an elderly aunt who had contracted some debilitating disease down in Atlanta. The plan was that Mary Ellen would really go to a Baptist-run home for girls in the mountains of North Carolina, set up to avoid the shame of unplanned births. She would have the baby, which would be given immediately to a proper Christian couple for adoption. Mary Ellen would reappear at school, but she would be held back a year and graduate with the next class. The boy would continue in school as though nothing had happened.

Mary Ellen had listened as both families came to the conclusion the home for wayward girls was the only way to deal with the situation. There was one thing she knew at that moment, that she was not going to go to some mountain hideaway for close to a year. She sat quietly and thought of how a cousin had handled her own unplanned pregnancy. The first week the cousin didn't have her period, she asked her parents if she could borrow the family car and visit a friend she had known from childhood, living in nearby Claussen. She picked up the friend and they drove to Pamlico, a half hour away, to an address on the backside of a pharmacy, down an alley off the three blocks everybody called "downtown." It was there that she had an abortion performed by a perfect stranger.

Three days before her parents were to drive her to North Carolina, Mary Ellen took herself to the same address in Pamlico with ninety-two dollars she had saved up from babysitting. She had just gotten her driver's license two months before, when she turned sixteen—she figured she would have no difficulty going the thirty-five miles to her destination. She took her mother's car, which usually sat in the driveway all week, and planned to be back before her father picked up the mother at the store in town and headed home.

The older Black man who opened the door let her in after she told him she had been referred by her cousin, a name he recognized. The room was devoid of any adornment and had very little furniture—a small cabinet, a long, narrow table, and a straight-backed chair. A sink hung from the wall adjacent to the table. The procedure was done quickly by hands well familiar from years of repetition. Hardly another word was spoken from the time she came through the door and handed him the money, in denominations of ten-, five- and one-dollar bills, all rolled up tightly into a tube.

Gil was spared the details of the procedure, but her mother said that she made it back home ahead of her parents at the end of the day. After they sat down for dinner, Mary Ellen told her parents that they didn't have to go to North Carolina, the problem was taken care of. They all ate dinner in silence—no grilling or questions. All they knew was that it was over, and that seemed to be enough. It never came up in conversation again.

For hours Gil's mother continued with a whole catalog of her life's trials and missteps, mostly about what she characterized as taking the wrong fork in the road at critical junctures.

Another thing she wanted to get off her chest and that had long been burning within her was that she felt she had made a terrible mistake by not going out and getting a job when she was young. She knew Gil's father made enough working for the railroad for the family to live on one salary. And there was Gil, just a child, who would somehow have to be cared for, but there were places for that. When she heard that, Gil assumed the "places" were after-school programs where somebody would pick the kid up from school and go to a public swimming pool, bowling alley or the library. Her mother was not making her argument with details. All she knew was that she should have gotten a job—not a career but just for a nest egg so that she would not feel stifled under the breadwinner who ruled the roost.

Gil's father was not the type to lord over his wife, but if the Missus wanted to buy a little something beyond groceries, she had to defend and justify it to the keeper of the purse. To hold in the resentment and regret for all those years showed Gil something about her mother she didn't know was possible—that her mother had more depth of feeling than was ever outwardly shown.

Gil said that her mother had to think about the times back then. She reminded her that it was a time when working mothers were frowned upon. Kids would whisper about a classmate, "Their mother works, you know." To most, a working mother was selfish, or there were money problems in the family.

Gil went on to say that there was a big shift in how women were to think of themselves around the same time of her mother's dilemma over a job—Women's Liberation was in full swing. If you had a job, traditionalists thought you were neglecting your children, whereas if you were a stay-at-home mom, Libbers thought you were neglecting your individual right to be your own person. It was a popular notion within the movement that you had the right to have a job or go all the way to build a career—you were every bit as entitled as the men. Gil and her mother talked about the difficulty of such decisions in the time the mother had to face them.

They talked into the night, and slowly the sandbags between them began to come down. From then on, the posture of the mother always giving advice, scattered with if-I-were-yous, changed. Gil felt the playing field leveling off and saw there could be a chance where she would feel secure in sharing issues she, too, struggled with.

By three in the morning, a transformation was near complete. They would always be mother and daughter, but the dynamic between them was about to make a major change. They had started with bourbon, but had switched to strong coffee to get through what they each considered important dialog. Both mother and daughter sensed the shift in their relationship. There would still be respect but also a healthier consideration for boundaries. The mother would accept that Gil was a grown woman, very capable of making her own decisions, and in turn Gil would not dismiss her mother as not having valuable insights based on personal experience.

There was a long hug, with no need to speak as to why the two women needed to put this exclamation point to the long conversation. Gil told her mother she was going to start calling her Chandler and they both laughed. Every year since her graduation from college the mother and friends from her dorm had gotten together at a rented beach house near Charleston. The eight of them—no spouses allowed—enjoyed a four-day weekend with no diversions from lounging about and sharing most everything about their lives that had happened since they had last met. They usually stayed in their pajamas, and were forbidden to waste time putting on makeup. They liked talking up their kids and dissing the husbands. They reveled in no one asking if they really needed that third glass of wine. As in college, they referred to one another by their maiden names—which was why Gil said that from then on, she was going to refer to her mother as Chandler.

———

FOR SEVERAL MOMENTS, as Gil held the fat envelope from her mother, she continued to feel a little apprehensive. As always, she had called just a few days before, so a letter was most curious. The envelope was thick, so she tilted back her chair, and put her feet up for what looked to be a long read. She put the little needlepoint bolster at the small of her back—the pillow read, *If It's Not One Thing, It's Your Mother*, a gift for her last birthday. Her mother had stayed up all night to finish the outside piping and put in the zipper in time to mail it to her daughter.

Before opening it, Gil again held the letter between both hands and for the first time noticed a change in her mother's handwriting, once enviable for the command of the pen in its fluidity, but now, not so much. Her mother was certainly aging.

Dear, My Darling Baby Girl,

This is your old mother here to say that with the goings-on at the State House over that damn flag, it has gotten me to thinking about just how I feel about it myself. I know you and your smart friends have it all worked out in your heads as to the meaning of the ruckus but I have never been a deep thinker (which you must believe is par for the course for an old hick) but it has put me to puzzling a lot about whites and blacks trying to just get along as I see it from my little perch as a true Southerner. I think I qualify because you don't get more Southern than Florence, S.C.

I don't want to go back to the flood, as Johnny Carson used to say, but it seems to me to have any opinion I have to start with my own experiences. Like my cousin Vic used to say, "Opinions are like assholes. Everybody's got one." As you may remember, he was a card and always had us laughing.

At my age, along with trying to make heads or tails of this modern-day world, I have found myself feeling I need to pass down to you some things from my life and about the time I lived it. Maybe it would be of some value to you if I laid out some things about growing up a Chandler. With you knee-deep in studying what you call Southern Culture all your adult life, I don't remember ever laying out before you the Chandlers, Southerners through and through in a time that so many outsiders look back at with scorn. It would be a shame to know so much about South Carolina history and not about your own people.

I took the family photo album out yesterday to see that frozen instant the shutter clicked to maybe get a glimpse of clues as to who they were beyond memory. I looked into their faces to see if there was anything I had missed—a sign of something other than time between then and now. There was a picture of my mother, your Nana, standing in front of some flowering bush, I think a gardenia, with me, a baby in her arms. I had to use the magnifying glass I keep next to me on the end table for fine print to make sure it was her because this was a young woman—happy, smiling, wearing dark red lipstick as best I could tell in the black and white photograph. I had to be reminded that at one time there had been girliness but what has been fixed in my mind is as she is today, with deep wrinkles from the South Carolina sun and hardship—typical of hardworking folks. At the bottom of the picture is the shadow of the photographer, I bet was Daddy. As I looked at it, it almost made me cry to think that he, too, must have been young, a new father, all full of vigor and hope.

In another small picture with wavy edges, most likely taken with our black box camera, was a picture of both my parents, your Nana and Pop Pop. It must have been taken in Kingstree because in the background is a pole hung with gourds, hollowed out for martin houses, just like I always remembered it. They must have been ready to go to church because she has her pocketbook in front of her, holding it by both hands on the handle. Daddy has his wide-brimmed hat pushed back on his head showing his very white forehead above the darker skin of his face made leathery by years of beating sun. His long-sleeve white shirt is buttoned up to his neck and there is a little paunch at the waist, likely from the sawmill gravy over biscuits and salt cured ham he insisted on having every morning for breakfast. And there is the spine curvature I never remember him without, from spending so many hours on a tractor seat. Both hands are resting on his hips with a lit cigarette between his fingers in his right hand.

The last picture, I stared at for a long time—of Sam and Johnny Mae. Do you remember them when you were a kid? This was the elderly Negro couple (calling them black is too modern. It was Negro or coloreds back then) whose family had worked there on the Chandler farm in Kingstree through generations. Sam was born right in the house in back of them in the picture. And he died there ninety years later. Sam used to say his grandfather remembered when Confederate soldiers passed down the road on their way to Virginia and the fighting.

In the picture, Johnny Mae, a beefy woman, is wearing a cotton dress with an apron. Sam is slim, and wears overalls with a crisp white shirt. Long after the electric iron replaced the solid cast iron relic heated in the fireplace, Johnny wouldn't hear of using the upgrade.

Johnny is not looking into the camera but is distracted by a small white child coming into the picture with outstretched arms—not much more than a streak because of the slow shutter of the Kodak box camera. That's you, my darling.

Sam is looking directly into the camera, and now, so many years later, I wonder what they were thinking, working their whole lifetime for the Chandlers. To us, Sam and Johnny Mae were not our blood family, but they were an extension of it. I can't think of growing up without them as a part of it.

Gil, maybe you got your curiosity about the past from me because I was always pestering family with what was it like in "the olden days." Especially, I liked to ask my grandparents, Mom Mom and Old Pop (they were both gone by the time you showed up) about what life was like in their time. I sat in wonder, hearing there was no such thing as television and other things that were so much a part of my life. When I got a little older, I calculated that their lives spanned from a time when the first airplanes they saw were barnstormers or flying circuses, they called them, when a show would come to town with crude planes that were nothing but canvas stretched over wooden slats. But on the other end, they lived to experience the first American astronaut to orbit the earth in 1962. Gil, what a leap for one generation!

When thoughts of the old folks come to mind now, my memories go beyond picking strawberries from their garden and Old Pop teaching me how to drive the tractor. These days I wonder what they were thinking. Did they ever question their relationship with "the coloreds" who were living so close to them? I think, no. Were they looking beyond their own little world? Probably not. The demonstrators are right to protest that remnant of the Civil War, the Confederate flag, and the reverence some whites still have for it. Obviously, blacks are riled. They are fed up with being treated as less than equal.

But it's hard to take the blaming. I think of our people as decent, with some prejudices, sure, but without malice toward others. When I tell you my personal experiences, I bring no judgment to my story, no analysis of good or bad behavior as if I have a handle on the human condition through the ages, which I don't.

I figured it was high time to share with you some of what I remember of my side of the family, the Chandlers' past, along with some things you may not know about my growing up during my generation. I'm taking the long way around the barn to tell you, I think it may give you some things to think about every day when you walk past that craziness of a demonstration over the flag. Maybe it will give you some clues as to what went on leading up to today.

Considering what you are witnessing there in Columbia right now, it will be hard for you to believe that from the time I was born until the early '60s, when I began to be more conscious of what was going on around me, no one spoke of race. I know, saying that is like telling a kid that we had no cell phones when I was growing up—they can't imagine it.

Certainly we were aware of blacks. They were an accent in the Southern landscape. This sounds harsh now, but when there was a total absence of familiarity as to who they really were, then the old women fishing a creek with a cane pole or field hands chopping tobacco—scenes that were commonplace—were more like props on a postcard. Somehow, somewhere, the lines had been laid down as to the rules of separation. The blacks knew their place. So that's how it was, with both sides appearing to accept it.

Gil, it will be hard for you to understand, but when I was growing up to ask me anything about the black people living literally across the tracks from us—it would be like asking me about Africans in the Congo. Like in one of my kid books, Little Black Sambo, their skin was black—that was all I knew about near half the population of Florence.

Johnny Mae and Sam were different from the Negroes on the other side of the tracks—they were like family. But when you think about it, they weren't really like family. Families fuss and squabble. They worked for us and didn't talk back. But still, there was affection and respect on both sides. Maybe that's the point—once you know someone up close, they fall out of the category of "unknowns" or "others." But I can't deny, the thing that was behind all attitudes regarding the black race was as common as the air we breathed. They were inferior to the white race. This supposed fact of life was not taught in terms of smaller brains, or God's creation as sub-par with whites or that they were created exclusively to serve—there were enough other signs for me to clearly get the gist. I didn't even think about it.

My first inkling that blacks and whites operated from two different sets of rules was when I was about seven years old and I asked Mother at the A&P in Florence why there were two drinking fountains—one marked "whites," the other "colored." She simply answered that each had their own fountain. She said it in the same way she would say the sky is blue. Chances are she had no other answer since in her mind "that's just the way it is." There was nothing in her voice of conscience or even of taboo. A short time after, I saw again that word "colored" on the public bus. This time it had an arrow above it pointing to the back. Those experiences must have made an impression on me, because I can see both the fountain and the bus as clear and exact as over fifty years ago.

There was plenty of support for the attitude that blacks had shortcomings. For me and my generation, there were clues all around in plain sight. When presented with images of bug-eyed, big-lipped Negroes on postcards in Woolworth's, it was pretty clear what the popular white viewpoint was—blacks were buffoons, harmless creatures, always scamming to get out of work. The black male was a tomcat always trying to put one over on his lady friend, who would eventually find him out and put a knot in his tail. A hugely popular television show, Amos 'n' Andy, aired until 1966, featuring a pair of black characters who lived in Harlem. That's not the South. The program was about two childlike, clownish Negroes who were always shuffling through life with some get-rich-quick scheme—Andy says to Amos that he is going to get rich by selling stamps which he will buy for ten cents apiece and sell for a nickel but he would make up for the loss in volume.

Florence, on what we knew as Highway 1 back then, was just down from the wildly successful tourist trap called South of the Border. Families traveling from the North to vacation in Florida would be driven crazy by their kids begging to stop for an "experience like no other" on a long and boring trip. At South of the Border, the kids could buy anything from a live baby alligator to a snow globe of the Last Supper. There was also a large selection of black kitsch—postcards with colorful banners reading Greetings from Dixie with Negroes eating watermelon, and pickaninnies covered in cotton sitting in picking baskets, or a Negro chased by a snapping alligator—or better, the alligator has him by his pants, exposing his naked behind. There was a selection of cheap figurines—black children with sprigs of hair tied up with strips of rags, sitting on a potty or coming out of an outhouse. The preoccupation with bathroom humor designed to be demeaning as possible set the tone. All these trinkets were bought eagerly with no negative judgment or conscience about the content. The joke was spread by vacationers traveling through the South heading home in the North with Aunt Jemima cookie jars featuring the big, red, waxy lips of a Negro mammy. The laughs were spread up and down the east coast and beyond. Sales were brisk. Few thought anything about it.

I would not be doing justice to my rambling on about this as an old Southerner if I didn't address the "n" word and my exposure to it growing up. The word nigger was used openly among my young friends because it was faceless. It had no power as it does today because the object of it was a people who blended into the background. But again, as far as Johnny Mae and Sam went, if I would ever have called them "niggers," I would have gotten my butt blistered. People who had "help" called them the "colored girl" or "colored man." In my memory, the word nigger was never used to hurt but as part of our everyday speech—Brazil nuts were nigger toes, kids piled on top of each other was a nigger pile, things were nigger rigged, a nigger sandwich was a chicken leg or pork chop between two slices of white bread—and there were plenty more.

Being mindless about the black race was one thing, but Catholics and Jews were not so lucky in my house. Mother was skeptical of Catholics and didn't mind letting you know. To her, they were like rabbits, unable to control their desire to pump out babies. The "Poop"—what she called the Pope—was a money-grubbing pale man in a beanie whose mission was to see everyone converted to his flock. When John F. Kennedy, a Catholic, ran for president, she was sure that the Poop would be running this country from the Vatican through his boy, JFK. There was a joke that they were going to change the coinage. It would say "In God we trust, in the Pope we hope." Catholics not permitting divorce and strictly marrying within the faith, Mother interpreted as thinking of themselves as better than everyone else.

I don't remember my parents actually saying anything derogatory about the one Jew in our school, Carol Meyer, but somewhere I picked up there were unexplained differences that cast an aura of mystery around her. That Jews don't believe in Christ in a town full of Baptists didn't help. And "Jews killed Christ" was a little ditty I picked up. I somehow, maybe through osmosis, understood that the Old Testament says Jews were the "money changers" and crafty merchants—which forever branded them as a breed to approach with much caution regarding business deals. But since Mr. Meyer was a bus driver, the presumption was never tested. However, that they were all smart held true because Carol was easily the smartest kid in our class, which to us validated the belief that there are natural born traits that are baked into the races.

Hurtful clichés that roll out so easily took on real meaning the night a bunch of us kids were playing Monopoly. Carol and I were in hot negotiation over some hotels and I blurted out that she was trying to "Jew me down." Everything went into slow motion and in an instant, I learned that words matter and can hurt. It was a good lesson, learned early—a mistake not to be repeated.

Writing it all down, more things have started to play in my head. Situations that now make me shudder at the memories. What seemed perfectly ordinary then puts my teeth on edge now. Daddy and Mom would drive the family down to Atlanta once a year to visit with Aunt Bess. Mostly we just sat around while Mom and Bess talked about old times when the sisters grew up on the farm in Kingstree, but always there would be Sunday lunch at Aunt Fanny's Cabin. The restaurant was decorated out in a strong theme of plantation life with an emphasis on gentility. But the draw for my family were the beef tips for Dad and the fresh roasted turkey with cornbread stuffing for Mom—with the gravy sopped up with yeast rolls that tasted every bit as good as the ones Johnny Mae made at home in Kingstree. And there were plenty of rolls and biscuits to be had, cradled in the apron of a black woman who was decked out to look like Aunt Jemima. Her job was to make her way around the dining room offering these wonderful rolls and biscuits fresh from the oven.

The menu was painted on a single board that hung from the neck of a black boy. He went from table to table displaying the menu to diners. He was dressed in period clothes—white blousy shirt, short black pants, and shoes with clip-on buckles—looking the part of a plantation houseboy. As he recited the specials of the day, he would do a little dance. What seems strange now is that the only thing that registered was how good the rolls were—no outrage, no pity, *no embarrassment. The insulting racial stereotyping went completely over everybody's head.*

Later, after I had gotten older and gone off on my own, I would go back to Aunt Fanny's if I was down that way. A few things had changed—the menu board was replaced with typical, plastic laminated menus—no boy and no jig—but the rolls were still offered in an apron and the Dixie plantation decor remained. By then, scattered throughout the restaurant were several tables of black patrons. I recently heard from friends that just six years ago the old owner died and the property was so valuable, his heirs sold it to a developer who built a forty-story commercial building where Fanny's had stood. There had been no pressure by protestors to close it down, outraged over the overt racial theme—just a decision based on a financial windfall.

I read somewhere that a black Atlanta social activist and early leader of the Civil Rights Movement was not surprised by whites not taking offense at the blatant racist overtones of the restaurant, but he sure was shocked that Fanny's ever had any black patrons. After thinking it over he said that likely young blacks just thought it was "cute." He had marched with King. Now years later, the younger generation seemed to take the parody of a slave time plantation in stride, which he thought an insult to all who had gone through so much on the front lines during the early days.

It seems so simple, but as it happened, it's not. Black oppression is a big ship to turn around, especially since whites profited so much from slavery and used terror and lies to justify the practice and the harsh coercion that went with it. We're still dealing with undoing those efforts that were so successful in painting a whole race as inferior.

Gil, I remember my grandparents and parents and I have to say that it all boiled down to "that's how it was" and even the decent common folks were willing to let things just be as they were. That's how it was when I came along. I know now the Klan was doing their dirty work and there were lynchings, but none of that ever crossed my life. Certainly, I'm not downplaying any of the horrible cross-burnings or other violence, but I can only tell of my personal experiences in my

South. And I don't think there is just one South. Other states like Alabama and Mississippi both have different stories based on different influences. I think it's unfair to put all the Southern states into one lump and call it the South as if each state operated in lockstep with the others.

I think our kin were like the majority of plain, decent folks from South Carolina at the time, not willing to jeopardize what was safe and comfortable, not thinking anywhere beyond what just was. Were they bad for not righting a wrong? To me, the demonstrators are trying to point a finger at all whites, going back hundreds of years and throwing a blanket of shame and blame on all for the legacy of slavery. Mom and Pop were close enough to the Civil War to actually know people who remembered it—only a generation away from the time of slavery itself. I think it's not realistic to expect the white race could change deep-seated prejudices, baked in from as far back as the early colonies, in a short time. That the white race could go from legally owning a human being to accepting blacks as equals in a few generations is too much to expect.

As I see it, the flag demonstration is blacks shaking up what we thought all along was the point when they should be content, now that they can vote, own property, etc. I think a lot of white people are perplexed because they think blacks got what they wanted but now they are overreaching. But just maybe it can happen.

It seems to me, blacks have gotten some political power over the past decades and have used it for changes like affirmative action, which some whites resent since they were happy with the way things had been. These days whites are walking on eggshells with what they say about race relations. Whites who used to run fast and loose with sloppy insulting talk about blacks are feeling the heat and are having to do something they never had to do before, watch their mouth or at least think before they speak. To use a saying from the old folks—blacks have moved up a few branches closer to the catbird seat. It seems sometimes like they are trying to dominate or take over, but maybe it's just that they are unwilling to tolerate the injustices any longer.

Gil, I guess the demonstration is not only about the flag, really, but way more.

So, my darling, what I have given you is what I know through what I saw and what I can remember of those before me. It's left up to you, with the advantage of your knowledge of history and your kind of methodical thinking to really make sense of the strong feelings that seem to be coming out over the Confederate flag that I think we both know hides a wider and more complicated story.

Gil I must say that as much as I have put thought to it, I am still stumped over how the black demonstrators have concluded that there is justification to demonize native Southerners and hold the living generation responsible for the past as well as our current situation, and to feel so much resentment and suspicion. From where I sit, there seems to be a strong desire to continually blame and hear back an apology from whites. No apology shouted from the highest mountain will do anything now. No one should be denying that slavery happened with devastating consequences. No one should be saying slavery turned out as anything other than a disaster. It hangs on as America's Great Shame. When will it be time to try to work together and continue plodding through, build on successes that have been achieved and work toward the goal of complete equality between the races? Maybe, my darling, you will see that time come.

Your Old Southern Mom,
Chandler

10

Rocky, hard going, lost
May 11, 1857

A FTER WALKING OUT OF NEWNAN and camping for the night, Medlin woke up ready to get on to Mobile. The day dawned bright. They had slept pretty well after enjoying supper, the campfire, and the brightly colored store candy the night before. They set out walking along the train bed, but late in the afternoon they climbed away from the track to try to find a road again, after Medlin realized that to board the train they had better get into a town by the road.

Always in the back of his mind was the farm, and his obligations that were being neglected. It had been almost four weeks since the first day of the season when he had started plowing the field. After that was done, he had rented slave hands as usual from the McLeod place for a couple of days to help him put in the seed. He knew a successful yield would not come without constant attention. He could picture the weeds already strangling the fledgling plants. Easily, the balance could tip when neglect took over. He had seen it happen when a neighboring farmer went through a sick spell and everything turned to ruin. A timetable began to play over and over in his head. If they got on a train to Mobile as Tom had suggested and everything ran smoothly from then on, there might be time—just barely time—to find success at the auction and get back home to the crop.

As soon as they had left Newnan on foot the day before, things had gone surprisingly easy. Considering all that was necessary to keep four people moving along—preparing meals and other necessities—Medlin was amazed to conclude that no matter the circumstances, all things could quickly become routine. The food preparation fell to Medlin and Celia. Almost immediately out of Newnan, without one word of direction, they had fallen into a pattern of individual responsibilities, silently determined.

Late in the evening they had filled the water bladders and canteen from the river so that next morning there would be water for coffee. Medlin set out rations of ground coffee that night for Celia to ready the pot for the fresh fire she would make in the morning.

When they first started to make camp, Jama watched Medlin hunt dry material for the campfire and took on the chore for herself. At the first sign of morning light the next day, the young girl began her scour for dry twigs shed from surrounding trees. A tangle of dry, stringlike fibers from underbrush was ideal to get a fire started quickly, but it was also a favorite of birds building nests. Medlin complimented Jama when she beat out her feathered competitors over the wispy fire starter.

In dealing with Hutto, Medlin kept the Colt in his left hand as he freed Hutto's wrists from the one set of shackles and then placed them on his ankles for the short walk away from camp into the cover of brush to relieve himself. Always, Medlin had Tom's warning in his head to "watch those niggers because they'll do anything for their freedom." Tom had often enjoyed repeating stories of how he escaped near death in one-on-one combat. A favorite tale was of the time when some slave got one wrist free and put him in a headlock with the chain wrapped tight around his neck. Tom bragged that he most certainly would be dead had it not been for the Colt, which Medlin now carried.

Nevertheless, Medlin could not help but be curious about the three slaves in his charge. His only experience had been on occasion when he rented a couple of slaves to help with field work. He reflected that although Negroes were so unfamiliar, life in many ways was all about them—at the gin and in private company when farm production came up, and that was often. Anytime there were cotton men around, the talk was of rising auction prices, runaways, and discipline. Though he owned none of his own, he did get riled when he heard of the Northerners' objection to the South's use of the African slave. What business was it of theirs?

———

ON THE SECOND NIGHT OUT OF NEWNAN, when they had been walking for hours after leaving the train bed but still not finding a road, Medlin knew they were lost. They came upon a large stream, and he decided that it was a good place to camp. They made a satisfying supper of the rabbit Medlin took with a lucky shot with the Colt. The animal was unaware of its fate as it was preoccupied with a lush patch of watercress in some shallows. Celia gathered some of that watercress for their meal.

With his stomach full on meat other than salt pork, Medlin felt conversational, and asked Hutto if he had been born on the Butler plantation. Hutto answered no, he had been born on Master William Aiken's place off the Edisto River—at a plantation called Jehossee.

Medlin asked if that was in South Carolina or Georgia. Hutto looked back with a quizzical stare. He had no concept of states. To Medlin, where a man was from was important—the root of his existence.

He picked up the green stick used to roast the rabbit and skittered off the picked-clean rib cage onto the ground. With his open hand he cleared leaf debris to expose a patch of bare earth. Using the stick, he drew a crude rectangle. In the right-hand side of this rectangle he marked off squares from top to bottom. He left the other side of the rectangle blank because it was only the right-side boxes he was interested in to make his point. Out to the right of the rectangle he drew several wavy lines, and announced this area to be the ocean. Hutto leaned in to inspect the drawing closely, and Celia came up and hovered over his shoulder.

Medlin held the stick over the big rectangle and said that it represented the United States of America. He pointed to the squares and told them these were states. Midway, he pointed to a square bordering what he called the ocean and said that this was the state of South Carolina.

Hutto looked at the box Medlin had just described as South Carolina. Anxious to lay out his thinking, Hutto recounted a time when he was in a boat that was taking Master Aiken to "Cheston" and along part of the way they were on big water. Medlin said he was likely going to Charleston and stabbed a spot where he said it would be on the dirt map.

—Hutto, you are from the great state of South Carolina!

Hutto got to his feet excitedly.

—I'm from South Carolina! Sir, did you say it was a great state?

—One of the greatest.

Hutto then asked questions about things he had long pondered regarding the world outside the confines of his home plantation. He asked what the North and the South were. He had heard some whispering about them around the night fire in the slave quarters.

Hutto said that he, his older brother—older by eleven years—and mother were treated well at the Jehossee place. His father was owned by the Grimbles, at the next plantation over. His father made the six-mile walk every other Sunday, to attend the church at Jehossee and visit with his family—his woman and two boys.

Hutto described his childhood surroundings as with ponds, full of bass and perch. And there was plenty of saltwater marsh and a wide river, the Dawhoo, coming off the Edisto where, when not working, they would catch fish, crab, and shrimp. Over what was caught that went to the Aiken table, the slaves were free to eat, and there was plenty for all.

Even as a child, Hutto said, he was very big for his age, and sooner than most children on the plantation he went out into the rice fields with his mother. His first job was to jump up and down and shout as loud as he could to scare off the rice birds, which, if given a chance, could make quick work of stripping the reeds.

Slaves of neighboring plantations had occasion to get together. A major topic of conversation was to compare treatment of slaves from one plantation to another. Plantation owners would have feared slaves socializing had it not been for their wish for the slave babies who often resulted from slaves commingling.

Slave unions were encouraged between different estates. If there was a shortage of desirable mates at one location, it made sense to allow passes to slaves to travel between plantations and so facilitate and encourage relationships and offspring. Hutto's father belonged to the Grimbles, and he worked and lived at their plantation.

Jehossee had a favorable reputation among slaves as being a place where God had smiled. Techniques to get the most productive work out of the slaves varied greatly from one plantation to another. The Aikens used a task system—each slave was daily given achievable tasks to be performed within a certain time. If they completed the task under the allotted period, the time remaining could be used at their own discretion. Slaves spent their free time tending their own gardens, raising livestock, or raising chickens. It was not unusual for a slave to make a little money by selling what they produced, like eggs. They even sold to the Master. At Jehossee, the task system was successful. Incentive was high to complete plantation work quickly and well so the slaves could get on with interests of their own. There was little need for punishment. However, stealing from the Master was not tolerated. When Old Master William found fresh peaches missing from his orchard, the perpetrator, if caught, was sure to get a ration of the lash.

Some planters thought the task system favored the slaves too much and chose intimidation through harsh discipline to try to get the most out of their slaves. For as many plantations as existed, there were as many different ways in which they were run. There were no laws established for the treatment of slaves—they could be beaten or killed, all depending on the whim of the Master or his overseer.

Life at Jehossee was most memorable for Hutto because of Master William Aiken's nephew, Elliot, who ran the plantation during the long periods when William attended other business in Charleston, thirty miles away. Elliot had showed a liking for the boy ever since the day he followed the noise of a commotion and come upon the scene the instant Hutto was dropped from his mother into the waiting arms of the plantation midwife. Elliott never forgot, and from then on took particular notice of the boy over all others on the property. Jig, Hutto's older brother, was included when special privileges were extended.

On occasion, even when Hutto was very young and not yet put to the fields, he and his brother accompanied Mr. Elliot and his friends bird and deer hunting across the 35,000-acre estate. They would take wagons, until the terrain was such that the party would have to continue on foot. Jig tended the dogs and ran ahead to scout for prey. Mr. Elliot entrusted Jig with carrying the gun not in use at the time—the long rifle for deer or rabbit, the shotgun for fowl. When they came across marsh waters or burr patches too onerous for Hutto to pass through, Mr. Elliot hoisted the young boy onto his shoulders, where he would ride until they reached more negotiable terrain.

By the campfire with Medlin, Celia, and Jama, Hutto continued his story, all the while staring into the fire, concentrating on an occasion in time that he had tried for many years to forget. But the more he talked, the more the details of that time resurfaced vividly.

He said that one day, Mr. Elliot, his brother, and two young men from neighboring plantations decided to follow up on what they had heard. A ten-point buck had been sighted in a pine forest about two miles off between the Dawhoo and the ocean. It was reported to have a body so large, the animal could be fed upon from the smokehouse for a good long while.

After some success in open fields with quail, the party traveled on foot a mile and a half from the wagons looking for the buck but decided that he had most likely gotten spooked by their shotgun fire. Meanwhile Jig, enthusiastic about spotting the buck, had gone way ahead. From a thicket he looked across a rivulet to where a tangle of scuppernong vines climbed out on a branch of a large live oak. The buck was up on his hind legs with his tongue fully extended, reaching for a bunch of mature scuppernongs up eight feet off the ground. Jig backed quietly out from the thicket where he had watched in amazement as the huge animal busied himself with the feast of wild grapes.

Jig ran like he had never run before through bramble and sedge and met the party just as they were deciding to return to the wagons. Mr. Elliot and his brother were very familiar with the description of where the buck was, and immediately fixed on a plan to flush the deer from the woods, out toward the beach, to hem him in. They would all fan out and move in on the buck. With the dogs driving him to the openness of the beach, the buck would be trapped. It would be an easy kill.

Everyone took off running. Hutto had great difficulty and could not keep up. The plan seemed to be a good one, but the buck unexpectedly broke away by leaping over a high line of yaupon, wax myrtles, and tangled sawbrier vines. The animal was in a frenzy and darted, full on, back across the open field. He would have been gone for good if Hutto, who had fallen behind, had not stumbled and lay entangled in bunch grass. He stood up and screamed when he saw the buck was bearing down. The deer was surprised by the boy popping up in his path. He dug in his front hooves to stop and made the mistake of changing his course back toward the ocean.

The three hunting dogs were running close behind, but the deer got to the beach first. He wildly sought to escape. Everybody was soon on the beach, the buck trapped between the ocean and the wide tidal creek running from the surrounding marsh, moving fast toward the sea through a deep channel.

The buck charged desperately toward the creek. When he got to the edge, the undercut gave way, and he fell into the water along with a large shelf of sand. At first, only one antler showed above the water, until he emerged with his front hooves stabbing the surface. As he bobbed up, he blew salt water from his snout along with slime that went whipping into the air. His mouth was gaping open with his tongue thrust out forward. The fast current had him moving quickly, out toward where the creek mingled with the sea.

By now everyone was on the bank of the tidal creek. Hutto finally caught up. Mr. Elliot shouted to Jig to jump in and turn the buck toward the beach. The boy ran a little way along the bank, leapt into the water and grabbed one of the antlers. With the help of the swift current, he was able to swing one leg over the wide back. Now, he had hold of the tines closest the head while everyone shouted for Jig to turn the buck to shore.

Where the tidal creek met the sea, a sandbar split the flow into two channels that passed around it, deeper and swifter than before. The deer's legs found the bar, and it struggled to climb out onto the surface. The enormous size of the animal could now be assessed for the first time. Jig seemed small in comparison. The boy was the Jehossee rider representing the Aiken horse for the annual plantation race, and he didn't seem this small on a fifteen-hand stallion. Along with the barking dogs, shouts to Jig to bring the buck to shore only scared the buck more. His pupils were dots within the exposed whites of the eyeballs, and both eyes looked as if they would pop from their sockets. His long tongue was now hanging out one side from his open mouth as he heaved for air.

The buck re-entered the water on the back side of the sandbar. Elliot directed Jig to let go, but instead the two stayed as one. Up until now, letting go of the animal seemed easy—an end to an adventure, a good story to be retold, forever. But now there was a desperateness in Elliot. Hutto sensed it and screamed.

—Let go, Jig! Let go!

He was jumping up and down on the beach. He even plunged into the water and attempted to get out to Jig, but Elliot waded in, grabbed him by his shirt, and dragged him to shore.

Hutto was sobbing while all the others helplessly watched for some minutes in stunned silence as the rhythmic bobbing of the rack and the black spot of Jig's head disappeared into the horizon. They stayed looking out to sea until it was near dark, and then at last, they started back. Everyone walked in silence except for Hutto, who went into a continuous moan and sob. Mr. Elliot lifted him onto his back, where the boy clung to his neck with his legs wrapped tightly around his ribs and cried until, exhausted, he fell asleep.

When they got back, Elliot took the sleeping Hutto to his shanty and gently placed him on the bed pallet on the floor. His mother tucked a blanket around him, and sensing bad news, went outside to hear it. She was told of Jig and the deer. It was a quiet night, with just the sound of a whippoorwill off in the distance—too pleasant an evening for such tragedy to be told.

Elliot and his brother went out to the beach the next day and walked a long stretch for any sign of Jig. By the time they got to where the tidal creek was flowing back to refill the marsh, close to high tide, they came upon the gnarly remnant of a big bush in the water—still with roots anchored into the sandbank. The water was now flowing almost imperceptibly, lapping against the bank. Caught in the bleached branches was Jig, still astride the deer. His shirt sleeve had been pierced by a tine just above the animal's ears, and that must have kept them tethered together on their watery journey. Where the water lapped at the bank, the bodies of Jig and the buck succumbed to the gentle ebb and flow, which gave the impression of animal and rider on a jaunt.

For days, Hutto pestered his mother as to his brother's whereabouts. Finally, she sat him down and told him of her version of Heaven. She said that life is a test for the hereafter. God put all creatures in this life to a test of worthiness to be accepted into a place of joy and beauty that's called Heaven. She told him that God had looked down on Jig and had decided it was his time to go. Hutto asked if it was the same as for his grandmother. His mother came back and said gently that God had decided that Jig would go to Heaven on a deer. When Hutto finished his story, he, Celia, and Medlin all sat quiet around the crackling fire. Jama had fallen asleep.

Medlin knew that tomorrow would be another exhausting day. Wanting to check the time, he pinched the stem of his watch between two fingers and lifted it from his vest pocket, as the entire length of the large gold chain came with it. As soon as the gold watch caught the light of the fire, Hutto stared in fascination. He had never seen such a thing before. He leaned forward to get a better look. Medlin noticed the attraction and slipped the toggle from the buttonhole of his vest. He handed the watch and chain to Hutto. Curious to Medlin, the big man seemed to be more taken with the chain than with the watch itself. As Hutto ran the chain through his large fingers, it was plain to see how he questioned its making—each link was attached so flawlessly to the next and so uniform, one to the other. It would not be the only time that Medlin would take out the watch and chain for Hutto to inspect. It would begin with Hutto asking for the time.

At first light the next morning, Medlin and his charges continued walking in search of a road that might lead into a town with a train station, where they could resume the trip to Mobile by rail. They heard a distant train whistle, twice, but did not find either a road or the train track. The character of the terrain seemed to be very gradually changing toward the less rocky, from what Medlin could determine. When he got a good view of the landscape far ahead, he saw that the ground was slowly becoming more planed out to flat open meadows. Still, it was pretty rough going in the wilderness, so when they stopped for a bit he wrote, *Still hard going*, for that day, May 12, in his diary.

After walking almost all day they came to a wide river and made camp at a place where the water was swift and seemed most anxious to find lower ground where it could become tranquil. To himself Medlin questioned his selection for the camp. The water, crashing over rocks, sounded almost too noisy to sleep through.

Rations were getting low, making it all the more important that very soon they must locate a town and provisions. Early the next morning, after having only coffee for breakfast, Medlin decided to break out on his own for the day to try to find some sign of a road. Alone, he figured he could cover more ground. He shackled Hutto by the wrists around the trunk of a tall but slender tree. He didn't quite know what to do with Celia and Jama, but finally decided to tether the two to each other with the leather strap used to attach pots and other gear to the duffle when they were on the move. He tied Celia's left wrist securely with one end, and Jama's right with the other, leaving a couple of feet of slack between. He put out two hanks of jerky and the last they had of biscuits. He picked up one water bladder, left a full canteen close to Hutto, and took off by himself.

About a mile out of camp, he started to feel good about being on his own. He hadn't felt like this since he left Clio, which he roughly calculated as somewhere over a week. Out there by himself with no one to take care of, to feed, he thought for a moment about just leaving the whole thing behind—finding the train heading back to Charleston and getting on. But what of Hutto, Celia, and Jama? What would happen to them? He wondered why he cared. But then he shrugged off the notion of abandoning the slaves and walked a couple more miles, mostly across open land. He wanted to stay within earshot of the river, which he could hear just on the other side of the tree line. By now the sun was hot and directly above. He could feel sweat beads letting go from the hair at his neck and running as far as possible, until his shirt took them into a big wet patch in the middle of his back.

The whole morning, Medlin saw only one simple clapboard building, that would have been home for someone, at some time, but it was abandoned now. He was disappointed not to find even a footpath, much less a wagon track, leading from the house out to any road. He wondered why there had not been some attempt to farm the land, but while walking across it he came upon patches of sloughing shale and figured it could be of no use to grow anything.

He angled his route back toward the river, and filled the bladder from the cold water that seemed to be much calmer here than upstream at the camp. With his spirits lightened after a good morning, Medlin was surprised when he suddenly felt a prickly sensation come over his body. He thought maybe it was the heat, so he took a long draw from the bladder. But then, in trying to cap it off, he fumbled with the stopper. His hand was shaking so much the stopper dropped into the water, caught the current, and started floating downriver.

Medlin had to chase the cork as best he could. He retrieved it just before it outpaced him. Taking the strap of the bladder he put it in place over his shoulder. He stretched out both hands in front of him and saw the uncontrollable tremor. There was nothing he could do about it, so he headed on again, a little away from the river, even more desperate to find a road or the train track.

He passed through an open meadow. He had questioned staying out in the sun over the tree-covered river route, but decided that the easy going of the open ground was the quicker—so better—option. When he came to the next stand of trees, he had to stop. Fatigue overtook him. His legs were quaking and barely able to support him. He sat on the trunk of a downed tree, closed his eyes, and sat perfectly still, hoping whatever had taken over would pass. He was so still, a possum passed just a couple of paces away without the slightest idea of his presence. The possum walking through brush sounded exactly like a stealthy human. Medlin reacted with a jolt when the sound of it broke through his trance. Then the possum picked up its pace and waddled on through the grass as quick as its short legs would permit.

Medlin felt as if there was an assault on an imaginary inner skin. Next the attack seemed to concentrate in his lower gut in stabs of sharp pain. Still sitting on the log, he tried for a position to relieve the extreme discomfort. First, he sat up straight and stretched upward, thinking that would relieve the pressure, which it did not. He settled on leaning way forward and resting his forearms on top of his knees. Sweat beads formed on his face like watery freckles. His whole body felt prickly again. This was familiar as a bout of the miseries, but this time it seemed worse than ever before.

He widened his knees and heaved bile onto his boots—all acid rather than substance, since he had taken in only a cup of coffee for breakfast. He convulsed into a series of dry heaves, and at the same time felt warm shit running into his pants. All went dark for what must have been a short time, because when he was again aware, his position had not changed. He had not tumbled forward to the ground but was still sitting on the log.

After a few minutes he recovered enough to get to the river, where he took off his boots and pants, and rinsed them off in the current as best he could. Then he walked back into the sunny meadow, where he laid the pants out on a patch of blue wildflowers among the cheat grass. The boots were laid on their side. Medlin stretched out, naked from his shirt-tail down. The Colt, still in its holster, lay nearby. He rested his hand on the grip, placed his hat on his face, and fell asleep.

Had it not been for the bite on his upper thigh from a large, russet-colored ant—it felt like a hot poker—he might have slept longer. Awake and feeling slight relief, he stood up and put on his pants and boots, which by now had dried. Returning to the river he filled up his water bladder again. For a support he picked up a bleached-out stick that he found in a logjam in the shallows, and continued walking.

Medlin went on for another half mile or so. With the attack of the miseries, confidence in his body was gone—he knew he was unsteady. In places where there was need for stepping high, he could not do it, and on two occasions almost fell flat out onto the ground. The third time, he fell directly on the Colt, which jammed hard against his rib cage. Pulling himself up, he steadied himself with the help of the river stick. When he tried to regain normal breathing, he found he had a catch of pain before his lungs filled completely with air. If he took half breaths, the pain was not so bad, so that was how he continued on.

As was his way, he started thinking about his overall predicament. It was easy for him to conclude that it was grave. The monotonous walking allowed his mind to fill with an endless list of obstacles to be overcome to find any success from selling the three slaves at an auction in Mobile. Within a short while, his head filled with so much that he went into a kind of a swoon and his mind went blank. He stopped dead and was just about to black out where he stood, when the sound of a train whistle cut through the air—one long blast, two short. The sound of it forced new focus, and he revived enough to carry on.

He thought he had the direction of the train pinned down, and kept walking in hopes of coming across the tracks. Some complications in the terrain prevented him from taking a direct route. After a while, he climbed up an incline and came to an overlook. There it was below, the railroad track sitting atop its raised gravel bed. Tears welled up in his eyes. He cleared them with a balled-up hand.

From his elevated vantage point, he saw that a wide road meandered up to the railroad track, and then they both trailed off in parallel into the distance. Now that Medlin had seen the road and the track, he planned to get back to camp and the slaves, and then early next day to get them to the road, which they would follow into the nearest town to buy a few provisions and find out where they could get on a train to Mobile.

Medlin made it back to camp with great difficulty. His ribs were bruised on the left side, and his legs were greatly compromised. He took out his watch, and as he had guessed, it was close to five in the afternoon. He looked at Hutto sheepishly when he saw what an uncomfortable position he had left him in early that morning, when he had been so intent on scouting on his own. The area around the base of the tree showed signs that the big man had moved considerably trying to settle in an agreeable position. After taking just a minute to make himself a cup of coffee, he would free Hutto from the tree.

Jama and Celia had waded out to a huge slab of granite that took up nearly half the width of the river. They had sat down on it, enjoying the cool flow on their legs. The granite was worn smooth by water washing over it for thousands of years, if not longer. It was shallow, only ankle-deep, but it was swift. They were both taking delight in trying to catch an occasional leaf or twig that, flowing with the current, came within reach of their cupped hands.

Medlin took the kettle to the river to fill it. Jama acknowledged him with a wave of her hand, restrained by the leather strap that still tethered her to her mother. By the time the kettle was filled, Medlin noticed that Celia and Jama started to cup water in their hands and were playfully heaving it toward each other, laughing. Medlin had been so preoccupied since leaving home that he had thought little about his family. Seeing the mother and daughter together, he pictured his own daughter and Lydia. Never had he witnessed the kind of playful fun such as the slaves had between themselves.

Part of the smooth granite was covered by strands of algae that whipped in the current, cold and slick. Celia and Jama both tried to stand up to return to the bank, trying to steady themselves against the swift current of the water and the slick algae. They both giggled, while they played the game to get their balance.

From the kindling pile Medlin took enough small twigs to make a teepee, and blew life into it until a good fire caught hold. He reached for the kettle and was about to set it on the ring of stones rimming the flame when he looked toward the river, where Jama had just let out a scream. Her feet had gone out from under her. She was sliding fast toward the edge of the slab of granite and about to be carried over into a deep pool. The leather strap jerked taut, pulling Celia headfirst in the same path. One after the other they were swept down a slide of water. They both disappeared, but soon surfaced ten yards downstream. Celia came up first, and was in front of Jama.

Medlin ran to the river and down the path alongside to get ahead of the two, who had no control as they were swept along in the current's frenzy to find lower ground. For whatever reason, there was no sound from either of them after Jama's scream.

Hutto, alarmed by Jama's shriek, sprang to his feet and shimmied the shackles up the slender tree trunk as he shouted their names. He made a desperate attempt to free himself, but the green wood of the tree was impossible to break despite all the energy and strength he applied to it. His view of the river quickly ran out.

Meanwhile Medlin found that his path was obstructed by a high mound of loose shale. An old avalanche had deposited plant and gravel debris in a slide down to the river. He frantically tried to make his way across it, but had trouble gaining traction. He could see the two where the current raced around another huge angular chunk of granite.

Medlin tried to stay upright as he made long, jumping strides over the loose shale, digging in with the heels of his boots, heedless of his painful breathing. At the far edge of the slide, his left boot hit the top of a big rock partly buried in the crumbly ground. The abrupt stop sent his body forward into a headlong tumble.

The next thing he was aware of, when he opened his eyes, were two small birds fussing in high agitation just above his head. They flicked their tails and darted around in the dappled, dim light of this strange environment. He was watching them with some fascination until one dove down to his face. He could feel its claw graze his cheek, then felt a sharp punch near his ear—a peck. It was enough to make him aware of the sound of the river. He drew his legs up, and felt restrained by branches. At that moment he realized he was hemmed in under a big chinaberry bush.

With some difficulty, he rolled onto his side and pulled himself out into the open. His hat lay to the side of the chinaberry bush, and when he reached for it, he felt a throbbing where his forehead met his hairline. When he put a hand to the spot, he felt something wet mixed with grit. Examining his fingers, he saw they were covered with blood.

Then he looked over to the river, and the reason why he happened to be there started to come over him in a wave of terrible dread. He got to his feet with as much deliberation as he could manage, and staggered downriver. He saw nothing of Celia and Jama as he made his way half stumbling along the bank. The river opened out to a stretch where it was not running as fast. Here it was wider, and the surrounding landscape was flatter. The water had room to flow with not so much need for violence. Then across the river, just before where it slowed down, he saw something inconsistent—a foreign color. A dull orange, not the color of the river. The color of Jama's shirt.

He waded in. At first the water was manageable, only knee-deep, but he had to struggle through a deeper channel that brought the water up to his chest. The going was slow, with his boots slipping on the slick rocks below.

The bodies had been pushed to the far side, and caught in the one last swift flow before the river went limp into what would have been a pleasant piece of water. He stood beside Jama's body, and was transfixed for a few moments as the water flowed all around her, moving her arms and legs as if she were keeping her body afloat on her own.

Celia's body had slipped between two big rocks and was held under by the current—all but for the one hand that had risen to the surface still tethered to Jama at the wrist. The flow nudged it back and forth in a sort of greeting, like a wave. Medlin let out one sob, which he sucked in, and held his breath. He had work to do.

With Celia secure between the rocks, he untied the leather strap and cradled Jama in his arms, waded back across the river and placed her gently on the bank. Once he freed Celia's body, he held her by one wrist until he got to the shallows, where he carefully lifted her and placed her next to her daughter. He relayed their bodies one at a time, to a place well out of sight of Hutto, until he could bring them into camp and lay them side by side in a sort of solemn presentation. He went into camp, and spread out a blanket so that they would be off the ground, and then went back to bring the bodies, intending to lay them side by side on the blanket. All the while, Hutto stood silent, still shackled helplessly to the tree. When Medlin gently laid the girl out, her skirt was hung up at the waistband. He adjusted it to lay properly in place over her legs. Then he brought Celia from where he had relayed the bodies—near the bottom of the slide where he had fallen earlier. He laid her alongside the daughter and carefully adjusted her arms, straight down, against her body.

He took the key from his pocket and unlocked Hutto's shackles, which had peeled off a layer of skin around both wrists when the big man tried, in vain, to free himself from the tree. Medlin walked out of the camp and away, hoping not to hear the sobs, but he could hear Hutto moaning anyway. He walked into a tall stand of bunch grass and sat cross-legged on the ground. Covering his face with both hands, he leaned forward, so far that the brim of his hat touched the ground and tipped off. He picked it up, buried his face in the crown, and cried as a child cries.

At twilight, Medlin went back to the camp. Hutto was sitting on the ground with his knees pulled up to his chest. The sides of the blanket

were folded over the bodies. A fire was made and over the flame the kettle was resting on the ring of river rock. Medlin made coffee and handed
a cup to Hutto, then fried up a strip of lean and added some corn mush
to the drippings in the pan. The two men ate in silence and spent the rest
of the evening staring into the fire.

Morning came. Medlin took the camp shovel, looking for a place to
dig a grave. A short walk from the camp, he came on a large sweet gum
tree with several root sprouts close to the base. Beyond where he thought
there could be interference from roots, he made a clearing, slashing away
low vegetation with the spade.

He started to dig. After a while Hutto came up and relieved him of the
shovel, but the tool was short-handled, and the scoop was no bigger than
his hand. It was too awkward to make progress. The thing was fashioned
for making fire pits at the most, so Medlin took back over the digging. He
dug a knee-deep rectangular recess in the ground—marginal to be deep
enough to elude the wild dogs and pigs that would follow the scent of
decay. They lined the hole with the blanket, placed the bodies side by side,
folded the blanket in across them and returned the earth into the hole.
Two river rocks were placed at the head of the grave. Both men stood in
silence for several moments. The sun was at Hutto's back. His big shadow
covered one corner of the fresh soil. Then he moved to one side so that his
shadow covered most of the grave. Medlin took off his hat.

—Ashes to ashes, dust to dust.

He had heard it somewhere before. It wasn't much, but the only thing
that came to mind.

Medlin went back to the campsite and divided what little food was left.
He wrapped it up in two pieces of oilcloth. Then he put everything they
had in a pile. The kettle went in one direction, the pot in the other and
and on until he stuffed half into the duffle, then rolled the other things in
the tarp. He paused for a few seconds when he picked up the leather strap
that had tethered Jama to Celia, then continued with binding one parcel
together with the kettle and a cup interwoven with the strap. Hutto stood
watching as Medlin busied through the exercise.

Medlin reached into his small rucksack and pulled out a paper that
was folded in quarters. He took out his diary and pulled the short pencil

from its attached loop. Next, he unfolded the paper. At the top, it read *W. Poulnott & Associates, Dealer of Commodities and Auctioneer*, with a Charleston address. It was a deed to one male field hand, Hutto in name. Underneath, *One female field hand, name of Celia.* Then, *One female child, Jama.*

Across all three names, Medlin struck a line with his pencil and in the margin wrote, *FREE.* He put a date of *May 14, 1857,* and wrote his name, *William R. Medlin.* He refolded the paper and handed it to Hutto along with the duffle. Picking up the bundle in the tarp, he straightened up.

—Hutto, from this moment on, you're a free man. I'm nobody's Sir. I'm a cotton farmer, and I'm going to get back to it.

Medlin shouldered his bundle, picked up the rucksack, and walked out of the camp and into open country, heading in what he hoped was the likeliest direction to the next town with a train station so he could get back to Charleston and on home.

His ribs on the left side, where he had fallen on the Colt, still kept him at shallow breaths. If there was a grade and he got winded, he had to stop and stretch his chest upward to work it out. Too, his legs were not right. He had to coax them to do their job when all they wanted to do was to surrender in fatigue.

The idea to buy and sell slaves for school money for Caleb had turned out to be a disaster. With the woman and child drowned and Hutto freed, he would go straight back to Clio. The unspeakable tragedy of the day before weighed on him heavily, but knowing he was physically bad off, and with the challenge of traveling, he tried to concentrate on what must lie ahead. He thought that if only he could get to a town, he might make it back to Clio. After going for days in the direction of Mobile, now he reversed course and tried to calculate the best direction to go to get home. It was time to start thinking of striking out east instead of south.

Medlin walked for what seemed like hours before he found a road. By now he was parched. He had only the canteen and one bladder to drink from, but he had drained them both dry earlier in the day. Around five o'clock in the afternoon, he came across a shallow stream. There was a channel of clear water, not much wider than his palm, making its way through muddy sludge. Submerging the canteen only stirred up the mud, so he carefully used his tin cup to transfer the water.

The day's travel was painful and not very productive. With any number of stops to rest and recoup what little energy he had, he could credit the day with only a few miles. He made an early camp. Food was not appealing, but more a necessity, so he ate a handful of berries he had come across during the day, along with a knob of jerky—not a satisfying pair, but at that point, taste wasn't part of it.

He spread out the tarp at the base of a cottonwood, with a pile of leaves under one end for a pillow. He slept a good stretch of time, but his rest was fitful, full of strange out-of-sequence bits and pieces of a recurring dream—all around the idea he was somehow stranded in unfamiliar territory. It was dark as pitch when he opened his eyes, thinking he had been disturbed by the mournful call of an owl holding to a near branch, but there was no owl. The sound had come from himself. He was coiled up in a ball and rocking back and forth. He stretched out and looked upward toward the stars, thinking he would identify the constellations, to take his mind off his condition, but the canopy of leaves from the cottonwood blocked the sky. The tarp, pulled up around him like a cocoon, was of little comfort against the bone-chilling despair he felt on this warm night.

Eventually he fell back to sleep. Once again, any restful sleep was dashed by another fantastical dream where he, Hutto, Celia, and Jama were on a sailboat in what must have been a calm ocean. Land was not to be seen in any direction. A small skiff floated by a short distance away. In this boat were his two boys, Caleb and Daniel. He called out to them to come alongside, but they just waved and floated on. A strong storm came up and tossed the sailboat around in the rough sea. Celia and Jama fell out of the boat but grabbed hold of the antlers of a deer. It was one of a whole herd of deer that swam by with ease. Medlin tended the sails while Hutto tended the rudder.

———

IN THE MORNING A shaft of sunlight came through the leaves of the cottonwood. Medlin opened his eyes, but he had to adjust to what reality he was returning to. Sitting up he found he was now covered with a blanket—the blanket he had given to Hutto, the one remaining after Celia and Jama were wrapped in the other and buried. He had not made a fire, but there was one burning, with the kettle perched above it. Steam came from the spout. There was no one but himself around. He pulled himself over to the kettle and poured a cup of water tinted greenish brown. When it cooled down a little bit he smelled it. It was fragrant and had a welcome taste—a taste that can be only described as unique to this tea. He knew of it as sassafras, a drink his grandmother made for what ailed you.

Before setting out again, Medlin spent some time sipping the tea, and checking his condition to travel. The tea did him good. With the addition of the blanket and kettle, he rolled everything up in the tarp. His legs were wobbly when he first tested them, but after assembling his gear, he felt fair to middling, so he managed to get out on the road again. It was a new day. Now that he had completely abandoned the thought of traveling to Mobile, he had to concentrate on getting home to Clio.

For the first hour, he was able to make good time. At one point, a train whistle sounded in the distance, but how much distance he couldn't tell. He was counting on it that the road he was now walking would lead to a town with a station. Monotonous walking cleared his mind, leaving him free to worry, to dredge up regrets or whatever his mind wanted to light on at the time. He thought about Hutto, who had evidently passed through the camp last night. Was the big man now off following a plan for his new life as a free man? Medlin hoped Hutto would realize that just because he had a piece of paper to back up his new status, there would still be the potential for continued enslavement—papers might be easily destroyed. Hutto would have to be cautious. Would he make his way back to South Carolina? Most likely Hutto could not travel safely that far on foot. Would he be able to hitch a ride on a train? Medlin tried to get it off his mind, but it kept coming back—would Hutto be all right?

Ahead the road swung to the left. As Medlin approached the curve, he could hear the loud voice of someone in high agitation. Whoever the man was directing his anger toward made no reply. As Medlin rounded the curve, he came up on an old man who had an overall appearance that matched the dull yellow sand of the road. His boots, pants, and shirt were all of the hue that would make him almost invisible, had he not a grimy red bandana around his neck. The pallor of his skin was dull like the rest of him and reminded Medlin of someone recently deceased.

With one hand, he tugged at the harness of a swayback draft, while the other hand gripped his slouch hat, which looked to be the tool used for discipline. As Medlin approached, the old man went into another tirade over the horse's stubbornness. Seems the animal had been part of a two-team used in the field, but when one horse died, and this one was relegated to the wagon, it got ornery and developed a mind of its own. The old man hit a few licks at the horse's head, and it retaliated with a couple of kicks. On the second kick, its heels caught the seat of the buckboard, which went flying. Then the old man went at it again in a whirling motion like a windmill.

Medlin was about to restrain the stranger, who looked as if he had been overtaken by a fit. But suddenly, the angry old man stopped cold and stared hard at something over Medlin's shoulder. Hutto had just come around the bend, stopping twenty paces away. He stood silent, with the duffle slung over his shoulder. The old man left the horse and reached for his rifle, which was on the floor of the wagon. Medlin put his hand on the barrel and said that he knew the man. He told of his being free, at which the old man moved the barrel around Medlin's hand, aiming it right at Hutto.

—There ain't no free niggers.

Medlin came up on the barrel and strong-armed it away from the old man.

—I'll give you fifteen dollars for your rig.

The old man said he'd take it. In that split second, he decided he didn't want to get into it with these two strangers.

Medlin retrieved the wooden seat, lined up the nails with the nail holes, and with the rifle butt tamped it back in place. He handed the rifle back to the old man, fished fifteen dollars out of his pouch, and threw his bundle and the rucksack into the back of the wagon. While he was climbing up onto the driver's seat, Hutto rushed up and jumped into the bed of the wagon, his legs hanging out the back, almost touching the ground.

11

GIL HAD DRINKS WITH CHIP and a visiting fellow researcher from the University of Florida to discuss a joint project involving Black Seminoles, descendants of the many runaway African slaves who found refuge with the Seminole Nation. With the Indian Removal Act of 1830, Andrew Jackson set about removing the Florida Seminoles—including the Black Seminoles—to Oklahoma, along with the rest of the Southeastern Indian nations. But after the 1930s, the Seminole Nation repeatedly sought to exclude Black Seminoles, to prevent them from sharing in federally awarded benefits. Then in 2000, the tribe won a big forty-six-million-dollar judgment against the United States, as compensation for the confiscation of their land in Florida that was established by the 1823 Treaty of Moultrie Creek. The Black Seminoles, in turn, sued the Seminole Nation over this settlement. The controversy was a hot topic for the university seminar, as the lawsuit was ongoing.

Chip had organized the meeting with Gil and the Florida colleague to divide the workload. The Caroliniana would present an introductory paper on the origin of Black Seminoles as slave runaways from plantations in South Carolina and Georgia, who took refuge with the Florida tribe of Seminoles. The U of F people would pick up the story when the fugitive slaves arrived in Florida, and describe the Seminole culture once there was blending into one tribe.

After an early dinner in the university executive dining room, Gil went back to the Caroliniana to retrieve material she had pulled relating to the Seminole project. She planned on propping herself up on her couch with a cold Michelob Ultra, to study a resource book from Special Collections, *Maroons: A History of Florida's Black Seminoles*. She would start right in.

When she walked out onto the Horseshoe, the evening air was light on humidity after an earlier rain. She was walking toward the State House grounds on her way to the parking garage, when at precisely seven thirty the cast-iron pole lanterns blinked a few times and came on in full.

Deep in thought about her Black Seminole project, Gil found her concentration interrupted when she came parallel to the State House steps, flooded in harsh television camera lighting. On the landing, midway up the granite steps, was the towering figure of Reverend Joe Pearl, speaking into a mic held by a local news anchor. Gil remarked to herself that with his ramrod posture and lacquered black hair, Joe bore a striking likeness to a cigar store Indian.

Just as Gil passed the steps, the TV camera lights abruptly went off, and the tranquility of the evening sky was restored. As she began to cross Gervais, the camera crew was already loading their equipment into a van, double-parked on the busy street. They moved quickly—likely trying to make it back to the station in time to prep their footage for the ten o'clock news.

Gil made a quick stop into Starbucks to pick up a slice of banana nut bread to satisfy her sweet tooth—not at all bothered by her intention to wash it down with a cold beer at home. It would be a strange combination for most people but had long been a guilty pleasure for Gil.

Navigating around the wooden barrier at the exit of the parking garage, Gil as usual took the quickest route, past the Crown Vic, and headed toward the steps to the fifth floor for the hike to her car. She was stopping at the first step to adjust the shoulder strap of her briefcase, when she heard behind her the gritty sound of footsteps on concrete. Someone was approaching her quickly. Even before the hand gripped her shoulder and swung her around, she felt the heavy weight of helplessness come over her. She almost lost her balance, and her briefcase slipped to the pavement.

Standing before her was a straggly looking young man, mid-twenties, with a tangle of blond hair. Even though he was close, he shouted at her in an uneven, nervous voice.

—Give me your money!

In a daze, she didn't respond instantly. He showed her he had a knife. It was not the size of a hunting knife, but certainly bigger than an innocent pocketknife. In fact, it was an open switchblade. She slowly knelt down to her briefcase to retrieve the File-a-Flex that held her money. Besides a few dollars, the worn leather case bulged with credit cards and a life's worth of contacts, both personal and professional. Instinctively, she knew she could not just surrender the whole thing, so, still in a crouch, she pulled out all the money she had. Her hand shook so badly that bills fell from her grasp to the concrete.

She was scooping up the scattered bills when she heard a muffled gasp. Looking up from her low position, she saw a large dark hand engulfing the boy's neck. The looming figure behind the blond youth almost entirely blocked the light from the fluorescent fixture above. About the only thing catching any light was the large pearl ring on the hand gripping the boy's neck. Gil recognized the owner of the Crown Vic, Reverend Joe Pearl Joy.

Gil fumbled for her cell phone to call the police, but her rescuer said in a calm, steady voice that he had another idea.

—Wait. I'm thinking of an idea of a higher calling. Here we have a chance to make this young man a disciple of God. Justice will be better served if he spreads the Good Word in the streets to others who have lost their way.

With one hand still around the youth's neck, the Reverend pulled him up so only his toes touched the ground. With his other hand, he loosened the boy's grip on the knife and took it in his own hand.

The young man's face was distorted, his eyes wide and wild in panic. His breathing was labored, the intake of air almost a squeak from the constriction of his air passageway. The Reverend's large face was pressed in close to the boy's ear. He spoke, almost in a whisper.

—Go you into the streets as a missionary of God Almighty.

Then, remembering his old wrestling days, he slowly and carefully cut into the center of the boy's forehead, making a Christian cross—as large as possible—from his hairline to his brow. The ex-wrestler had learned in the ring that a hidden razor blade, applied to the thin skin of the forehead, would not be painful, but would make it bleed like a stuck pig and create quite a show. Blood ran down freely into the mugger's eyes and open mouth, and it looked as though he had been bludgeoned to within an inch of his life.

The Reverend released his grip. The youth dropped to the concrete in a heap, then struggled to get to his feet. Unsteady, he ran out into the street as the Reverend yelled after him.

—Go spread the Word!

Then he let out a big laugh. Car horns broke through the quiet night, indicating that the boy had probably run into the path of traffic.

With his middle finger, the Reverend pressed the safety catch on the knife, and with his thumb expertly eased the blade back into the closed position in the slot in the handle—all in one, efficient motion. The knife went into his pocket. When he pulled his hand out, he extended it to Gil.

—My name's Joe. What's yours?

The handshake was hearty and natural, as though nothing had just happened. Gil, standing now, had difficulty getting out her name. She hardly recognized her own voice when she finally forced it from her throat.

—Gillian Culkin.

Gil gave her full name, instinctively.

Joe insisted on walking with her up the four flights of stairs to her car. He opened her car door. As she sat behind the wheel, looking dazed, Joe asked if she could use a drink. Without hesitation she said yes, she sure could use a drink. She noticed her hands were shaking. They decided on driving to the nearby Walmart, where she would leave her car and ride in the Vic to a place Joe promised would fix her up.

After leaving Gil's car, they drove about three miles into an area unfamiliar to Gil. However, the scene was recognizable—a neighborhood in transition. It was like so many places with modest houses previously lived in by older Black people until the recent influx of White thirty-some-things, who bought in on the cheap and didn't mind putting in the sweat equity and funds to bring an old house around to where it was a little gem.

There had been recent media coverage about gentrification, about the fate of established Black in-town neighborhoods. Property values had escalated, and rents and taxes had gone way up. Low-income Black people who couldn't afford the taxes, or just couldn't resist cashing in, sold and moved on. Where did they move to? No one seemed to know or care.

After a couple of blocks, the gentrifying residential area opened into a commercial district that must have been the hub of activity in the neighborhood back in its day. There was a connected chain of enterprises—an old-school hardware store, a barber shop, a pizza joint and an antique store—side by side in a two-story red brick building.

Joe pulled into one of a half dozen parking spaces in front of the only freestanding structure, a one-story, cinderblock building that looked of no particular pedigree. It was painted dark brown. Across the front, in turquoise, was a stylized graphic, positioned on a forty-five-degree angle, of a man playing a piano wearing a porkpie hat. In one of the few windows was a neon sign in big red letters saying *Chester's*, and below, in smaller letters, *Two Times*.

They entered the dimly lit place that anybody would call the friendly neighborhood bar. Of what little light existed, most came from backlit panels of magenta-colored plexiglass behind rows of liquor bottles on glass shelves in back of the long wooden bar. The remaining weak light came from wall-mounted fixtures over each of the half dozen booths of red faux-leather bench seats with butcher-block tables.

Joe shouted a greeting to an older man wearing a hat with a narrow, turned-up brim, who was drying glasses with a bar towel. Joe called him Ches. The man shot back.

—Hey, JP, that ain't Nikki you got there.

—How many times do I have to tell you? That's over a long time ago!

—You want the usual?

—Yeah. And bring the lady the same poison. She could use it. She's just had an encounter of the knife kind.

Chester brought two tumblers of a brown liquor over rocks.

—Now why would anybody want to terrorize this nice lady? Maybe Nikki, but not this lovely thing.

—I told you, we can't bring that woman up again.

—Okay, okay, JP.

Chester headed over to where three men were readying instruments to play music, although Gil and Joe were the only patrons. The room was otherwise empty.

Gil was a beer drinker, but whatever Ches had served her, it had done its job on her nerves after two short sips.

Joe was not coy. He didn't mind revealing that she had long before come across his radar.

—Miss Gillian, how come you walk past the State House twice a day?

She was taken aback that he had noticed her pattern. She wondered if Joe had an agenda and put her antenna up to test if he was coming on to her. She answered him rather stiffly.

—I do research for the Caroliniana Library in Southern History and Culture.

—Culture, now that's a wide term. Boil that down for me.

—Well, I study patterns of human behavior and beliefs as influenced by historical events, specifically in South Carolina.

—Let me bring up some recent history. Did the university assign your parking spot to me?

Gil was looking down at her drink, avoiding eye contact, but she quickly looked up as soon as he mentioned the parking space. Joe had an amused look on his face and seemed happy he got a rise out of her.

—How did you know?

—I caught you stink-eyeing my car one day.

Joe had his own way of laughing. After he saw he had caught Gil off guard he tilted his head down and closed his eyes, his wide shoulders rising and falling, punctuating each measure of the laugh. Gil was now laughing at herself.

—Don't be mean. I've been parking in that ground-floor spot for years. I don't take well to change.

—You'll be happy to know, I'll be outta there soon. I'm involved with the demonstration. The legislature can't hold out about taking down that flag much longer.

At the moment, Gil was not paying attention, did not answer, because she was distracted by the amber-colored drink and wondering why she had so long resisted hard liquor over beer. She knew so little of liquor. She had no idea if what she was drinking was bourbon, scotch, or whiskey. She asked what it was. Joe verbally danced around, not giving her a straight answer, so she asked Chester, who had gotten up from the piano to check on them. He walked over with a bottle that had old-style lettering spelling out *Rebel Yell, Small Batch Rye.*

—You mean to tell me the Reverend Joe Pearl Joy drinks something called Rebel Yell? I can't wait to march up there to the State House tomorrow and announce for all to hear that you drink something called Rebel Yell.

Chester said that he had to hide it under the bar out of sight because no self-respecting Black dude would drink anything with such a name. Joe looked a little sheepish, but then they all had a good laugh.

Joe went to a more serious demeanor.

—Yes, you'll be able to go back to parking in your spot again because the Vic will be long gone.

—When I walk past the State House, you always look so in the thick of it. This has to have changed your life in some ways. Are you going to be able to just go back to normal after this is over?

—The demonstration has definitely changed my life. It's made me a more serious man. I've never been an activist, but of course being Black you can't avoid the glaring disparities everywhere and you know things have to change. When the NAACP made me their spokesman—to handle the press and all—I wasn't naïve or vain enough to think they picked me because of anything but my curb appeal—from my years with the TV show and before that in wrestling. I took it on because this is a big stage. The showman in me couldn't resist. And way deep down I felt a sense of responsibility and saw this flag thing as a real opportunity to contribute to my people. But then when I got up in front of the press and saw them taking notes for a news story to be printed or aired, I started to realize I couldn't just run off from the mouth—I've had to start thinking seriously what this is all about and how I can most effectively tell the story. I gotta tell you, when you see yourself on the national news and you get that you're the guy—you're the face and what's coming outta that face is the official truth as it now stands—it's scary. Gil, you say you're professionally involved with the study of human behavior and the influences of historical events—it sounds like you think you can get at the root of why things work out the way they do. That's amazing. But I wonder if anything can really be explained . . .

His voice trailed off and Gil felt she had to say something, although for the first time she hesitated to say that things can be fully explained by history.

—I'm not sure. In academia you get to study and learn a lot, and you can understand some things about how some things happened, but for example nothing I ever learned in a book could teach me what it's like to walk in your shoes. I can't imagine what it's like for a Black person to go into a room and feel the need to size everyone up as to their possible prejudices. So in complete honesty, I can never hope to understand what it's like to be Black, no matter how much I study—far from it. I can sympathize, but I doubt if you want sympathy. I can only try to help make a better society, to do what's right. But—and this just amazes me now—I never felt the need for things to change much before this Confederate flag issue. Not only can I say I, too, have never been an activist—in the beginning I really didn't see what all the fuss was about. When it went national and seemed to turn into a trial of the South, I took my head out of the sand. The press quickly saw an opportunity to make it about the extremes—the tattooed radical White supremacists running around waving Confederate flags sure made for eye-popping visuals shown across the country. That led me to thinking about the South and most especially to ask myself a couple of questions: How were my own ancestors to blame for holding the Black race down? And how am I myself to blame today?

—It seems both of us are working at understanding, but we're coming at it from different angles—you're looking at the history. I'm more in the present, in the trenches. I accept the past is present, but I've got to motivate people to make change now!

—I absolutely see where you're coming from, but I can't get away from trying to understand what brought us here to the present day. It's the academic in me that wants to create the outline with bullet points.

—Okay, what's your Roman numeral one?

—I hate to be so obvious, but I'd have to start with the promise that "all men are created equal," and that thereafter, extraordinary efforts went into creating controls—in both law and custom—to assure Black people would remain in forced labor, as property. There's been a centuries-long campaign to promote the notion that Blacks are not equal, and that they're innately inferior to Whites. And, I think it's completely outrageous that Blacks are still having to fight against that false image!

Gil took a deep breath. Above all she did not want Joe to misunderstand what she was trying to say. It was certainly not that she herself consciously believed Black people were in any way inferior. She knew that the idea of inferiority was just an idea—a false idea—that had been a powerful historical force. At the same time she realized that she and her kin were products of the culture where Black people were seen as "less than," and she regretted the fact. She continued talking.

—Damn, as I say that, you just have to cringe at the extent powerful men will go to get the world jerked around to benefit them!

—Yeah, I think you're right. At the core is a demand for simple equality or equity. To a White man who asks, "What do Blacks want anyway?" the Black man's answer is, "The same damn thing you want!"

—A simple enough demand, yes, but the road from the first Africans in Jamestown to now is full of contradictions, complexity, and of course hypocrisy. Plenty of hypocrisy.

—Yeah, but I don't have the time to give a history lesson! I have to tap into the hot buttons of the now.

Gil chuckled wryly.

—To be limited to two minutes on air to make a point would frustrate the hell out of me. As a historian I've been taught how to connect the dots by evaluating the influences that evoke human responses in one way or another, and that takes time. Maybe I rely on history too much to find answers to understand race, but I like to put events in the context of the time in which they happen. To me, it's been helpful to learn what was popular thought way back when.

—What do you mean?

—A good example would be how popular literature offers insight into the characterization of Black people, how imagery promoted the idea of inferiority. Two extraordinarily successful books influenced how readers thought about "Black character"—*Uncle Tom's Cabin* and *Gone with the Wind*. In both bestsellers, mischaracterization of the Negro as a simpleton perpetuated—perhaps unconsciously—the notion of inferiority. Even when intended to be sympathetic toward the Black race, the portrayal was a mischaracterization. Harriet Beecher Stowe wrote *Uncle Tom's Cabin*, the sentimental story of a character who was subservient, childlike, innocent—Uncle Tom. He, along with rambunctious pickaninnies and the mischievous Topsy, reached a tremendous audience and carried on the demeaning image of the Negro, despite the author's intention, which was to highlight mistreatment. In 1852 *Uncle Tom's Cabin* was outsold only by the Bible! So powerful was its message for Abolition that many say it laid the groundwork for the Civil War. Nevertheless, readers were shown a series of characters who very clearly were depicted as "inferior" to Whites. Then *Gone with the Wind* told a story of loyalty, faithfulness, and devotion between slaves and slaveholders, using sentimental characters—childlike scatterbrains and kindly, gentle old darkies. Both books were wildly successful. Of course no one should see them as factual portrayals, but they tell us about the authors and the population for whom they were written when they were written. Unfortunately, images of the Negro as trifle'n and shallow-minded were presented in both books, and the residue still hangs on in the minds of some Whites.

—Gil, I have to make a confession. When I was in the wrestling business, my promo guys said I should take on the persona of a King Kong. Now I'm very ashamed to say I went along with it. I took to coming in the ring pounding my chest. When I got a little wiser and became truly aware of how I'd played "Black man as ape," I was mad at myself for not being outraged right off and refusing to play that part. Then I really started to pay more attention to the subtleties of the put-downs that are all around.

—Yes, it's the subtleties just accepted out of hand that are so silently harmful. And no matter how unconscious somebody might be about their attitude, which is formed by the culture they live in, there is only one word for them if they feel superior to another race—supremacist. There's no pretty way to put it. As a White person, I'm really startled to think of a "supremacist" as somebody other than a rough, hard-looking character waving a Confederate flag. In a way my own mother can be a "supremacist." I can't believe I just said that, but I know it's true. And me? I'm struggling trying to understand these cultural influences and still do what's right.

With a pang, Gil thought of the trainer who had applied for a job at her gym.

—Since we're in a confessional mood here, my mother had a rough time, and she did some not-so-mom things when I was growing up, but I long ago gave her a pass when I took account of her upbringing. Not that I'm all that anxious to say there's justification for your mother's "supremacist" attitude, but you may want to think about her past as it got her to that place.

—Now, if you're talking about influences of the past on the present, that's where I live! I absolutely agree with you about trying to look at behavior through the eyes of those who lived it. As one of my professors used to say, "History is human." He explained that people through history were reacting to influences of *their* present—what we now call the *past*. He tried to pound into our heads that people in the past didn't know how things would turn out. They didn't have the advantage of foreseeing what effects their decisions would have on the future. When folks look back to this time in Columbia in the year 2000—at what they will call *back then*—I would give anything to hear what they say. I think I know one thing and that is, answers will be found by understanding the times and what made people act the way they did.

Joe looked interested, so Gil went on.

—Once I started getting immersed in the history of this state, it became clear that practically everything in South Carolina relates to the issue of race, how race comes into play. By the time civil rights was being fought in the streets in the fifties and sixties, there were eye-popping news-reels, which had a great deal to do with changing minds, when everything in the visual media was out there for all to see. However, before that, hundreds of years of slavery had to be told by somebody's written word—someone's account and opinion of events. Almost all these writers were White men. Thank goodness, research continues to sharpen the accuracy of what was written and tell a fuller story. I hope this doesn't bore you because God knows I can run on and on about this stuff! I'm trying to make sense out of it as we talk about it, but generally I have to have some conviction about what I'm saying before I throw it out there to anyone who'll listen.

—Yes, like I was saying before, when I started seeing reporters writing down whatever I said, I knew I'd better be clear about my convictions and feel very confident about what I say. I represent folks who've been fighting for Black causes since way before Martin Luther King and young people who'll carry on long after the flag's gone. It's a huge responsibility, and I feel it. I couldn't forgive myself if I didn't do my absolute best.

—I've been born and raised in South Carolina, like you—but different of course. And I have a confession to make. Until now it's always been easy for me to do what I do—research, which often involves race—and feel totally dispassionate about it because I didn't think it touched me personally. But when the flag issue morphed into an all-out assault on Southerners, it forced me into alien territory. I've begun to notice the racial connotations of most everything I come in contact with just in my daily life. For the first time, I'm getting a glimpse of what Blacks have to deal with—and how racism permeates the Southern and indeed the whole American landscape.

—Yes, it's all around. For instance, just my own size cuts both ways. Whites feel they better not mess with me, and at the same time it escalates the fear that so many Whites feel toward Black people in general. I have to be sure to be friendly where some White lady may think she's isolated with this big Black guy, where she feels if she has to call for help no one will hear her. And of course White people are always pulling their possessions like a purse or laptop in closer if a Black dude is passing by. I might not look like the type that would be offended, but it hurts my feelings. What they don't realize is that I would be quick to help if there was a need. Once I saved a little kid from being hit by a car. The mother didn't even thank me. Instead, she pulled a five-dollar bill out of her purse. What?! She didn't see me as a human being who acted on a human instinct?

Joe sounded mad just remembering the scene, but then he changed his tone.

—Gil, since you're White, you've had the luxury to walk around the struggles of Black people. I commend you for saying right out that for the first time in your life you have taken notice of racism today. You've hinted that you realize that racism isn't just a Black problem, and that if you're part of these United States, you must be part of the solution. But remember, if you grew up Black, all your life you would've faced affronts like these.

—Yes, now I've taken my head out of the sand, I have to say that finally I do see that racism is still very much alive and well in this country. We all go around in our own little worlds thinking a certain way—reinforced by our friends and colleagues—that reality is just as we see it. Then the flag comes along and we find out that plenty of people don't share our same reality. It's a shocker to find out the divide's as wide as it is. I'd say a big part of the problem is because there's so little familiarity between the races. As recent as my mother's day—she had almost no contact with Blacks her whole life. She tells me that a whole decade after *Brown v. Board* supposedly ended school segregation, she had only one Black classmate, and that wasn't until her senior year. Not wanting trouble, the school principal spread the word that he was "Hawaiian." And there have been no Blacks in her social circle. As for me, it's about the same. There were a few Black kids in school of course, but people seemed to stay pretty much to themselves. As much as we all, both races, talk about integration into a mixed society, there seems to be a natural tendency to stay with your own kind. Blacks and Whites seem to gravitate to different restaurants, churches, clubs, bars, even sporting events. Not having occasion for open conversation about race—or anything else—only perpetuates the problem. And anyway, people are so anxious about offending, it's just safer to not bring it up. I'm embarrassed to say it, but I've never had a talk like this with a Black person before.

—Yeah, I know what you mean about separation. The whole time

I was growing up, it was beat into my head that all White people want to keep you down—nothing good can come from Whites in your life. That's strong stuff that sticks until you have some positive experience that gets you to thinking another way. I bought it until I came into the sights of a White lady when I was seventeen. She had a huge influence over my life, which makes it all the more confusing when I have to deal with a bunch of rednecks every day at the State House.

—Joe, I've come to this issue by way of geography—the South. I want to understand how the South got to such a place of divide between the races and, regarding my family, what role they've played.

—But my mission's different. As I said, my focus is more on the present. Equality *now* is what it's all about for me!

—You know, everyone who's ever had anything to do with race has been put in front of a camera over this flag thing. The other day I heard an interview with Andy Young, who was a close confidant of King, congressman from Georgia, ambassador to the UN, and mayor of Atlanta—so he knows a thing or two. Well, he shared something to think about. In this TV interview on NBC's *Meet the Press* he said—and I have to paraphrase—he felt sorry for the White supremacists who are at the lowest rung of the economic ladder, the poorest of the poor. I thought, has this man lost his mind? He continued, saying he felt sorry for these White men who were seeing advances made by Blacks while they experienced no progress in their own lives. He was talking about the extreme of the haters, generalizing, but there's truth to it. There are so many towns where the mill shut down or where men are still in the coal mines getting black lung. Have you ever heard of a White supremacist from a progressive environment? No. For the most part they're from the small, dried-up towns where the chance of the good life has passed them by. Lyndon Johnson may have hit the nail on the head when he said, "If you can convince the lowest White man he's better than the best Colored man," there's some contentment in it for him. Now his world is changing and he has less chance to look down on someone else. Blacks are more than ever getting a chance to share the catbird seat, and the Confederate flag wavers see it and resent it.

—I never would've thought of it that way, but it does seem to make sense. Still, it's hard to have any empathy for people who have implied or told you to your face, you're no good. And I'm not just talking about these small-town yahoos. Let's keep in mind there are haters walking around in tailored suits, too. There are plenty of crackers in the State House. But, Gil, what's the catbird seat?

—You haven't heard that old Southern expression? The catbird, kin to the mockingbird, gets its name from being able to mimic the meow of a cat. But the saying comes from the fact that the catbird likes to sing from the top of the tree, so to be in the catbird seat means you have the advantage of being at the top. It's like sitting pretty.

—So are you saying it's a struggle between Whites and Blacks to be on top?

—It's some Whites' fear of having to share the top or give up any part of their superiority. Whites have worked hard to keep the Black man in an inferior position, beneath them. After Emancipation, during Reconstruction, Blacks gained some control in elected offices, which White supremacists wholeheartedly resented. Through intimidation by the KKK and Jim Crow laws, any gains were quickly snatched back.

—Gil, it's pretty amazing that after Black folks have been fighting for equality for so many years, it's the Confederate flag, of all things, that brings such a big issue out in the open. This nonsense about the flag representing pride is just a big smoke screen! Insisting the Civil War was fought not over slavery but over states' rights is just plain wrong! Really, is it so hard to understand? All the Confederate states wanted the right to have slaves. Everything else—pride, standing up for states' rights—is trying to put an innocent slant on the Confederacy, which was willing to go to war to keep slaves.

—But, Joe, remember that plenty of Southerners have ancestors who fought in the War, so they might feel they have a stake in the Confederate flag. However, there's a lot they don't know or understand. It's complicated. The War was spurred on by men of influence—mostly big planters getting rich on cotton or others living on cotton, like traders and shippers. They were the ones who stood to lose everything without slavery. If you look at how many plantation owners actually had large slave holdings, there were only about three hundred in all the Southern states. These were the powerful movers and shakers running politics. They were the ones ginning up the dirt farmers and the sons of dirt farmers to go to war, inspiring them to fight. For the most part, the foot soldiers owned no slaves. It was drummed into them that the North was out to change every aspect of the Southern way of life, so they fought out of Southern pride, not specifically about defending slavery. I'm no scholar regarding the Civil War, but to me, what the War was about—pride or slavery—depended on your point of view, whether you were a rank-and-file soldier or one of the planter class. Over the years I've had to read plenty of Confederate soldiers' letters home. I've never read one that mentioned fighting to preserve slavery. The letters were all about missing home, or missing their mother's cooking, or longing for their sweetie. I think the issue of pride is tied up with the romanticism and sentimentality that the pro-flag people attach to the notion that someone is willing to die for a cause. Sadly, especially when you consider over two hundred and fifty thousand Confederate casualties, the War was set in motion to preserve the wealth of a very few. But in the end, it was about both slavery and pride.

—Damn, Gil. What do I do with that? What you're saying now is confusing.

—Well, welcome to my world. I do agree with you, what the War was fought over seems to have little to do with going forward.

Joe sat up and leaned in. He reached into his breast pocket and pulled out a small notepad that had a loop holding a short pen and wrote, *Pride or prejudice—little to do with going forward.*

—So where *do* we go from here? For my folks on the Black side of the demonstration, their world is about today. For the most of them, their view is limited to things like job opportunities, the struggle to get decent health care, cops stopping them for no other reason than that they're Black and maybe look like they're up to something. That's the story I've got to get a handle on. As for pride or prejudice, that's way down on the list of concerns. Discrimination is what my people are concerned about—every day. They see White women shifting their purse around when a brother is about to pass. They watch Black women wearily getting off of public buses in the dark after cleaning some White woman's floors. But if this time the discussion starts with the flag—if that's what has people talking, so be it. Do Black folks want to have to see the Confederate flag on top of a tax-funded institution where our state laws come out of? No, of course they don't! It's just another slap in our face! It's just another eyeful of a bunch of White folks lining up against us! Sometimes it's more subtle, but with the flag there's no ambiguity. Heritage or White supremacy, they feel a kinship with that flag and are demonstrating for it. You hear people defending the flag, saying it doesn't represent hate at all. They say they want to see the flag because they're proud that their great-grandpappy fought in the War with honor under that flag. I've never been there, but I doubt that in Germany anyone would dare fly a Nazi flag because old Gramps was a proud member of the SS!

—I've wondered about that parallel myself. There doesn't seem to be open, public debate over the hate so great that millions of people were gassed, for God's sake. I know that old-timers who served over there—saw the horrors of war, which they still carry with them—hate the people they fought against, but they're dying off. And their descendants don't seem to be passing up the Mercedes if they can afford it. But again, I have to think of my own ancestors in all this. One of the reasons I'm confused is that I can't avoid knowing my own kin—who I think of as decent people—have somehow contributed to where we are now. On top of everything, Northerners seem to think Southerners have some hate gene, a wired-in outright hatred for Black people. There's this demonization of the South I need to make some sense of. You know, Malcolm X's family was terrorized by the Ku Klux Klan in Omaha, Nebraska, and his father was murdered by White supremacists in Michigan. That's not the South!

Now, Joe sank back into the banquette, comfortable in thinking that they could talk openly. He had been feeling a little wary, because discussing race could make tempers flare.

—I know a lot of Whites think Blacks want things given them by Big Daddy, the US government—that we live in a culture where everyone has perfected ways to ride a scam to free money giveaways. There's some of that, but it's nowhere near as common as most White people like to think. I imagine there are a whole lot of deadbeat Whites on the government tit. However, the vast majority of people, Black or White, just want to work and provide for their families. None of these folks want to sit on their ass, but damn, anyone with dark skin in America has to climb out of such a deep hole!

Again Gil pictured the young man who wanted a job at her gym. She didn't bring him up to Joe, because the more she thought about it, the more she was mortified and ashamed. After a moment, Joe went on.

—Blacks might be able to be served in any restaurant now, but few have made it to the table in boardrooms. On top of everything, look at education! What elementary or high school curriculum includes an honest portrayal of Black history? None, would be my guess. There's plenty of material about the colonists fighting the English for independence, and then just a pass-by on the Civil War. Slavery, maybe the most consequential issue of American history, never gets just treatment. It gets passed over almost like it never happened. Black history is erased, and we continue to live with discrimination and racism every day!

As Joe was going on about the lack of valid Black history in schools, Gil was still thinking about the Black trainer. Until the Confederate flag issue put a spotlight on the realities of racism, she would never have agreed with Joe that racism was still taking a heavy toll on Black people, continually wearing down self-esteem and causing such enormous frustration. She was upset that she had been so concerned about the probable discomfort of the clientele at the gym with a Black trainer in their midst. Discomfort, for God's sake! She hoped Joe didn't detect the distraction in her eyes, but Joe was still talking, and he seemed to be getting pretty worked up.

—Yeah! And then that word *reparations* keeps coming up. It scares some Whites, and I can see why. People look at it as nothing but a big cash handout. No, that's not it at all! It's a way to dismantle the roadblocks thrown up against Black people from day one to keep us down and poor! Instead of cash to individual descendants of slaves, there should be money so we have equal opportunity to a good education and jobs. Good God, it's the same argument made way back in 1964, when everybody thought it was the end of segregation. Here it is 2000 and there are still all-Black schools in Columbia, not because of legal segregation, but now because of White flight to private schools or the White suburbs. That leaves underfunded public schools full of Black kids. And the problem isn't the Black kids; it's that the schools are so underfunded. With adequate resources Black folks do just fine, segregated or not.

—Yes, that's something the *Brown v. Board* ruling didn't foresee.

—You bet. And let me make a point here. Whites tend to throw up what they think is a utopian world where any kid from the ghetto can get scholarships and go as far as they want with drive and hard work. But, for one thing, the special person with uncommon drive and ability is rare anywhere. Let's face it, most of the population is made up of average Joes and Janes. And then if you're Black you're being told you're inferior all your life. We might not be told to our face that we don't cut it, but it's impossible not to absorb exactly that from our environment—crap schools, parents who long ago accepted the reality of poverty, a vast public that has been brought up on—and has bought into—the myth of Black inferiority, a stereotype of underachievement. Gil, you wonder about the bad rap the South has to fight against. But don't you think it's deserved? How about lynching, the KKK, cross-burning—all Southern inventions. Yes, I have a problem with all of it! Any thinking human being would be repulsed by all the stuff that's been heaped on Black people from the beginning of this country, and, in many ways, continues today. The hate can't be explained away or, God forbid, justified, though I'm sure there are plenty of people who've written books thinking they can explain away hate!

—But, Joe, hate isn't the whole story. I'm working on a project right now at the Caroliniana, transcribing the diary of a South Carolina cotton farmer, what they call a dirt farmer. He was living in the time of slavery and, Joe, he clearly was no hater.

—Yeah, okay, but let's get back to today, the year 2000. The only thing that keeps me plugging along are those young people at the State House. Most of the older folks have been beat down and see no sense in coming out. The group I fall into, the mid-age Blacks, are up to our eyeballs in frustration and are hanging on because we see in the young ones the glimmer of hope that things will change. I'm scared for the kids, though. If they, too, start to see the futility and get what I call the dead eyes, they're doomed.

—Joe, I think this is where you can help the most. You can be the one to keep the heat on. The White resistance, the Dixie flag wavers, have to see that you're not going to back off. Many Whites think you want to take over—that Blacks are demanding not only equality but beyond, that they want superiority or domination over Whites. That Blacks with power will treat Whites the way Whites have treated them, and they're afraid. Remember the catbird? I really do think that some Whites are desperately afraid they're going to lose their position at the top of the tree—and they're unwilling to share.

—Well, dammit, they're going to have to share!

—Yes you're right. But as I see it, hollow rhetoric shouted from both sides is only going to make things worse. That said, I realize that sheer outrage has its place. Some movements started with the loud and mad—those who chained themselves to immovable objects, willing to be hauled off to jail. When the feminist movement first started in the sixties, the bra burners were on the front lines and grabbed attention. It took a while before they crafted a message that was not so angry and presented it in a way that the opposition could open up to listening. Same thing with the gay and lesbian movement. The first wave of protestors came off as pretty hard, but then they settled down to a presentation more conducive to understanding and change. I think you sell yourself short when you say the NAACP tapped you only because you're a public figure. I think they chose you as their front man because they feel confident that you're the right person to present a clear message about the necessity for change now.

Joe was not one to take such a compliment easily. To lighten the situation, he called out to Chester in a mocking way to come top off Gil's tumbler with Rebel Yell.

Unfazed, Gil continued.

—I do think this flag thing has a chance to start a turnaround. But it might be slow, like turning around the *Titanic*. And even though I say that, I have a problem with Blacks who complain that nothing has happened in the minds of Whites, that it's still the same old story. Hell, my own mother remembers when there were Coloreds- and Whites-only drinking fountains. There HAS been progress from Whites thinking Negroes weren't good enough to share fresh water from the same spout—that's a huge change, to my mind. And there's change daily, but of course it's ever so slight, almost imperceptible, and that's where the young folks are going to have a problem—with the slow speed of change. I think they just have to keep the heat turned up. It's easy for the public to chase after the next shiny new issue.

—Gil! First you built up my enthusiasm, but now you're bringing me down again with this talk of slow change.

—Yes, the slow pace is frustrating, but change IS happening, Joe.

Joe turned toward the bar, where Chester had gone back to wiping glasses.

—Ches, you've been around, you see things. Are there more white breads coming in here?

Chester came around the bar and over to their table, still wiping a glass.

—JP, I thought two years ago I was going to have to close down. You know I was raised right here. My daddy converted a laundromat into a jazz bar and it was swingin'. When I came of age I took over. Well, the old ones started dyin' off and the place started getting pretty lonesome. Then young Whites started movin' into the neighborhood and they started stragglin' in here. One night, a young White dude came in while we were jammin'. He said could he sit in on the piano. We didn't expect much but let him do it just to be nice. He started in with the boys and I gotta tell ya, I thought Thelonious had riz up from the dead and found my little joint. Where had this guy learned to ride the keys like that? Well, damn, he said he'd played piano as a kid but he really sharpened up at USC. Seems they've got a jazz department over there. That young fella started comin' in every Wednesday to jam, and pretty soon we got busy as hell. I had to get my daughter in here to cook up wings and onion rings to go with all the beer. JP, I started makin' money for the first time in a LONG time. And the kids are great—a real good mix of White kids and brothers. And now the girls are comin' in too. They're decent folks—no drugs. Only a few ever get carried away on the beer. They call me Pops. My daddy is probably rollin' in his grave. It's a new day, J. I never thought I'd see it.

—How come I didn't know about any of this?

—You tape your show on Wednesday. I see you usually on Monday with Nikki.

—I told you, never say that name around me again! And by the way, I think that glass is plenty dry by now.

Chester shrugged good-naturedly. He returned to the back side of the bar. Gil looked at Joe with one of those satisfied I-told-you-so looks.

—See, Joe? Right here there's been change. But to me it will take two or three more generations till our society quits noticing skin color.

—Two or three generations! How am I supposed to deal with that? How can you struggle now, knowing there will be no real change for generations? That's too much! How am I supposed to stand up in front of the press and demonstrators demanding something that's not going to happen until my nephews' unborn kids grow up? Huh?

—But if you look back in history, real social change has never been a sweeping replacement of assumptions and beliefs that people had been immersed in since birth. Instead, changes have come about through pressure on those in power. I doubt you can change the minds of the White supremacists behind the barriers at the State House. The big changes are going to come from laws passed and enforced that will make the radicals have to change their behavior. First, elected lawmakers are going to have to get the message that equality or rather equity is the will of the public. The Nineteenth Amendment, *Brown v. Board*, the sixties' Civil Rights Act—all were put in place to ensure equal treatment for everyone in the United States, but they didn't come about until a lot of people made sacrifices, risked their personal safety, and dedicated their lives to change. And as we well know, just because laws are passed, it's not over. The aftermath of all those landmarks came with tireless and sometimes unsuccessful work put in to enforce them.

—Okay, Gil, but also we can't think that even the majority of the big issues are in the past—voting rights tilted against Blacks, for example. Unjust penal system disproportionately filled with Black prisoners. Cops using undue force and even killing people and on and on—all issues that have barely begun to be solved. On top of these there are now so many subtle and not so subtle efforts like gerrymandering and voter IDs that pick away at Black rights.

Gil leaned forward as she became more juiced up.

—Look, I'll say it again. Protesting over the Confederate flag was the event a lot of people were waiting for to highlight the fact that Blacks REFUSE to continue to accept the position of inferiority. The flag as a symbol of the Civil War flying over a government facility is the perfect time and place to take up the fight.

—Right, you're making everything sound so orderly and rational. But before you continue, I think we've got to address why Blacks are so fired up. These people are about to blow because first their ancestors were enslaved for over two hundred years and then they've been forced for over a century to tolerate what's been done to them ever since slavery ended! You can't just chalk it up to a hiccup in history when owning another human being was necessary for a particular country's economy to thrive. Blacks are where we are now because we were forced into slavery to pick the White man's cotton! But, Whites have forgotten all that and are waving the flag to once again remind us darkies of our place as supposedly inferior beings!

Joe's voice was intense, and Gil got a little angry.

—Joe, I have to ask, do you want to work toward change or do you want to bring out the slave card? As you said before, Whites have got to get over thinking Blacks are inferior, naturally lazy, and looking for some entitlement program—all stale mischaracterizations thrown out there so that people don't have to actually think. Well, in my opinion, Blacks have got to get over blaming and accusing at every turn, mostly as it relates to slavery. We've all got to get beyond the tired rhetoric about inferiority and about slavery, name-calling, and blaming. Slavery has come and gone. In its wake is lots of damage, for sure. But if Whites and Blacks can approach the issues of today without all the finger-pointing about slavery, there's a chance for real change.

—Gil, that's a nice thought, but this whole damn flag thing shows that too many Whites are still White supremacists! And when you know that slavery is the root of all our race problems today, it's very difficult to present the case for equal treatment with a sea of Confederate flags in front of you! And the flag wavers have only one thing on their mind—to rationalize why it's okay to fly that damn flag from the State House!

—Joe, please get over that part of it! As I see it, your job is way bigger than the flag. It may be the thing that got people stirred up, but now's the time to move on and make it clear that Blacks aren't looking to run over Whites but they do insist on claiming the same rights as anyone else!

Gil, all of a sudden feeling helpless and frustrated, and maybe fueled some by the Rebel Yell, stood up and threw her sweater over her shoulders as she fired off a parting salvo.

—Joe, it looks to me like you're getting carried away by your own anger. If you think those mostly White legislators are going to take kindly to a blast of Black rhetoric, you're mistaken. See ya 'round the State House!

Then, she turned and stalked toward the door. But as she walked out into the cool air, there was the Vic, and that was when she realized her car was still at the Walmart. She turned around and went back inside at a much slower pace, knowing she would have to swallow a bit of crow. Joe, looking very relaxed, had both arms spread out across the back of the red banquette with one leg fully extended out into the aisle, making him look bigger than ever.

—Well I declare, fancy meeting you here!

Still drying glasses, Chester witnessed Gil's approach.

—JP, you've sure got the touch. I think that's how it was the last time I saw Nikki.

Gil slid into the seat and faced Joe with a sheepish grin. It wasn't only her car—she knew she had been wrong.

—Sometimes I get too carried away. Sorry I stormed out like that. Please, can you forgive me?

Joe drew in his leg and leaned in, crossing his arms on the table.

—You didn't really think I'd lose it in front of a bunch of old White legislators, did you? My whole life, whether in the ring or the pulpit, has been to maintain a presence for one thing—to convince. I'm ready for it. Gil, you've given me some things to think about tonight.

—I've learned plenty, myself.

Then Joe drove her back to her car, and she thanked him for saving her earlier from the creep in the parking garage, which now seemed so long ago.

12

Pleasant Hill to sell watch
May 15, 1857

THE OLD SWAYBACK HORSE pulling the wagon was not much faster than a man on foot. After a couple of monotonous hours they came upon a wooden sign nailed to a post. The crude lettering announced *Pleasant Hill 2 mi.* Medlin had very little money left in his pouch after buying the buckboard and broken-down horse earlier that day. He regretted having given Tom most of the money left over from the auction for safekeeping. Other than a couple of dollars, the only thing of value he had left was his father's watch. That would have to go if he could come across a place in the next town of Pleasant Hill where he could strike a deal for cash. For appearance as they rode into the town, Hutto, sitting with his long legs still hanging over the back, was shackled to a side rail of the wagon.

To Medlin, Pleasant Hill had the look of Bennettsville back home. Coming into town he saw the similar separation of those with and those without money—the wealthy to themselves on one street, and the less well-to-do a few blocks over. As they turned into the big open square, Medlin, as a man of cotton, saw right away that both towns were laid out to accommodate the clutter of wagons, piled high with the week's pick on trading days during the harvest. However, unlike in Bennettsville, smack in the center of the Pleasant Hill square was a statue of some man of local interest, raised up on a stone pedestal. The monument evidently represented someone important to have been placed right where wagons had to take precautions to negotiate around it.

Pedestrians hustled around the square to do this or that, among stores selling necessities and shops offering more discretionary items. One such had in its window a mannequin wearing a bright-colored frock and an elaborate matching hat decorated with feathers. This caught the curious eye of Hutto.

Medlin eased the wagon into the flow with other wagons going about their business, like ants on a mission. He needed to come upon some likely concern where he could sell the watch. Usually where there was cotton business there would be someone trading all commodities. Too, if a trade of the watch came off, there would be cause to find a grocery, so Medlin also kept an eye out for a store.

There was always the threat that the story of the slave traders missing from the train had caught up with their travels, so Medlin was hoping to pass with little notice. That was certainly his aim, but the White stranger accompanied by such a man as Hutto caught people's eye, and no one had any self-consciousness about stopping to stare.

Medlin saw what looked to be a likely place for supplies—Hudson's Grocery and Dry Goods—and steered the horse to a hitching post directly in front. Hutto stayed in the back of the wagon. With Medlin in the store, several people passing nearby stopped to satisfy their curiosity about the big Negro sitting alone in a wagon right there on the square—something never witnessed before. Townspeople had seen plenty of slaves, but mostly from a distance as they worked the fields, or if a gang was shuffled through town at a trot to wagons bound for Canton, the closest town with a train station, with daily trains heading to Mobile and the slave auctions. But with this one sitting stony and all alone in such close proximity, there was a rare chance to inspect the oddities of the hair and skin of an African up close. Many broke purposefully from their intended route to join in to gape at the specimen, until they swelled to a crowd.

Hutto sat still as a post, with his head tilted down and eyes toward the ground. A fly landed on his cheek and dabbed at the stream of sweat that had first formed on his scalp and then let loose to gravity, running down his face and dripping onto his trousers. The fly made the short flight to his ear, and followed its creases and folds all along, darting its tongue to lap up more sweat and smut before it wandered all the way into his ear. Hutto could feel the bug's feet and hear the buzzing wings until it was almost unbearable to keep still, but then all of a sudden it flew out and away.

A young boy, emboldened when the adults showed no conscience or shame in their staring, wrangled through trousers and skirts, approaching Hutto so close as to be almost between his knees.

—Are you a nigger giant, like my mom says? She declares you're the biggest nigger in the whole wide world!

The crowd laughed. Hutto didn't answer a word, but just kept looking down at the ground. Meanwhile, the mother, who had briefly lost sight of her boy, pushed through the crowd, grabbed her son roughly by the arm, and worked her way back through the onlookers and away.

Inside the store, the clerk told Medlin the watch trade could be accomplished just across the square at Landrum Brokerage. Medlin looked around, decided the store had everything he needed, and said he would return when he had money in his pocket. Outside, he found a small crowd gathered around the back of the buck. Hutto was motionless with eyes still downcast to keep from any engagement. Uneasy about the crowd, Medlin decided to take Hutto with him across the square to Landrum's.

He was just digging into his pocket searching for the key to Hutto's wrist shackles when the sound of mayhem broke out. Way down the street several dogs were packed up trailing a bitch through the traffic of slow-moving wagons. They decided to work off their frustration and set to yapping and snapping at a team hauling a wagon full of cabbages. The two-horse team went into a frenzy kicking and bucking, and when there was no relief in that, they took off. Other wagons hastily pulled over to get out of the way. In all of the commotion, the driver lost the reins, which fell loose around the runaway horses' hind legs. This spooked them even more. The whole team and wagon raced wildly down the street. Cabbages spilled out of the back and went rolling through the watching, stunned crowd like cannonballs. A few men stepped out in feeble attempts to put a stop to it, but when they saw the whole thing coming at them, they realized the futility, and stepped back into the comfort of those who chose to just watch in amazement.

With all eyes riveted in the direction of the spectacle, no one noticed when a little girl, a toddler, spurred on by recent success at first walking, tentatively put one foot in front of the other. The child tottered out from the crowd gathered around Hutto, who was still shackled to the wagon, into the path of the out-of-control rig. The people were now turned away from Hutto, watching the runaway wagon headed their way. As she realized she was alone for the first time in her young life, the little girl clung tightly to her doll and froze in place. Meanwhile, the onlookers scattered to the safety of the sidewalk.

Sitting on the back of the wagon, Hutto saw it all. He jerked on the chain of his shackles with no result. Then, with all his might, he clasped his hands together and with one big swinging motion snapped the wooden rail and was free of the wagon. With only a split second to lunge for the toddler, he grabbed her as gently as he could and got her out of harm's way before he himself went down headlong in a cloud of dust. A near hysterical young woman, obviously the mother, ran to her child, who, more scared than hurt, was sitting there bawling, with tears running down her cheeks through the heavy layer of dust covering her head to toe. The mother snatched up the child and ran over to Hutto, screaming hysterically that he had put his hands on her daughter. She began to kick him as he tried to stand to get back to the wagon. Others gathered around him, and some kicked and flailed away with canes and umbrellas.

Medlin, with his back to the street looking for the keys to unlock Hutto's shackles, missed what had happened in the very few moments it took for everything to unfold. As soon as he became aware, he pushed through the crowd around Hutto, and found him with crossed wrists, still shackled, trying to protect his face from an all-out assault by the growing crowd, who, against a defenseless prey, did not consider the head and face of their victim off-limits. With Medlin there to break things up, the crowd dispersed, satisfied they had made the point that Negroes best not ever touch anyone outside their own kind in Pleasant Hill, no matter what the circumstance.

Hutto stood and felt his face wounds. Fortunately there was nothing too bad. As they started crossing the square to get to Landrum's, Hutto noticed the little girl's doll, crushed by hooves. There was a small porcelain arm that lay in one piece. He picked it up, rubbed it across his shirt to get rid of the dirt, and slid it into his pocket.

In the middle of crossing the street, suddenly Medlin decided to get Hutto out of the mainstream of activity on the square, so they got back in the wagon and drove down a side street off of the square. They came to an alley that ran along behind Landrum Brokerage. Medlin stopped at a likely place to leave the horse and rig. For a small fee the animal would be stabled overnight. It wasn't much of a place—no yard to speak of—but there was enough room to park the wagon outside the small four-stall barn. Medlin agreed to pay a dollar and a half for the place, including two buckets of feed and fresh water. For an additional quarter, Hutto could sleep in a stall next to the horse, upon assurance that he was to be shackled.

The stableman held out his hand to collect the money, to be paid in advance. Medlin fished from his drawstring pouch near what was required and then the man waited for him to scrounge loose change from his pocket to complete the deal. Now Medlin was flat broke. This added much seriousness to selling his watch, which he hoped would not put him at a disadvantage with a potential buyer who might sense his desperation.

Medlin unlocked the shackles from Hutto's wrists and put them on his ankles. Next, he bound his wrists with a leather strap. They took off walking and found their way to the front door of Landrum's.

Medlin entered with Hutto shuffling close behind, stopping just inside to get his bearings, and to let his eyes adjust to the dim light after the bright sun outside. Upon seeing Hutto, the man hired for security slid his finger onto the trigger of his shotgun, which had a shortened barrel for effectiveness at close range. Aim was not critical with this firearm.

There was a high counter of wood paneling artfully made by a knowing craftsman, with finishes way beyond its purpose to shield the clerk standing behind it. Upon examination, any man would conclude that the appearance of the place was meant to awe and give the impression that Landrum's was top drawer. But Medlin was not aware of anything other than getting his head straight to make a satisfactory deal. He had to get enough money for the watch to make it back home to Clio.

Announcing his purpose to the clerk, Medlin was directed to go on up to the second floor. He took Hutto and approached the wide set of stairs. The tall, bony man with the shotgun ushered them up the steps and past a fancy stained-glass window picturing a big shield above an emerald green banner with a short message in a foreign language. On the second floor, they stopped in front of a pair of heavy mahogany doors. The bony man rapped ever so lightly, and was answered from within by a booming voice commanding them to come in.

Medlin and Hutto stood several paces back from the large desk, where Happy Landum was looking over some papers. He appeared to be a man used to life behind a desk, a big desk, an impressive desk, but his face—most especially his eyes—told of a life of difficulties. He looked tired. He slowly took in the scene in front of him, trying to conjure an explanation for the bedraggled White man and the giant Negro standing one pace behind.

Before asking Medlin his business, he inquired about the circumstances that had brought him to Pleasant Hill. Happy had learned this technique long ago as a way to first put a man at ease before any deal-making. Without giving much information, Medlin spoke of the auction in Savannah and—although he knew it wasn't true—of his intention to make it to the Mobile slave exchange.

Hutto took in the conversation between the two White men while he stood motionless, hardly seeming to breathe. Happy had already heard about the incident that had just happened in the street below, but he didn't mention it. He was uneasy, just because of the presence of a Negro in his office for the first time.

For a while, the conversation meandered, while Medlin, still standing, shifted his weight from one foot to the other, as Happy questioned him about things of a more personal nature—where he was from, whether he was a slave dealer by trade—until Happy asked Medlin what state of mind had brought him to his office. When Happy asked about Medlin's state of mind, Hutto, without hesitation, unable to help himself, took a step forward and, before Medlin could answer, announced proudly that they were from the Great State of South Carolina.

Happy instinctively moved his hand toward the top drawer that he always intentionally left partially open. His Smith and Wesson lay there ready, but when he saw there was no danger, he broke into an open laugh—the kind where all restraint was abandoned and the body and mind gave way to the pure joy of hilarity.

Medlin, seizing the moment, took the watch from his pocket and shoved the timepiece with its chain across the desk toward Happy, who was wiping a tear of laughter from his eye. Medlin asked what he would give him for the watch. Happy picked up the watch and felt the substantial weight. The way it felt in the hand made him think he might like to keep it for himself, and not pass it on for profit. A deal was struck that Medlin felt was fair. The amount should be enough to get back to Clio, and then some.

Happy lifted a tin box from a drawer in his desk and opened it to reveal three stacks of currency. He counted out the agreed upon price, and laid out ten-dollar bills side by side for the seller to quickly assess that it was the correct amount. Medlin scooped up the bills, shuffled them into one stack, folded that in half, and stuffed it into the right front pocket of his pants. He looked squarely into Happy's eyes and gave a subtle nod to acknowledge the satisfactory exchange.

Medlin and Hutto went down the stairs and out into the street. Now there was more than enough for supplies. In his relief to have some money again, Medlin forgot about Hutto being clearly visible to the townspeople so soon after the recent events and headed directly across the open square to the dry goods store. Medlin expected Hutto to keep up. He looked back and motioned rather impatiently for him to come on. Hutto was looking at the ground and shuffling slowly along. Medlin held up, to determine the reason for his sudden change in demeanor. When Hutto raised his eyes, Medlin searched them for some sign as to what could have come over him since they left Landrum's, and, in an instant, realized it was the watch chain.

Medlin stood stock-still for a moment, then grabbed ahold of the leather strap securing Hutto's wrists and pulled him back in the direction of the brokerage office. They entered the lobby, where Medlin approached the guard and told him to keep an eye on Hutto while he went back upstairs. The bony guard flinched but did not refuse the assignment. Medlin took the steps two at a time. When he got to the big mahogany doors, he opened them without a knock and found Happy transferring the heavy gold watch onto his old chain. Medlin stepped quickly to the desk and scooped up the chain he had walked in with earlier. He told Happy that the deal was for the watch only—not the chain—and walked out. Back on the square, Medlin told Hutto to hold out his hand. Without saying another word, he dropped the chain into Hutto's palm. Then they walked over to the store.

It felt good to accumulate food staples on the counter—cornmeal, salt pork, hardtack biscuits, and a little jar of honey. The honey was a luxury that Medlin felt drawn to because of having money in his pocket. He also fancied a shave and a haircut. Even more important, he craved some conversation, which he had not enjoyed for what seemed like a long time. Rarely did he partake of liquor in Clio, but now a couple of whiskies would suit.

The sun was getting low when they got back to the stable and found the horse eating peacefully in a stall. The wagon sat protected just inside the fence. Medlin pulled from the renewed supply of vittles an ample meal for Hutto. As he had arranged and paid for with the stableman, Medlin set Hutto up in one of the stalls for the night. He had already decided he would spend the evening in town on his own, maybe sleep in a hotel. He untied the strap around Hutto's wrists, leaving the hands free. Shackles were removed from Hutto's ankles and placed in the stall, on the ready if someone would happen by. Hutto understood that the irons could be quickly positioned on the ankles, unlocked, but would give the impression that he was still under control.

Walking down the street in Pleasant Hill, Medlin marveled as to how lighthearted he felt. He had in tow no one who would prompt stares. When he reflected on it further, there was no Lydia to criticize if he happened to want brown liquor and conversation with other common folks like himself—maybe other dirt farmers looking to refresh after a day in the field. He made a pass down one side of the street and up the other, looking through the windows and doors of the few social establishments the town had to offer, and decided on a bar called Down the Hatch.

———

WITH NOBODY PASSING BY THE STABLE, Hutto dared to wander about the area within the fence. There was not much to look at that he had not seen at both Jehossee and the Butler place. Inside the stable, the smithy, shoeing equipment, and some carpentry tools were all familiar, as well as the walls with pegs for hanging tack. He stood in front of a work counter and looked at all the fiddly bits and pieces scattered across the scarred surface, which showed signs of many uses over the years—small holes from the leather punch, saw cuts on the edge, gashes from who knew what all.

There were several small metal rings lying on a wooden shelf above the workbench. He picked one up and put it on the counter, then fished from his trouser pocket the gold watch chain Medlin had given him, and the porcelain doll's arm he had picked up out of the dirt in the square. He took a tool hanging on a nail and forced open the little ring where the ends of the wire met. His fingers were large and clumsy. With some difficulty, he looped the ring through a link in the gold chain and then through a hole in the shoulder end of the porcelain arm, where twine had united it to the doll's body before it was wrenched off in the commotion. With pliers he found on the counter, he pinched the ring closed again, and held up his handiwork in the little bit of light left in the day. Then he noticed the bucket of jet-black paint used to coat buggy springs to prevent rust. Carefully, he dipped the doll's arm into the paint, pulled it back up and waited for the excess to drip back into the bucket. He found a low nail in his stall, where he hung it to let the paint dry. He lay down close to it. He did not know what time it was but figured it was still pretty early.

Hutto was not accustomed to idle time. Even at the plantation there were fires to tend, repairs around the cabin, and everything else necessary to keep life steadily rolling on. But he took pleasure in the time on his own there in the stable and decided on a doze. Feeling in the dark, he heaped up some straw for a pillow. With the blanket Medlin had left him, he lay down and quickly dropped into sleep.

He had no way of knowing how long he had been asleep before he was awakened by a light movement next to his shoulder. He abruptly sat up and saw two white cat's feet that seemed to be floating in the darkness. There was but a single shaft of moonlight, coming through a gap in the wall planks. He made out that the white feet belonged to a young cat, all black as pitch except for its paws and whiskers. The cat jumped up into his lap and stretched its white front paws up to his chest, craning its neck to sniff everything it could reach. Its white whiskers shone bright like streaks from shooting stars.

—Cat, where did *you* come from?

He reached to Cat's head to give it a pet. The ears went flat and the whiskers lay back to accept the big hand. Purring started, and Hutto had a chuckle over such tremendous volume that came from such a small creature.

After a while Cat got down off his lap. It began to wander around the stall. Coming across the gold chain hanging low on the wall, Cat began to bat it around until it came off the nail. Hutto felt around in the straw, found it in the dark, and held it up to the beam of moonlight. He gently felt the porcelain arm, by now completely dry. Cat leaped at it while Hutto held it suspended, gleaming in the sliver of light. Once again, he tried to fathom how someone could make such a fine, delicate thing as that chain. Cat seemed to take such joy in it that Hutto gently swung it in and out of reach, as the little animal made leaps and wild jabs, all along with ears pricked forward and whiskers extended in full attention. Energized, Cat went on to play wildcat-in-the-jungle. Hiding alongside Hutto's leg, it pounced headlong onto his moving hand or foot, latched on and engaged in playful biting. This went on for a while, until Cat was worn out. Hutto unbuttoned the top of his shirt and lifted Cat, unprotesting, to where it curled up against his chest and fell asleep.

Where it was supposed to attach to a watch, the gold chain had a small delicate clasp that was very hard for Hutto's fingers to manipulate. He struggled to fasten both ends of the chain together and then barely succeeded in sliding it over his big head. He lay down on the straw bed, and very quickly fell into a deep sleep.

Sometime later, suddenly Cat scratched Hutto's chest in a wild move to free itself from inside his shirt. There were voices that sounded as though people were out in the yard and coming in the direction of the stable. Hutto heard a woman's voice saying things, as best he could make out, to coax a man into the building. Pulling himself into a crouch he peered from the stall, and on out the opening at the end. There was just enough light in the yard from the moonlit sky to make out that the woman was holding tight to a man's waist. He had his arm around her shoulder. She was struggling to keep him upright and moving forward toward the stable. The slurred voice of the man did not give it away, but the slouch hat did—it was Medlin.

The woman kept coaxing that if he could make it inside, they would have a good time. As the two staggered inside from the yard, the woman let go of her hold and shook off Medlin's arm. Medlin fell in a heap on the dirt floor. Two other shadowy figures, two men, rushed into the stable. One dropped to his knees and started going through the unconscious Medlin's pockets. They were jittery, in anxious chatter just above a whisper. It was so dark that Hutto could barely make out that the one on his knees had a drawn pistol and the other, hunched over his companion, was carrying a long rifle.

Just at that moment Cat sprang out of the stall as a rake fell against a pail. Hearing the clatter the man with the pistol, in a panic, whirled around. He took a wild shot. Cat was hit squarely in the chest, propelled up against the wall, then dropped to the floor, dead.

Hutto lunged out of the stall toward the two men, who in the extremely dim light were paralyzed at the wholly unexpected sight of a giant coming toward them. The woman screamed, ran out across the yard, and disappeared into the alley.

Hutto let out the holler of a man possessed, with his eyes wide open and teeth fully exposed. Grasping the two heads, one in each large hand, he slammed them together with tremendous force. Their bodies instantly went limp and crumpled to the ground.

Medlin was now coming to and struggling to stand, as he tried to recover his wits. Hutto took charge and grabbed everything he could carry from the stall and wagon, first stooping down to pick up the long rifle. Finally, he grabbed the shackles looped over the open stall door.

It seemed likely that the woman would sound the alarm. She was clearly not one of Pleasant Hill's finest citizens, but any tale she would make up would be believed over outsiders. Not even considering that there might be time to hitch the horse to the wagon, Medlin and Hutto took off on foot.

13

T HE ISSUE OF THE CONFEDERATE FLAG brought out all
sorts of efforts in Columbia to have what was pegged as "open
dialog" regarding race relations. There were forums with facili-
tators making sure everyone had a chance to offer ideas for unity. CNN
taped an "open forum" at the Civic Center for a nationwide feed. Gil
watched it on TV. She didn't know what to expect, but nothing she
saw seemed successful if you measured success as feeling satisfied that
you learned something, were influenced to be sympathetic, and gained
insight into the struggles of the Black experience. She came to one
clear conclusion—the subject was too charged for any open dialog, too
charged for anyone to feel comfortable opening themselves up to articulate truth-telling about their personal experiences and observations.

The CNN open forum was nothing more than a nationally recognized,
Black on-air personality roaming the room with a hand microphone asking not particularly enlightening questions. She put the microphone to
an older White man in bibbed overalls. He had a well-worn hat, which
he held with his two hands in front of his chest. Before she could ask him
a question he started to cry. He wanted to be forgiven for the way he had
been raised—to hate Black people. Not knowing how to come back to
that, the CNN correspondent quickly moved on with her microphone.
The whole thing was not informative, just awkward.

USC put on their own race event using a panel of experts. As much
as she knew about the history of her state, including its participation in

slavery, Gil was hoping for a fresh perspective so she could move along her own thinking. She felt she had come to a standstill. But the USC panel turned out to be disappointing—the same old academic rhetoric. One panelist talked about the social construct of racism. Another spoke about the difference between race and ethnicity.

It was clear to Gil that beyond the shelter of theories based in sociology and semantics, no one was willing to stick their neck out and talk about racism in 2000 and how to deal with it. She wondered about USC students taking classes in Black studies and how frustrating it must be to be fed the dry statistics and theories with protests going on just a couple of blocks away at the State House. She thought about how maybe she, too, was hiding behind academia. She certainly did not feel totally comfortable trying to articulate to JP about how she personally felt about race. And for her, there was the big issue that was always hanging heavy on her mind: What were the role and the culpability of her own Southern family in all this?

After the first time Gil talked with Joe at Ches's, they made a point of meeting to continue talking mostly about race over a couple of Rebel Yells. Both were eager to share their evolving ideas and personal observations. Gil thought what a shame it was that this one-on-one was so rare between Black folks and White folks. Her mother had told her that lack of understanding in her generation was due to absolute unfamiliarity between the races.

The demonstration grew as the number of people weighing in on the subject of race grew. Every evening a news segment on the goings-on in Columbia aired on national television. Joe's role as lead spokesman for Black people's demand that the flag be taken down from the State House grew as well. He appeared calm and thoughtful in interviews, and though Gil got a kick out of recognizing her own words once in a while, it was mostly all Joe. His presentation was impressive.

As the demonstration snowballed, Gil started to think about what lasting effect it might have in changing minds. Clearly the Confederate flag issue had brought the subject of race out in the open for many who earlier had been indifferent or ambivalent. *The New York Times* had a front-page story, headlined "What's Up in Dixie?" and *Time* Magazine had just run a major story, showing the Confederate flag on the cover. Gil could tell that the North was looking on with both curiosity and amusement. To them, it was a Southern issue. Northerners had fun watching the mud fight in somebody else's mudhole.

But Gil was focused on how people would be moved one way or another, and how the issue would be recorded in history. How would it play out? She knew about the women's movement and how far the demonstrations in the '70s had gone to change minds and laws on gender equality. She would have thought that the big steps would have closed the gender gap, but at a conference just two weeks before, the president of Harvard University had publicly stated that men outper-formed women in math and science because of biological differences. He used as an example giving his young daughter two toy trucks, which she treated as dolls and named mummy and daddy trucks—which he deduced was because of built-in gender bias. It was shocking to see such thinking was still out there in 2000.

Gil had told Joe she thought it was only a matter of time before centuries of prejudice against Black people in America would be drowned out of the culture. However, without vigilance in changing minds, nothing would happen. It would take a constant pounding on the public with demonstrations and pressure on legislatures for things to change.

Gil herself began to take notice of everyday slights toward Black people in her own life. Certainly the issue of the Black trainer at her gym weighed heavily on her. She winced when she heard the occasional joke about Black folks. She was conscious that all her work colleagues were White. And she did not have to look too far back in her upbringing to remember things like the explanation she had been given of why there were no Black NFL quarterbacks. She was told it was because they were not bright enough to deal with the complexity of the position.

She also got to realizing how people of a different race were often thought of as one big entity—"them"—and not as individuals, making it easy to paint with a broad brush a whole segment of society. Somehow the population would have to get away from generalizing so much and drop the "us and them" mindset.

The roaming microphone approach of CNN was a disaster to Gil's mind, and so were lectures by reputed experts. To her it just further deepened the divide as each side piled up the sandbags. At the three or four race equality events Gil attended, the outcome was the same—Black people hammered on the horrors of slavery. Without much to counter it with, White people grew resentful over being blamed, and over the demand for retribution. In the end, there was not the promised open discussion, but only a lot of mutual resentment—no progress toward mutual understanding. So far, discussions one-on-one—like those she had with JP at Chester's—seemed to Gil the only way to make progress, but God, that would take forever!

Change was certainly glacial. Just in that year, 2000, South Carolina became the last state to ratify a bill establishing a national holiday commemorating Martin Luther King. Leading up to the ratification there had been a few stabs here and there at coming to grips with the race issue.

———

IN THE SMALL TOWN OF LAURENS, the First Tuesday Book Club met to select their next book. It was February, which happened to be Black History Month. This led the group to consider books written by or about Black people in America. They settled on a biography—*Jesse: The Life and Pilgrimage of Jesse Jackson*. They selected it for two reasons. The book had just come out, putting Jesse on all the national talk shows, and more importantly, he was from Greenville—just down the road. They chose the book despite a tale circulating around town relating how Jesse as a young man worked as a waiter in a popular tearoom in Greenville's Topper Hotel. A *Life* Magazine article had reported that Jesse would spit in the soups of patrons who had shown no kindness to him, before he delivered the plates to the table. Each of the ladies in the book club had been to the Topper as a young girl, usually with a grandmother who thought of the tearoom as a training ground for good manners—napkin in the lap, both knife and fork placed across the plate to show you had finished your meal. Everybody did some quick math to see if their visits might have coincided with Jesse's tenure there.

Later, in discussing the book, the women were fascinated and shocked about Jesse's life as one of their own South Carolinians from the other side of the tracks. His world, so close in geography to theirs, was so far apart from their own experience. Quickly their discussion gravitated to the personal. Everyone in the book club grew up in an upper-middle-class White neighborhood, and most had known each other all their lives. All had Black maids as "help" in their households. In the vernacular of the time, the Black maid was referred to as the "Colored girl." Everyone boasted that they were very close to her, and most admitted proudly that they were closer to her than to their own mother. The ladies were quick to say that their maid was a "member of the family"—she sat in the front row in the church at family weddings.

All members of the book club felt satisfied that they had had warm, nurturing experiences with Black folks growing up. But then someone asked a question: Did they realize that while their Colored girl was serving dinner at all holidays, or traveling with the family to their second home on the lake, or staying over to nurse a feverish child, these women were not at home with their own families, and that the needs of their own families sometimes went unmet? The personal recollections stopped as everyone contemplated this revelation. It was a new thought, one that had never crossed their minds.

The club members had something to think about, and, moved by Jesse's story, they wanted to do something to improve race relations in Laurens. They decided on common ground—religion. It was a natural, since both Black people and White people in Laurens valued highly the church experience. The fellowship, traditions, and of course the spiritual aspects were of great importance for both communities. After some effort it was arranged that on a certain Sunday the First Presbyterian and Bethel AME churches would exchange congregations. Each side would benefit from the full experience of visiting another church. The service would include the pastor, his sermon, and the choir. The usual fellowship lunch would be served after the service.

So it was on one spring Sunday morning that over two hundred White worshippers showed up at the Bethel AME Church, and even more Black folks entered First Presbyterian.

———

BETHEL'S REVEREND WILSON was dressed in a splendid white robe with a kente cloth shawl in an Obaakofo Mmu Man pattern. The ecclesiastical vestment catalog said it meant, *One person does not rule a nation.* It was chosen specifically for this day. His sermon was about two worlds as described in Matthew 5:9. One world was a fallen world where conflict was ignored or suppressed by the use of force, threat or intimidation. The other world was God's Kingdom where it was a blessing to bring together peacefully people who were in conflict. The Reverend intended to hang his sermon on the fact that, as he saw it, all of America was at the fork in the road. The question was whether the country was going to continue to ignore the race conflict or work to bring people together. As he began, Reverend Wilson was pleased with how he set up the proposition of the two worlds. He felt he was laying out nicely the beat, which he thought essential as background rhythm for his delivery. The White congregation recognized both his cadence and the way he held on to certain words as very similar to Martin Luther King. In the beginning he was masterful with the tenor of his voice—forceful to make a point, soft for reflection. Things were going well until he sensed something was off.

The Reverend usually had a way of knowing that he was engaging his parishioners by their response, as customary in all Southern Black churches. He was used to a cacophony of "Amens," "Thank you, Lords," and clapping, or to seeing individuals, feeling the Spirit, standing with their arms in the air swaying their bodies—but this White congregation was completely silent. The Reverend began to doubt his ability to connect. He looked directly at one person in the second row, thinking if he could establish some intimacy by narrowing his audience to one it would get him through, but when that woman began fiddling with her purse to retrieve a mint, he started feeling panic.

He began to hear his own voice, and questioned his delivery to the extent that he had difficulty staying on message. This led him to an outright reading from his written sermon, something he had never had to do before, since the participation from his flock always spurred him on to lead from his heart and always made him feel like the Lord Almighty was speaking directly through him. Mercifully the service came to an end and the choir immediately began "Let's Gather at the Waters of Jericho." The Reverend raised his arms, looked to the ceiling, and secretly gave thanks that he had somehow gotten through it.

At the meet and greet at the front door as the congregation poured out, the Reverend was astonished by the enthusiastic reception from the White folks. The men gave him a hearty handshake. Some of the women even gave him a hug. All said something to the effect that the sermon was most inspiring. Even the children did not sneak past to the freedom of outdoors but stayed with their parents for the opportunity to see the Black man up close and get a good look at his vestments, so colorful and different. The parents were a bit embarrassed when their children stared intently into the face of the Reverend as he leaned down to their level and shook their hand. The children had never seen a Black man at such close range and most especially they had never until now had physical contact with a Black stranger. The large bald head, with facial features that seemed to be carved from some ebonized wood and sanded to perfection, and with the booming voice still resonating—all these gave the children the impression of an African chieftain.

———

OVER AT FIRST PRESBYTERIAN, meanwhile, the Black visitors filed in and settled down, while taking in all that was a White man's church. There was a large stained-glass window featuring a seated blond Christ. The white-faced children at his feet all looked up adoringly into the face of their Heavenly Savior. Pipes, some the size of stovepipes, rose beside the console of the enormous organ that filled the left side of the chancel. The organist was dwarfed by the instrument, but he put out a powerful sound that was not so much a tune or melody as a heavy hum that vibrated the floor.

The choir and pastor entered simultaneously from separate doors. After a welcome, prayer, and choral piece, the pastor climbed the three steps to the raised pulpit, where he loomed well above the congregation. So far, it was all as expected by the Black visitors. The pastor wore a cream-colored robe with a plain light-blue sash. His hair was cut neatly as it had been since high school. That, and wire-rimmed glasses, made a very pale overall impression. His voice had a conversational tone so that anyone with a hearing issue pivoted their head to favor a good ear and try to catch what he was saying.

He started with, "We must be prepared," and paid it off by telling the story of a Black soldier from South Carolina who had just, posthumously, been awarded the Medal of Honor for a heroic deed during the Vietnam War many decades before. Grateful witnesses to the event—along with his family—had never given up on the recognition due the dead soldier. Forty-three years passed before the medal was presented to his ninety-year-old mother at the White House. Through arduous scrutiny, the US Army verified the eyewitness accounts of how the twenty-year-old soldier sacrificed himself by diving onto a live grenade when it was thrown into the middle of the cramped earthen dugout he shared with five other soldiers. His body took the full power of the grenade, leaving his comrades with only minor shrapnel wounds. There was barely enough of his body left to put into a coffin.

The pastor said that after reading of this award in the paper, he began to think about how the hero had only an instant to respond, with no time for contemplation, no chance to weigh his options or consider the consequences. Where had his instantaneous resolve come from? The pastor looked to the Bible for answers. He saw that in Jesus's life, he and his followers were tested continuously and reacted selflessly, no matter the consequences.

The attention of the Black congregation had been grabbed by the powerful story, even though the pastor's voice was low and uninflected. They leaned forward in the pews, waiting to hear any secrets of the soul to which the pastor might give clues.

He next said that he himself, as a young man, had had a weekend job working the front counter at an auto shop for brakes and alignments. One Saturday, there was a steady flow of customers and a backup of half a dozen people lined up waiting for his attention. A man bullied his way to the front.

—I need a full set of brakes and I don't want any nigger working on 'em! Niggers always screw things up.

Upon hearing the word "nigger," the entire congregation sucked in a breath and held it. No one had escaped the sting of the word sometime in their lives, but to hear it in this public setting, most especially from a White man using it so matter-of-factly, caught them totally off guard. The pastor had considered not using it, or watering it down to the N-word—but what was the point of the story without the word's full power? The pastor confessed that he had certainly been unprepared—young, scared for his job, had been taught that the customer was always right. He had written up the order with a note to have a White mechanic perform the work. Meanwhile everyone waiting at the counter had looked off in different directions or fiddled with something in their hands. No one had spoken up.

—I wasn't ready.

All the people in the congregation sat motionless.

—We all need to practice every day doing the right thing when we see injustice so that we can act without thinking, just as that hero did when he threw himself on the grenade. God will be our guide.

Next, the pastor read several passages from the Bible that spoke to readiness. And then it was over. He came down from the pulpit to a lively piece. The organist's feet pumped the pedals wildly and his fingers ran up and down the keys. The pastor moved down the aisle at a fast pace, matching the quick tempo of the organ. The congregation had heard a sermon far more powerful than what they had expected.

Months later, the two women organizers of the church swap, one from First Presbyterian, one from Bethel, ran into each other at a grocery store. Upon seeing each other, they approached for a greeting. Each freed up a right hand in case the other would initiate a handshake, but it didn't come. They each mentioned that the church swap was a positive and meaningful experience, and both agreed they must do it again, but it never happened.

———

WHILE THE ADULTS were not making much progress among themselves, something was going on in the schools. From her two newspaper subscriptions—*The State*, the paper of the Upstate, and *The Post and Courier* of Charleston—Gil started picking up on a subject being bandied about:

how school kids should learn about slavery. The debate was about whether they should be taught at home or at school. Evolution and sex education were two other topics that seemed to pop up, then die, only to come around again later. With the Confederate flag controversy heating up, some grade school teachers added teaching about slavery to their lesson plan. No school system wanted to touch the subject by requiring teacher training and course material. Individual teachers who tried to address slavery wandered into dangerous territory. Dangerous, because the subject was so charged. There was, at least, potential for a firestorm in the media.

Just the year before, it had been reported that a fifth-grade teacher did what she had done for years. She took her students on the annual field trip to a nearby cotton farm. The class of ten-year-olds, after handing in the permission slips signed by their parents, were bused to a field of cotton, where a Black man in overalls and a straw hat, carrying a small drum, was waiting for them.

Burlap bags were handed out. To the beat of the drum—as slaves had done one hundred and fifty years earlier—the kids began to pick. The Black man sang a song similar to a plantation work song: *I like it when you fill your sack. I like it when you don't talk back. Make money for me.*

The cotton picking was competitive. The loser had to drag around the huge bag called "Big Mama" for the rest of the field trip. The man with the drum answered the kids' questions according to what had been passed down to him from ancestors who worked this same land through many generations.

It was over in an hour, without incident. The kids got back on the bus and returned to school. But someone had taken a video. Things went quickly downhill. One parent got hold of a copy of the video showing her son picking cotton, and it didn't sit well. The mother gave the video to a local TV station, and from there the reactions exploded. Anyone who even remotely had anything to do with race relations felt they needed to weigh in with their take on the incident. One member of the Legislative Black Caucus made a statement that "slavery was a system of violence and oppression, not to be treated like a game." The NAACP asked for an apology from the school and got it.

Gil thought that there was certainly a need for proper educational programs to be developed and widely adopted. She asked herself, if adults can't find some common ground to working on diversity and racism, how can children learn about these things?

But the older kids seemed to be ahead of the adults. In light of the Confederate flag controversy, students at School of the Arts in Columbia overwhelmingly elected to stage *To Kill a Mockingbird* for their annual production. The backlash came swiftly. The school principal said there were complaints based on words in the script, which made some people "uncomfortable." The objectionable word was *nigger*. At the same time, it was brought to the attention of the school administration that the book was in the curriculum and on the shelves of the library. It was yanked immediately.

Meanwhile, the students hung fast to wanting to stage *Mockingbird*. The whole student body was surveyed. A big majority of both Black kids and White kids thought it was an appropriate selection, especially in light of the goings-on at the State House. The administration reconsidered and said they would allow the production if the objectionable word was replaced. The students came back and argued that if *Mockingbird* as written made people "uncomfortable" that's exactly why they chose it.

The student president wrote an opinion piece for the school paper, making the point that many state legislators were trying to protect the Confederate flag on the State House in spite of the fact that this flag flying atop a public building surely made Black people "uncomfortable." As it turned out, the drama students performed no play for that year, in protest. Some students were more eager than adults to confront issues of race and diversity.

During the same period, it was reported that the football team of the mostly White Academic Magnet High School, just outside of Charleston, celebrated a win over their majority Black rivals by smashing watermelons, long a demeaning symbol in the lexicon of Black history. All hell cut loose. Almost immediately, parents, the media and the NAACP got involved in a whirlwind of newspaper articles and local television pieces. The district superintendent of schools quit after the school board criticized her, saying she waffled on an immediate response. The football team coach was fired but was soon reinstated when the students and parents rallied behind him. The coach then sued district officials for treating him "in a racially disparate manner as a White male."

After the watermelon incident, the students at Academic Magnet took it upon themselves to face the issue of race, head-on. They formed Students Advocating for Multicultural Education or SAME. The organization established an after-school tutoring program at a nearby low-income, mostly minority, elementary school. SAME was active in bringing in speakers to address diversity and inequality. The students started a facilitating board on race called the Discovering Diversity Panel to stage and monitor open discussions. At each event the auditorium was packed. The school principal freely admitted that the students were courageous in tackling uncomfortable topics that the adults simply could not handle.

14

On foot out of Pleasant Hill, Alabama
May 16, 1857

T HE KILLING OF THE TWO YOUNG MEN in Pleasant Hill set off a firestorm of activity in the town. It had never had such a thing as a double murder except the time Bobby Masters put a bullet through his wife and the Johnson kid on account they were caught together in the marital bed, for which he got off scot-free as the jury thought it was justified, given what had befallen Ol' Bob.

It did not take much to gather a search party to go run down the two strangers. Happy Landrum advised them that by his recollection, the two were headed to Mobile and the auction houses, so the riders galloped south.

Even before the killings, the oddity of a Negro and White man traveling in what had been observed as a suspicious manner, almost friendly like, made its way through the town as soon as Medlin and Hutto were sighted.

The townspeople referred to the strange pair simply as "the two." People thought of little else from the moment the odd pair appeared in town. After the evening meal, several wives who had never shown any interest demanded that their husbands teach them how to put a bullet in the chamber of the house gun that had long lain ignored in the top drawer of the buffet. Within hours after the strangers came into town, men took to belting on their sidearms, and in carrying out their chores that evening, they kept their hand on the grip when they entered their own barns or sheds. Even the family hound, only occasionally set to tree a coon, was tethered to a porch post to sound the alarm in the event the two targeted the house. That night, children crawled into bed with their parents.

As to the reason for the alliance of such an unlikely pair, speculation fluctuated wildly. The White man could be under a spell. Most thought surely he suffered from a malady of the brain. Otherwise, what could account for it?

People thought that no White man would fall in step in common with a Negro—couldn't, on account he, by nature, was a follower. It was a common belief that an African's brain was not developed as necessary to carry out anything but the simplest tasks, and that was with instructions from his natural superior, the White man.

As a girl, Mrs. Haverford, from an old established family in Pleasant Hill, had studied a book titled *The Origins of Early Savages of the Continent of Africa* while attending the Normal School for Girls in Birmingham. From what she recalled from her long-ago school days, she speculated that witchcraft might be at the root. She remembered reference to a strange tribe of exceedingly tall men, who could cast a spell potent enough to control the most violent subjects. Their practice was applied to animals of an African jungle, but possibly that same thing was at work here. Perhaps the innocent White man's brain had been taken over by a spell. This notion, once whispered by Mrs. Haverford at the Pleasant Hill Dry Goods Mercantile, was immediately repeated and spread like a brushfire.

The cotton crop was not, for once, the topic of every conversation. It was early in the season, and so far, the plants had not experienced the extremes of rain—too much, too little—that would send the cotton men to street corners and the feed store for comfort in knowing they were not alone in their fears. They always hoped everyone was in the same predicament while knowing it was unchristian-like to wish bad luck on others. But no never mind. Misery did love company. With the season's crop in rare harmony with nature, room was left for idle talk about the unaccountable strangers.

When the murders became known, most talk centered on the suspected murderers and not the murdered. Two young men had been killed, for what reason was not known. But for the townspeople, the deaths of these particular two were no loss to humanity. Known in Pleasant Hill as unsavory characters, the two were from Brawley, a nothing town a few miles away, and—as the old saying went, birds didn't "shit in their own nest"—they traveled to Pleasant Hill to carry out their boozing and nothing else to the good. The larger town offered more opportunities to satisfy their predatory nature to bamboozle, and on occasion injure, just for the sport of it.

The two young men, drawn together through mutual attraction to devilment, had known each other from childhood. They did little or nothing in their short lives to earn sympathy at their demise, and though no one would say it out loud, everyone felt they deserved killing. If details had been known about the colliding heads that sent them to the Hereafter at precisely the same instant, all would have agreed it was part of the Divine Plan for all of Earth's creatures. However, to the people of Pleasant Hill the two Brawley boys were in some fashion their own, and it was not for strangers to have their way with them.

Happy Landrum had a big role in the drama, because he was about the only person who had actual dealings with the pair. He had the chance to observe their behavior at close range while striking the deal for the pocket watch. When recounting the story, he greatly jiggered the details, since nobody was holding him to the purity of truth.

Happy was a natural storyteller. The chance meeting with the strangers could not have come at a better time. Happy had become complacent and dull, often having his daily ritual of bourbon and branch sitting alone at a back table in the Jerome before heading home to his hapless and dull wife.

Now, in just a short day, life was different. The afternoon following the double murder, when he observed that Happy walked in at five fifteen surrounded by a crowd, the Jerome manager showed him to a front table instead of his usual place in the back. Then he brought Happy a big glass of bourbon at no charge. The table was rimmed with excited men all jockeying for a position to hear the story about when the White man had entered the Brokerage to sell a watch. Most had already heard some version, but no one commented or cared when the present account deviated wildly from what they had already heard. For a few hours, Happy was a town celebrity, and he enjoyed the limelight enormously for the short time it lasted.

———

IT WOULD SEEM A TOTAL DENIAL of ancestral inclination that Thomas "Happy" Landrum would be of the family to which he was born. All other members of the Landrum family were incapable of viewing life around them other than precisely as it was—dry and witless. No other Landrum had the least desire to engage in conjecture or interpretation, as that would require wandering into the dangerous territory of questioning the workings of God Almighty, who had set things out, not to be challenged.

The family Bible had a pasted-in engraving of the Landrum crest, with its green sash displaying the ancestral motto *Disce Ferenda Pati.* Under this, written freehand in pencil, was the English translation, *Bear Patiently What Must Be Borne.* Only Happy would take notice of how such an axiom could travel hundreds of years through the ancestral pipeline and still describe the family so very accurately.

He himself was a complete contradiction to the Landrums. They were farmers—a calling he resisted from an early age. He found farming too solitary. He desired to be among people who found him amusing and good company. As soon as his father no longer had the power or patience to force him to stay on the farm, he moved into a furnished room in Pleasant Hill. He took a job as a clerk at Peoples Bank, which occupied a desirable location, mid-block on the side of the square that caught the morning sun—a favorite spot for the old folks to sit on the benches beside the front entrance to the bank, where they could avoid the morning chill and gossip at leisure.

Most would consider the bank job deadly dull, but the young Happy made the most of it from the start. Each transaction came to him for filing. He read and digested everything that passed through his hands. The job put him in the way of understanding the complete flow of commerce throughout the town and the surrounding countryside. No will, deed, or loan passed through without his inspection.

The complexity of wills and land deals fascinated him. After a while he was given the latitude to handle some low-level transactions. He saw everything as a puzzle and manipulated all the pieces to forge the best deal for everyone concerned. After many transactions, he started to put forward his own solutions that more often than not were somewhat out of alignment with the bank's timeworn way of doing things.

An increased demand for cotton from Britain caught Peoples by surprise. The unforeseen insatiable market for cotton had the planters in a panic to keep up. For the first time ever, men of cotton in Pleasant Hill found themselves in a whirlwind to produce for the dizzying high prices offered. At the gin they were giddy over what they called "crazy money" flying around. More land, more slaves, more equipment were all needed in a hurry. They crowded into Peoples for loans. The understaffed bank, not prepared for the sudden volume of business, had to turn to the one man in their employ who had not succumbed to complacency and a very slow pace—Happy Landrum.

The energetic young clerk operated with such inventiveness it alarmed the officers, who were powerless to rein him in. With all the business he was handling, there was nothing they could do but relax their inclination to force the young man to follow strictly the narrow lane of tradition. If Happy's approach was sometimes unorthodox, clients found the transactions more than satisfactory. They were glad to be in the hands of such an inventive financial force with fresh ideas. His deal-making seemed to have no limit. He assembled a group of the most influential planters and businessmen in Pleasant Hill into a partnership to open a much-needed new gin.

Moreover, no deal was too small. On the contrary, he saw the small deal as a place to show his most creative solutions, adding to his reputation. And he did everything with flair. He coordinated an even swap of three mules for a field slave, with the transaction taking place right out in front of the bank—a spectacle for all the townspeople to witness. Though he did not have the title of officer, the bank felt compelled to extend to Happy a small commission per transaction—the same as enjoyed by seasoned loan officers. It irked some who had been at the bank for years, but they were powerless to keep the young dynamo to the slow pace to which they had long been accustomed. Happy was of indispensable value at Peoples in the time of the cotton rush.

Banking men who intended to spend their whole careers at Peoples were ill equipped to change their mindset to this new way of conducting business as established by Happy. Before long, the young man was masterminding almost all deals, with the old guard left the menial job of expediting the documents.

Eventually it was clear the bank bosses were not going to promote Happy—a bachelor to boot—to a lofty title with a matching salary, even if they were giving him a commission on every deal he made. It was not in him to wait for the bank to direct his fate. He was not going to wait stoically—as his father had waited for rain—for the bank to make him an officer. No *Disce Ferenda Pati* for him.

He had been putting away cash received for brokering deals outside the bank. Such deal-making was frowned upon, but by now any desire he felt to play according to others' rules had long since vanished. Neatly stacked bills filled the pasteboard box hidden under the bed in his rented room. His purpose for the stash was uncertain until one day he looked across the street from Peoples and spotted a sign advertising commercial space for sale on the other side of the square. At that very moment, he knew he must open his own mortgage, loan and brokerage establishment. For weeks, as he contemplated his future, it uplifted his spirits to take the long way around the square on his way to Peoples in the morning just to cup his hands against the large glass window to have a look at the interior of the available space. He looked forward to the day when his former employers could not help but observe the steady flow of customers whom they had lost to their former clerk.

He bought the whole building and started Landrum Brokerage. Happy had the notion that an appearance of quality promoted feelings of security for prospective clients, so he decked out the establishment in fine-finish wood paneling, surfaces of Italian marble, and floors of polished stone. He thoroughly enjoyed outfitting the building in all the impressive finery.

Over many years in business, Landrum Brokerage handled thousands of transactions. Happy made a lot of money, bought a big fine house and stocked it with furnishings chosen to impress, including a wife selected using the same criteria.

By any standard, he should have been a contented man, living out his life in security. However, Happy was not content. What was once exciting became routine and dull. With wealth came boring complacency and predictability.

Once, he had enjoyed the feeling of accomplishment and had an honest desire to strike a deal with all parties satisfied with the outcome, but over the years, with more cotton money—lots of it—came the hardness as grace fell away to be replaced by suspicion and greed. Then there came to him those who wanted to win for winning's sake or, worse, just wanted to get an upper hand for the sport of it, as though making a deal was some kind of game with scores. This new way of doing business made Happy weary, and that weariness turned into disillusionment.

But when Medlin walked into his office to make a deal, Happy was put into the frame of mind of a gentler time. He could see in the young stranger's face no sinister or sharp expression, but rather a purity of purpose he had not seen for a long time. Somehow, he felt kindly toward the odd pair, and a little protective of Medlin, who he sensed was just a decent, simple man. Medlin reminded Happy of a kinder and gentler time in business. But now two youths had been killed and the strangers were suspected.

———

MEDLIN AND HUTTO REALIZED that they would be the object of an all-out hunt after the incident in Pleasant Hill. Every professional slave tracker who happened to be within the region, along with farmers turned vigilantes, would be on the move in a pack, riding with purpose to rid this usually peaceful land of the scourge. In fact, there were eighteen riders in all, with, to a man, the knowledge that whoever fired the fatal shot would be an instant hero. What they did not know was that they were headed in the wrong direction.

Entering Pleasant Hill to sell his watch, Medlin had kept to the story that they were heading to Mobile, but in reality, as soon as he and Hutto buried Celia and Jama, that notion had changed and was replaced by the determination to head straight home to Clio. He didn't have it in him to continue the journey to the coast and the slave auction. Celia and Jama's drowning had thoroughly soured him on the scheme of making quick money. He would never have tried such a thing but for Tom's push. Too, the miseries were coming on with more frequency. He could no longer pass his illness off as something that he would overcome. It was clearer by the day that something was really wrong within his body—he would have to try to make it back to Clio and the farm.

As soon as they left Pleasant Hill after the killings, Medlin knew that there was simply no way to get to Clio other than to find a town with a train station and board a train to Charleston. Foot travel all the way was out of the question. They would have to take their chances. He knew that word would be circulating regarding the killings in Pleasant Hill and also about the earlier disappearance of the slave traders from the train out of Charleston. Still, the two would have to find a town with a train station.

Hightailing it out of Pleasant Hill in the dark, they had stayed well off the road, and for a few hours held up in a dense stand of laurel near a stream.

When it was light enough to read, Medlin fidgeted around in his rucksack and pulled out the train schedule he had picked up in Charleston when buying the tickets for Mobile. It was a foldout affair, with a front title panel that read, *S.C.C. & R.R. Company*, and under that, in smaller letters, *South Carolina Canal and Rail Road Company*. The printed schedule was limp from humidity and suffered from being cooped up with fatback and the like. It had the character and texture more of a rag than paper.

As Medlin inspected the schedule, trying to determine where they were, Hutto looked over his shoulder, sensing it had great significance. Medlin ran his finger along the schedule in the direction of Charleston. He located Maryville, where they had all left the train in the middle of the night—it seemed so long ago now—and then Newnan. But there was no sign of Pleasant Hill, so Medlin had to make a pure guess as to where they could be now and tapped his finger several times to make the point to Hutto, who comprehended immediately.

They continued on the move in a northeasterly direction as best they could tell from the trajectory of the sun.

As they walked through thick brush and woods, they came in and out of contact with a road, of great interest since it could lead to a town and maybe to a train station. There were occasional stretches of road when they felt safe to climb out from the dense cover of foliage and walk a spell until they could see or hear someone coming their way and take cover again. They were now on such a piece of the road, where Hutto evidently felt inclined to walk at a faster pace. Medlin told him to go on ahead, which he did. But Medlin was getting weaker every minute, and soon he lagged behind a good twenty paces, although he was determined not to stop in such a vulnerable place. Ahead, Hutto went out of sight around a curve, which inspired Medlin to go into a half-staggering trot to catch up.

Once he cleared the bend, he saw Hutto standing perfectly still, faced by a man on horseback. The man leaned on the saddle horn, looking as if he had no cares—casual except the right hand was holding a rifle with a finger on the trigger. Medlin slowed to a walk and got closer, to see the man was dressed in a dark blue suit and well-cared-for boots. The man had his head tilted with his hat brim shadowing most of his face. From his vest pocket hung a gold chain attached to a timepiece that, due to its large size, crowned from the watch pocket. Medlin immediately recognized his father's watch.

Happy Landrum readjusted to sit more erect, and remarked that the search party from Pleasant Hill had in his estimation chosen the wrong direction out of town—to the south because they believed the story about the auction in Mobile. He said that from his many years in reading the stories behind stories to measure a man's true intentions, he figured Medlin to be headed north to "the Great State of South Carolina."

He offered that if they followed the road another near ten miles, they would come into Canton, where there was a train that came through bound for Charleston. With that, he spurred his horse, circled around the two men in the road, and, tipping his hat, wished them safe travels.

After meeting Happy, Medlin and Hutto continued on the road for a little while, ready as before to take cover if they saw or heard anyone. But soon Medlin decided that it would be better to stay off the road altogether. He had no fixed plan as to traveling in the safety of darkness or in broad daylight. As a matter of fact, any planning was impossible. It was pretty clear that their progress was going to depend strictly on Medlin's ability to walk. The miseries came on more and more frequently and the shooting pains in his gut lingered longer after each bout. It would be hard for him to make the ten miles to Canton, on or off the road. Medlin was losing his ability to high-step through the brush. His legs were no longer fully within his control. The miseries in his gut seemed to affect his extremities.

About this time there was a shift in the relationship between the two—subtle but defined, with a definite beginning. It started after another fall when Hutto silently helped Medlin up from his knees to a stand. There was a moment of confusion as Medlin tried to get his bearings. Sure that he was again steady on his feet, Hutto walked on ahead. In that one gesture, it was plain between them that Hutto would take charge from then on. He would now decide the route and when and where to camp. Medlin did not resist—he welcomed it.

Keeping to Happy's suggestion about Canton, the two stayed fairly close to the road. When they risked taking to the road again, they met a man driving a produce wagon, who stopped to chat, sticking mostly to the weather. He offered Medlin a big bunch of fresh collards as a friendly gesture between fellow travelers, which Medlin happily accepted. Soon after that, they heard the sound of pounding hooves coming from a distance and had hardly enough time to slip into the woods and watch as five mounted men of unknown purpose galloped by.

At twilight, Hutto suggested that they make camp by a bend at a nearly dry riverbed. It looked like a good campsite. They climbed down what must have been an animal path. As soon as they made it to the bottom, Medlin sat down and surveyed how he would grade his condition, between feeling puny and at the end of his tether. He sat perfectly still in hopes of warding off the convulsive fit that seemed to be ever nearer, fixing on some mud daubers busily stocking up on moist earth from the undercut of the bank directly across from where he sat.

As Hutto busied himself with the fire and other chores in putting a meal together, Medlin made no excuses for not pulling his own weight but sat transfixed by the activity of the mud daubers hard at work, envying their singular purpose to build mud houses and live in harmony and simplicity.

Hutto headed into a thicket of laurels to find more firewood. When he had traveled a little way from the campsite, he heard the distinctive sound of a good-sized animal. Suddenly, a wild hog lunged out from the dense underbrush. It stopped short in the middle of the trail ahead, where it shuffled and stomped its hooves in a frenzy. The powerful animal looked about to charge. It was close enough for Hutto to know a sudden strike could knock his legs out from under him, which could be fatal. With hackles standing up like a mad dog and spittle coming from the mouth, with tendrils of slime hanging from its tusks, the boar made short lunges in Hutto's direction, but each time stopped short, digging its small but powerful hooves into the ground. Apparently, the animal was waiting for just the right moment to charge full-on. With one swift motion Hutto took off his shirt and wrapped it tightly around his right arm for what was coming—a final attack. He barely got into a crouched fighting stance when every bristle on the animal flared out like a porcupine and it charged.

When the hog was but a few feet away and bearing fast, a loud shot sounded and the animal abruptly veered off with a squeal that lasted through a series of convulsions until it lay, legs skyward, its nostrils flaring with a few last heaves of air, snot, and blood. Then it lay motionless.

Hutto gave it two kicks to check for life before turning around to look in the direction of the shot. For a moment he could not make out anything, but then saw what first appeared to be a modest-sized man. However, the hat with a bright-colored bandana tied around it gave it away that it was a woman. She lowered the revolver held with both hands, and, casual as if nothing had happened, said they should butcher the hog, though from its wildness it would be tough, but good eating all the same. With that, others stepped from the thicket just behind her. There were six adults in all, four men, the woman in the hat, and a young woman with a baby in a sling of cloth that she held close.

Back in the camp, Medlin, alarmed by the shot, picked up the rifle Hutto had taken off one of the men in Pleasant Hill, and rested it across his lap with his finger on the trigger. Soon Hutto emerged from the woods walking backward carrying the front two legs of the hog, while another man had the hindquarters. When the rest of the party came into view, they froze at the sight of the White man with the rifle, but came on when they saw he had not positioned it to fire.

With no explanations passed to Medlin, three men went to butchering the boar while the others built up the fire to accommodate the meat. In time, the fire was flaring with fat dripping from hams hanging from greenwood skewers. Side meat lay on hot rocks around the fire.

Hutto caught drippings in the pan and, when the time was right, poured in cornmeal mixed with water. Then the pot with the gift of collards was placed on the coals directly under the dripping fat. Slivers of crackling were added into the cooking cornmeal. Hutto made a small portion of cornmeal mush and offered it to the baby's mother, who used her finger as a utensil. The hungry baby took the mush easily this way. Hutto found three short logs and placed them around the fire. Some squatted on their haunches, rotating the sticks of meat directly over the flames. Mother and baby busied with breastfeeding. Top meat was cut back when done and piled high on the only spare plate available, with Medlin served on the other. Corn cakes were dished out as soon as they finished cooking, with everyone served in ample portions. Nobody said much while they ate.

Medlin, too, sat in silence, but watched with interest as the others showed reverence toward the food and one another. There was no grabbing or gorging. As the food was passed around, everyone took a modest share and no more, even though they had seen only a very little foraged food and stagnant water for days.

Though hungry in the extreme, no one gorged, but they all savored every bite. It was the same with coffee, passed around in a single shared cup after Medlin was handed the other one. Everyone sipped with deliberation, so as not to take more than the others.

With immediate hunger satisfied, the old woman told the tale of the group, and the circumstances that had led to their present condition. All but the old woman were from two neighboring cotton plantations somewhere north of Mobile. Their masters, first cousins, had allowed for Sunday visitations to encourage unions and increase the population of their slave stock. These cousins had a falling out, after which visiting was no longer permitted, resulting in breaking up established families. Fifteen slaves decided they would run away to lands east where they had heard Seminole Indians would fold them into their society. As they were making their way, they were set upon by their former overseers. Seems they had been betrayed by another slave, whom the overseers had beaten almost to death to gain information.

A skirmish between the runaway slaves and the White slave trackers resulted in four deaths—three slaves and one overseer. The twelve slaves left alive scattered. Four, plus the mother with the baby, joined up again after two hard days in Alabama swampland. The old woman went on to say that she had been living alone in the swamp ever since she herself became a runaway, years before the group showed up in her part of the gator- and snake-infested terrain, where no White man was desperate enough to venture. She decided that her life, closer to an end than theirs, had served no higher calling for a long spell—had not ever served much of purpose—so she told them she would lead them as far as her body would allow. She made but one rule, and that was that no matter how hard the going, they could not jeopardize the lives of the others. They all promised not to act in a manner where they would think singly to save themselves and compromise any of the others. She went further and told them that she would be carrying the revolver that she had retrieved from a White man she had managed to kill during her own break to freedom, and that they would be shot dead if they showed cowardliness.

There had been near capture of the runaway party in two instances, but the old woman was wily, and her well-tuned instincts had saved them. As she told the story, both Hutto and Medlin looked over this woman who was dressed in coarse britches—also no doubt taken off a dead man—and guessed the said gun was settled in the hand covered by the blanket lying loosely over her arm. Too, she was older than they first thought. Maybe upward of seventy.

As more coffee was passed, the conversation became downright friendly, and before long, the stories were flowing. Medlin withdrew quietly from the group, lay down on the tarp and, wrapped in the blanket, listened to the talk now that everyone felt comfortable about the company. He found it amusing that Hutto's voice took on a different rhythm and delivery along with a dialect he had sometimes heard among field hands. The atmosphere around the campfire was a relief after so much foot travel through dangerous territory. The young mother at times let the baby feed from her breast.

Medlin dozed off and on for a while, but would suddenly wake up when everyone broke into a fit of laughter. Several times, Hutto signaled for softer outbreaks for Medlin's sake, but as a new round of dueling stories began, all restraint again would fall away.

All of the stories were of life on the plantation, just about the only world the slaves had ever known. The stories that drew the most laughter were of putting one over on the bosses—stories of cunning and cleverness where the slaves seemed innocent in the event they were caught pinching, say, an apple, from the master's private orchard, or caught napping.

The old woman had been a house slave, so her recollections were about life with the master's family. Her main duty was the care of the two young daughters. She said that though she had heard of close relationships elsewhere, her charges were mean to her and often lied to the mother, who on many occasions took off after her with a willow switch. The old slave woman said she got her revenge by telling the girls tales of ghosts within the house, which frightened them to such a degree they would huddle together every night in one bed and shake uncontrollably, waiting for the ghosts to finally achieve their mission to eat them, one extremity at a time. Just as with all the other stories, everyone convulsed with laughter. Even the baby joined in, with her little legs kicking. She bounced up and down, and her outstretched arms flapped wildly in spasms of joy.

The strangers ignored Medlin, settled outside the circle and lying down. He decided that sound sleep was out of the question, and just lay enjoying hearing the runaways' stories and seeing into their world. He lay on his side with his back toward the fire and the group, but he was listening to every word. He found it interesting to hear of life from a whole different perspective than he had ever experienced. Though he did not grow up on a plantation where there were plenty of slaves to observe firsthand, it was assumed by the majority of White people that Negroes were dim-witted, with no comprehension of God's idea of family, or of self-pride. Most especially, it was a conviction that they had no capacity for the least bit of intellect. Put plainly, it was thought they were just not complete human beings. With no impulse to come to any particular conclusion or articulate a contradiction, Medlin was astonished that these people did not at all fit the picture of these people as dumb-minded.

After a long time of storytelling, whose purpose Medlin deduced was to top the last tale as in a back-and-forth game, Hutto, who had been thoroughly enjoying the verbal sparring with the rest, commenced with his contribution. Everyone fell silent to hear from the big man who had not, up to this time, revealed anything about himself. He started by saying he was not from their region but from a place that only recently did he know to be the Great State of South Carolina before he was sold and moved to another state called Georgia. Medlin saw that Hutto had learned well from his lessons around the campfire regarding the states.

As his tale went, the master and his family on the Jehossee plantation in South Carolina were, on balance, very kind. He would often go along on hunting outings and on occasion he would be taken to town to help tote parcels back to the wagon. But the bosses who ran all the slaves were extremely hard and unpredictable in their quick swings to violent behavior.

There was a White overseer who had two Negro drivers. Although these two had risen from being common slaves to a position of power, they, too, had to watch their step. Hutto said one of the drivers made the grave mistake of taking a grievance against the overseer directly to the master, who gave the overseer a thorough dressing down. When word of this got back to the others, everyone knew something was coming. Both drivers increasingly had mistreated their own people once they had gotten the upper hand. It was just a matter of time before the driver would be punished by the White overseer for going over his head to the master. Struggles to maintain power were common on every plantation. This was not at all a situation unfamiliar to the runaways around the campfire. To some degree, most slaves on the plantation suffered under the hand of the one above them.

Hutto went on to tell how one evening, all the slaves were called out to a raging bonfire within their settlement. The overseer announced to all that no one should ever go to the master for anything, and if they did there would be consequences. With that, he grabbed the offending driver with the help of the other, and, using a forked stick, forced his hand into the flames. The flesh up to the wrist began to first wrinkle, then bubble, until it began to fall off into the fire, where it flared up and threw off a sizzling sound. Meanwhile the driver shrieked in pain. The bones of the fingers grew naked of flesh, then charred, and ever after looked like a heron's claw. According to Hutto, he himself was hardly more than a boy at the time.

Hearing that this horror had come to someone who they thought well deserved it, some of those around the campfire began to howl their approval, clapping their hands together. Hutto, too, was enjoying his own story as he recalled that the blacksmith made for the driver a sort of hand tied on with leather laces. Medlin, lying there quietly, had been entertained by the stories of minor mischief, but the story of the burnt hand and the hilarity with which some reacted to the tale stunned him. That they had experienced such brutality and violence was a great shock, and it came to him just how much their lives were different from his own.

Medlin, with his back to the fire and the storytelling, took out his diary and pencil. It was dark, but he could just make out the page. He had already written *On foot out of Pleasant Hill* that morning, but now he thought for some time about what he would add and decided on *Six Negroes and a baby came into camp for a meal*—which somehow didn't seem adequate to chronicle the day, but it would have to do.

By early morning the next day, the fugitives were bustling about the camp, preparing to set out. Hutto passed around coffee, and then offered some of what remained of the hog meat. One of the men wrapped it up tight in a kerchief for when they would be once again on the move with little to eat. Hutto poured out a couple of cups full of dried beans into another kerchief and gave this to the fugitives. His offering was graciously accepted.

They left in single file, thanking Hutto in low tones for the hospitality. Everyone nodded in the direction of Medlin, who removed his hat and made a subtle gesture back.

The two remaining, as was their routine, rolled up the tarp and blanket and strapped them to the duffle. Tins were rinsed, and, along with remaining food, stowed away. On this day Medlin was poorly, but could move around with some effort. Relieving himself in the brush took more time than usual. The shooting pains in his gut were fierce. If it were not for the absolute necessity of keeping on the move, he would seek some relief by lying, wrapped in the blanket, motionless—but that was out.

Hutto was scattering the fire when they heard a shot. It seemed to come from only a few hundred yards away in the direction the visitors had taken. A woman screamed and men were shouting. The sound of horses running in a fury and dogs barking rounded out the noise.

Medlin threw the Colt belt over his head and right arm until the gun was positioned for use. Hutto grabbed the rifle. Both men took off running in the riverbed, toward the commotion. Whatever had happened, it was all over. They dared to raise their heads, only to have to drop back down as a riderless horse jumped directly over them and headlong into the ravine. The horse planted its front legs and the rest went over in a somersault. The whole thing ended with the animal slamming hard into the opposite bank. Medlin and Hutto stood and waited to see if it would recover, stand and make off. Instead the horse flailed its head and neck wildly trying to right itself. After several attempts it managed to stand, but when it tried to run, the right front leg swung from the knee independently and in odd directions. The horse continued down the riverbed as best it could, until it fell and laid its head down in submission.

Medlin and Hutto found a break in the bank and climbed out. Nearly crawling, they made their way to a clearing in a stand of pines. Not hearing anything, they felt safe enough to stand upright, to make sense of what had happened. From the looks of things, there had been plenty of action to trample all the low vegetation the way it was. A grease-stained kerchief lay on the ground. Evidently the dogs had gobbled up the meat. Pieces of clothing lay strewn about here and there—a crude shoe, a ripped sleeve. And there was a dead White man in a heap with blood still coming from an open hole in his chest. From his clothes it was obvious he was of the rough trade of a slave tracker. There were no others dead upon the first inspection. Medlin and Hutto felt no shame in going through the dead man's pockets for anything of value he might have on him. A plug of tobacco and a rag tied with a few dollars and change were all that was salvageable. Nothing of his clothing was worth taking.

Without saying so, both Medlin and Hutto came to the same conclusion, that the people in camp earlier had been set upon by trackers and hauled off. With the old woman not worth the effort to capture, they were surprised the shot heard earlier was not meant for her—but she was not there. Too, how did the dead man get shot? They both hoped she killed him and made off.

They started to go back to camp, retrieve their belongings and head out, but as they left the clearing they spotted a bundle of cloth partly buried in the disturbed earth. Hutto leaned over to retrieve it, thinking maybe it was something they could use. He was lifting it up when a small, lifeless arm fell into view. He crouched, laid the bundle on the ground and gently unwrapped the cloth, to find it was the baby. Dead. Trampled by hooves. They both stood staring, with nothing to say that would place any meaning to it.

Hutto went silently and returned with the camp shovel. They dug a hole as deep as they could so scavenging animals would not pick up on a scent, wrapped the small body carefully in its cloth, placed it in the hole and covered it over. They left the little unmarked grave in silence, retrieved their things from the campsite, and headed off walking in the riverbed where the horse still lay with its eyes wide with wonder. It would have been the right thing to do—what people do when times are right—but they couldn't risk the sound of a shot to properly put it out of its misery. With events coming as they were, nothing seemed to make much sense.

CHAPTER

15

GIL MET A FRIEND at the terrace cafe of the Columbia Museum of Art. After lunch they made a pass through the latest featured exhibit—*Georgia O'Keeffe: Her Carolina Story*—before saying their goodbyes on the steps of CMA and heading back to their offices. On her way back to the Caroliniana, Gil noticed that the activity around the State House was in high gear. Being that it was a Friday, Gil was surprised to see so many demonstrators, until she remembered that this was the day Joe Riley was to finish his march from Charleston and address the crowd from the State House steps. Both sides knew the press would be there in full force, so great efforts were made to have a big turnout.

Various factions of White supremacists were out in impressive numbers. They had learned a long time ago that the press was a great vehicle to spread their message. They were usually covered heavily, as they had appeal for reporters looking to find people to tell their hate story. Any number of the White supremacists sported tattoos of a racist nature, and were very willing to spew their racist rhetoric when the cameras came on. Two chapters of the South Carolina KKK were standing together, yelling blatantly racist slogans as they waved Confederate flags on long poles extending above the crowd.

There was a loose contingent of Black citizens, not affiliated with any organized association, hanging together. Several signs, hand drawn with Magic Marker on Day-Glo poster board, were held up by people in this group. A few Black demonstrators were willing to engage in shouting

matches with White agitators roaming around spoiling for a fight. However nothing much developed.

There was a big crowd of White people who did not think of themselves as radical supremacists. Most of the signs they carried indicated the
notion that the flag represented their Southern heritage. When pressed
by reporters, they answered that it was their belief that the removal of
the flag was about pride, not prejudice. To them, the flag commemo-
rated fallen ancestors who died for a cause they believed in. They feared
that once the flag came down, the Civil War monuments would be next.

The demonstration had grown exponentially, because so many people felt it was important to show their support either for taking the flag
down or leaving it up. When the press started to report on the size
of the demonstration, neither side wanted to be outnumbered by the
opposing side.

The crowd representing the NAACP position was the bigger. Since
the NAACP was the organizing force behind the demonstration, their
members enjoyed the run of the place, and on this day, they were busy
straightening up their tables of handout material and in general tidy-
ing up, expecting the imminent arrival of the mayor of Charleston, Joe
Riley. They had a two-way radio, and learned that Riley was right then
walking over the nearby Congaree Bridge. He was close to finishing what
was being referred to as his march from Charleston to the State House to
show his support for the removal of the Confederate flag. It wasn't really
a march at all, but a 125-mile five-day hike all the way from Charleston
to Columbia. However, *march* sounded more important, like Sherman's
March to the Sea or the Selma March.

In office continuously since 1975, Mayor Riley was a much-admired
figure in Charleston. When he announced that he would walk to Columbia in solidarity with the NAACP, he struck a chord with local celebrities
and just plain folks who thought it was an honorable gesture, so dozens
of them decided to join him. Seventy-five people laced up their walking
shoes and started out on the five-day trek. Everyone was enthusiastic.
Everyone had done some preparatory training, even if it was just a
leisurely stroll through their neighborhood to test out their new sports
shoes. But at the end of the first day, the realities of such a trip set in.

Many went home to rest up and tend blisters, but then arrived four days later by car to rejoin Mayor Riley on the outskirts of Columbia to walk in solidarity as they faced the crowds and the press at the State House.

Joe Riley himself walked every step of the way. Already an avid runner, he was surprised when he got blisters on both feet, but he carried on. All along the way, the little procession encountered onlookers shouting out their support or otherwise. Many people waved and called out, "Go, Joe, go!"

On the other hand, pickups displaying oversized Confederate flags were common. In the truck bed, sitting in folding chairs, were jeering White people who had waited for hours to give Joe the finger. One man carrying a big Confederate flag ran up on the mayor and yelled at him belligerently.

—I dare you to take this out of my hands!

Riley would later say of the protesters that he felt they were basically good people, with opinions counter to his own, and that he was confident of his safety. Nonetheless, at all times he was flanked by two plainclothes Charleston policemen in flak jackets. And, if anyone who saw Riley for the first time thought he was stockier than he looked in the newspaper, it was because he, too, was wearing a bulletproof vest.

––––––

IN HIS LONG CAREER as mayor of Charleston, Riley was a champion for fair treatment of Black people. It was so much a part of the persona of the five-foot-five mayor that he was given the nickname Little Black Joe.

Riley's first real look at racist discrimination was, of all things, while he was playing Little League baseball at age eleven. Across town from where the future mayor grew up was the all-Black neighborhood of Cannon Street, where in 1955 there was a great deal of excitement when for the first time the coach from the local YMCA signed up his team to play in the Charleston Little League tournament. Black kids and White kids for years had played baseball without incident in sandlots all over Charleston, but when it became official that the all-Black Cannon Street YMCA team intended to square off in competition against all-White teams throughout the city, it was a different story. Under pressure from parents of White players, both the tournament organizers and Charleston County officials canceled the tournament.

Undaunted, the Black coach entered the team to play in the South Carolina state tournament in Greenville. All sixty-one White teams withdrew from that tournament. The coach then entered the Cannon Street team in the regional tournament to take place in Rome, Georgia, where the winners from eight Southern state tournaments would play to determine which team would compete in the Little League World Series in Williamsport, Pennsylvania. The resistance was again fierce. The governor of Georgia, Marvin Griffen, made a public statement.

—If youth baseball could be integrated, so, too, could schools, swimming pools, and municipal parks. One break in the dike and the relentless sea will rush in and destroy us.

The regional officials ruled that the Cannon Street team could not advance on forfeitures and therefore was disqualified to play in the World Series. But in what the officials saw as a magnanimous gesture, they invited the team to Williamsport as honored guests. There the young Black boys sat in the stands and watched as their dream to play in the Series was realized only by White teams.

The story of what happened to the Cannon Street team traveled through Charleston. Joe Riley never forgot this blatant discrimination he heard about as a young boy. Fairness and sportsmanship should have been present on the baseball field in 1955, but they weren't.

———

AS SHE WAITED, MRS. THALIA JOHNSON had plenty to do before Mayor Riley would come bounding up the steps of the State House to address the crowd. She was the director of the Columbia Chapter of the NAACP, and everyone wanted her attention. On this day, something strange had come over her, so she stopped for a moment, took her emotional temperature, and tried to diagnose the unfamiliar, gay mood. She was happy. That was it. It had been so long since this lightness and feeling of satisfaction had washed over her.

Thalia Johnson could pinpoint the first time she had ever felt so uplifted. It was the moment when she first felt she belonged to something—something that gave purpose to her life, something that meant she was not just settling as her parents had done for so many years. That moment was when, at age eighteen, she had walked into the office of the NAACP on Simpson Street in Columbia and asked if there was anything she could do to help, even if it was only in the evening or on the weekend when she wasn't working as a laundress at the Pierpont Hotel. From that moment on, she felt she belonged.

Back then, the "Advancement of Colored People" did not sound out of place because back then Black people were called "Coloreds." When she told the young ones that, they looked at her as if she dated back to the days of Methuselah.

———

THE NATIONAL ASSOCIATION for the Advancement of Colored People was founded in 1909 with an almost all-White executive board. In that day and time, Black people had little or no clout to start such a thing on their own. The exception to the all-White board was Black writer and civil rights activist W. E. B. DuBois. In forming the NAACP the founders were reacting to a deadly race "riot" in 1908 in Springfield, Illinois, "the Land of Lincoln," when a reported mob of five thousand White people attacked the Black neighborhood, murdering sixteen residents—including two who were lynched. Though the founders of the NAACP were most outraged by anti-Colored violence, they expanded their mission to "remove all barriers of racial discrimination through democratic processes."

In the early days, emphasis was on establishing branch offices. Within the first five years, three hundred local branches blanketed the country. At the same time, the organization built a legal team that won victories in the courts regarding discriminatory voting practices and admitting Black people into the military. For thirty years they tried in vain to get the United States Congress to explicitly outlaw lynching and to require action by law enforcement. Although several times they came close to getting bills through to make it law that lynchers must be prosecuted by the federal government, the Southern bloc was too powerful and squashed all efforts, so nearly a century after the NAACP was founded and as thousands were victims of lynching, there were still no federal laws specifically addressing lynching. It was left up to local authorities to deal with these crimes—and often they did not act at all appropriately.

In the 1940s, when Congress showed no appetite for dealing with the constitutionality of equal rights for all Black citizens, the Supreme Court seemed ready to take on the challenge. Maybe there would be the long-awaited showdown over the issue of inferiority that went back hundreds of years.

FEW TIMES IN AMERICAN HISTORY had need and remedy so successfully aligned as in the pairing of civil rights issues and Federal Court Justice Thurgood Marshall. Born in Baltimore in 1908, the year of the Springfield riot, Marshall was the son of parents who were both descendants of slaves. His father, a train porter, saw and experienced much discrimination firsthand. However, he taught his two sons to appreciate the US Constitution, especially the principle of protecting the rights of all citizens. He taught them to argue. He relentlessly challenged Thurgood and his brother, making them prove every statement they made. Young Thurgood learned the importance of logical thinking, which he carried into his career in the law. The father often took both boys to the Baltimore courthouse to witness cases in progress, and then they debated around the dinner table everything they had seen. Later, Marshall credited what he learned at home as being the foundation of his appreciation for debate.

After graduating with a law degree from Howard University, Marshall established a private law practice. He represented the NAACP in one of his first cases. The case involved a young Black man with excellent credentials, denied admission into the University of Maryland Law School because of its segregation policy. This case was the beginning of Marshall's twenty-five-year affiliation with the NAACP.

In 1940 he founded and was executive director of the NAACP Legal Defense and Education Fund, which backed many cases he argued before the United States Supreme Court. No case was more momentous than *Brown v. Board of Education* in 1954, when he successfully argued that racial segregation in public education was a violation of the Equal Protection Clause.

Thurgood Marshall eventually became the first African American Supreme Court Justice, serving from 1967 until 1991. Marshall was the ninety-sixth Supreme Court Justice. President Lyndon Johnson nominated him, saying this was "the right thing to do, the right time to do it, the right man and the right place." For all the significant things that Marshall accomplished to help along the advancement of all Black people in America, his name was forever tied to the NAACP.

The NAACP was, from the start, committed to advancing their cause through the court system, but it was slow slogging. The younger, new members who came on with energy and enthusiasm found the waiting time to be tedious. They had hoped to be part of the action, but while Marshall and the rest of the legal team were battling it out in Washington or regional courthouses, the downtime was a spirit breaker.

Meanwhile, there were other organizations that popped up with their own brand of activism. The Southern Christian Leadership Conference really caught on in late 1957 with Martin Luther King Jr. as president. The NAACP and SCLC had the same goals, but their methods differed radically. King was for nonviolent direct action, whereas the NAACP thought civil rights should be fought for through the courts—a much slower process. The NAACP traditionally promoted leadership from the top—elite educators, clergymen, and professionals. They were skeptical of marshaling ordinary Black folks in mass demonstrations. They preferred the leadership to be front and center. King and the SCLC's philosophy was to include everyone, to send the message and share the passions in a collective voice. Even though the two groups worked well together on some things, their opposing methodologies were too great for them to be completely in accord.

King's direct actions and mass demonstrations made events more visual. The images of fire hosing, attack dogs, and clubbing of Black demonstrators—including children—were a strong lesson to the mass public watching television in how and to what degree the "American problem" existed. The NAACP could not compete with the dynamism of King and the press. In the end, the new blood went to the SCLC, and

the NAACP lost membership and momentum. But Thalia Johnson stuck
with the NAACP.

––––––

As Miz Johnson arranged tables and tidied up the stacks of
pamphlets at the State House, waiting for Mayor Riley, she started to
think back on her pre-NAACP days. She was seventeen when she rode
the thirty miles into Columbia from her home in Elma with her parents
in their '41 Ford. They made the drive every other Sunday to see her
mother's mother at a dreary senior home in the middle of town. As they
left the car and walked through a park to get to her grandmother's, there
was a Black man standing on a bench preaching to a handful of people.
It was most curious because this was in the 1950s when "Coloreds" well
knew that it was best for them to maintain a low profile. Thalia and her
parents did not stop, but she got the gist of his message. He seemed to be
worked up about having to prove who he was to vote. He punctuated it
by asking, "Am I not a man?"

As they walked past, her parents picked up their pace so as not to be
confused with people interested in his message. On their return to the car
after their brief visit to the senior home, the orator was sitting by himself
on the bench tending to a split lip with a handkerchief soaked in blood.

This was in the 1950s, when South Carolina became the first state to
require identification to vote. The reason given was that this would cut
down on voter fraud, but exhaustive studies proved fraud was extremely
rare, so the real reason was obvious. The requirement was clearly
designed to keep the poor minorities away from the polls.

Back home in Elma, Thalia quietly decided on her own to approach
every Black man and woman within walking distance of her house to
see if they had some form of identification. If they did not, she had a list
of acceptable documentation. Many had no birth certificate or driver's
license, but an electric or water bill would do if it had their name and
address on it.

Elma lay thirty miles south of Columbia. Any money passing through
Elma was from cotton. According to the census the town's population was
eighteen hundred, but likely that number was not accurate, since most

people in Elma were suspicious of any door-to-door canvassing by the government, and so kept their doors closed when the census takers came around. The proportion of have-nots to haves was great. The haves were White, and if they had not run off to greener pastures after graduation from either USC or Clemson, they followed in the footsteps of the generation before them—always in the cotton business. Some owned ancestral cotton farms or managed large spreads. The town ran on cotton.

The majority population was Black, descendants of sharecroppers who in turn were descendants of slaves who had worked the same land. If they were not sweating in the cotton fields, then these Black people serviced the needs of those who were making money from cotton. Thalia's father, Big Jim, worked at the gin in the elevated position of cotton grader.

Had it not been for the fact that Jim played as a young boy with Mr. Bobby Stanley, the owner of the gin, he would be a loader along with other Black people. The two grew up together, fished together and bird-hunted together. They drove wild all over the property in the work truck, out of sight of Buck Stanley, Bobby's father. But there came a time when it was just not right to mingle with Colored kids. If you did, you were a "nigger lover," and nobody wanted that label. So, without any conscience about it, Bobby abruptly stopped any sign of friendship with Jimmy. However, when Buck handed over the cotton gin business to his son, Big Jim became the grader. At the yard, Bobby was Mr. Stanley to Jim.

Thalia's mother, Bess, worked at the laundromat, one block off the main street in town. During her many years at the laundromat, Bess experienced everything that could happen to the ten washers and eight dryers. With one old screwdriver held together with duct tape, she could bring to life any machine gone down. She also worked the front counter and took in bundles of dirty clothes from a few people who were willing to pay a premium for her to wash, dry, and fold them by the end of the day. Without exception, these patrons were White.

Bess and Big Jim's eldest daughter had run off to Atlanta with a new boyfriend, leaving three kids, all under five years old, to be cared for in Elma by the grandparents. At the laundromat Bess barely made enough to pay a babysitter to take care of them. Where she made extra money to make life worth living was from work she just sort of fell into—laundering and ironing White ladies' legacy bed linens. What began with one order grew to a little side business that closely rivaled the earnings of her day job.

It started when a friend who worked as a housekeeper brought in two sets of sheets and pillowcases of the finest quality Bess had ever seen. The friend tended the home of the president of the only bank in Elma. The Missus was very demanding, and would hear no excuses regarding a broken-down washing machine on wash day, so that day the housekeeper brought the linens to the laundromat and left them with Bess. Bess ran her hand over the luxuriant, soft bedclothes that had worn to the consistency of silk. When a monogram emerged, she held her breath at such beauty and craftsmanship. The elegant curved, continuous line that intertwined the three initials must have been worked by an artisan with skill perfected over a lifetime.

Bess knew that wealthy White people collected things for the "glory box" of a daughter approaching an age to marry and already being groomed to run a household and staff. An expectant bride's mother and grandmother would assemble fine things for the trousseau. They might comb through Europe, purchasing only the best quality goods to accompany the young bride into marriage. Bess did not know it, but these linens had been purchased and monogramed in Belgium. They were delivered to the dock, where they waited along with all the other finery purchased throughout Europe for the travelers boarding the ship for the voyage back to America.

Quickly, after Bess took in the first order, word got around as to her excellent handling of the linens. Her weekly clientele grew to four households. Bess would close the laundromat at six thirty as always, but would stay on and use the machines to carefully wash the linens on the gentlest cycle. Then she would use six dryers and spin the linens only until damp, never trusting such fine things to a complete cycle of scorching heat. The owner of the laundromat lived in Columbia and rarely swung by during the day to check on her, so she felt in no danger of losing her job over using the machines after hours.

The damp linens would go into a large basket to be carried home for careful ironing. Thalia would help by holding the long lengths of linen off the floor while Bess meticulously ironed each piece. Ironing over the monograms, she placed a damp cloth between the linen and hot iron so as not to scorch the delicate stitching. After each fold, she made another pass with the iron so that the final piece was flat, crisp and tailored. Her patrons were pleased, because the work showed that someone in service took particular care of their precious possessions.

Just as word got around fast that Bess could make up fine linens well, it took only a few days until all of Elma was aware of Thalia's efforts to increase the Black voting roster. Only a teenager, she had not a clue there could be backlash or even danger in what she was doing. And, going door to door in her Black neighborhood, she was surprised that some people shut their doors, afraid White folks would take offense if they listened to her.

For the most part, she felt safe, but when after a few days she expanded her mission out of her neighborhood, and had to walk on less traveled roads to get to the more rural population, she realized that she was vulnerable. On occasion a slow-moving car followed her for a hundred yards, then sped by her. Young White boys hung out of car windows, yelling obscenities as they passed. Each time, they were a little more brazen, so she started to make her way through the woods, out of eyeshot of traffic on the road.

Thalia's parents were well aware of danger, as Black friends told them the Whites were not at all happy with Thalia going around ginning up the Black vote. But Bess and Jimmy never made any mention to their daughter or asked her to quit her efforts. Instead, they chose to let the young girl find out for herself that black skin is never rewarded with fairness—a lesson they had both learned the hard way.

Thalia was sure to be home in time on Tuesdays and Thursdays to help her mother with ironing the linens, but one Tuesday she arrived back from her canvassing to find Bess sitting on the back porch snapping pole beans. There were no linens in sight. As to why, Bess said that her clients had decided they no longer needed her services—they would get their Colored girls to handle the linens from then on. That night was Thalia's time to learn a hard lesson that would stay deep within her. It was the moment when she had to make up her mind to go with the grain or against it.

———

ON THE LANDING HALFWAY UP the State House steps, Thalia—or Miz Johnson as she liked to be called—continued busying herself placing folding chairs and tables, not willing for any of her volunteers to make decisions of arrangement on their own. She thought to herself that she hadn't been with the organization for this long to let them take over in any way. There was never any chatter about her bossiness behind her back, because all knew her time went back to King, and that alone was reason for respect.

From her position on the landing, Miz Johnson caught sight of the woman with the red hair, the same one she had noticed walking by the State House twice a day. Miz Johnson often appeared to be in a dither, but nothing much ever escaped her consciousness. She noticed that the Reverend Joe, too, was aware of the White lady and her comings and goings. In a conversation with herself, she acknowledged that the Reverend was not married so he could take up with anyone he wanted to, but right now he had a job to do—this flag thing was too big for anyone to get distracted. Joe Pearl had walked into her life and by God, he needed to keep his eye on the prize. It would be up to her to have him always looking forward.

Miz Johnson thought to herself that on top of everything, Reverend Joe was a fine specimen of a Black man whose appearance couldn't hurt in selling their story. To her, his greatest weakness was that he seemed too sensitive to the opinion of others—not always the right people—who had not gone down the long road to do right by their people, as she had done. To bring Joe around, this would be her job. Her crown and glory might well be to be the woman behind the next modern-day Messiah whom the movement desperately needed. King, alone, had not pulled himself up to the mountaintop without the efforts of others, behind the scenes, strategizing every move. She had been close enough in the old days to observe that Martin was the word man, but when to speak out for the maximum impact was always a decision made by others in the tight group of handlers.

Rosa Parks was another one who had the organization behind her. She didn't just one day decide she'd had it with White people keeping her from sitting in the Whites-only section in the front of the bus. She had been active in the NAACP for a decade before she was arrested for civil disobedience, for not relinquishing her seat to a White passenger. The NAACP had chosen her as a spearhead, the one to challenge Alabama segregation laws, and thought that she would be willing to become a controversial figure, that she had the dedication to go the distance in the legal battle to come. She made the personal sacrifice and suffered the consequences of defiance in order to demonstrate that Black people were fed up with being held down as second-class citizens.

Miz Johnson's thoughts drifted back to all the legendary stories of the successes during her early years of service at the NAACP, and she felt the personal sacrifices were all worth it. She would have to keep her eye on the redhead to be sure she didn't get her hooks into Joe and manipulate him in the wrong direction. This White lady could not be allowed to mess things up—there was too much riding on it.

———

GIL ARRIVED BACK AT THE OFFICE after lunch at the art museum anxious to get back to the Medlin diaries. They would be a refreshing interlude between projects that usually required resources scattered within the university's vast library system and frequently way beyond. For the most part this project should be a skip through records easily retrieved on her computer. If she had to take the short drive over to State Archives, she wouldn't mind—Gil loved to reconnect with people she had known for years. And she certainly would be happy to take a walk to the courthouse, just a few blocks away, if she wanted to put her hands on original documents written with a quill pen. Often copies of these were not legible on the computer.

Before turning to the Medlin diaries, Gil followed one of her hard-and-fast habits—making hot tea. She dropped a bag of ginger black tea into a prissy porcelain cup from her grandmother's china, and prepared to start on the diaries. The cup, with its transfer image of some grand English manor house, always made the ritual feel special.

As she settled down to work, right off she could see why the descendants of William R. Medlin had no attachment to the two leather bound diaries. The writing was illegible to anyone not accustomed to making sense out of the chicken scratch written almost one hundred and fifty years before. Gil had seen dozens of these early diaries and had gotten good at deciphering words written most often in a hurry and for the writer's eyes only.

In Gil's experience, diaries fell into two categories—if you didn't count Civil War diaries, which were in a special class all their own. The diaries in one category were dedicated to recording sentiment—describing a relationship or social occasion, or memorializing a special moment. These were usually written by romantic young women. The pen stroke was often exquisite—in a hand trained at an early age to produce a lovely note that showed good breeding.

The other category of diary was strictly utilitarian, usually written hastily by a planter or farmer—recording weather conditions, production yields, expenses, or any other information that could show patterns and trends maybe helpful for the business of the next year. These were the work of men who were not at all concerned about sentiment. The writing was often done on the fly, with no consideration for whittling a fine pencil point or fancy penmanship. Art was of no importance—only information. Gil already knew that W. R. Medlin was a cotton farmer, so she figured the project would be cut-and-dried—she would transcribe the penciled notations and follow up with a couple of pages of narrative on William R. Medlin of Clio, South Carolina.

She started in to get an overview of the Medlin family lineage. Processes for building family genealogies had changed radically and become much easier since the computer showed up. Several enterprises had taken on the task of assembling vast amounts of information for quick sharing, after the era of amateur and professional historians who tramped through courthouses and record rooms looking to build family histories.

Gil signed into the university's account with Ancestry.com and searched for William R. Medlin. Up came some basic information—he was born on January 7, 1814, in a town called Clio, in Marlboro County, South Carolina. His father was Joel, and his mother, Mary. His wife was named Lydia. In the 1850 census there were three children, two sons,

Caleb and Daniel, and a daughter named Clara Anne. Gil clicked on William's father Joel and found that he and his wife, Mary, had lived in Cumberland, North Carolina, just across the state line from Clio. Gil knew that a move from one nearby town to another was not unusual, as often people were looking for better land. Likely Joel and Mary moved from Cumberland to Clio as a young couple.

When Gil saw William's mother listed as Mary Unk, she recalled with a smile that when, as a young inexperienced summer intern at USC, she had first come across the name Unk, she had remarked to her advisor that Unk was a name she had never seen before. After hearing a couple of giggles around the room, she was embarrassed when it was explained that Unk stood for Unknown—Mary's maiden name was unknown.

Gil covered two earlier generations of Medlins. With just a couple of clicks she found them in Virginia. She assumed that the early migration of the family originated in Virginia and the Chesapeake Bay region. That pattern of migration looked similar to that of so many early Irish settlers like her own family, the Culkins. But it was too early in the research for her to come to any conclusions.

She had seen it many times—the families came to America during a mass migration in masted ships from England, Ireland, Scotland, and Wales. Several hundred thousand came to worship as they chose, work their own land and keep the bounty of their labor—all denied them by the Church and Crown in their homeland. The largest number came into Philadelphia and then dispersed throughout the states of Pennsylvania, Delaware, and Maryland. It was only a matter of time that as the numbers of immigrants swelled, land to the south became a temptation.

What came to be known as the Great Wagon Road—once a trail for huge herds of buffalo, and then an Iroquois trade route—served as the main thoroughfare for a mass movement of humanity traveling south into Tennessee, the Carolinas, and Georgia. The Great Wagon Road went from Philadelphia to Augusta, 735 miles in all. It split at Big Lick, Virginia, later to be known as Roanoke. One road went upland into Knoxville. The other branch went through the Piedmont of North Carolina across the center belly of South Carolina and terminated in Augusta on the boundary of Georgia and South Carolina.

All manner of transportation was put into action to carry the worldly goods of the newcomers down the Wagon Road. There were carts and wagons of every kind, up to the over twenty-foot-long Conestoga wagons requiring six pairs of horses to pull them along. Depending on the final stop, the trip could take a minimum of two to four months.

Gil's assumption that the Medlins were part of the Great Migration from Britain seemed to be validated when she came upon Richard Medlin (1660–1700) of Redruth, Cornwall, England. She brought up several sites on Redruth to see if there were any clues as to why Richard would decide to put himself and his wife, Rachel, through the hardship of extreme travel to come to the complete unknown in America.

Gil read that John Wesley traveled to preach twenty-two times in Redruth, where he found a very receptive audience to promote his new brand of religion—Methodism. His notion that every man in his lifetime could by his own efforts reach a blessed state struck a favorable chord with the people of Redruth who were fed up with the Church of England's tenet that God spoke only through the clergy. Maybe Richard Medlin wanted to be free to practice the religion of the Methodists in the American Colonies, where the doors of tolerance were swung wide open—but Gil found no hard evidence of this. She figured it would remain a mystery how and why Richard came to America and raised his family in New Kent, Virginia.

Returning to Ancestry.com, Gil clicked on the tab for *Public Member Scanned Documents*—a space dedicated to material posted by a subscriber doing research on a particular family. Up came an announcement that an amateur historian was soon to publish a book on the first Medlin to come to America, Richard. There was also a two-page synopsis of the contents of the book. Richard and Rachel were Quakers who left England in 1682 on the ship *Carolina*, which passed through the Barbados and then sailed on to Charleston, South Carolina, where they had been granted a hundred acres of land on what was later known as James Island. Gil held her breath over what she was reading. The Medlins were Quakers who had come first to Charleston, a place they knew to be tolerant of their religion, and not through Philadelphia like most all other British, Scottish, Irish, and Welsh immigrants.

The amateur historian speculated that Richard and Rachel did not stay long in the Lowcountry, but left out of fear of raiding Spaniards coming to the region from Florida. In any case, the records showed that they left the Lowcountry and traveled north, where they settled in New Kent, Virginia Colony, and raised a family.

Gil jumped from her chair, stamped her feet, and threw her arms up as though she was set upon by a swarm of bees. She broke all the rules of library etiquette by shouting out at the top of her lungs.

—I *love* my job! Sorry, everybody, you know how I can get carried away.

With a big grin, she remarked to herself that out of all the thousands of early settlers who traveled down the Great Wagon Road, the Medlins were the only ones she had ever heard of who went *up* the Wagon Road. As she flopped back into her chair, she couldn't help but think that nothing was totally predictable in history, and that was why she loved it so much.

16

Hutto gone
May 20, 1857

FTER MEDLIN AND HUTTO buried the trampled body of the baby, they went back to their campsite without a word, gathered up their belongings, and headed out toward Canton again. They made slow progress—only a very few miles that day before making an early camp. They figured they had several more miles to travel, according to Happy Landrum's estimate that from the time they chanced to meet him they had about ten miles on the road until they would encounter a train station at Canton. If Medlin were in better shape, they would have reached Canton by now, but there had been several interludes that day when they had to stop for Medlin to regain his strength, after his legs gave out and he just dropped to the ground unable to go on. The miseries were frequent and violent. Puking joined bowel eruptions. Hutto tried to remedy these with teas of wild herbs foraged along the way, but they didn't help much.

Although so much was foreign, there were some plants familiar from South Carolina, and it was with those plants that the teas were concocted. Sassafras and wild ginger root tea were of modest benefit against a condition that could not be cured by anything administered in the field, but the warmth of the cup and the rest provided Medlin some comfort. Both Medlin and Hutto soon came to the realization that their effort was just to get Medlin back to Clio—not to be nursed back to health but to die at home. Both had the instinct that whatever the problem, there would be no recovery.

Medlin still carried the shackles. In the event they were about to pass by people working a field or to encounter others riding in a buckboard, he quickly applied them to Hutto's wrists so that suspicion did not arise that they were traveling under any condition other than as master and slave. But most of the time it was just the two of them, struggling to make it another mile up the road toward the train.

After another day of this very difficult travel, Medlin figured that if Happy Landrum could be believed, they must be over halfway to Canton and the train that would take them to Charleston. Medlin told Hutto that from Charleston they would take another train on to Bennettsville and then somehow they would get from there to Clio.

By the next morning Medlin was so weak that he could barely walk, even with Hutto carrying all the gear now. They made it only until midmorning before they had to stop and make camp. Medlin lapsed into incoherence but then woke in the evening with a little renewed energy, enough to carry on limited conversation. They spoke about things beyond Hutto's experience—a world outside of the confines of the plantation. Hutto also wanted to know more about trains now that he had several experiences with them and his fear was not as strong. Who made them and how was it determined where they would travel? Once Hutto got started, there seemed to be endless questions until Medlin was exhausted and he dropped off to sleep.

Next morning, he was able to travel for only an hour, when he could go no farther that day. Some distance from the road Hutto found a wide stream with fresh water, ideal for a camp. He put everything down, and with his big hand anchored under Medlin's upper arm, he helped him maneuver down the embankment and into the shelter of an undercut from a time when the stream had swelled. The big man had to lift Medlin almost off his feet because of the weakness in the legs. There was a natural gravel bank where he propped Medlin against a rock, while he climbed back up to the road for the gear. The clearing along the stream was cool under a high shaded wet rock face. Moss and ferns were fond of the conditions and grew profusely on out-cut landings and in crevices.

Hutto made a fire and heated a cup of sassafras tea from a supply made the day before and stored in the bladder. He scrounged through the duffle and rucksack but found only a sliver of jerky and some dregs of ground coffee at the bottom of the tin. In the late afternoon, with Medlin in such a poor state, Hutto said he was going off in search of food. Maybe the woods would be holding some berries and wild apples, or—even better—a gopher tortoise might make a mistake and wander into a clearing to become easy prey.

Hutto took the empty rucksack, negotiated a dry crossing over the stream and followed a deer trail up to the rocky ridgeline opposite the camp. At the crest, he saw that the terrain opened onto grassy meadowland. He crossed it until he reached a good-sized field of corn. After a while he came to a meandering line of willows mingled with hemlocks beside fast-moving water—bigger than a stream, almost what anyone would call a small river. Approaching the edge, he stood on the bank and saw that by the looks of deposits of dry debris among the rocks on either side, the water was not at its full height.

He sat on a rock, pulled off his shoes, rolled up his pants, and then walked knee-deep into the water. It was cold, but it felt good. He felt good. It had been a long time since he felt free to dally—free to watch the natural world in motion. Hutto now had the rare occasion to just look out over the land—to feel the coolness of the water on his calloused feet and to notice the calls of birds darting throughout the hemlocks.

Before he continued on to find food, he stood in the water thinking of what it would be like not to go back to camp—to just keep going on his own. He began to picture what he would do from that moment on. He had a fleeting thought to try to make it back to South Carolina alone, but dropped that notion since he had not the slightest idea how he could travel so far without benefit of the train and the company of a White man. Recalling the fate of those they shared their camp with a few days before was certainly no encouragement. And then, there was Medlin.

Without at first being conscious of it, Hutto was watching two dark shadows below the surface of the clear water. The silhouettes resisted the swift flow, which convinced Hutto that they were only submerged roots or slender, elongated rocks. But one "rock" moved out of sight into deeper shadow and returned with a third, and then they were all still, somehow resisting the current. Now it was plain that they were fish that could live in the cool, fresh water.

He returned to the bank, put on his shoes, and headed upriver. He traveled on a little while until the river took a sharp bend into a stand of trees. From beyond the trees rose a narrow plume of blue-gray smoke as from a chimney—not the splayed-out pattern as from a campfire. Getting closer, he saw a small house with several outbuildings. Approaching on an angle to the house to avoid being in full view from any window, he came up against the exterior wood cladding and made his way to the back. The house was built up off the ground by about four feet, possibly to avoid damage from a seasonal overflow of the river. There was a porch off the back door where two mongrels—half coon dog, half something wild—were eating from a large crock bowl. They were too busy eating to notice Hutto taking up a crouched position below the porch. They were making quick work of meaty pork rib bones in a slurry of rendered lard and cornmeal.

Hutto slowly rose to where his head cleared the floor so he was in view of the dogs, an arm's length away. Their heads swung in Hutto's direction, their leathery ears slapping against their jowls. With a low growl, they both showed their teeth, cornmeal dropping to the porch in wet globs of mush. Hutto stayed perfectly still, but curled his lips, showing his own teeth. He opened his eyes wide, and he too uttered a low, guttural growl. Intimidated, both dogs slunk down the steps and under the house, looking out of their droopy, watery eyes.

From the rucksack Hutto pulled the hank of waxed cloth that once carried jerky. With one motion of his big hand he scooped up the entire contents of the bowl—meaty pork bones and corn mush—and placed it in the middle of the cloth. Then he pulled up all four corners and tied them tight.

He crossed the yard to an outbuilding with one end cantilevered over a sluice run of fast water on the river. He slid open the door that was on rollers suspended from a track. Inside, it was dim, almost dark. There was a big window overlooking the river and a pair of high-up narrow openings on each side, but none let in much light, as they were all covered with cobwebs laden with mill dust.

He walked the long, narrow building toward the window. There was a grinding stone attached to a shaft that went down to the water where, when engaged, a paddlewheel powered the whole thing. Now the stone lay idle in a horizontal wooden frame on four sturdy legs. As he approached the contraption, mice scattered in all directions. Within seconds, they disappeared into every available crevice and crack.

Opening a flap on the rucksack, he used his hand and forearm to sweep in the cracked corn that was scattered about. With his fingers he fidgeted meal from the catch trough and negotiated it into the pocket of the rucksack until it could hold no more. On his way out, he picked up several empty gunnysacks and a roll of heavy hemp twine.

Meanwhile, back in camp, Medlin sat as long as he could leaning against the rock where Hutto had left him. With the sun now not much more than a faint glow coming through the trees, the spot by the stream grew cold. The fire went out when he closed his eyes for a while, but Hutto had put the blanket nearby. Medlin pulled the blanket up around himself. Before it turned totally dark, he looked again at the train schedule. He took out his diary to catch up where it had been left blank for a three-day spell. The diary would not permit neglect, as there was a space dedicated to each day. There was not much to account for other than laborious walking and attacks of the miseries. Desperate to put down something in the blank spaces, he just wrote *Walked*. For this day, May 20, he contemplated on a diary notation and finally decided on *Hutto gone*.

He had been thinking about being left ever since the long shadows came and there was no sign of the big man. Medlin ran the scenario through his head, and it seemed to be a logical conclusion. He convinced himself that if it hadn't been for him, Celia and Jama would still be alive. There was no reason for Hutto to stay, especially since his condition had become such a burden, and by all signs it would only get worse. Medlin struggled a bit but was able to put the duffle between himself and the rock where Hutto had left him, collapsed against it and, feeling hopeless, fell asleep.

Something awakened Medlin, but he couldn't respond until he came out of a kind of a stupor. There was little to remind him of his circumstances—it was pitch dark. He was on his side in a crumpled position as if he had no spine. His face was in the gravel. He pulled himself into a sit and had to brush away pebbles stuck to his cheek. They left indentations in his flesh. The sound of the stream brought back that he was in camp.

Footsteps in gravel told of someone coming close. He patted the ground to find the Colt, but with no success. Then he heard a voice in the dark.

—Sir, where are you?

Hutto was able to scrounge what was needed to start a fire that soon blazed bright. Medlin got his bearings, but it bothered him that he had fallen so deeply asleep.

Hutto had a rolling boil of water in the pot and poured in meal from a pocket of the rucksack. He stepped out of the light of the fire and returned with a handful of fern fronds. While he fiddled around the fire, he told Medlin about the river, the fish, stealing the dogs' food, all about the mill and scooping up meal. At one point, he knelt at Medlin's side to show him the abundance of meal in the rucksack. Words poured from Hutto about his time away, but Medlin, still in a fog, remarked little. However, he was moved by Hutto's enthusiasm, and was swept along in the telling of the tale, enough to bring a smile to his face. Under his amusement he was glad to put away the fear that Hutto was not coming back. He was too weak to put thought as to why he had returned.

Talk stopped for a time as Hutto concentrated on a construction of green twigs, with the aim to build a platform suspended well above the flames of the campfire. He dipped the ferns into the stream and placed them in a heap on the rack. Soon, they let off a plume of white smoke. He went on to tell Medlin about the fish that lived in the cold water of the river. He said that on the way back to camp from the mill, there were streaks of sunlight that lit up the wings of bugs flying low over the river. Pools were dimpled and full of fish feeding off the insects that touched on the surface.

Hutto told of crossing the river and working his way over to an outcrop directly at the tail end of the feeding pool. He waited for the fish to resettle and resume feeding after they scattered when they first sensed foreign movement. He said that when the time was right, he swiped at a surfacing fish, caught it at its underbelly, and threw it onto dry land. With that, he plunged his hand into the rucksack, grabbed the fish behind its gills and raised it triumphantly high in the air. At the same time, he let out a big laugh. Medlin, too, got caught up in the story, and did as well as he could with a laugh that ended in a spasm.

Hutto cut off the head, tail and fins, and gutted the fish as he would a shad. He placed it deep inside the pocket of smoking ferns. In a short time, Hutto was pinching off chunks of flaky white meat and feasting heartily. This, and the pork ribs cooked in cornmeal with lard, were a welcome change from jerky and salt pork.

Medlin was only able to pick at some white meat of the fish before his bowels went into convulsions. He lay still on his back, motionless, hoping his body would remain neutral, but it didn't happen. He pulled his knees up to his chest, rocked back and forth and moaned until his gut settled enough so he could stretch out again.

The storm came up with little warning. It began to rain hard, and heavy lightning lit up the trees overhead. Some bolts of lightning struck very close by, making the whole camp turn blinding white for a split second. Hutto wrapped Medlin in the blanket and drew the tarp over both of them. They huddled tightly together—Medlin cradled in Hutto's cavernous chest. Soon the stream swelled and overflowed the bank, enough that Hutto had to reposition the two onto a grassy plateau up from the gravelly bank. Medlin was in and out of consciousness, and often let out an extended low moan. Once again, they were huddled to one another, with the tarp covering them against the rain. To anyone who might have wandered into the camp, the mound made by the two men would be mistaken for a boulder. The only thing that would betray them was the moan.

Very early the next morning Medlin became faintly aware that Hutto was busying on something as he cut down two sturdy birch saplings and pared off everything that was not part of the final wooden shafts. To these he strung burlap with twine until he had a crude litter. He was rough with it, to test durability, and was satisfied it would hold together. Medlin was totally unaware of the bright sun, and that the rain had cleared out some of the humidity. The only thing that came into his consciousness a little later was the gentle sway of his body in a hammock of coarse sacking, and the sound of something being dragged along the road.

G IL SAW THE DEMONSTRATION at the State House for what
would be the last time—the Confederate flag was coming down
at two o'clock. After so long, she wanted to see it through.

She started wondering about what, if anything, she may have learned
from the whole to-do about the Confederate flag. In her spare time, she
had been digging into the history of racism and now she started reviewing
what she had learned so far. The flag was to come down, and she naturally
wanted some closure. Up to that point, whatever professional project she
undertook had a beginning that would set up the premise and a middle
to tell the story, and then the end would pay off in a summary of how
the story was concluded. However, in non-professional life and the flag
situation, Gil felt some uneasiness about having come to the end without
drawing a clear conclusion. It was unsettling.

She had approached the flag issue aiming, as she always did, at
understanding something through research and analytical thinking, but
this time her habitual approach didn't work—something was missing.
She thought there could be a clue in her favorite James Baldwin quote:
"The great force of history comes from the fact that we carry it within
us, are unconsciously controlled by it in many ways, and history is literally present in all that we do."

One question had stuck in her mind right from the beginning of the
demonstration—was the South itself totally responsible for the lingering sting of racism in America? Finally, she had turned to her mother,

who had spent all of her life in the South. Gil had called her the day
before—as always, on Friday—asking her directly what growing up in
the South meant to her. Her mother, ever ready to go down memory
lane, offered a rolling reel of snippets from what she called "my raising
up in the South."

She talked about church, and how every Easter Aunt Bea would buy
her an outfit from Reuben's in downtown Florence—a complete getup
from tip to toe. One of her favorites was a straw hat with a pink grosgrain
ribbon hatband, and a fancy flowered dress that reached almost down to
her white patent Mary Janes. The mother made it clear it was the simple
pleasures that made up most of the character of the Southerner.

Then there came a change in her voice. To her it was an important
point, the most important point, so she said it slowly and emphatically.

—Honey, the South was mostly poor people who depended on the
dirt and stuck to it. All our people, and most others we knew, had a little
land that had come down through generations. There was always that
tie to the land. Even if you had a full-time job like running the hardware
store, you always set aside some time to put in a little corn or some beans.
Very few people left to find something better, or at least if they did move
off, it usually wasn't far.

She kept talking, as Gil tried to imagine her mother's world.

—Nobody had money, so we had to rely on our imaginations. There
was no arena for sports and no theater for plays. There was one movie
house in town, where most all us kids went to Saturday matinees for
nine cents. Some lucky ones had an extra two cents for a Tootsie Roll
Pop. Colored people went to the movies too, but they had to sit up in
the balcony.

Gil's mother shifted back to the importance of church and family.

—There was always a sit-down Sunday lunch, for the whole family. It
was after church, so the men and boys all wore fresh shirts and long pants.
For women and girls, fresh ironed dress or skirt. Nobody ever missed Sunday lunch unless they were in bed sick. There would usually be a roast,
but always there was a dish of Johnny Mae's deviled eggs with sweet pick-
les sliced thin as paper. Another of my favorites was her tomato aspic with
minced celery and a dollop of Duke's on top. Johnny Mae would cook the

meal, serve us, then slip out the kitchen door to Sunday dinner with her own family. Of course, she never sat down with us.

Gil wondered if Johnny Mae did the Sunday dishes when she came in to work on Monday morning.

Gil's mother ran on for an hour about square dances at school, picking pole beans fresh from the garden for that same night's supper. Catching lightning bugs, putting them in a jar with holes in the lid made with an ice pick. Gil listened intently. She did not want to break in to cut it short, since her mother was relishing each memory of growing up in the South. In the end, Gil's impression was that there was not open racism, much less conscious expressions of White supremacy, among her mother's people or those they knew. And as she thought of the redlining or the police killings all over the country, she remarked again to herself that racism and White supremacy were not to be found exclusively in the South, despite the attitude of the national press covering the Confederate flag.

Though she enjoyed hearing her mother's memories, Gil could not admit to her mother's South being exactly her South. For Gil's upbringing, her mother's square dances and hayrides were replaced by hanging out at the Pizza Hut, and pool parties. As for fireflies, no one could account for why they had disappeared—some said the nearby pulp plant had something to do with it.

Gil noticed her mother did not mention Black people, beyond Johnny Mae, as having any part in her description of growing up Southern, except that they had to sit in the balcony at the movie theater. But Gil was hardly surprised at this after her mother's long letter, where she had declared that she knew almost nothing at all of Black life on the other side of the tracks. And, on the matter of an improvement regarding race relations, Gil could not claim much of a change toward more diversity in her own life. In high school there may have been close to a dozen Black students, but they did not mingle with the White students. They seemed to prefer hanging around together. Same with the White kids.

For the first time, Gil considered how both she and her mother were unconsciously aloof from race. In Gil's opinion, not knowing any Black folks to any degree could no longer be an excuse to put your head in the sand and ignore the concerns expressed at the demonstration. She came to the realization that White people could no longer have it both ways—they couldn't claim ignorance and at the same time put a deaf ear to the glaring mistreatment dished out for four hundred years. Now here they were in the year 2000 and still the efforts to perpetuate the notion of inferiority persisted. But the race problem had at last come home to roost. Many decades of inequality in schools, job opportunities, health care and on and on had finally emerged all wrapped in the Confederate flag. Throughout the United States there were millions of frustrated, often poor, often under-educated, often underemployed and often disrespected African Americans who had had enough.

Gil was not ready to assume—as so many in the North seemed to assume—that America's racial problem was strictly a Southern prob-lem. Racism and White supremacy were particularly evident in the South, but they were by no means unique to the South.

The flag supporters insisted on a very narrow view of the conflict over the flag. They cast the flag as the symbol of their proud legacy from an honorable and prideful period of their past to justify its place flying over the State House. Those holding that view missed the whole point of the demonstration. Moreover, they sidestepped the bigger issue, the South's—and not only the South's—practice of slavery and rac-ism, ignoring the powerful fact that throughout United States history, the Negro was not considered, by most White people, fully a man. And even in 2000—well over a hundred years after Emancipation—the false idea of inferiority persisted in many minds. Race was not the problem, but racism and White supremacy definitely were. The Confederate flag was a symbol of both.

Gil continued to think about the role of both North and South through the centuries of systematic racism that had the effect of keeping the Black people in a powerless and inferior position. Before the War, as the North became urban and industrial, the South continued to be agrarian and more and more heavily dependent on slave labor. There was a growing population of free Negroes in the North, but their disposition to be com-patible with White society began to be contentiously debated, and the contenders were not always predictable.

Lincoln, "the president who freed the slaves," thought throughout his whole political career that the differences between the races would always be too great to overcome. Though he believed that all should enjoy the fruits of their own labor, he was firm that the Negro should not be able to vote, serve on juries, or intermarry with White people. Lincoln was not in favor of the Negro having the same equal social and political rights as White people. He concluded there would always be animosity between the races, so it would be best if Negroes left the country and colonized in Liberia, West Africa. Thinking they could never live in harmony with White people, Lincoln said that it would be best all around if the Africans would be "sent back to their country of origin."

Even though Gil thought the Civil War itself was not the be-all-and-end-all with regard to understanding inequality, after reading about Lincoln's attitude she had questions as to the motive of the North with respect to freeing the slaves. The South's position on slavery was unequivocal—it was to preserve the slave labor that was at the very core of the wealth and financial stability of the Southern states. But what was the attitude of the Northerner regarding slavery? Aside from the abolitionists, whose mission was clear, concern about slavery did not seem to be felt above the Mason-Dixon Line. History did not bear out that the ordinary citizen of the North had cause to go to war to defend the rights of slaves, but rather they got caught up in Lincoln's push to preserve the Union. Gil questioned what evidence existed to demonstrate that Union soldiers thought the freedom of the slave was worth fighting for.

As for the Union generals, what about the treatment of thousands of ex-slaves who joined the fourteen-mile caravan of William Tecumseh Sherman, when he and his army passed through the Confederacy on his March to the Sea? As Sherman proceeded toward Savannah, there were no provisions, plans, accommodations, or laws in place to follow through on the promise to end slavery. Sherman, having cut off Confederate supply routes, marched into Savannah trailed by thousands of slaves who had simply walked off plantations as the Union Army burned their way to the sea. Unwilling to continue feeding and caring for them, Sherman ordered the Negroes onto ships and indiscriminately unloaded these ex-slaves to fend for themselves in unfamiliar territory all along the coast of Georgia and South Carolina.

Gil saw that at the end of the War, assimilating freed slaves into a functioning White society was on no one's mind. The government had nothing in place even to start the process. Soldiers, from both North and South, just wanted to go home and rebuild their lives. The upshot was that four million freed slaves had nowhere to go and nothing to go to. There was no "forty acres and a mule." To Gil, it appeared the Negro had no champion after the War—not in the North or South.

Gil thought she had a handle on the causes and effects of the early story of the African slave in America, but it was when she had started to trace the history after the Civil War that she was surprised at the complexity of that part of the journey and also at how much she did not know. When she read all she could about the fate of freed slaves after the War, she saw how significant the period known as Reconstruction was in the whole picture of Black history. She wondered how she could have known so little about a period that had such profound repercussions in modern times. She was surprised to see, after the slaves were freed, just how persistent and successful White people were in holding the Negroes down—and that they were still, in 2000, using the centuries-old argument of inferiority. What happened to prevent freed slaves from assimilating into society?

After 600,000 troops lost their lives in the Civil War, it was astounding to Gil to find how little was done to carry through with integrating ex-slaves into society. She recalled a scene in Booker T. Washington's *Up from Slavery*. He told of the time, when he was a small boy, that the Union man came to the still-working slave plantation where he lived to read the Emancipation Proclamation. At first the slaves were overjoyed, after years of praying that the day of freedom would come. They began dancing and chanting about freedom at long last. Meanwhile, the master and his family were all assembled on the porch, hearing the same thing. The family was crying. After a while, both the slaves and White family settled into quiet reflection as everyone started to think about in what way their lives would change. A pall of uncertainty settled over all the people gathered. Then both slaves and masters, in near silence, retreated back to their houses to contemplate just what Emancipation would mean for them. Washington's account seemed to set the stage accurately for Gil, especially considering all that she had read about the aftermath of the War, when it was clear that next to nothing of a roadmap had been developed to assure a successful transformation to freedom for four million ex-slaves.

As the dust was settling after the War, efforts began to put the nation back together. The daunting job was to try to reconcile the divide between the Union and the defeated Confederacy. Southern states had battled to defend and preserve slave labor all the way back to the Constitutional Convention in 1787. Now the War was over, but the Confederates were not at all reconciled to their defeat. They still viewed the Negro as inferior, and his labor as necessary to their way of life.

How to get the Southern states back into Congress and functioning in unison with the other states once again was the immediate challenge for the federal government. At the same time, the promise to end slavery seemed to have been made good. But it was naive to assume that Reconstruction would be about reconciliation and protecting the freedom and civil rights of the newly emancipated former slaves. As with most of Black history, especially after the Civil War, the road to equal rights for the ex-slaves would turn out to be complicated and rocky.

Right off, immediately at War's end, the still all-White Southern legislatures enacted Black Codes to replace the social controls of slaves lost through the Emancipation Proclamation. Newly freed slaves were subjected to new laws designed to maintain norms of White supremacy as before the War. Black Code laws severely undermined the freedoms of emancipated slaves. They were obstacles thrown up to restrict movement and labor so that Negroes could not move freely or eke out a living. Some Southern states restricted freedmen from owning property or working in certain skilled trades. At every turn, ex-slaves were subjected to laws that made life very difficult.

Northern states retaliated against Black Codes. Congress passed the Civil Rights Act of 1866, over Johnson's veto. The Act guaranteed citizenship to everyone born in the United States. Next, the Reconstruction Acts in 1867 provided for military protection for the voting rights of all males without regard to race.

The Reconstruction Acts required all states to ratify the Fourteenth Amendment, which guaranteed equal protection for all citizens under the law. Reconstruction laws paved the way for Negroes to enter into government for the first time, and they soon won elections to Southern state legislatures, as well as to the United States Congress. In the new environment of 1868, Negroes made up the overwhelming majority of voters in the South, electing large numbers of Negro officeholders. South Carolina led in the numbers of Negroes voted into office at three hundred and sixteen. In all, during the period of Reconstruction, six hundred Negroes were elected to state legislatures.

With Negro participation, federal and state governments developed a solid record of accomplishment. They heavily promoted economic development and passed legislation that gave Negroes the right to buy land, serve on juries, and enter into contracts.

With the ratification of the Thirteenth, Fourteenth, and Fifteenth Amendments to the United States Constitution, citizenship rights and equal protections to former slaves should certainly have been on solid footing. However, the Southern states in bad faith ratified the Amendments only because ratification was the condition for them to be readmitted into the Union. The Southern states were not through with resisting freedoms for Negroes—far from it. The most consequential of the Amendments, the Fourteenth, which guaranteed voting rights, the right to hold public office, and the right to protection against physical harm, would be the new battlefield for White Southerners to resist freedoms extended to Negroes. All three amendments would be the object of future legal challenges. Reconstruction might have been a period when the chaos of war subsided and the country could heal, but it didn't happen. Considering what was to come, Reconstruction was barely a start to advance toward equality.

Seeing Negroes voting and elected to positions of political power galled White Southerners—especially since they had just spent five long years defending their belief that Negroes were property. Blacks were still considered by White people to be inherently inferior, and, worse, sub-human, even if they could no longer be thought of as chattel. White Southerners persisted in believing that the Negro was too ignorant to take part in government. The Southern press portrayed the houses of government with Black participation as "monkey houses" and published cartoons with monkeys dressed in waistcoats running wild in government chambers.

Organized Southern White supremacists resorted to violence. When the federal government loosened their vigilance to protect freedmen, in the mid-1870s, violence erupted below the Mason-Dixon Line. Thirty-five Negro officeholders were assassinated, with little effort by local authorities or the federal government to bring the killers to justice. The Ku Klux Klan focused attention on controlling the polls, and their efforts were effective in scaring off voters. Advances made immediately after the War that added so many Negroes to State Houses all over the South reversed quickly when the Klan energized supporters of White supremacy to engage in widespread terrorism, intimidation and lynching. Political control returned back to White people, to White supremacists.

At the time of state elections in 1870, White candidates regained their dominance in the South, so that almost as soon as Black legislators were elected, their momentum reversed. Gil was dismayed to see how quickly Black inclusion in government had been turned around.

Negroes were again vulnerable. They had legal protection, according to the three constitutional amendments, but the laws were not enforced. As could be expected, it was an especially violent, dangerous time. There were five years of extreme lawlessness, until in 1875, President Ulysses S. Grant proposed a group of civil rights measures known as the Enforcement Act. It looked to be just what was needed—"to protect all citizens in their civil and legal rights," guaranteeing equal access to public accommodations and public transportation. Congress signed off on a watered-down version of Grant's proposal. In the end, with Blacks too powerless to fight effectively for a strong version, and with no real passion for it among Whites, Grant's Enforcement Act, like the three constitutional amendments, was ignored and ineffective. This Enforcement Act of 1875 would be the last federal civil rights legislation until 1964. There would be no relief for another three generations.

The last gasp of Reconstruction came when President Rutherford B. Hayes pulled all the remaining federal troops from the South. Without federal troops to provide any protections whatsoever to Black citizens, White supremacists were free to stifle the advances of Negroes all over the South. Segregationists went to court to challenge the law protecting the rights of Black people from being denied access to public accommodations—hotels, public parks, theaters. In 1883 the US Supreme Court ruled eight to one that private business owners had a right to control who could come into their businesses. Twenty years after the Civil War, Black people were still not on equal footing with White people—far from it. The 1883 Supreme Court decision sanctioned Whites-only spaces, and paved the way for Jim Crow laws that further openly allowed for racial discrimination. More than another decade would pass before civil rights for Black people would be again seriously addressed—and then the outcome would be extremely unfavorable.

Thirty years after the Civil War, in 1896, came one of the most significant cases in the long and bumpy ride toward the realization of civil rights—*Plessy v. Ferguson*, considered to be the worst civil rights decision ever handed down by the US Supreme Court. Before it was replaced or superseded by the Civil Rights Act of 1964, *Plessy* was a precedent for subsequent bad law. The case involved a Black man, Homer Plessy, who boarded a Whites-only passenger car of the East Louisiana Railroad when there were cars designated for Coloreds. The Supreme Court upheld the constitutionality of the segregation of public facilities as long as there was an "equal" alternative available. The Court ruled that it could not eliminate social distinctions based on color—it was not unconstitutional to make decisions based on race—but that it could mandate equal facilities. This ruling became known as the "separate but equal" doctrine. Separate public schools, restrooms, parks, would all be part of the parallel societies as determined in *Plessy v. Ferguson*.

However, even in this the governments, once again, failed at every level to carry through their responsibility regarding the Black population. They would provide and maintain White facilities and let those for Black people, such as there were, fall into ruin. Black children were issued hand-me-down books from the White schools. Black parents were expected to provide transportation to and from Black schools, while White students were bused to school at taxpayers' expense. Black schools were not maintained. Soon, separate but equal was no longer equal. In fact, separate was never equal.

Gil thought back to her mother's long letter. Separate but equal was of her mother's era when Black people were in their own schools, across the tracks from White people. The paths of her mother and Black folks never crossed because Black people were on their own path—separate and definitely not equal. White people were comfortable, so they felt no need to change things. Gil's mother did not feel keenly the racial disparity because there was no chance she would walk in their shoes. This was what her mother meant when she said that was just the way it was—they went along to get along and didn't have to face any ugliness. Most White folks had not the slightest idea of or concern about Black people—who were often in the majority. White people were not directly affected by the Black condition, so they ignored it.

———

BEFORE INTERSTATE 95 — "AMERICA'S MARVEL," which cut straight down the middle of South Carolina—travel in Clarendon County was mostly along dusty roads passing through pine forests and tobacco or cotton farms and over rickety bridges crossing blackwater swamps. By 1950 more than seventy percent of the population in Clarendon County were Black descendants of African slaves. Most of the land in and around the town of Summerton was leased by Black tenant farmers—land that had very likely been worked by the same family since before the Civil War. Two-thirds of the Black tenant farmers earned under one thousand dollars per year.

Despite the preponderance of Black students in the 1940s, there were far fewer schools for Black kids than there were for White kids. There was an adequate number of White schools, which the students could get to easily either by a short walk or a school bus ride. The White schools were solidly built, mostly of red brick, with cafeterias, large assembly halls and well-equipped science labs. Colored schools were fewer and very far apart. One look at these schools and it was easy to see that separate but equal mandated in *Plessy* had been blatantly ignored. Most Black schoolhouses were wooden, and only large enough to hold two classrooms. Most of the Black schools in the more rural areas of the county had no electricity or running water.

To get to and from Scott's Branch School in Summerton, Black students had to walk as much as five miles, twice each day. Sometimes some schoolchildren had to ford swollen streams. After a young boy drowned in the recently created Lake Marion reservoir that had cut off a Black community from the school, Black parents attempted to remedy the transportation problem. The Reverend Armstrong DeLaine took up donations from parents of Scott's Branch students to buy a second-hand school bus, but the only affordable vehicle was constantly down for repairs and the Black community could not keep up the expense on their meager incomes. So, in 1947, the Reverend encouraged parents to sign a petition urging Clarendon County school officials to provide a bus for Black students—a modest request considering the White schools had been provided with more than thirty buses. The parents of the Black children were denied the one bus they asked for. They were told that the Black community did not pay enough taxes to support it.

The petitioners—farmers, a gas station attendant, and domestic workers—experienced swift reprisal. Most immediately lost their jobs. Their credit sources were pulled from them. There were drive-by shootings. Reverend DeLaine's church and house were burned to the ground. In the attack on his house, he was shot at and in self-defense he fired back. For that, he was charged with assault, and, once he fled the state, could not return to the county for fear of arrest. For their safety, the majority of the remaining petitioners moved out of Summerton, where they had spent their whole lives.

The NAACP had heard about the gross injustice and thought it might be the case they had been waiting for. This had the potential to go all the way into the national spotlight—to show the racially biased treatment of Blacks next to the treatment of Whites. So, the organization sacrificed most of their resources for what they knew could be a long-protracted battle. Thurgood Marshall, a young lawyer, wrote a petition to challenge the Clarendon County school bus policy and filed it against the South Carolina State Superintendent of Schools with the US District Court in Charleston.

In the pretrial hearing, Marshall focused on the legality of unequal, segregated conditions within the public school system. He laid out that by denying the school bus, the Superintendent of Schools in Clarendon went against the separate but equal doctrine established in law. However, by the time the actual case was presented, Marshall had enlarged the scope to boldly challenge the constitutionality of *Plessy v. Ferguson*, and that put into question the broader issue of segregation itself.

Marshall challenged *Plessy*, a ruling by the US Supreme Court from 1896, on the constitutionality of racial segregation. His was a brave decision, and a big gamble. But he thought the chance he was taking was worth it. To strike down *Plessy* would pave the way to dissolve the devastating Jim Crow laws that had denied Black people access to public accommodations like restrooms, parks, restaurants and drinking fountains.

The three-judge panel hearing the case in the Federal District Court in Charleston ruled against the plaintiffs, two judges to one. When Marshall appealed the case in 1952 to the Supreme Court, the Court tacked on delays to bundle Marshall's case with four other similar cases on desegregation. The South Carolina school case was the first to be filed with the Court. However, so that this case would not appear to be just another Black grievance against the South, the Court named the whole proceeding after a Kansas case—*Brown v. the Board of Education of Topeka, Kansas.*

It was five years after the 1947 request for a school bus in Summerton when Marshall addressed the Supreme Court on December 9, 1952. It had been a grueling wait. Most of the original plaintiffs in the bus case had suffered greatly in many ways. Thurgood Marshall himself often had to travel through South Carolina, preparing for the case, constantly watching over his shoulder. When Marshall approached the bench to present the case for desegregation, the weight of all Black people in America was on his shoulders. As he began making his case to the Supreme Court, he was on the threshold of a new era.

White people who were vehemently against desegregation had a lot to lose if *Brown* did not go their way. If *Plessy v. Ferguson* went down, hopes for a continued segregated society would go down with it. The White supremacist Southern culture as it was in 1952 was in great jeopardy—facing a fate that many could not imagine. The year 1952 was already more than three generations away from the Civil War, but it was not unusual for some old folks to remember hearing stories about cannon fire in the distance or the sight of a troop of Confederates heading northward.

All who followed the case speculated on the bias of the Supreme Court justices, scrutinizing their records to see which direction they might lean. There was no certainty about the majority decision, but most thought it would be a close split. The segregationists thought they could count on the decision of Chief Justice Fred Vinson, who had clearly shown himself in the past as a strong supporter of *Plessy*, but Vinson suddenly died of a heart attack just before the case was to be heard. When the Court reconvened in the fall of 1952, there was a new Chief Justice—Earl Warren.

————

WARREN'S EARLIEST JUDICIAL AND POLITICAL experience had been in California, where he had been State Attorney General and Governor. His background showed both liberal and conservative leanings. His legal experience was stellar, but California was a long way from the South. As to desegregation, he, like most other White people from outside the South, had little experience with the deep divide regarding race.

His first direct personal experience came shortly after he arrived in Washington from California. As a history buff he decided to tour Virginia Civil War battlefields. The first night his Black driver dropped him off at a hotel. The next morning, Warren asked the driver where he had stayed and was told he had slept in the car because no hotels accepted Black folks. It was impossible to tell if the experience had any influence on Warren's thoughts on civil rights, but it was known that he repeated the story to others.

————

WHEN ORAL ARGUMENTS STARTED, Marshall had what he thought to be a sound strategy to incorporate both social and political implications of the case. He put these implications into constitutional concepts that the justices could clearly understand. His case against separate but equal was a simple one. The Reconstruction constitutional amendments—the

Thirteenth, Fourteenth, and Fifteenth—were clearly written to abolish slavery and guarantee equal, protected rights. He spoke in straightforward language and argued that racial segregation through separation was "unreasonable" and "made no sense"—terms never before heard in the Supreme Court that was most accustomed to hearing arguments based on precedent.

He then departed in a risky direction to present evidence based on social science data. He cited twenty-nine different scientific sources to support that school segregation denied children the ability to fulfill their full potential. Marshall drew on the doll test studies of psychologists Kenneth and Mamie Clark, which demonstrated that Black children raised in a segregated environment suffered damage to their self-image. The Clarks tested Black children from segregated schools. They showed the children two dolls—one White, one Black—and asked which doll was prettier, nicer, had the best hair, which one they would rather be. Ten of sixteen Black children preferred the White doll.

Marshall also declared that segregation was hypocritical in view of the country's foreign policy message. He pointed out that diplomats representing the US government spoke of the country's policy on human rights abroad, but the United States did not practice it at home. The country was in the midst of a Cold War with the Soviet Union. Marshall argued that the discrimination was eroding America's international image. In this he touched a familiar note with several well-traveled justices who commented on having made the same observation firsthand on trips abroad. Justice William Douglas commented that the first thing he was asked on a trip to India was why America tolerated lynching.

Thurgood Marshall, who would himself eventually be sworn in as the first Black justice of the Supreme Court, concluded his argument by saying that the only justification for segregation would be if it were judged true that "Negroes are inferior to all other human beings."

Had the argument depended strictly on law and precedent, the state would have prevailed in *Brown v. Board*, but momentum was shifting in the country, away from strict property rights toward equal civil rights, and the Court was shifting with it. The Warren Court decision came down on the side of *Brown* for the reason that separate, by definition, was not equal. Marshall successfully convinced the Court that *Plessy* was no longer able to deny Black people equal treatment.

Chief Justice Warren thought the Court's decision should override *Plessy* to demonstrate and maintain the country's core belief in liberty and justice for all. He thought the decision should be announced quickly before segregationists had time to plan their resistance. To show strength and solidarity in this important ruling, Warren felt strongly that the Supreme Court decision should be unanimous. He lobbied the other justices hard and got what he wanted. Warren wrote the opinion himself. He wanted it to be clear with no room for an avalanche of different interpretations later. He would write plainly that no one could be deprived of the equal protections of the laws guaranteed by the Fourteenth Amendment.

Many people were stunned by the Court's decision in *Brown v. Board*. Some were overjoyed, but many segregationists took it badly that Black people were elevated to equal status under the law by the highest court in the land. For them, it was a bitter pill that would not go down smoothly.

—————

TRYING TO FIND OUT what her mother could recall about civil rights while growing up, Gil had told her about the Summerton case that went all the way to the Supreme Court—how the Reverend DeLaine, the filling station attendant, and the maid who changed beds at a motel all got run out of town, and how their houses had been torched. Her mother said she had no idea of that ugliness coming down on those people.

When Gil had gone on to tell her mother about how Black people had fought in court for equal protection—rights to have access to parks and public restrooms, to stay in a hotel, to buy an ice cream cone where they wanted to, she knew some of it would go over her mother's head, but she wanted to paint in a wide swath the difficulties and injustices that Black folks had endured in towns all over the South like Summerton and just under the noses of White people right there in nearby Florence.

Gil's mother got where her daughter was going with all this talk of Southern White resistance.

—Darlin', you don't think your people had anything to do with that. Your granddaddy worked every day with 'em, side by side, on the farm. What could he do for them to get their own school bus? Like I told you before, we were simple folks, didn't know history like you do. We didn't know life should be any different than it was. I hope you don't think we were mean with any of 'em. I know, your generation has a whole different idea about the world and how it ought to be, but you have to step back and realize that we didn't have the time to sit around philosophizing about rights—we just had how things had come down to us. Don't think we didn't try to be decent. We may not have invited Hattie and her family over for supper, but we didn't act all high and mighty around her. She was a proud woman and we respected that. We did the best we could.

———

TEN YEARS AFTER *BROWN V. BOARD*, another very important milestone along the long road to equality was reached. Newsreels showing President Lyndon B. Johnson signing the Civil Rights Act on July 2, 1964, had every bit the look of a landmark occasion when everybody present appreciated finally putting things right. Johnson handed out one hundred commemorative pens—Bobby Kennedy, whose brother John had originally proposed the bill, was handed a pen. Martin Luther King Jr. got a pen, as well as J. Edger Hoover, who had been hostile to King for years, claiming to be convinced that King was a pawn of the Communist Party and keeping him under constant surveillance.

When Vice President Johnson assumed the presidency, after the assassination of John F. Kennedy, the spotlight was on him as to the future of civil rights. Johnson had a dilemma—he could lose the presidential election coming up in November if he went against the South on segregation. Through his whole political career, he had demonstrated resistance to expanding civil rights. In a crowd of Southern cronies, he was known to tell demeaning jokes about Black people. Now that he was president, no one could say how he would respond to the strong push to advance civil rights that he had inherited. But Johnson left no question when he addressed Congress, five days after Kennedy's death. He plainly stated that he intended to carry through what JFK had started.

As a true Texan—Southern, gregarious, a popular "good ole boy"—Johnson knew how to get what he wanted. He spoke as he always spoke and did what he felt he needed to do to get his way. There was a story told about how just before the civil rights bill was to be voted on in the Senate, Johnson ran into Sam Erwin from North Carolina. He greeted his former colleague.

—Sam, we're gettin' ready to vote on the nigger bill. I'm counting on you votin' with me on this thing.

With Lyndon Johnson's skills to cajole, persuade and sometimes threaten, the Civil Rights Act of 1964 passed into law. After 1964 the issue of civil rights dropped off the front pages.

By the time the 1980s rolled around, fifteen years after the Civil Rights Act of 1964, segregationists were assuming that all complaints by Black folks had been satisfied and efforts to demand equal treatment were a thing of the past. White supremacists thought they had given in enough under court orders and other pressures. They might have thought all was calm in the land, but they had not counted on the Confederate flag in Columbia bringing so many issues back into view.

———

AFTER MONTHS OF DEMONSTRATION in Columbia over the flag, the NAACP had worked out a plan with the state legislators that satisfied both parties enough to announce the flag would come down. The compromise was that the flag would be removed from the State House and that a smaller version would be flown above the prominent and elaborate Confederate monument that was within sight of the State House—the flag would still fly on state grounds but not on the State House itself. No one got exactly what they wanted, but after so many months everybody was weary and ready to go home, to call it quits. With organizing, laboriously working through the legislature, and the demonstration itself, everyone was exhausted. Both the NAACP and representatives of the state felt they could leave with their dignity intact.

Meanwhile, with little notice, the old guard White legislators passed a Heritage Act—prohibiting alteration or removal of state historical monuments without a two-thirds vote of both chambers of the general assembly.

———

THE FLAG WAS TO COME DOWN at two o'clock. The organizers published the precise time for the national news feeds to sync with their affiliates around the country. Gil wanted to catch some of the planned program put on by the NAACP. She knew Joe Pearl would be at the State House and she wanted him to see she was there for support. They had met at Chester's a few times after the first night when they had gotten into it over their thoughts about the flag. To hear what each had to say was one thing, but the real kick for both of them was that two people—one Black, one White—could talk together about race without defensiveness or suspecting that the other was pushing an agenda. It was comfortable, satisfying, and gratifying, and that was important and enough.

Over the weeks and months since the whole thing started, flag supporters and opponents had staked out their territories. On the east side of the wide concrete walkway leading to the steps of the State House, the opponents of the flag congregated, holding homemade signs with messages supporting their position that the flag must come down. In addition, someone had gone to a printer and ordered signs silk-screened with the word *SHAME* in blue against a white background, to oppose racism. Folk singers had carved out a clearing in the crowd, and Gil could hear them singing *The Night They Brought Old Dixie Down*.

On the west side of the walkway was a boisterous crowd of flag supporters, holding up some signs scrawled in marker. But their message was mostly broadcast through the Confederate flag itself, of which there were at least a couple hundred of various sizes. One huge flag maneuvered through the crowd was the size of a living room rug—nine by twelve. The smallest were flags on sticks waved by little kids carried on the shoulders of their parents. Several local news stations had helicopters taking turns flying over the crowd. They all found the giant flag an attention-getter and fed the image all over the country. Even the English *Guardian* would have an aerial shot of it on the front page the next morning.

Gil was making her way through the crowd and heard her name being called out from the steps above her. It was Joe. He motioned for her to come up to the landing, halfway up the steps of the State House. By the time she got to the NAACP ceremony, it was already in progress, so she stood in back of the rows of folding chairs rented for the occasion. The governor, the mayor of Columbia, several members of the state legislature, the highest-ranking officer of the regional office of the NAACP, Joe, and an attractive Black woman sat in the first row of chairs. In the second row were people who were of local nonprofit organizations sympathetic to Black causes.

In the third row were people affiliated with the local chapter of the NAACP, including a woman whom Gil had noticed on her daily walk past the State House on her way to the Caroliniana. The woman was always busying around from the time the demonstration first began. Gil took notice that the woman was clearly committed to the cause, as she seemed to have her hand in every aspect, whether it was tying banners to railings or being deep in conversation with others who were obviously organizers brought in from "off."

Gil took a seat in the back row just when Joe got to the speaker's podium. She couldn't help but notice how much more confident he appeared than when she first saw him on television. He took from his breast pocket the small notepad he seemed to always carry as she had first seen it at Chester's. With just a few notes in front of him, Joe launched into a concise, well-composed synopsis of events addressing the public's need to remove the Confederate flag from the State House. He artfully maneuvered through what could have been a minefield of divisive rhetoric. Through his choice of words he presented the solution as being good for all humanity. Knowing his remarks would be broadcast nationally, he pointed out that the removal of the flag demonstrated there was a new, progressive South, willing to put racism behind it. He knew this was a stretch, but no one could challenge him and not risk sounding backward.

Gil was pleased to hear him incorporate a few things they had talked about at Chester's. He said that the occasion that brought everyone there that day would never have happened if it were not for the bravery of those folks in Summerton that led to *Brown v. Board of Education*. Tears welled up in Gil's eyes because they had talked at length about *Brown* and how it was the mother of all equal rights rulings since it was first decided.

Joe had tried to argue that everything that had ever happened for Black rights was through civil protest, but she had come back with the importance of the quiet path of court action. They both realized that were it not for the gas station attendant, the reverend, and the hotel maid in Summerton, *Brown* would never have seen the light of day.

It was one thirty when the NAACP program was over, and time had come to clear away the chairs and get ready for the flag to actually come down. Miz Johnson jumped up the second it was over and started barking orders for her young volunteers to fold the chairs and stack them, precisely as she instructed. Gil watched her and noticed that she passed up the schmoozing to deal with the tedium—the tedious tasks that most ran from but had to be done.

After all Gil's reading about civil rights legal battles, with the NAACP in the middle of it all, she saw this elderly Black woman in a new light. With Summerton just up the way, she had to have been involved at the time of *Brown*. She may even have met Thurgood Marshall—she was the right age. Obviously she was a worker bee, the kind of person who didn't wait around for someone to tell her what to do—she just did what needed to be done without being asked. That didn't mean she didn't have a dialog running through her head about the shortcomings of others, but this did not keep her from moving forward. Gil would not have been surprised to learn that she had volunteered to assist in any way she could for the landmark *Brown* case—to run documents up and down dusty back roads between Summerton and Columbia before I-95 made it easy. Before email and fax, somebody had to get the stuff around and she was the one who would do it because she was a doer—it was in her DNA.

As she helped stack chairs, Thalia Johnson's mind went to the aggravation she had running with national NAACP headquarters in Maryland. Why had they sent that wimp from the regional office and not someone more important? Events didn't get much bigger than this. This flag thing had consumed her for months, and that bunch in Baltimore didn't see fit to send Kweisi, the national president. She thought to herself, *My God, we're broke, but they don't see this for what it is—a way to get back into the game with big issues and the potential for donations flowing in again.*

She knew the NAACP had gotten stale and had lost influence. Dedicating all her time for the organization—for decades—to getting out the vote had worn her down. But getting this damn cracker flag off the State House had given her new life and had brought in new, young members. As much as she thought Kweisi Mfume was a dandy with those four-hundred-dollar suits and celebrity friends, he did have drawing power—but Baltimore blew it by not getting him down to Columbia. As she folded the last chair, the old thought again crossed her mind, *This might be my last year.*

Gil waited while Joe shook hands with people queued up to exchange greetings. When she found an opening, she stepped in to say hello. He introduced the woman who had sat alongside him at the ceremony. She was the Nikki whose name Gil knew from the talk at Chester's. This was not the badass that she had heard so much about. Instead, Nikki was an attractive woman who struck Gil as someone who did not suffer fools lightly. Nikki said that she had heard good things about the evenings at Chester's and that she noticed Joe had learned a thing or two. Gil grinned. Then she saw that there were other people who were hovering around trying to get a word with Joe, so she stepped back.

It was now only a few minutes before two o'clock. As was her way, Miz Johnson started to herd together everybody on the landing to hold hands in a big circle as the flag was lowered. She swished her arms back and forth as she went through the crowd as if she was shooing chickens to get everybody rounded up in place. There were Joe, Nikki, local political types, and the NAACP contingent closing the circle.

Making their way up the steps to join in the celebration on the landing were two young teenage Black girls, on either side of a very old Black man, practically lifting him off his feet to clear each step. The girls were dressed in contemporary duds of the day—one wore a short denim jacket, the other a short-sleeved hooded sweatshirt in Day-Glo orange. Both had long straightened hair. The old man, 101 years of age, had been a tenant farmer in Edisto, South Carolina, working the same land his grandfather had worked as a sharecropper after being dumped by Sherman on Steamboat Landing with nothing more than a few pieces of tattered clothing wrapped in a bandana. The great-grandchildren of the old man thought he should see the Confederate flag come down, so they drove from where the family had moved in Virginia so that he would see it firsthand.

Joe beckoned for Gil to come over and join him and Nikki. But Gil saw Miz Johnson looking for a place in the circle, and so she grabbed her by the hand and made sure she was next to Joe. Somebody needed to show respect to the woman who had brought the whole thing together. A smile of appreciation and accomplishment came over her face—maybe the first time in many months she could feel relieved and proud.

Gil was at her right, leaning toward her ear and trying to speak over the buzz of the crowd.

—This wouldn't have happened if it weren't for you.

Miz Johnson looked at the redhead next to her, taken aback that someone, a White girl at that, had acknowledged anything about her. She squeezed Gil's hand. They didn't say anything, but for a split second they felt a genuine connection.

At exactly two o'clock, the Confederate flag started descending the flagpole. It was lowered at a slightly uneven pace as though by human hands, which it was—by two Citadel cadets, one White, the other Black. Anyone could see the irony: White Citadel cadets had fired on Fort Sumter on April 12, 1861, starting the Civil War.

For the sixty seconds it took to lower the flag out of sight, there seemed to be a common sentiment between both factions—the flag had drawn them to the same place, each with opposing views, but there was some satisfaction that those views had been heard. When the flag was down, a deafening roar came from the crowd, estimated at over ten thousand. The cadets folded the flag and ceremoniously handed it to the state museum director. That particular flag was to be taken to State Archives, where it would reside until a plan could be made about where it would be permanently displayed. There had been some talk about building a whole museum exclusively for displaying that flag to the public.

A smaller version of the Confederate flag was carried through two rows of state troopers to the nearby Civil War monument. When it was raised up the thirty-foot pole, a loud cheer went up from the flag supporters.

Miz Johnson spoke to herself as the flag was raised.

—Over my dead body will that stay. Next year they're going to hear from me!

Everyone on the landing left. It was over. Gil sat alone on a step and watched the people in the crowd dispersing. Minutes earlier they had been participants in the final part of a rowdy, boisterous demonstration that had lasted for months. Now they were no longer two opposing sides but just plain folks, heading home. Trash barrels were overflowing with signs and placards, with city workers trying to clear it all away. A breeze caught a couple of banners and blew them across the grounds.

The only people lingering were in a group encircling the Confederate monument, savoring the moment, not ready to give it up and go home. Gil could see that they were silent with a kind of reverence like at a funeral. Confederate re-enactors, standing perfectly still with period muskets, were stationed on all four sides. Several onlookers turned to go, but not before saluting the flag fluttering above. A middle-aged man wearing a replica of a Confederate kepi was kneeling on one knee with his head down in prayer.

Still sitting on the steps, Gil rested her elbows on her knees and held up her head in both hands, contemplating what had gone on here. She had not changed her mind since she told Joe at Chester's that equal rights was a promise, slowly to be redeemed over decades after it was given. She thought that truly equal rights were inevitable but that it would still take time to achieve them, secure them. The flag coming down was the end of another chapter in the long story of struggle. Gil recalled that she had read somewhere that in 1964 Lyndon Johnson, just before he signed his name to the civil rights bill, said that the Founders knew freedom would be secure only if each generation would renew and enlarge the meaning of it. Maybe the battle over the Confederate flag was advancing the meaning of freedom and was finally reflecting the aspirations of some of the Founders—who had been hampered by the various limitations of their time.

Around the Confederate monument, people lingered on, still not able to let go. Their reverence remained, with all conversations in low tones in contrast to the noise of the crowd that had filled the grounds around the State House an hour earlier. Gil did not know about the motives of others, but she, too, felt compelled to stay on, and enjoy the quiet and the slight coolness of dusk, and most especially to take a moment, as her mother liked to say, to "settle herself."

CHAPTER

18

LYDIA WAS HANGING THE WASH ON THE LINE when she looked toward the field. Never had she seen such neglect. Weeds filled the furrows. She could not make them out from this distance, but she could imagine tendrils of all sorts choking the powerless young plants that were just getting their start—struggling toward the sun, barely knee-high after the better part of May had already passed. And she could see that the fencing of post and wire was a solid mass of bramble. She shook her head in disapproval and turned to hang another sheet on the line.

There had been rain, the kind most favorable to farmers—not torrents, but steady showers that rolled in about every three days. Rains that would come, nourish, and return just in time when the plants were again thirsty. Rarely did the Good Lord bring the blessing of such perfect weather conditions, but His Divine Gifts were not shared with Medlin, who had been gone now over two weeks. She set the empty laundry basket down on the porch, sat in one of the rockers, and began to think about how she was going to manage the place by herself if Medlin did not come back.

Of course this put her on track to once again get a good mad on regarding her husband. Lydia could come up with plenty of Medlin's shortcomings—which she often did, no matter the company—but she knew he would never abandon his responsibilities. Fear began to well up in the pit of her stomach. She thought angrily that if Tom hadn't stuck his nose in where it didn't belong, this fool scheme about buying slaves to make quick money would never have materialized. She muttered to herself.

—Here we are in a big pickle!

Both the boys were of an age to help, but Lydia and Medlin had agreed—though they agreed on precious little—that the sons should not be made to farm. Caleb, three months out from seventeen, was a tinkerer—always in the shed inventing something or improving where he thought fit. Twelve-year-old Daniel, when not in school, would leave the house in the morning and not come back until the day was gone. Often he would bring home fish he had caught or rabbits he had snared. He was more a hunter than a cultivator of soil. So neither boy had the slightest idea of the workings of a farm. They did not know the difference between a coulter and a share.

The girl was the exclusive project of Lydia to mold. God as witness, Clara Anne was going to marry well and her mother would put her through the training—same as she had gotten from her own mother. Certainly, there would have to be adjustments made. Clio wasn't Bennettsville, and there would have to be some maneuvers around the fact the girl was a farmer's daughter. Her season was not for a while, but it was never too early to start to get the girl's skills up to snuff. Lydia's plan had been to move with Clara Anne into Bennettsville, the year before her coming-out season and stay with her own parents in their big house, where she herself had grown up. She could take advantage of the elevated status of the girl's grandfather, who ran the bank. But lately some irregularities had been discovered at the bank at the highest level, implicating her father. He assured his wife and daughter that it was just a misunderstanding that would soon blow over, but so far it was still hanging over their heads with no end in sight.

Lydia went into the house and put the iron in the firebox to heat up, then cleared the table and laid down a heavy cloth to protect the wood surface from the hot iron. She knew ironing sheets was an extravagant gesture, if not ridiculous, but it was a sign to Clara Anne of the finer aspects of a well-ordered home—something she would enjoy in marriage. Of course, then, a slave would be doing the ironing. A bedsheet was dry on the line, so she retrieved it and folded it in half, smoothing it out over the ironing cloth. She protected her hand from the hot handle of the iron with a dishrag, then tested to see if the iron was hot enough. A few drops of water flicked onto the face sputtered and danced, showing the iron was ready for service.

Just then there was a pounding of boots on the porch. Daniel shouted excitedly through the screen door.

—There's a big nigger comin' by the house!

All the while he looked back as he followed the large black head showing just above the skip laurel hedge between the house and the road in front.

Lydia looked out the window and saw the same. The hedge was of a good height, so to see the Negro's head clearing the top, anyone would guess the man was of abnormally large size. Even more alarming was that he definitely appeared to be unsecured. Instinct told her he would have to be stopped.

She called out to Clara Anne to stay close to her and ordered Daniel to roust Caleb from the shed and get to the barn where the two boys should arm themselves with any farm tools that could act as weapons if she needed their help.

Lydia pulled the rifle from the sliver of space behind the sideboard, where it was standing upright resting on the butt of the stock. In a drawer was the wooden box where all the loading paraphernalia was kept. She threw open the hinged lid and started fumbling for the paper packets of black powder. She glanced out the window again to see if she had time to load and get a shot off. Now she could just see that the tall man was laboring in his advance. He looked to be struggling with something that was slowing his pace—something low and still out of sight behind the hedge.

Medlin had once showed her how to load the rifle, a very long time ago. Now she wished she had paid more attention, but she never thought the time would come to use it.

Lydia leaned the barrel in the crook of her arm to free both hands to tear open the powder packet. Her hands were trembling like a leaf. Most of the powder went down the barrel, but some made a black streak down the front of her skirt. There was no time to speculate if there was enough powder to ignite. She pulled hard at the ramrod affixed along the side of the barrel, but it wouldn't budge until she remembered to swing open the catch lock. The ramrod packed down the powder, and she held the rifle against her breast with her left hand while the fingers of her right hand drew out of the box a mini ball and wadding. The ball flew out of her trembling fingers, fell to the floor and rolled off. Right away, Clara Anne reached into the box and retrieved another. Ball and wad were rammed down the barrel, and the rifle was ready.

Lydia knew she had but one chance, so she dropped to her knees, rested the barrel on the windowsill and sighted the target. Medlin had taught her to aim slightly ahead to account for the delay of the flight of the ball. And he had said squeeze the trigger, don't jerk. The big stranger was in near perfect position now as he fully cleared the rise. She cocked the hammer with her thumb while she kept steady pressure on the trigger. She blew out any air in her lungs between her teeth, held her breath, and began to squeeze. She tensed, expecting a recoil, but found the trigger took a lot more effort than she expected. Only one eye was open to isolate the target down the barrel, but then she opened the squinted eye to check positioning. That's when she saw her target was pulling a crude litter with a burdensome load—an outstretched White man, covered up to his neck with a tarp.

———

HUTTO LAID MEDLIN ON THE CRISP, WHITE SHEETS. He then turned toward Lydia, handed her Medlin's money pouch, quietly left the room and went out in the yard. Everybody in the family was of the same mind that Medlin looked so frail and childlike. His eyes fluttered a bit. He opened them for just a few seconds, surveyed the surroundings, and closed them again. No one could tell if he recognized any of them. Clara Anne squeezed his hand and announced that she thought he may have squeezed back.

Lydia made a determined gesture with her hands sweeping toward the door for everyone to leave the room. She told Clara Anne to warm some broth and bring it in the pap bowl. Lydia stayed in the room with Medlin and closed the door on everyone else. After that no one but Lydia entered the sickroom. She felt a doctor could do no better than she could in bringing Medlin around if it was God's will that he should live. A basin of warm, soapy water came and went several times along with bowls of broth and biscuits softened to mush. The food went back out hardly touched. Lydia gave no reports when she came and went from Medlin's room, but that was no surprise as it was her way.

As soon as he had the chance, Daniel pestered Hutto as to where his father had been. The only answer Hutto gave was that they had been on a train and then did a lot of walking, then got on a train again and then did some more walking. With that, he told the boy all that he knew, because he had no knowledge of reasons. Even to Hutto any overall plan was a mystery. He was dimly aware of Mobile and another auction as Medlin's original destination. Slaves were meant to obey and to follow—to what fate always remained unknown.

Some supper was brought to him on the back porch by Daniel. He ate at a small table put there mainly for shucking corn or snapping beans. Daniel stayed close by Hutto out of curiosity. There was a certain fascination with the big man. Daniel knew only one thing about Africans and that was they were from Africa, which he had seen on a map, and he knew that the Dark Continent was very far away. The boy thought that Hutto must know something about the big land across the ocean, so he filled the air with incessant questions. As with most children his age, the answers were of no consequence—the point was to show he knew enough to ask. Puzzled by how Hutto took his supper, Daniel asked why he ate just staring at the blank wall of the house, and was told he didn't look out over the landscape because he knew what was out there and had seen enough of it.

With Wylie and Baugh out to pasture, Hutto made his bed in an empty stall, with the tarp laid down over some straw. He had no thoughts as to what the next day would bring, but he had seen right away that Medlin's cotton needed tending. So, when he brought Medlin home, just as at the Jehossee and Butler plantations, the future was all about the immediate requirements of the crop, the needs of the young plants. At Jehossee the life of the rice plants had been his whole occupation—spring meant cleaning the canals to make way for the planting. Then came the planting, the weeding, and the first cut. Next came threshing and, finally, sacking. And then, all over again the next year.

When he was sold to the Butler place, he had to learn about cotton. Life was different but the same—the particulars as to cultivation between rice and cotton were different, but the nature of work was the same—up very early, taking direction from the driver, then working all day. At the end of the day—if the sun still lingered in the sky—there could be an opportunity to work a personal patch of ground. Then supper and falling into bed bone tired, only to start it all over again before sunup. To a slave, hopes and dreams of a personal nature—to feel independent or fulfilled, to have choices—were out of range.

Hutto briefly tried to imagine a life beyond the boundaries of the plantation. Medlin had clearly told him he was free, but he could not envision what freedom would be like. He sensed that being free meant fending entirely for yourself—where could he live and what could he do? Dragging Medlin on the litter down the road, he had thought about the few hours he had spent out of camp on his own to scout for food when Medlin was too sick to function. He had felt joy then—was that freedom? He couldn't think about that experience as permanent. Work as a slave was all he knew. Such had been his life, the soil and the crop.

In the morning Hutto woke up and got to work early. Enticed by a handful of corn in a pail, Baugh approached him with no resistance. He slipped a halter into the bucket and when the mule leaned in for the corn, he drew it over her muzzle and ears and had it buckled during the animal's preoccupation. The same thing worked on Wylie. When Hutto got them to the barn and tied outside to a rail, he went to work with a coarse grooming brush on their manes, tails and fetlocks—all tangled with burrs of a wide variety designed to snag and hold on. As he worked the brush through to long, silky results, both animals gave out blasts of air from their flared nostrils and elastic lips, in approval. Lydia came out of the house only once and spoke to Hutto to ask where Medlin had been for so long. He answered as he had to Daniel.

After he finished grooming Baugh and Wylie, Hutto walked over to the window of the room where Medlin lay. As he stood on the ground outside, he could easily look in. The sash was slid open as high as it would go. The canvas shade was pulled down, more than halfway so that all he could see was the side of the mattress with a white sheet tucked in tightly. There *was* a forearm hanging over the side of the bed, with a pasty hand coming from the sleeve of a linen nightshirt. The hand was the color of a plucked chicken and seemed lifeless. With the sun rising behind his back, Hutto's silhouette filled the window to its edges. He spoke to Medlin in a low whisper.

—Sir?

After a while, when there was no answer, Hutto began to turn away, but then he heard Medlin's faint but almost angry voice.

—I'm not your Sir. I told you, I'm nobody's Sir. Besides, you're free now. You're Mr. Sir, yourself.

Then there was another long pause before Medlin shifted to a stream of words said by a man who knew there was little time to get out everything that he had to say. It started clear but as his energy began to run out, it faded, and the words got to be not much more than a slight variation to his shallow breathing.

—I've been layin' here with nothin' to do but think, and when I wasn't out of my head, I tried to figure what purpose my life's been on this earth. I was an honest farmer. Only one time I strayed from that honest work and went against my nature, against the needs of the farm, thinking to make quick money. I did harm and for that I'm sorry. Sorry to have brought harm to you and your family. And sorry for me who will carry the heavy burden of guilt for this harm to my grave, which is not far away.

Medlin's voice was now almost inaudible. He stretched out his hand and touched the windowsill. For a moment Hutto covered it with his own big hand. As Medlin's hand started to slip, Hutto increased his grip and held on. With the last energy he had, Medlin pulled back, a gesture for Hutto to lean in closer.

—My name's William Medlin.

His voice was more part of an exhale that hung in the air until everything went silent except for the call of a crow out in the yard. Hutto realized that Medlin had breathed his last.

After standing by the window for a few moments, Hutto turned and went to the barn, where he had left Baugh and Wylie hitched to a post.

He untied the drafts and led them across to an opening in the fence, where he had the plow waiting. He had already found a whetstone and with it put a sharp edge on the coulter blade that he planned on running along the furrows to free the plants of vines in the first chop.

The two mules put up no resistance as Hutto hitched them to the plow. As he slid his hands up the leads, he came across notches cut into the leather, which he reckoned were hold markers put there many seasons earlier by Medlin. Hutto slid his hands farther up to a place comfortable for his long arms, and with all assembled and ready, he flicked the leads. Baugh and Wylie lunged forward.

19

G IL HAD BEEN EXCITED as she completed work on the background of the Medlin family. Now she had to pick up on William R. and what he had been up to in 1857, the year of the diary. The first page, preprinted with the year *1857*, had a few ruled lines where William had written in his name, town and state:

William R. Medlin

Clio

South Carolina

It took Gil days to write out in long hand what William had put down until he mysteriously quit toward the end of May. She had an intern type up her transcription and make a good photocopy of the diary, so it would not be necessary to handle the delicate original beyond what was absolutely essential. Each page had a preprinted date followed by ruled lines for the entries. The last few entries were extremely terse, maybe one word or just a short phrase. His last entry was on May 20.

The brief notations were written in lead pencil. When he let the pencil wear to a blunt point, the entries were almost impossible to read. Evidently, he found it necessary to whittle the pencil to a fine point only about once a week. Then the hand-printed letters became clear and legible for three or four entries. Often it had taken Gil several passes to make out what he had written in what she called chicken scratch.

His use of capitalization seemed whimsical: *went to get my Cutting Knife sharpened.* It bordered on comical as to what he thought required an initial capital letter. Spelling was inconsistent. He used the word *commenced* often and he rotated between one and two M's. Gil chalked it up to the fact that the diary was for William's eyes only and he knew what he meant.

Recording the weather was of particular interest, since he was a farmer and rain or the lack of it was so important. Weather conditions were incorporated into most entries. The range of description of weather conditions was wide:

fine
agreeable
more pleasant
disagreeable
seasonable
hot
cool
cool rain & sleet
cold & windy
frost & ice rain
large rain

William was a church man. Most Sundays he noted going to church to one of three different houses of worship—one in Clio, one in Bennettsville, and one in the neighboring town of Dunbar. He noted the names of the preachers who gave the sermon. There was never an indication as to whether Lydia and the kids accompanied him.

There were entries showing domestic activity such as *Col Edwards comes to the house to rid Lydia of two teeth* and *Lydia & myself had our ambrotype taken*. The only straight leisure practice that came up time and again was fishing. He must have loved to fish. He may have done it alone because he never mentioned companions: *Went to Edens Mill Fishing & caught 25 Brim* and *Caught a 10 pd Cat fish*.

In February, William's diary referred to a serious disease that spread among some of the people he had noted who had *borrowed a wagon* or *sold me 10 pounds* of *flour*. The particularly virulent fever, which Gil thought may have been typhoid, was referred to as *putrid bilious fever*. This mystified Gil. She searched for any reference to a recorded outbreak at that time and found none. However, whatever it was, it was deadly. There were weeks when William visited friends and neighbors who had come down with it. There was a period of deaths and funerals.

In early March, he himself was *taken down sick*. During a two-week period he was too feeble to elaborate in the diary of his condition beyond the note, *sick*. Then he was *on the mend*. A week later, *taking a relaps*. It must have been severe, because he wrote, *Doctor comes twice today*. He was again *mending*, and noted his appetite was back, *commenced eating some ham*. He survived his illness well enough to be able to work again.

Gil looked at documents about the early history of Clio and found the existence of three civic institutions—the Masons, the Temperance Union, and a chapter of the South Carolina Agricultural Society. William R. Medlin was enrolled as a member of all three. In the diary there were numerous entries noting meetings, celebrations, and speakers. He was busy.

This diary seemed to Gil to be like so many she had seen over her career, merely listing the day in and day out tedium of a mundane life.

William appeared to be a simple farmer, living a simple life except for an odd period of a little more than two weeks just before the diary abruptly stopped. Gil was curious about the flurry of travel in the spring with nothing written to explain why. In what was usually a very busy time for a cotton farmer in preparing, planting and tending the field, William noted train travel.

Before the May 5 entry—*Tom & me board the Eastern for Charl & Savannah*—was his note *Tom comes and stays at the house for two days*. In Gil's research into background material, she had found a sibling, Thomas G., listed as a trader of commodities. There was no clue to the purpose of their travel together. Gil speculated that Tom may have accompanied William on travel to Savannah, and then back north to Charleston, but he was no longer mentioned after William wrote *Board Wm Javey for Mobil* on May 9.

It was a long shot, but Gil brought up archival issues of *The Savannah Daily Republican* for the days around the time William was there. Among articles about what was news from New York and Washington and local pieces reporting that cotton prices had hit an all-time high, she found a prominent advertisement boldly headlined *Slave Auction of the Major Butler Estate*. It announced that Asbill & Smythe would be pulling their regular first Wednesday and Thursday of the month auctions and replacing these with a *special auction on Thursday and Friday, May 6th and 7th*. The auction would not be held as usual at their yard, but because they expected a large turnout it would be held at the Big Oval Race Track. The Butler estate was divesting its holdings of slaves, said to be 463 of *prime stock*.

Gil knew of some records that could help her see if William R. Medlin had been involved in the Butler auction. She was fascinated by the history of these records, about how they themselves had escaped oblivion. When Sherman made his destructive March to the Sea, he met with little resistance on entering his destination, Savannah, Georgia. Many people had already fled the city in a panic, carrying whatever they could. Reporters representing Northern newspapers arrived just before Sherman and scoured the city for anything that would play well in their papers, whose readers were eager for firsthand accounts of a crumbling Confederacy.

Gil was familiar with the story of the legendary Davis Thompson of the *Chicago Daily Tribune* and how he knew that Asbill & Smythe was the largest dealer in slaves in Savannah, so as soon as he got to town, he headed straight to the offices of the trading company through all the anxious people hurrying in the streets. He found a large padlock on the iron gates but climbed over, broke a window and crawled inside the office. There were years of documents strewn all over the floor—an indication that someone had looked for anything of any value and then left in a hurry. Thompson grabbed whatever he thought would be fodder for his report to the paper. At the back of the office were half a dozen holding cells with their doors thrown open. He looped a set of shackles over his arm—an arm already laden with documents. Thompson made off with as much as one man could manage. The series of articles about his experience in Savannah, written for the *Tribune*, boosted his career to legendary status. He later wrote a book about his firsthand experiences during the Civil War that remained one of the best sources for research on the period.

The university had a copy, which Gil got her hands on. She went immediately to the chapter on the things Thompson took from the

Savannah auction office, a list of the materials he was able to scoop up. As Gil glanced down the list, she was thrilled to see that one of the items was the ledger of the *1857 Butler Auction*. Thompson explained that he had been enticed to grab this because it was intact and bound with cord—easy to carry. Gil couldn't believe her good fortune, but now she would have to run down what had happened to that auction record over the 135 years since Thompson acquired it.

Gil went on the hunt for the auction ledger. She called the *Tribune* and asked for anyone in Archives. This was a wild reach, but it might send her in the right direction. A young voice came on the line and Gil said she was looking for some information about a reporter with the paper who wrote in the time of the Civil War.

In Gil's experience, cold calls could go in one of two directions—the person had no idea what you were talking about and, worse, couldn't care less. Or they had a sense of what you needed and took joy in joining the hunt with you. This call was a success. The young woman actually knew of Davis Thompson because she had gone to the University of Chicago, where she majored in nineteenth-century American history. She went on to say that one of her professors had published, through the university press, a book on the history of Chicago newspapers.

———

DR. DRAGO AT THE UNIVERSITY was extremely helpful. The descendants of Thompson had donated the papers in his estate to the Chicago Historical Society, where Drago had actually gone through all the material himself. He remembered the Butler auction ledger, still bound with the original string. Gil thanked him, hung up, and leaned contentedly back in her chair, thinking once again that she couldn't have a better job.

Drago had said that the Butler auction record had been transcribed. Gil asked for a PDF from the Historical Society. She was spending way more time than required on the Medlin project, but there was no way in hell she was not going to follow through with finding out if William R. Medlin was registered to bid at that auction on May 6 and 7, 1857.

The next day Gil had the PDF of the Butler auction ledger on her screen. The first four pages were the contract—the binding arrangement between Asbill & Smythe and the Butler estate—to dispose of the Butler Negro stock. The broker and seller were both represented by legal counsel. Within the arrangement were issues of commission and the latitude of the auctioneer to lower prices for less desirable individuals. There was verbiage regarding the expectations of the seller and adjustments if goals were not met. Next were over fifty documents submitted by potential buyers listing securities to show financial fitness to purchase. William R. Medlin was not among these.

Then there were dozens of pages listing each of the slaves with lot number, name, age, skill and flaws, if any, such as *Pompey, 31, rice hand—lame in one foot; Lettia, 11, cotton, prime girl*. The final pages, completed after the auction, had lot numbers with names of buyers and hammered-down prices. Gil put her finger on the column of lots and slid it down the page, looking for William R. Medlin.

On the Friday, the second day of the auction, the last entry was what she was looking for: *Lot #461, to William R. Medlin, $200; Lot #462 to William R. Medlin, $0; Lot #463 to* William R. *Medlin, $0.* Gil looked back to the pages that listed the description of each lot. *Lot #461* said, *Hutto, 32, prime field hand, strong. Lot #462* was *Celia, 23, prime woman field hand. Lot #463* said, *Jama, 11, prime girl.* Gil looked at the prices fetched for prime field hands and found most went for over one thousand dollars. Why had Hutto gone for only $200 when other prime hands were going for over $1,000? Why had the two females been listed as prime but brought in no price?

Now that she knew William had bought three slaves at the Savannah auction, the travel to Mobile made sense. By the late 1850s, the soil in South Carolina was almost played out. The demand for cotton was increasingly being met in Alabama and Mississippi, where the soil had not yet been dogged to death. That meant a rush was on for more slaves in the Gulf states. Auction houses in Mobile were doing brisk business. To Gil, it appeared William could have been heading south, looking for top dollar for his slaves in a Mobile auction. But in his diary, there was no mention of Mobile after the May 9 entry *Board Wm Javey for Mobil.*

Gil realized she could not solve everything, that some mystery would remain. She was still puzzled as to why a lone dirt cotton farmer would up and buy a couple of slaves. It was far more common for a slave trader to follow a robust cycle of constant buying and selling. That William, out of the blue, went and bought three slaves, even if he was intending to sell them in a hurry, did not make complete sense to Gil.

To bring the project to a close, she wanted to try to find out what had finally happened to him. In 1860, when the War started, he would still have been of prime age to join the Confederate Army—three years beyond the 1857 diary. She looked at the 1860 census and there was no sign of William R. Medlin.

Now she recalled that there had been a second piece in the archival box Chip handed her. This second piece looked on the outside just like the other in style and size. However, when she opened it, she saw it was not a diary but rather an account book with printed, ruled lines to record expenses. The hand that wrote the first entry—*June 15, Share blade $17.45*—was in the heavy hand of a man. The entries that followed were more delicate, in the hand of a woman clearly schooled in penmanship. Gil deduced that Medlin was no longer in the picture by the middle of June of 1857, thinking he probably had died. She guessed his widow, Lydia, had taken over, but first was shown how to use the account book by a male figure, an acquaintance or maybe a relative—someone who took the time to help teach a widow how to carry on, alone.

Of the three children, Caleb was the only one who surfaced in documents on record. Gil ran down a reference to scholarship money given by the Agriculture Society of South Carolina to Caleb F. Medlin to attend South Carolina College in engineering. With some digging she found that Caleb, along with most of the other students, joined the Confederate Army right after the War began. He was a casualty in 1861 of the Battle of Bull Run, the first major battle in the Civil War.

Gil found something interesting and puzzling in the Marlboro County records. The name Hutto—a name William referred to twice in his diary and likely the same slave called Hutto whom he bought at the Butler auction in Savannah—was listed in a property inventory that showed up in the county records. Inventories were usually prepared to support a loan or for tax calculation. Along with a wagon, two draft mules and some farm equipment was listed one slave, *Hutto, field hand, value $1,500.*

Gil wondered why Hutto was in the Marlboro County records. Had William perhaps brought him back to Clio with him, instead of taking him to Mobile? And what of Celia and Jama?

Coming back from a weekend visit with her mother in Florence, Gil decided to turn off Interstate 95 at the Bennettsville exit. She followed the road through a mixture of farmland and intersections with strip centers and fast-food joints. Bennettsville looked like so many other small towns. The road ran into a square with the county courthouse sitting in the middle of a pattern of sidewalks, all leading to its wide set of granite steps.

The small-town Southern courthouses were always red brick, often with a dome, and sometimes there was a marble Confederate monument with a soldier leaning on a long rifle, on an elevated base—every bit the image so memorable in *To Kill a Mockingbird*. Gil drove three quarters around the square and turned off at the sign *Clio 3 miles*. Just before she got to Clio, she pulled off onto the shoulder and unfolded a detailed map of South Carolina. She had circled with a yellow marker where she thought the Medlin farm had been. In Columbia she had gotten the intern to go to the Tax and Property Department, just two blocks from the Caroliniana, to find the Medlin property in the big, unwieldy, bound plat books. The state was in the process of scanning the plat books for online viewing, but Gil got a kick out of thinking the intern needed to see what life was like before computers.

She drove through the town, which had not much more than a four-way stop, pausing by the Zion Baptist Church cemetery to take a picture of William's gravesite to put with her report. After some looking, she found it. Rod iron scalloped edging hemmed in two graves of very different styles. William R. Medlin's plain stone had the dates *1814–1857* chiseled below the name. A smaller but fancier stone, to the right, had an urn on top that was carved out of one piece of granite. It read *LYDIA BRISTOW MEDLIN* followed by her dates. There was room to the left of the two graves for three more, but the grass lay undisturbed.

Next, Gil drove down a couple of miles of county roads until she thought she had located the spot where William had worked a thirty-five-acre cotton farm. She turned off at *Meadow Manor Estates*. She could tell this was a brand-new development because past the first fully built house there were unsold lots with green metal boxes at the street, ready for utility hook up. It was easy to see that the landscaping had not been planted very long because it hadn't had time to catch hold yet. The one house, just inside the entrance, was of buff-colored stucco with shutters in a French farmhouse style. The front door was grand in size, as if from a fortress, with heavy strap hinges. There was an ornate metal decorative cage over a small viewing window. All the metal looked hand forged, made especially for this particular door. The owners obviously had an affinity for the houses of Normandy—possibly a taste that grew out of a trip to that French region.

There was a man on a riding mower doing swipes across the front yard. When he came close, Gil got out of her car and flagged him down. He turned off the mower and came over to her. She told him who she was and what her interest was with the land within the development. He told her that he was the developer of Meadow Manor and knew the property well from all the excavation that had to be done early on. He invited her into the house to meet his wife who was "interested in history." They sat in the air-conditioned solarium porch at the back of the house and sipped sweet tea as Gil told them about her Medlin project.

The man said that he had seen the name in the original title search but did not know anything of the Medlins. He went on to say that when he first saw the property, both a small house and a little barn had already collapsed, with the roofs lying on top and covering anything that was left of the structures. After he bought the property, his crew bulldozed everything into a pile. He said he went through it looking for any planks of heart pine, and except for a few salvageable pieces of pine, there were only a couple of bits of bric-a-brac that he pulled out, but nothing of any value.

Gil was about to leave when the man looked sheepishly at his wife.

—Should we tell her what we found?

He said that there was an enormous live oak right where they had planned the main road through the development, so he decided to cut a roundabout and have traffic go in a circle with the tree saved in the middle. When they went to work, one of the crew, operating a Bobcat, struck something. After some shovel work, they found it was a whole human skeleton.

—This was a big sucker. There was no headstone or casket, so we figured it was a slave. Oh, Lord, we didn't tell anybody 'cause there's nothing will shut down a construction site quicker than finding buried remains of slaves. I found that out the hard way on a job in Bennettsville when a few Black folks went to the authorities and told them they thought there was a slave graveyard somewhere on the site. They shut us down for weeks while they looked for graves, but they didn't find a one. I learned my lesson on that job. So I just told the guys to get rid of it and from there on out, I didn't want to know a thing about it. I took something off it and if you promise not to tell the slave police on me, I'll give it to you because we find it kinda creepy.

His wife chatted with Gil while he disappeared to somewhere in the house. He came back with an object concealed in his clenched fist and motioned for Gil to hold out her hand. He dropped into her palm a long gold chain with a strange object hanging on it. Gil lifted it up to the light to get a closer look. It was a porcelain doll's arm, painted black.

—Miss history lady, I bet you've never seen anything like that before.

Gil agreed.

On her way to the front door while thanking the couple for their hospitality, she passed a mahogany hall table with a Chinese ginger-jar lamp and a stand holding a framed watercolor painting of a French landscape covered in poppies. She did not notice the antique crackled sugar bowl, filled to overflowing with silk violets that covered up where one of the handles had been broken off sometime in the past. It was decorated with a delicately hand-painted wing feather of a red woodland grouse.

The End

ACKNOWLEDGMENTS

The Catbird Seat did not arise out of a crowded support system of seasoned literary types giving wise advice. Instead it came out of an isolated existence passed mainly in two local libraries. I spent many hours writing in the South Carolina Room in the main library of Charleston County and in the iconic Charleston Library Society. The latter was founded in 1748 by a group of men who felt strongly that the citizens of Charleston should benefit from books and not exist as uneducated "savages."

I want to extend my appreciation to the staff of the venerable Caroliniana, the library of research archives and special collections in the library system of the University of South Carolina in Columbia. Their assistance in showing me techniques for conducting research was vital in describing the work life of one of my main characters in *Catbird*.

Of the many books I used for research material, there are some that stand out. Henry Louis Gates, Jr., kindly recommended a book written by his Harvard colleague, Sven Beckert: *Empire of Cotton: A Global History*. This was an invaluable source in understanding the rise of cotton, its impact on slavery, and how it changed the world's economy. Walter Edgar's *South Carolina: A History* is both thorough and definitive. Theodore Rosengarten's *Tombee: Portrait of a Cotton Planter* is a revealing and honest account of the life of a South Carolina planter. Finally, I could always count on David McCullough's writing as a guide in trying to make historical writing engaging, not boring.

Thanks to Deedie Cooper, my life-partner of forty years, for not objecting to my working long hours on *Catbird*, a preoccupation that went on for more than two decades.

I extend boundless gratitude to my friend, Sheila Low-Beer, for editing and for her unending persistence even when my own energy flagged. Early on, she offered to write a few comments in the margin of a sample chapter I had given her. From that time on she has been by my side, pushing me forward through the endless hours. Without her, *Catbird* would never have made it to the printed page. My gratitude has no end.

ABOUT THE AUTHOR

Rebecca Hollingsworth was raised in rural Florida, which she says was every bit as backward as any place in the Deep South. With a degree in graphic design from the University of Florida, she moved to New York City in 1968 to work in advertising. After several years she turned South again, this time to Atlanta, her home for the next thirty-five years. Growing restless after fifteen years in advertising and design, she started a service business in Atlanta, which she ran successfully for twenty years until a nationwide company purchased it, allowing her to retire at age fifty.

She moved to Charleston, South Carolina, a history town that offered endless avenues of exploration into the past. Her philanthropic work assembling a collection of slave artifacts for the Ryan Slave Mart Museum in Charleston grew out of her interest in the institution of slavery. From there she started trying to understand influences on modern-day Black/White conflicts. In the year 2000, flack over the Confederate flag flying from the dome of the State House in Columbia forced Hollingsworth and other Southerners to face the complications of race as they never had.

Born in 1945, the author vividly remembers seeing White and Colored drinking fountains as a child. *The Catbird Seat* offers rich personal observations and historical research that bring to the reader a deeply thoughtful and honest perspective on race, not likely to be found elsewhere.

April 22

April 23

April 24